Charles Egbert Craddock

In the Stranger People's Country

Charles Egbert Craddock

In the Stranger People's Country

ISBN/EAN: 9783337028756

Printed in Europe, USA, Canada, Australia, Japan

Cover: Foto ©Andreas Hilbeck / pixelio.de

More available books at **www.hansebooks.com**

" IT WAS AN ATTITUDE THAT COMMENDED A TEMPORIZING POLICY."

(See page 255.)

IN THE "STRANGER PEOPLE'S" COUNTRY ❧ A NOVEL ❧ BY CHARLES EGBERT CRADDOCK ❧

With Illustrations

NEW YORK

HARPER & BROTHERS, FRANKLIN SQUARE

1891

ILLUSTRATIONS.

IN THE
"STRANGER PEOPLE'S" COUNTRY.

I.

WHO they were, and whence they came, none can say. The mountains where they found their home —their long home—keep silence. The stars, that they knew, look down upon their graves and make no sign. Their memory, unless in some fine and subtle way lingering in the mystery, the pervasive melancholy, the vaguely troublous forecast and retrospect which possess the mind in contemplating this sequestered spot, unhallowed save by the sense of a common humanity, has faded from the earth. None might know that they had ever lived but for a dim tradition associating them with the ancient forgotten peoples of this old hemisphere of ours that we are wont to deem so new. For this is one of the strange burial-grounds of the "pygmy dwellers" of Tennessee; prehistoric, it is held, an extinct diminutive race; only Aztec children, others surmise, of a uniform age and size, buried apart from their kindred, for some unimagined, never-to-be-explained reason; and a more prosaic opinion contends that the curious stone sepulchres contain merely infant relics of the Cherokee Indian. All I

1

know is, here they rest, awaiting that supreme moment when this mortality shall put on immortality, and meanwhile in the solemn environment of the Great Smoky Mountains the "Leetle People" sleep well.

Quiet neighbors all these years have they been. So quiet! almost forgotten. In fact, the nearest mountaineers start, with a dazed look, at a question concerning them, then become mysterious, with that superstitious, speculative gleam in the eye as of one who knows much of uncanny lore, but is shy to recount.

"I do declar' I never war so set back in my life ez I felt whenst that thar valley man jes' upped an' axed me 'bout'n them thar Leetle Stranger People buried yander on the rise," declared Stephen Yates, one July evening, as he stood leaning on his rifle before the door of his cabin in the cove. His horse, reeking and blown, still saddled, bore a deer, newly slain, unprotected by the game-laws, and the old hounds, panting and muddy from the chase, lay around the doorstep.

A young woman of twenty, perhaps, with a pale oval face and dark hair, and serene dark gray eyes, was on the rickety porch, leaning upon a rude shelf that served also as a balustrade; she had a cedar piggin in her hand, and the cow was lowing at the bars. On the doorstep there sat a rotund and stalwart, but preternaturally solemn young person, who now and again, with a corrugated countenance, gnashed his gums. His time and energies were expended in that trying occupation known as "cuttin' yer teeth," an acquisition which he would some day

"LEETLE MOSE."

value more highly than now. He sought, as far as
an abnormally developed craft might compass, to
force, by many an infant wile, his elders to share his
woes, and it was with a distinctly fallen countenance
that his father hearkened to his mother's parenthet-
ical request to "'bide hyar an' company leetle Moses
whilst I be a-milkin' the cow."

Yates did not refuse, although a braver man might
have quailed. It was his hard fate to regard "leetle
Moses" as a supreme fetich, and to worship him
with as unrequited an idolatry as ever was lavished
on the great god Dagon. He only sought to gain
time, and continued his account of the conversation:

"He 'lowed ef he hed knowed afore ez they war

buried hyar, he'd hev kem a hunderd mile jes' ter view the spot," he said, his eye kindling with a recollection of the " valley man's " enthusiasm.

His wife hardly entered into it at second-hand. She regarded him with a slow wonderment stealing over her face.

" War—war he 'quainted with enny of 'em in thar lifetime ?" she demanded, hesitating, but seeking to solve the valley man's reason—" them Leetle Stranger People ?"

" Great Gosh ! Adelaide !" Yates exclaimed, irritably, contemptuous all at once of the limitations of her standpoint. " Ye stay cooped up hyar 'sociatin' with nobody but leetle Mose till ye hev furgot every durned thing ye ever knowed. The Leetle People hev been dead so long ago nobody 'members 'em—not even old man Peake, an' he air a hunderd an' ten year old—ef he ain't lyin'," he added, cautiously.

Her face flushed. There was fire in her serene eyes, like a flare of sunset in the placid depths of a lake. " I'm willin' ter 'bide along o' leetle Mose," she retorted. " I never expect ter see no better company 'n leetle Mose ter the las' day I live, an' I never *did* see none !"

Yates shifted his weight uncertainly upon his other foot, and surveyed with a casual glance the wide landscape. The sense of supersedure was sharp at the moment. He had been in his day a great man in her estimation, and now " leetle Mose," with his surly dejection, with only a tooth or two—and with these he would have gladly dispensed—with his uncertain gait and his pigeon-toes and his nearly bald head, was a greater man still. He and his mother

were a close corporation, but, for the sake of his own
fealty to the domestic Dagon, Steve Yates forgave
them both.   He went on presently :

"The valley man hed jes' hearn tell ez them Leetle People war buried hyarabout.   I .never seen a
man so streck of a heap ez he war, an' he axed me
fool questions till I felt plumb cur'ous a-talkin' 'bout
them Leetle Stranger People buried thar on the
rise."   Once more he turned toward the slope that
embarrassed, half-laughing glance—in which, however, there was no mirth—betokening a spirit ill at
ease, and secretly shrinking from some uncanny,
irksome fear.

Her eyes mechanically followed his to the purple
slope so still under the crimson sky.   Higher up,
the mountain, shielded by the shadow of its own
crags from this reflection of the west, showed a
dark green shade of an indescribable depth and richness of tone, never merging into dusky indefiniteness.
Through a gap in the range to the east were visible
the infinite blue distances of the Great Smoky peaks,
their color here and there idealized by the far-away
glamours of sunset to an exquisite roseate hue, or a
crystalline and perfect amethyst against the amber
horizon.   Down the clifty gorge—its walls of solid
sandstone, cloven to the bare heart of the range by
the fierce momentum of the waters — the bounding
river came.   One mad leap presented the glittering
splendors of a glassy-green cataract, and in its elastic spray an elusive rainbow lurked.   Its voice was
like that of one crying in the wilderness, so far
might its eloquent iteration be heard.   The Little
People, in their day, might have given ear to its

message and pondered on the untranslated tidings, but now they did not heed.

Only the dwellers in the mountaineer's cabin hard by listened at times to the pulsing rhythm, as alive as the metre of a great poem; and, again, in duller mood, its sound was but as silence to those who cared not to hear. The dark little house seemed small and solitary and transitory here among the massive, enduring mountains, beside the majestic flow of the waters, and the rail-fence enclosed the minimum of space from the great unpeopled wilds.

. "I 'lowed ter him they never walked," Yates said, presently. "Ez fur ez I know, they hain't been seen, nor none o' 'em set out ter walk, sence they war put thar fust. Nobody ez I know purfesses ter hev seen enny o' the Stranger People's harnts."

He repeated this with simplicity, evidently desirous of giving the pygmy dwellers their bounden due.

"I 'lowed ter him," he continued, "ez folks hed let them be, an' they hed let the mounting folks be. Nobody wanted seeh cur'ous harnts ez folks o' thar sizo ter git ter walkin' at this late day."

There was a vague chill in the air—or was it in the moral atmosphere?

"What be *he* a-vagrantin' sound fur, inquirin' 'bout them as be dead an' done with the livin' long ago?" she demanded, a touch of acerbity in her tone and a restless look in her eyes.

"He 'lows ez he's jes' kem hyar along o' Leonard Rhodes ez be a-'lectioneerin' fur floater fur the Legislatur'. An'. him an' Rhodes air frien's, an' Rhodes hev got some lan' in this county ez hev got one o'

"'WAR—WAR HE 'QUAINTED WITH ENNY OF 'EM?'"

them Injun mounds on it, an' he hev let this frien' o' his hev men ter dig an' open it ter see what they could find. I seen 'em arter it ter-day; this hyar man 'peared mighty nigh ez excited ez a Juny-bug; I noticed he never dug none, though, hisse'f."

He paused for a moment, chewing hard on his quid of tobacco; then he slowly laughed. "The folks he hed hired ter dig 'lowed he war teched in the head, but he 'peared sorter sensible ter me— never teched a spade, an' 'twar a hot day."

"What did they find?" asked his wife, breathlessly.

"Dirt," Yates said, with an iconoclastic laugh, "a plenty of it. He 'peared toler'ble disapp'inted till he hearn 'bout the Stranger People's buryin'-groun'. Adelaide"—he raised his voice suddenly— "that thar idjit o' a man, he 'lows ez them Leetle People warn't grown folks at all—jes' chil'n; I tried ter tell the fool better—jes' leetle chil'n!"

He glanced quickly at her, as if prepared for the shock of surprise which must be elicited by this onslaught upon the faith of a whole community. Somehow, as she again fastened her eyes on the sombre declivity, her face wore the look of one whose secret thought is revealed in words. In the few years that she had lived here, a stranger herself, in some sort— not accustomed, as was her husband, to a lifelong vicinage to the pygmy burial-ground—she had developed no receptivity to that uncanny idea of a race of dwarfs. Always as children she had thought of the Little People; she had made no effort to reconcile this theory with the strange fact that no similar sarcophagi, enclosing larger frames, were known of far or near; she found no incongruity in the idea that infants should have been thus segregated in death from all their kindred; it seemed a meet resting-place for youth and innocence, thus apart from all others. They were children — only children; all asleep; asleep and resting! With the strange fascination that the spot and its unique tradition exerted upon her, she would glance thither from time to time throughout the day, pausing at her task to follow the shadow of the clouds sweeping over the purple slope, and to listen to the whir of bees in the still noon amongst the sweet fern and to the call of the glad birds. When she sang in fitful fragments a crooning lullaby to her own child, who had made all childhood doubly dear and doubly sacred to her heart, she was wont to watch pensively the tender glow of evening reddening there, so soft, so brilliant, so promissory of the splendid days to come that it needs must suggest that supernal dawn when the Little People should all rise to greet the rising sun that they had seen set for the last time so long ago. In bright, slanting rows, as swift, as ethereal, as dazzling as the morning mist transfigured by the sun's rays—with her prophetic eyes she could behold them, rank after rank, coming down the slope in this radiant guise; meanwhile they slept as securely as her child slept in her arms, their waking as certain.

The picture recurred to her thoughts at the moment. "They will all rise before we-uns at the jedg-mint-day," she said, her far-seeing gray eyes clear and crystalline upon the unmarked place.

"Laws-a-massy, Adelaide!" cried her husband, in a tone of expostulation and alarm, with a quick glance over his shoulder, " what ails ye ter say sech ez that—ez ef it war gospel sure?"

Her eyes came back reluctantly to him; the question had jarred upon her reverie. " Ye air 'bleeged ter know that," she retorted, with a slighting manner. " The sun strikes through the gap an' teehes the Leetle People's buryin'-groun' a full haffen hour an' better afore it reaches the graveyard o' the mounting folks down thar in the shadder o' the range."

He listened ponderingly to this logic, his chin resting upon the muzzle of his rifle; then, with a noiseless shifting of his posture, he looked again with a cautious gesture over his shoulder. He was a hardy hunter, of a vigorous physique and but scantily acquainted with fear, but this eerie idea of a thousand or so adult pygmy Tennesseeans astir on the last day, forestalling the familiar mountain neighbors, robbed immortality for the moment of its wonted prestige.

The oppressive influence even laid hold on his strong frame, and he extended one powerful arm at full length, with a futile effort to yawn.

" G'long, Adelaide! G'long an' milk the cow!" he exclaimed, with the irritation that was always apparent in his manner when perplexity seized upon his brain—a good organ of its kind, but working best in the clear air of out-of-door contemplation. He was a man of sound common-sense, but with no endowment for furtive speculation, and purblind gropings, and tenuous deductions from flimsy premises. He heaved a great sigh of relief to remember the cow—the good, homely cow—at the bars.

Adelaide had slowly taken up the piggin. " Ye

hain't told me why that thar valley man sets so much store by the Leetle People. I'll go arter I hear that word."

"Waal, I ain't a-goin' ter speak it," retorted her husband, with a threatening conjugal frown. "I ain't a-goin' ter let leetle Mose be kep' up hyar till midnight a-waitin' for you-uns ter milk the cow. It's cleverly dark now."

"Leetle Mose" was a name to conjure with; even the wife denied herself the luxury of the last word, so lost was she in the mother. She put the piggin hastily upon her head, and went, with the erect, graceful pose that the prosaic weight fosters, down the winding path beyond the spring to the bars where the red cow stood lowing.

The household idol, sitting upon the step with a grave, inscrutable countenance, silently watched her departure, then suddenly set up a loud and bitter wail of desertion. It was in vain that she paused and called back promises of return, albeit he understood well the language which so far he refused to speak; in vain that his father came and sat beside him on the step, and patted him with a large hand upon his limited back. It was a good opportunity for the lamentation in which "leetle Mose" was prone to indulge. He had a reputation that extended far beyond his ken—for the fence bounded his world—not, however, that he would have cared. He was known throughout many a cove, and even in the settlement, as the " wust chile ever seen, an' a jedgmint, ef the truth war known, on Stephen an' Adelaide Yates fur hevin' been so fly-away an' headstrong in thar single days—both of 'em wild ez deer,

an' gin over ter dancin' an' foolishness." It was
with a certain grim satisfaction that the settlement
hearkened to the fact that they were "mighty tame
now." Thus Dagon's filial exploits lacked no plau-
dits. His mental capacities, too, received due recognition. "He be powerful smart, though; he won't
let 'em hev no mo' comp'ny 'n he can help. I reckon
he knows they wouldn't 'tend ter him ef they hed
ennything else they *could* 'tend ter. Sometimes that
chile be a-settin' on the front porch sorter peaceable,
restin' hisse'f from hollerin'," his maternal great-
aunt Jerushy chronicled to a coterie of pleased gossips, "an' ef he see a wagon a-stoppin' at the gate,
or a visitor a-walkin' up the path, he'll mos' lif' the
roof off with his screeches. An' screech he will till
they leaves; he hev mos' made *me* deef fur life. I
useter spend consider'ble o' my time with that young
couple"— and there was an ousted suggestion in
Aunt Jerushy's manner. "It makes his dad an'
mam 'shamed fur true, his kerryin's on; they air
bowed down ter the yearth!"

The widespread strictures on their idol were very
bitter to the parental worshippers. Often, with a
troubled aspect, they took counsel together, and repeated in helpless dudgeon the criticism of his kindred and neighbors. It was powerless to shake their
loyalty. Even his father, whom he chose to regard
with a lowering and suspicious mien, unless it were
in the dead hours of the night, when he developed a
morbid craving to be trotted back and forth and up
and down the puncheon floor, was flattered with the
smallest tokens of his confidence.

He had an admirable perseverance. He sat still

weeping in the midst of his pink fat with so much distortion of countenance and display of gums, and such loud vocal exercises, when Adelaide returned, that she cast upon her husband a look of deep reproach, and he divined that she suspected him of having gone to the extreme length of smiting Dagon in her absence, and despite his clear conscience he could but look guilty.

"Oh, Mose!" he said, outdone, as he rose, "ye air so mean—ye air so durned mean!"

But the callow wrath of the "leetle Mose" was more formidable than the displeasure of the big man, and his heart burned at the short reply of his wife, a sarcastic "I reckon so!" when he protested that he had done nothing to Mose to which any fair-minded infant could have taken exceptions. The vocalizations of Dagon were of such unusual power this evening that his strength failed shortly after supper, and he was asleep earlier than his ordinary hour, for he was something of a late bird. Belying all his traits, he looked angelic as he lay in his little rude box cradle. When the moonlight came creeping through the door it found him there, with a smile on his rose-leaf lips, and both his pink hands unclasped on the coverlet. Adelaide, despite the silence and studious air of preoccupation she had maintained toward her husband, could but beg Yates to observe the child's beauty as she sank down, dead beat, on the door-step to rest, but still keeping one hand on the rocker of the cradle, for motion was pleasing to "leetle Mose," and by this requisition he doubtless understood that he could absorb and occupy his elders, even when he was unconscious.

"He's purty enough, the Lord knows," the dejected father assented, as he sat smoking his pipe at a little distance on the step of the porch. "I dun' no', though, what ails him ter take sech a spite at me. I do all I kin ter pleasure him."

Adelaide experienced a vicarious qualm of conscience. "He ain't got no spite at you-uns," she said, reassuringly, in the hope that her words could speak louder than Dagon's actions. "It's jes' his teeth harry him so."

"An' ye didn't useter be so easy sot agin me." Yates preferred this complaint after a meditative puff of the pipe. There is a melancholy pleasure in the rôle of domestic martyr. He was beginning to enjoy himself.

"I ain't sot agin ye, but *somebody* hev got ter take up an' gin up fur leetle Mose. Men-folks hain't got no patience with leetle chil'n."

"I never knowed what 'twar ter gin up afore," he protested. "I ain't done nuthin' else sence Mose war born. Don't go nowhar, don't see nuthin' nor nobody."

He smoked languidly for a few moments, then, with decision: "Thar ain't no use in it; we-uns mought jes' ez well hev gone ter the infair over yander in the cove at Pettingill's ez not ter-night, an' got Aunt Jerushy ter bide with Moses till we kem back."

"Moses would hev hollered hisself inter a fit; he jes' stiffens at the sight o' Aunt Jerushy."

"Waal, then, we-uns mought hev tuk Moses along; I hev seen plenty o' babies sleepin' at a dance an' camp-meetin's, an' even fune'ls. I'll bet thar's a right smart chance of 'em over at Pettingill's now."

"Mought cotch measles from some of 'em, too, or whoopin'-cough," said his wife, conclusively.

There was no help for it. Seclusion with their Dagon was evidently their fate until "leetle Mose" should be grown to man's estate.

There was a long pause, in which the mercurial and socially disposed Yates dimly beheld the lengthening perspective of this prospect. He had been a dancer of famous activities and a joyous blade at all the mountain merry-makings, and he had married the liveliest girl of his acquaintance—with no little trouble, too, for she had been a mountain belle and something of a coquette. He sometimes could hardly identify with these recollections the watchful-eyed and pensive little mother and the home-staying wife.

"I wouldn't mind it ef Moses didn't treat me so mean," he resumed, all his sensibilities sorely wounded. "I do declar' I be kep' hid out so in the woods that I war plumb flustered when I seen them valley men this evenin' down thar at the mound. I wouldn't hev been s'prised none ef I hed jes' sot out an' run from 'em an' hid a-hint a tree like old folks 'low the Injuns useter do whenst they seen a white man."

"Ye never 'lowed ez what set that valley man ter talkin' 'bout the Leetle People," she said, seeking to divert his mind from his unfilial son, and to open a more congenial topic. Her eyes, full of the moonlight, turned toward the slope where the sheen, richly metallic and deeply yellow, rested ; the rising disk itself was visible through the gap in the mountains ; much of the world seemed in some sort unaware of its advent, and lay in the shadow, dark and stolid, in a dull invisibility, as though without form and void.

The moon had not yet scaled the heights of the great range ; only that long clifty gorge cleaving its mighty heart was radiant with the forecast of the splendors of the night, and through this vista, upon the mystic burial-ground, fell the pensive light like a benison.

Yates, too, glanced toward it with a kindling eye and an alert interest.

"He 'pears ter be a powerful cur'us man.   Somebody 'lowed he war a-diggin' fur jugs an' sech ez the Injuns hed—leastwise them ez built the mounds; he 'lows 'twarn't no Injuns; and Pete Dinks tole it ez how the jugs mus' be like that'n ez Felix Guthrie 'lowed war in the grave o' one o' the Leetle People."

He paused.   She turned her white, startled face toward him, her eyes distended.   Her voice was bated with horror—a mere whisper.

"What grave ?   How do Fee ondertake ter know sech ez air in the Stranger People's graves ?"

In his instant irritation because of the problem of her mental attitude he lifted his voice, and it sounded strident above the droning *susurrus* of the cicada, which filled the summer night with a drowsy monotone, and the insistent iteration of the falls.

"Gloryful gracious, Adelaide, surely ye mus' hev hearn ez how one o' them big rocks in the water-fall thar fell from the top wunst, an' crashed down inter the ruver.   An' it kerried cornsider'ble o' the yearth along the ruver-bank with it, an' tuk off the top slab o' the stone coffin o' one o' these hyar Leetle People. They hain't buried more'n two feet deep.   An' Fee —'twar on his lan'—he had ter move his fence back-'ards, an' whilst he war about it he got that slab an' put it whar it b'longed, an' kivered the grave agin.

An' so he seen the jug in thar with the bones. The jug hed shells in it, Fee say, an' the skeleton hed beads round its neck. That all happened, now ez I kem ter study on it, afore ye an' me war married."

His acerbity had evaporated in the interest of the narration, and in the evolution of an excellent reason for her ignorance of these things that had happened previous to her advent into the neighborhood. He did not notice that she took no advantage of the excuse to upbraid him with his readiness to find fault, and that she made no rejoinder as she sat, her head depressed, her whole attitude crouching, her dilated eyes fixed with a horror-stricken fascination upon the pygmy burial-ground, in that broad, lucent expanse of the yellow moonlight which was still streaming through the illuminated gorge of the mountains into an otherwise dusky world. The events of the afternoon were reasserting themselves in his mind. He laughed a little as he reviewed them.

"Fee hed been huntin' with me ter-day, an' this valley man—I b'lieve they 'lowed his name war Shattuck, an' he air a lawyer whar he kem from; he don't dig fur a living—whenst he hearn 'bout that, he say, quick ez lightning: 'Would ye know the spot agin? What made ye leave the jar thar? What made ye put the slab back?' An' Fee—ye know how crusty an' sour an' cantankerous he be—he say, 'Them Leetle People air *folks*, an' I hev no call ter go grave-robbin' ez I knows on!' That thar Shattuck turned fire-red in a minit. He air a mighty nice, sa-aft-spoken, perlite man, though spindlin'.' An' he talked mos'ly ter me arter that—Fee stood by an' listened—an' I liked Shattuck middlin' well. He 'lowed ez 'twar important ter know fur the history of the kentry—an' he did sound sorter like he war vagrantin' in his mind—ter know ef them Leetle People war grown folks or jes' chil'n. He b'lieves they war jes' chil'n, but ef he could see jes' one skull he could tell."

Adelaide gasped; she reached out her hand mechanically and laid it upon the feet of the baby curled up in his soft, warm nest. Her husband's glance absently followed her movement, but he went on unheeding:

"An' Fee, standin' stare-gazin' him, ez sullen ez a bar with a sore head, axed, 'How kin ye tell?' ez much ez ter say, 'Ye lie!' But Shattuck war perlite ez ever. 'Many ways; by their teeth, for instance—their wisdom teeth.' Then he went a-maunderin' on 'bout a man he knowed ez could jes' take a bone o' a animal ez he never seen, ez lived hyar afore the flood, an' tell how tall 'twar an' what it eat—I do declar' he did sound like he war crazy, though ho *looked* sensible ter the las'—an' this l'arned man could actially medjure an' make a pictur' of sech a animal out'n a few bones. An' Fee, he jes' stood listenin' long enough ter say, 'Them Leetle People never done me no harm, an' I ain't goin' ter do them none jes' 'kase they air leetle an' dead, an' can't holp tharse'fs. They may hev hed a use fur thar teeth in thar lifetime; I hain't got no use fur 'em now.' An' he whurled around an' put his foot inter his stirrup an' war a-goin' ter ride off, whenst the valley man cotch his bridle an' say, 'Ye hev got no objections ter my excavatin' on yer land, though?'"

Yates laughed lazily. "I do declar' 'twar too durned funny. Fee didn't know what the long-tongued sinner meant by ' excavatin',' an' I didn't nuther till arterward. But Fee, he jes' wanted ter be contrairy, no matter what, so he jes' say, powerful glum, ' I dun' no' 'bout that,' and rid off down the road. An' this Shattuck, he jes' stood lookin' after Fee with his chin cocked up in the air, an' he say, ' That's a sweet youth !' He speaks out right plain an' spunky fur sech a spindlin' man. Everybody laughed but Rhodes ; _he_ looked mightily tuck back ter hev his friend making game o' the mounting folks. Fee's vote counts jes' the same ez ef he war ez pleasant ez a basket o' chips. So Rhodes, he sorter frowned up an' say, ' Ye don't onderstan' Felix Guthrie. He air a good-hearted man, but he ain't been treated right, an' it's sorter soured him. He's good at heart, though.' An' this Shattuck 'peared ter take the hint ; he say sorter stridin' about, off-hand, an' that leetle soft hat o' his'n on the side o' his head, ' I mus' make frien's with him, then ; I mus' git on the right side o' him.' An' up spoke one o' them Peakes—they war holpin' ter look on at the few ez war willin' ter dig—'The only way,' he say, ' ter make frien's with Fee Guthrie air ter fondle him with a six-shooter.' Shattuck laffed. But Rhodes, he be a-shettin' him up all the time, an' a-hintin' at him, an' a-lookin' oneasy. Rhodes air skeered 'bout his 'lection, ef the truth war knowed."

He stretched his arms above his head and drew a long sigh of pleasurable reminiscence. " We hed a right sorter sociable evenin'. I'll be bound they air all over yander at the infair now. I know Rhodes danced at the weddin' the t'other night at Gossam's, an' they do say he kissed the bride, though they mought hev been funnin' 'bout'n that."

He looked at her once more, noticing at last the absorbed, intent expression of her lustrous, thoughtful eyes; the thrill of some feeling unknown to him was in her hand as she laid it upon his, and asked in an irrelevant, mysterious, apprehensive tone, " What do ' excavate' mean?"

" Hey?" he exclaimed. He had already forgotten what he had said, in the flexibility of his shallow mental processes, and recalled it by an effort. "Shucks! Jes' dig—that's all. Folks hev got a heap o' cur'ous words o' late years."

Her grasp tightened convulsively on his arm, "'Mongst the graves o' the Leetle People?"

He nodded, looking at her with vague surprise and gathering anger.

" He sha'n't !" she cried, finding her voice suddenly, and it rang out shrilly into the soft, perfumed night air. " It's in rifle range—the Leetle People's buryin'-groun'. I hev got aim enough ter stop his meddlin', pryin' han's 'mongst them pore Leetle People's bones. An' I'll do it, too," she added, in a lower tone.

Her grasp had relaxed, for he had sprung to his feet and stood looking at her, infinitely shocked, the image of the unoffending gentleman and scholar, whom she threatened, in his mind, all unaware how it differed from the ghoul of her ignorant fancy.

" Adelaide !" he exclaimed, with that accent of authority which he seldom assumed, " hesh up ! Tech that rifle, an' I'll turn ye out'n my door !"

She, too, was standing ; she turned a stony face, white in the moonlight, upon him as if she could not realize his words, but her eyes were slowly kindling with a fury before which he quailed.

He was, however, in every way the stronger, and the gravity of the crisis taught him how to use his strength.

"Take them words back," he reiterated, as if all unaffrighted, "or I'll turn ye out'n my house forever, an' ye'll leave leetle Mose hyar, for *he* b'longs ter me!"

The fear that had quivered in his heart seemed suddenly translated into her eyes; they looked an eloquent reproach, then, suddenly, all the fire was quenched in tears, and she sank down sobbing by the side of the cradle, leaving him standing there triumphant, it is true, but finding bitterness in his victory. He sat down, presently, in his former posture, feeling ill-used and reproachful and indignant. It was difficult to resume the conversation in the tone which he had maintained, and as she persistently wept, he resorted to reproaches.

"I dun' no' what in Canaan is the reason ye an' me can't git along 'thout quar'lin'. We never used ter quar'l none in our courtin' days, an' "—as a fresh burst of sobs acquiesced in this statement, he hastened to put the blame upon her—" ye never used ter talk so like a durned fool." The chilly sensation which her threat, so full of horror, had caused him, renewed for the moment its thrill.

"'Tain't like a fool," she declared, lifting her tearful face. "Ef 'tis, then the law's a fool—the law, ez ye set sech store on. Ain't the law agin diggin' up folks's bones? I ain't a-goin' ter do nothin' 'bout'n it, but ef ennybody war cotched at sech in the *mount-ing*-folks's buryin'-groun' they'd hev a few ounces o' lead ter tote off inside of 'em ef they could git away at all, an' ye know they would."

The difference of their standpoint — his normal views unconsciously modified by the talk of the scientific theorist, in which sentiment was easily subordinated to the acquisition of valuable knowledge, none of which could he adequately impart at second hand to her, quivering as she was with the idea of sacrilege and the sanctity of the tomb—baffled him for the moment; he hesitated; he found no words to convey the impressions he had received; then he gave way to the anger always the sequence of the antagonism of opinion between them.

"Ye don't sense nuthin', an' ye dun' no' nuthin', an' ye can't l'arn nuthin'."

"I don't want ter l'arn sech ez ye 'pear ter pick up in the settlemints," she retorted, with spirit. "Robbin' the dead an' sech! I'd ruther stay at home an' jes' 'sociate with leetle Moses—a sight ruther."

"I hedn't!" he declared, roughly. He rose to his feet. "I don't hev no peace at home. I reckon I mought ez well go whar I don't get quar'led with ez much. I mought jes' ez well be at the infair ez hyar."

"Jes' ez well," she sarcastically assented.

He stepped past her into the room to lay aside his shot-pouch and powder-horn, as not meet accoutrement for a festive gathering.

"Ye hed better kerry yer rifle. Ain't ye 'feared ef ye leave it hyar I mought take aim at suthin' in the Leetle People's buryin'-ground?" she said, looking up at him from her lowly seat on the floor, her eyes hard and dry and bright.

"Edzac'ly—fool enough fur ennything," he declared; but it was empty-handed that he stepped out into the moonlight.

She made no effort to detain him; she did not call him back. He paused when in the shadow of the great hickory-trees about the spring, and looked up at the little house. The moon was above the mountains, nearly full and radiant. Trailing luminous mists crept over the summits after it, and caught the light. All the world shared in its gracious splendors now, and the great gap, the gorge of the river, bereft of the unique illumination its rugged vistas had monopolized while all was dark about it, seemed melancholy and pensive, of reduced prominence and blurred effect.

The dew glistened on the slanting roof of the little log-cabin; the vines swayed duplicated by their moving shadows, and where the moonlight fell unbroken through the doorway he saw, against the dark background of the interior, Adelaide, still sitting on the floor beside the cradle, and he heard the monotone of the rockers as they thumped to and fro.

He heard it long after distance had nullified the sound. The wayside katydids sang their song in chorus with it; the tree-toad shrilling stridulously but bore it a burden. Even the roar of the water-fall was secondary, however it might pervade and thrill the wilderness. More than once, as he went along the dark and dewy road, he paused doubtfully, half minded to retrace his way. "I oughtn't ter hev tuck Adelaide up so sharp. Sence she hev hearn the notion ez them Leetle People war jes' leetle chil'n, like Mose, she'll set mo' store by 'em, jes' ter complimint him, ter the las' day she live. I'd hate ter be sech a fool 'bout leetle Mose ez she be." He shook his head solemnly as he stood in the road, fragrant with the odor of the azaleas in the undergrowth and the balsamic breath of the low-hanging firs, which were all fibrously a-glitter wherever the moon touched the dew in the dense midst of their shadows. "An' she 'pears to think herse'f gifted with wisdom now'-days, an' sets up ter make remarks ez sobersided ez ef she war risin' fifty year old. 'Fore she war married she never hed no 'pinions on nuthin'—ez frisky as a squir'l an' ez nimble. An' now'days she ain't got nuthin' but 'pinions, an' air ez sot in her doctrines an' ez solemn ez the rider, an' ez slow-spoken."

While he still hesitated, there came into his mind a foretaste of this slow diction, fashioned to reproach or to ill-disguised triumph in sedulously casual phrase, that would greet him should he return home, his threat of attending the infair all unaccomplished. He would have been glad enough to be sitting once more upon the low step of the little porch, with Adelaide and the cradle of the slumbering Dagon close by; but the pleasures of the festive gathering, grown all at once strangely vapid and sterile to his imagination, lay between him and the return to this calm domestic sphere; otherwise he would relinquish all pretence of conserving those elements of primacy which he should arrogate and maintain.

"It's time Adelaide hed fund out who's the head o' this hyar fambly. 'Tain't her, an' 'tain't leetle Mose, an' she ain't a-goin' to l'arn no younger."

II

In those open fields near the Pettingill cabin where the infair was in progress, the moonlight seemed to reach its richest effulgence. There was something in the delicate blue - green tint of the broad blades of the waving Indian corn, where the dew lay with a glitter like that of the whetted edge of a keen weapon, which was not revoked by the night, being of so chaste and fine a tone that it comported with that limited scale of color which the moon countenances. With the unbroken splendor upon this expanse, all the brighter because of the deep sombre forests above and the dense dark jungle of the laurel below—for the corn stood upon so steep a slope that how the crop was cultivated seemed a marvel to the unaccustomed eye—it was visible a long way to Stephen Yates as he approached on the country road; even after he had crossed the little log foot-bridge over the river, and commenced the steep ascent of a wooded hill, he could still catch glimpses now and then of this dazzling green through the heavy black shadows of the great trees, from the foliage of which every suggestion of color had been expunged. Another light presently came from a different direction, goading the dulled and preoccupied mind of the young man into fresh receptivities. A sound arose other than the tinkling metallic tremors and gurglings of the mountain stream — the sound of a fiddle ; a poor thing enough, doubtless, but voicing a wild, plaintive melody, which pervaded the woods with vibrant rhythmic tones, even in the distances, where it wandered fitfully and faint, and now and again was lost. It issued from out a great tawny flare, under the dense boughs of the trees, that grew a brighter yellow as Yates drew nearer, soon resolving itself into the illuminated squares of the doors and windows of the Pettingill cabin. More than once figures, with gigantic shadows that reached high up among the trees, eclipsed these lights, and suggested to him the superannuated spectators of the festivity, looking in upon it from porch and window. Certain masses of shadow began to be differentiated amidst the dusky, tawny vistas in the darkness, now only vaguely asserting an alien texture from the heavy shade of the foliage, and now becoming definite and recognizable as sundry household furnishings, evicted and thrust upon the bare ground to make room for the dancing. The loom cut a sorry figure standing out under the trees. Dimly discerned, it seemed to wear an aspect of forlorn astonishment, consciously grotesque and discouraged. And then, as the path wound, it receded to obscurity, and his attention was bespoken by the spinning-wheels close by the wood-pile, all a-teeter on the uneven flooring of the chips, and now and again, as if by a common impulse, awhirl in a solemn, hesitant revolution, as some tricksy wind came out of the woods and went its way.

A sinuous turn of the river brought it close to the

Pettingill cabin, and in the darkness he could see the stars, all come down to the earth, the splendid Lyra playing in the ripples. A flare, too, from the festive halls glassed itself in certain shallows; the rainbow hues of the warping bars hard by were reflected on this placid surface, and the great gaunt frame for the first time beheld its skeleton proportions. The rhythmic beat of the untiring feet on the puncheon floor of the cabin pulsed with the palpitations of the stars; the fiddle sang and sang as ceaselessly as the chanting cicada without, and the frogs intoning their sylvan runes by the waterside. All the night seemed given over, in a certain languorous, subtly pensive way, to the rustic merry-making of the infair, and only Stephen Yates felt himself an intruder and out of place. As his step fell upon the porch, in its most secluded and shadowy corner, he winced to note the quick, alert turning from the window of a shaggy gray head, and the keen, peering eyes of the hospitably intent father of the bridegroom who made the feast.

"Ye, Steve!" he cried out, "what ye kem a-sneakin' up ter the house that-a-way fur? Howdy! howdy!"

This stentorian welcome, pitched high to drown the sound of the dancing and the long-drawn cadence of the violin, diverted the attention of the by-standers, who, their faces unfamiliar in the combined effects of the high lights from the windows and the deep shadows of the darkness without, all turned to gaze at the new-comer and to assist at the colloquy.

"We-uns hev all been a-gittin' married round hyar lately. Whar's that purty wife o' yourn? Lef' her

at home?" Genuine dismay and covert rebuke
were in the very inflections of the host's voice,
although he sought to make it as hearty and effervescent as before. " Lef' her at home? Ter mind
the baby? Waal, we air a-goin' ter miss her, but
mebbe the baby would hev missed her mo'. Waal,
ye air welcome, ennyhow."

"They tell me, Yates," remarked one of the by-
standers, with the pious intention of making himself
disagreeable, " ez you-uns hev got the meanes' baby
in the kentry. Plumb harries ye out'n house an'
home with the temper of him."

" I have hearn that, too," affirmed another, the
gleaming teeth of his half-illumined face attesting
his relish of the abashed attitude of the forlorn Benedict. " I hev hearn 'way down ter Hang-Over
Mountain big tales 'bout'n the survigrous temper o'
that thar brat o' yourn. They 'low they kin hear
him holler plumb ter the Leetle Tennessee."

The others exchanged glances of derision. The
goaded father plucked up a trifle of spirit.

" He *may* have a survigrous temper, an' he *do* holler; he hev got the lungs ter do it; fur I tell ye
now he's a *whale!* He air goin' ter be the Big
Man o' these mountings—a reg'lar Samson!"

"Sure enough?" demanded the host, who, in his
double character of entertainer and father, showed
more interest in " leetle Mose " than the bachelors felt,
except as he subdued his paternal relative and rendered him ridiculous.

"Yes, sir! Git him to stand on his feet, sir, an'
I tell ye his head will reach that high." Yates measured off a length of the post at least twice the height

of Moses. "*He's a whale!*" And, with a gravely triumphant nod, he pushed boldly into the room, although he knew that the rows of elderly women against the wall were commenting upon his "insurance" in appearing without his wife, thence proceeding, doubtless, to tear the character of the "leetle Moses" in such manner as that flimsy and much rent and riddled fabric was capable of being further shred.

The floor trembled and elastically vibrated to the tread of the dancers. The fiddler was seated in a rickety chair, precariously perched upon a table that evidently felt also the recurrent thrills of the measured pace. An intimation of the reverence in which his genius was held was given in the generous glass at the feet of the musician, never allowed to grow empty, however often, with a dexterous downward lurch, he caught it up and applied it to his lips in the intervals of the "figures," which he cried aloud in a stentorian voice. The big boots on his long crossed legs swayed above the heads of the company; his own head was not far from the festoons of red peppers swinging from the brown beams, his face was rapt, his cheek rested on the violin; his eyes were half-closed, and yet his vision was clear enough to detect any effort on the part of a passer-by to perpetrate the threadbare joke of appropriating the glass at his feet devoted to his refreshment. Then the fiddle-bow demonstrated a versatile utility in the sharp rap which it could deal, and its swiftness in resuming its more ostensible uses. There was little laughter amongst the young hunters and their partners. They danced with glistening eyes and flushed cheeks and a solemn agility, each man-

date of the fiddler watched for with expectant interest, and obeyed with silent alacrity. They were all
familiar to Steve Yates, looking on from the vantage-
ground of his twenty-two years at the scenes of his
youth, as it were; for in this primitive society the
fact that he was a married man rendered him as
ineligible for a dancing partner as the palsy could
have done. Only Leonard Rhodes seemed something of a novelty. He hailed from the county town,
and was a candidate for the Legislature. In the
nimble pursuance of the road to success and fame
he mingled in the dance, and he would have esteemed
it fortunate could his devoirs have always been as
congenial. He affected a pronounced rural air, although even his best manners were further from the
cosmopolitan standard at which he habitually aimed
than he himself realized. He was a tall, well-built,
brown-haired young man, with a deeply sunburned
face, a small, laughing brown eye, a reddish-brown,
waving beard of a fine tint and lustre, which he
usually had dyed a darker tone to evade the red
shade considered so great a defect in that region.
Owing to the length of his absence from his home
in the interests of his canvass, and the lack of the
village barber and his arts, its color had quite regained
its pristine value. He wore sedulously his old clothes,
which, upon his handsome figure, hardly looked so old
or so plain or so democratic as he would fain have had
his constituents see them, or, indeed, as the garments
would have seemed on another man. He danced
impartially and successively with every girl in the
room; and it was well for his political prospects,
doubtless, that he had such elastic and tough re-

sources for this amusement at his command, since the neglect of any one of the fair might have resulted in the loss of an indefinite number of votes among her relatives of the sterner sex. His opponent, a family man forty-five years of age, was in disastrous eclipse. The elder candidate could only stand in a corner with some old codgers, who were painfully unresponsive to his remarks and his jolly stories, and whose attention was prone to wander from his long, cadaverous, bearded face as he talked, and to follow the mazes of the dance.

Yates bethought himself of Rhodes's friend, the archæologist, and catching sight of him lounging in a window opposite, his face lighted with the first suggestion of pleasure that the evening had offered. He made the tour of the room gradually, pausing now to keep out of the way of the dancers; now darting mouse-like along the wall in the rear of a couple advancing to the centre; now respectfully edging past a row of the mountain dowagers seated in splint-bottomed chairs, and talking with loud, shrill glee, bestowing but scant recognition on the man who had left his wife at home. At last, after many hairbreadth escapes, he reached Mr. Shattuck, still lolling upon the window-seat.

"How hev ye been a-comin' on?" Yates demanded, looking down at him with a pleased smile.

For Mr. Shattuck, without the affectation of rustic proclivities, made his way so fairly into the predilections of the mountaineers that his friend Rhodes, who held himself a famous tactician and full of all the finer enterprises to capture public favor, had asked more than once how he managed it.

" I *don't manage* it," the other had said.

He was a man of some twenty-eight or thirty years of age, of medium height and with a slender figure, clad somewhat negligently in a dark suit of flannel; he wore a small, soft, blue hat with an upturned brim, which left his features unshaded. They were very keenly chiselled features, not otherwise striking, but their clear cutting imparted delicacy and intimations of refined force to his pale, narrow face. He had a long, drooping brown moustache, and his hair, cut close, was of a kindred tint, but darker. His eyes were full of light and life, darkly gray, and with heavy lashes, and as they rested upon the scene, unique to his experience, for he was city bred, one might never have divined the circumstance of initiation, so ready an acceptance of it all in its best interpretations did they convey. He made apparently no effort to assume this air and mental attitude. As he looked up his glance was singularly free and unaffected.

" I'm taking it all in," he said.

Yates, his fancy titillated by a fresh interest, his blood beginning to pulse at last to the rhythm of happiness in the air, for which the old fiddle marked the time, grudged himself so much pleasure which Adelaide could not share. His heart was warm with the thought of her; a subtle pain of self-reproach thrilled through his consciousness, and presently her name was on his lips.

" My wife," he said, with unwonted communicativeness to the stranger, " she's a great hand fur sech goin's on ez this; an' sech a dancer! Ye mought ez well compare a herd o' cows ter a nimble young fawn ez compare them gals ter Adelaide."

As he roared this out with all the force of his lungs above the violin's strain and the recurrent beat of the dancing feet, his enthusiasm re-enforcing the distinctness and volume of his speech, the careless Mr. Shattuck became slightly embarrassed, and looked about from one side to the other, as if fearful that the colloquy might be overheard. But no one seemed to notice except a certain long and lank mountaineer standing hard by, grizzled and middle-aged, who bore earnest testimony to the same effect, leaning down toward Shattuck to make himself heard.

"Yes, sir; a plumb beautiful dancer; light on her feet, I tell ye! The purties' gal ennywhar round hyar. I hev knowed her sence she war no bigger'n that thar citizen over yander."

He gave a jerk of his thumb toward a year-old child on the outskirts of the crowd standing at the knee of his grandmother, who supported him in an upright posture by keeping a clutch upon his petticoats, while he bobbed up and down in time to the music, thumping first one foot and then the other upon the floor, emulating and imitating the dancers, participating in the occasion with the zest of a born worldling. His grave face, his glittering eye, his scarlet plumpness of cheek, and his evident satisfaction in his own performance combined to secure an affectionate ridicule from the by-standers; but he, and indeed all else, was unobserved by the dancers.

"Ef I hed thunk Adelaide would hev put up with sech ez you-uns, Steve, I'd hev tried myself," protested the elderly bachelor, "though I ain't much of a marryin' man in gineral."

Yates received this with less geniality. "Ye

needn't hev gin yerse'f the trouble," he retorted. " Haffen the mounting tried thar luck, an' war sent away with thar finger in thar mouth."

" An' 'mongst 'em all she made ch'ice of a man ez goes a-pleasurin' whilst she be lef' ter set at home like a old 'oman," and with a nod, half reproach, half derision, he strolled away.

A mild form of pleasuring certainly, to watch the solemn capering of the young mountaineers to and fro on the shaking puncheons, the vibrations of which, communicated to the tallow dips sputtering upon every shelf and table, caused the drowsy yellow light to so fluctuate that with the confusion and the wild whirl of dancing figures the details of the scene were like some half-discriminated furnishings of a dream. Such as it was, Yates's conscience gave him a sharper pang, especially when he thought of her as he had seen her last, the quiet, pure moonlight falling fibrous and splendid through the open door upon her grieved, upturned face as she crouched on the floor beside the sleeping child, angelic in his smiling, pensive dreams. Yates felt that he had been harsh; he felt this so poignantly that he gave himself no plea of justification. All that she had said seemed now natural and devoid of intention ; only his alert censoriousness could have called it in question—and he had been her choice of all the mountain.

" Adelaide ain't keerin' fur sech ez this," he said, loftily. " A nangel o' light couldn't 'tice her away from leetle Mose. She fairly dotes on all the other chil'n in the worl' jes' out'n complimint ter leetle Mose. I hed a plumb quar'l with her this evenin'," he added, turning to the archæologist with a smile, "arter I hed told her ez ye reckoned them Leetle People buried thar on the rise war nuthin' but chil'n. She jes' fired up, sir, an' 'lowed ef ye went a-foolin' round them with yer fine book l'arnin' an' diggin' up thar bones, she'd pick ye off with a rifle. Leetle Mose hev made her mighty tender to all the chil'n."

Shattuck glanced up with a good-natured laugh; he recognized only fantastic hyperbole in the threat, and Yates once more experienced a qualm of self-reproach to realize how seriously he had regarded it, how heavily he had punished the extravagant, meaningless indignation.

"The only trouble I fear is getting the consent of the owner of the land," Shattuck said, easily, and his eyes reverted to the object that had before absorbed his attention. It was not the maelstrom of "Ladies to the right." Yates, following the direction of his intent gaze, experienced a trifle of surprise that it should be nothing more striking than Letitia Pettingill, the daughter of the house, standing in the doorway silently watching the dancing.

"A scrap of a gal" she was esteemed in the mountains, being a trifle under the average height, and delicately built in proportion. The light flickering out upon the porch barely showed the dark green background of hop-vines in the black darkness without. Her dull, light-blue cotton dress, defined against this sombre hue, was swaying slightly aslant, the wind breaking the straight folds of the skirt. Her complexion was of a clear creamy tone; the hair, curling on her brow, and massed at the nape of the neck and there tied closely, the thick, short, curling ends hanging down, was a dusky brown, not black; and her eyes, well set and with long dark lashes and distinctly arched eyebrows, were of that definite blue which always seems doubly radiant and lucent when illumined by an artificial light. Her small straight features had little expression, but her lips were finely cut and delicately red. She held up one arm against the door-frame, and bent her inscrutable eyes on the quickening whirl.

"Waal, what Fee Guthrie kin see in her or what she kin see in Fee Guthrie ter fall in love with one another beats my time," said Yates, with a grin, commenting openly upon the focus of the other's attention.

Mr. Shattuck evidently perceived something of interest in her; he did not lift his eyes, but he rejoined with freshened animation:

"Guthrie? The young 'bear with the sore head' who owns the pygmy burying-ground?"

"That very actial bear," cried Yates, delighted with this characterization of his friend and neighbor. "His old cabin thar's 'bout tumbled down; 'twar lef' him by his gran'dad, an' he lives up on the mounting with his step-mam; but he owns that house too; his dad's dead. Some folks 'low," he continued, rehearsing with evident gusto the gossip, "ez he don't keep comp'ny with Litt Pettingill. He jes' sot by her wunst at camp-meetin', 'kase him an' her war all the sinners present, an' that started the tale ez he war courtin' her; everybody else war either convicted o' sin, an' at the mourner's bench, or else shoutin' saints o' the Lord, prayin' an' goin' 'mongst the mourners. I never hearn tell o' nobody keepin' comp'ny with Letishy Pettingill; I'll be bound it'll take a heap better-lookin' gal 'n her ter suit Fee Guthrie."

"I should like ter know where he'd find her," observed Shattuck.

Yates turned to bend the eye of astonished and questioning criticism upon the unconscious object of their scrutiny.

"Ye 'low ez Litt Pettingill air well-favored, stranger?" he demanded at last, in amazement.

"Very pretty and very odd. I never saw a face in the least like hers."

"Waal!" exclaimed Yates. "Litt Pettingill's beauty air news ter the mountings. Some folks 'low she hev got a cur'us kind o' mind. Some even say she air teched in the head." His tone seemed to intimate that Mr. Shattuck, in the face of this fact, had reason to reform his standard of taste.

That gentleman shook his own head in contemptuous negation. "Never in this world. Never with that face."

"Waal, ye can't size her up now," insisted Yates, "leetle ez she be"—with a grin—"whilst she be a-standin' still. Ef ye war ter see her a-movin' an' a-turnin' roun', she's ez quick an' keen-lookin' ez a knife-blade in a suddint fight, an' mighty nigh ez dangerous. She looks at ye like she *warn't* lookin' at ye, but plumb through yer skull inter yer brains, ter make sure ye war tellin' her what ye thunk. She talks cur'ous, too, sorter onexpected an' contrariwise, an' she never *could* git religion. That's mighty cur'ous in gal-folks. I ain't so mighty partic'lar 'bout men Christians, though I'm a perfesser myself, but religion 'pears ter me ter kem sorter nat'ral ter gal-

folks.   'Tain't 'kase she's too religious that she ain't
a-dancin'.   It's jes' 'kase nobody hev asked her.   She
ain't no sorter fav*orite* 'mongst the boys."

Mr. Shattuck suddenly glanced up, half laughing,
half triumphant, for the little figure in blue had just
been led out to the centre of the floor, and the doorway was vacant save for a large brindled cur that
stood upon the threshold, wagging his tail and
watching the scene with a suave, indulgent, presidial
gaze, as if he were the patron of the ball.   To be
sure, her partner was that man of facile admiration,
the candidate Rhodes, but Shattuck experienced a
vicarious satisfaction that it could not be said that
she had not been asked to dance at all.

He watched the couple as the set formed anew,
and noticed that Rhodes, with his sedulously rustic
air, was beginning in the interim some conversation, stooping from his superior height for her reply.
He rose suddenly to the perpendicular, an almost
startled surprise upon his face as he stared ; then
he clapped his hands with a jocular air of applause,
and his round laugh rang out with an elastic, un-
forced merriment, which suggested to his friend that
he was finding the ways of policy not such thorny
ways after all.   Shattuck wondered vaguely if this
demonstration, too, were of the affectations of propitiation, or if what she had said were clever enough
to elicit it, or merely funny.   His eyes followed the
little blue-clad figure as she began to dance — her
untutored movements all in rhythm with the music,
as an azalea dances in time to the wind.   Now she
drifted about with short, mincing, hesitant steps, now
with flying feet and skirts whirling, as if responsive

to the circling impetus she could in no wise resist. She looked almost a child amongst the burlier and coarser forms. With her delicate hands, and her tiny feet, and her spirited face, and the faint blue color of her dress, she bore an odd contrast to the buxom beauty of the other mountain girls, clad in variegated plaided homespun. Her blue eyes were alight and glancing; her parted lips were red; her feet hardly seemed to touch the floor as her hands fell from one partner's grasp, and she came wafting through the party - colored maze, with outstretched arms, to another.

For the fun was waxing fast and furious with the added and unique diversion known as "Dancin' Tucker." The forlorn "Tucker" himself, partner-less in the centre of the set, capered solemnly up and down, adjusting his muscles and his pride to ridicule, which was amply attested by the guffaws that ever and anon broke from the spectators. However nonchalantly each temporary "Tucker" might deport himself in his isolated position, the earnest-ness of his desire to escape from his unwelcome conspicuousness by securing a partner, and his sin-cere objection to his plight, were manifested always upon the fiddler's command, "Gen'lemen ter the right," when he might join the others on their round, dogging the steps of the youth he wished to fore-stall, both balancing to each lady in succession. If, by chance, the "Tucker" succeeded first in catching a damsel's hands and swinging her around at the moment that the magic command " Promenade all !" sounded on the air, he left his pillory to the slower swain, who must needs forthwith " dance Tucker."

The traits of character elicited by the "Tucker" rôle constitute its true fascinations, and are manifold. One nimble young hunter seemed almost stricken with the palsy upon his isolation, or gradually petrifying, while he sought to dance alone in the middle of the circle, so heavily did each foot follow the other as he hopped aimlessly up and down; the expression of his eyes was so ludicrously pitiable and deprecatory, as they swept the coterie of the dowagers who lined the walls, that they screamed with laughter. The instant "Promenade all!" sounded upon the air, he made a frantic burst for liberty so precipitate that at the moment of touching the hand of the damsel of his choice he suddenly lost his equilibrium, and fell with a thunderous crash quite outside of the charmed periphery. Amidst the shouts of the company Rhodes caught the relinquished hands of the waiting lady, and triumphantly gallopaded away, thus escaping the ignominy of "dancin' Tucker."

And then Rhodes bethought himself suddenly of that future seat in the legislative halls of the State. Shattuck laughed to divine his anxiety as the meditative gravity gathered upon Rhodes's flushed and distended countenance; his white teeth, all on display, suddenly disappeared. His hand doubtfully stroked his beautiful undyed beard. There was something worse even than dancing Tucker at the infair. With every sharpened sense and every heightened emotion normal to the estate of candidacy, he was appreciating with how much less philosophy, with what scanty grace, indeed, he could endure to dance Tucker before the people at the polls in the

November election. As the rueful "Tucker," with every bone shaken, gathered himself up slowly from the floor amidst the screaming and stamping elders —even the dancers and the fiddler had paused to laugh — his face scarlet, his lips compressed with pain, his eyes nervously glancing, unseeing, hither and thither, like a creature's in a trap, Rhodes stepped out from his place.

"This ain't fair," he said, taking the "Tucker" by the arm; "you were ahead of me, and I'd have been left if you hadn't tripped up. *I'm* Tucker by rights, an' I always play fair."

The "Tucker" looked at him with a doubtful, red, frowning face; but as Rhodes jocularly took his place in the centre, and the violin began a *pizzicato* movement, as if all the strings were dancing too, with a long sigh of relief he accepted the situation, and presently joined in the laugh at the lorn candidate-Tucker.

The fact of an ulterior motive is a wonderfully reconciling influence. Leonard Rhodes was dancing his way into the ballot-box, and thus it was that he thought it consistent with his dignity to seek to be an especially comical "Tucker." But the essential humor of the character of "Tucker" is his unwillingness to be funny, and his helpless absurdity and eagerness to elude his solitary dance. Human nature is so complex that even those whose profession it is to know it can predicate little even upon its most fundamental facts. As Rhodes bounded about, now and then executing a double-shuffle and cutting a pigeon-wing of an extraordinary agility, and more than once intentionally suffering an opportunity of securing a partner to escape him, remaining "Tucker" through several rounds, Shattuck heard comments among the by-standers altogether at variance with the candidate's expectations. "That's all done a purpose!" "He makes a tremenjious fool of hisself!" "*He* don't expect ter git married in this kentry!"

Shattuck wondered by what subtle unclassified perception, appertaining to candidate-nature, these unexpected results were at last borne in to Rhodes's consciousness, since he was unable to hear the whispers by reason of the noise of the dancing, or, in the midst of his absorbing saltatory activities, to mark any change of aspect among the spectators. His jocund face grew gradually incongruously grave and troubled as he bounded about with undiminished agility. These were muscular forces now, however, at work, sustaining his continuance—mere strength—instead of the joyous elasticity and animal spirits that had at first made him so light. When, finally, it was possible to bring his penance to a close, his politic monitions had all become confused and contradictory, and he made as blind and vehement a rush for the nearest opportunity as if he had been merely one of the young mountaineers, with no further or deeper purpose in participating in the pastime than the pleasure of dancing. His eyes seemed suddenly opened to his precipitancy as he stood successful among the couples, equipped at last with a partner, and flushed and tired and panting. A wild acclamation of jeering joy had arisen among the spectators, who during Rhodes's incumbency had grown tired and lost zest, for it was seldom, indeed, that

Felix Guthrie "danced Tucker." As the young mountaineer, lowering and indignant, stood looking at Rhodes, the genuine mirth of the situation was communicated once more to the dancers, to the violin, and to the spectators, and the whole infair was throbbing with a new lease on life. The tallow candles, sputtering on tables and shelves, which had occasionally bowed almost to extinction before the passing breeze—the whole party vanishing in these momentary eclipses—seemed now endowed with freshened brilliancy; the fiddler changed the tune to a merrier; the odor of apple-jack, newly drawn from the barrel, was imbued with zestful suggestions as the jug was passed among the on-lookers; only to Leonard Rhodes did the hour seem late, and the room hot, and the violin dissonant, and the company frowsily rustic and distasteful, and himself an un-lucky devil to have his fate and his best and highest aspirations and his chosen walk in life at their arbi-trary will. No candidate, making the crucial test of personal experience, ever felt more doubtful of the wisdom of republican institutions than did Leonard Rhodes, realizing the fatuity of his choice for dis-placement, on meeting the gaze of Fee Guthrie, whom he had constituted "Tucker" for the nonce, for Guthrie's aspect gave no room for speculation as to the real sentiments with which he regarded the position.

As Felix Guthrie stood in his conspicuous place, both the strangers were impressed with the large symmetry of the scale upon which he was built, its perfect proportion, its graceful ease. His boots, reaching to the knee, were of a length and weight

that might have been an effective bar to any display
of agility on the part of one less accustomed to such
cumbrous foot-gear.   His brown jeans coat was but-
toned to the chin and girded about with a leather
belt, in which there were a pistol and a hunting-
knife—in fact, the only preparation which he had
made for the dance was the removal of his spurs and
his hat.   His face was deeply bronzed by the sun
and the wind, somewhat too square, but otherwise so
regularly cut that the features were inexpressive, save
for the long brown eyes, with their lowering, suspicious, antagonistic gleam.   The full, dark, straight
eyebrows almost met above them.   His hair, of a
rich yellow color, falling in long, loose, feminine
ringlets on either side of this large, surly, aggressive
face, had an almost grotesque effect, so far is our
civilization from the days of the lovelocks.   It hung
down on his collar, and curled with a grace and
readiness that were the envy of more than one of his
partners.   He was known far and wide as an "ugly
customer," in reference to his surly and belligerent
traits of character, which rather overshadowed his
physical endowments.   Rhodes, however, had no
fear of him, save for his political influence, for he
was a man of some hereditary consideration, and of
substance—of more than moderate means, according
to the standard of the cove—and in no wise had he
ever been known to be placated or to forgive an affront.   It was with a heavy heart that the candidate
began to dance to his doom, which he now felt was in-
evitable, wishing that he could have the immunity of
his opponent, whose age had rendered him ineligible
for mingling in the festivities of the infair.   His

eyes ever and anon wandered to the "Tucker," who was beginning to dance too, not vehemently, but with a wonderful softness and lightness, considering his ponderous accoutrements, his curls all in commotion, delicately waving and oscillating about his fierce, intent, unsmiling face. This was a "Tucker" of unique interest and value. The windows were full of the loiterers without; the spectators about the walls laughed breathlessly, and now and again stood up to catch an unimpeded glimpse of him amidst the dancers moving to the fiddler's mandate.

The musician was a wise man in his generation, and understood the human nature amongst which his lot was cast. He had kept sundry "Tuckers" dancing, as mechanically and unwillingly as if they trod on hot iron, long, long after they had despaired of ever hearing again the "Gen'lemen ter the right" which gave them their chance, often elusive, to escape. But he made Fee Guthrie's "Tucker" a short rôle. The spectators were hardly accustomed to him in the unbeloved character when the sudden command "To the right" smote sharply upon the air, and the circle was awhirl anew. Felix Guthrie, in the midst, manifested none of the precipitancy of his predecessors. His eyes were aglow; his feet moved softly in certain "steps" of his own invention; his whole attitude was one of expectancy, of abeyance. Scanning continually the revolving crowd, he looked like a panther ready to spring. When the word came at last, and he darted forward, the whole attack was most accurately adjusted to the moment. He had chosen to forestall Rhodes, who was balancing to Letitia Pettingill. There was only an instant's difference in the quick movements, but instead of "swinging" the man who came first, according to the rules, she suddenly swerved aside, passed under Guthrie's outstretched arm, and, with a radiant face and sapphire eyes, held out both hands to the candidate, who, bewildered, clasped them, and the two swung round in the customary revolution, leaving Guthrie "Tucker" as before. He stood as if petrified in the instant's silence that ensued. Then, as a great clamor of laughter and surprised comment arose, he sprang upon Rhodes, his grip on the candidate's throat. Rhodes, himself of a brawny strength, had put forth its uttermost to defend himself. A wave of wind went through the room, flickering all its candles and blending the fluctuating shadows. In their midst the bewildered guests saw, as in a dream, Guthrie deal, with the butt of the pistol clasped in his hand, a blow upon the candidate's head. The next moment the sharp crack of the discharged weapon pealed through the room, and the puncheons trembled with the heavy fall as Rhodes came down at full length on the floor. The violin quavered into silence, the crowd drew off suddenly, then again pressed close about the insensible figure; the wind once more went through the rooms, with all the shadows racing after; and only the baby, still dancing in the corner—although he, too, had stopped a moment and winked hard at the clamorous, jarring tone of the pistol—was unaware that "dancin' Tucker" at the infair had ended in bloodshed, and that the gayety was over for the time.

III.

Shattuck sprang up, crying out, "Stop him! Don't let him escape!" as he rushed to lift his friend's bleeding head from the floor. Despite the turmoil of his emotions, he appreciated with all his keenly tutored senses the antithesis of the effect of Felix Guthrie's massive immobility as he stood hard by wiping the blood from the butt of the smoking pistol.

"Stop him!" he retorted; "hedn't ye better wait till I set out ter run somewhar?"

There was a bravado in the situation not altogether distasteful, Shattuck knew, to the spirit of the backwoodsmen, and although there were muttered reproaches amongst them, no one laid hands on Felix Guthrie, still looking about to the right and to the left with lowering eyes, and still wiping the blood from his pistol with the soft brim of his hat, that it might not rust upon the weapon to its injury.

The most vehement expressions of reprobation came from the host, who loudly upbraided Felix Guthrie for his lack of "manners," and bewailed the omen of the incident, as he knelt beside the wounded candidate with one of the limp hands in his.

"Thar ain't been nobody died on these puncheons sence Sandy McVeigh called my gran'dad ter the door an' shot him down in his tracks! Thar's been cornsider'ble quiet hyar' sence. The old man war a powerful fighter an' a tartar, an' the neighborhood war peacefuller with him out'n it than in it, ef I *do* say it myse'f. An' now Fee Guthrie kems hyar a-killin' folks ter spite the infair—whenst we hev hed sech luck with the weddin' an' the supper an' all—an' stain up these old puncheons with a bloody death one more time !"

His gray shock head bobbed about over the prone figure, and as he made his unique lament he sought to stanch the wounds, still bleeding profusely. He rose with a sudden alacrity when, on the outskirts of the crowd, a heralding cry announced that the doctor was coming. Even then it was a question of propriety and hospitality which took precedence with him.

"Let's git him onto a bed, boys ; quick! quick! Don't let Doc Craig kem hyar an' tell the whole kentry-side ez we-uns let Mr. Rhodes die on the floor 'kase I don't vote on his side. I wonder I never thunk o' it before. Let's git him onto a bed."

Shattuck's objections to moving him were overborne in the turmoil. A dozen strong fellows seized the prostrate figure, and it was lifted as if it had no weight, and swiftly borne up the narrow stairs to be laid upon a bed in the roof-room. Shattuck, feeling helpless in the midst of these coercive circumstances, could only follow, his protests grinding between his teeth, almost unconsciously metamorphosed into curses. But as he rose step by step on the steep narrow stair blockaded by the crowd pressing after the wounded man, and the roof-room came gradually into view, he grew more content, so palpably for the better was the change. The window at each gable end stood open; into one fell the silvery splendor of the moon; the other was dusky with shadows, though beyond he caught the interfulgent rays amongst the sycamore leaves. The batten shutters swayed gently in the wind. The air was full of vaguely prophetic intimations of dawn. A pigeon that had nested in the niche between the chimney and the wall was astir for a moment, and cooed softly. The dust and glare of the room below seemed far away. The tent-like roof and the simple furnishing—a bed, a cedar chest, a few garments and some large wolf-skins hanging to the rafters—all were made visible by the gracious courtesy of the moon.

Shattuck fancied that he heard his friend sigh faintly as they placed him upon the great soft feather-bed—the whole structure of an uncommon stature, but promising ease and comfort in proportionate amplitude.

He made haste to seize his host's arm. "Send them all down," he said, in an imperative whisper; "you and I are enough to take the doctor's instructions. He needs air and quiet; send them all down."

To his relief, Zack Pettingill seemed to appreciate the suggestion. He turned abruptly to the great shadowy figures of the mountaineers, repeatedly lifting both arms and letting them fall with emphasis, as if he were driving a flock of sheep or poultry before him.

"*Git out*, boys," he said, in his most clamorous drawl. Shattuck's nerves recoiled from the rasping tone. "We-uns don't want the doctor-man around hyar preachin' an' namin' the devil like he seen him yistiddy—always skeers me out'n my skin ter hear 'bout *him* so familiar—an' sayin' we air crowdin' round jes' out'n cur'osity an' smotherin' the man an' ain't done all we could fur Candidate Rhodes. I wisht Rhodes *could* hev tuk another time and somebody else's place ter git shot! *Git out'n hyar*, boys!" And as he advanced upon the retiring crowd he once more lifted both arms high and let them fall.

"Hesh!" said one of the retreating mountaineers, in a warning tone—he had descended three or four steps of the staircase that entered the room at one corner, his head and shoulders still visible above the floor. "The doctor's a-comin'." The dusky figures pressed close after him. He glanced up once more, his face suddenly illumined with a vague flicker. "*With a candle*," he added, under his breath, as if he imparted significant matter.

Shattuck drew a long sigh of relief. At last he would be able to see his friend in proper care, and would be free from that terrifying sense of responsibility which sorely harassed him, hampered as he was by the unaccustomed conditions of the place. He would have the aid and sympathy of a man of some education, and on whose judgment he could rely—one of his own nationality at least; for he suddenly felt an alien amongst these men, whose springs of action so differed from his own.

He waited breathlessly, watching the light grow stronger, casting a gigantic shadow of the tousled head of the master of the house upon the walls, as the heavy tread came nearer. The host leaned down to take the candle from the doctor's hand, and in

4

the flicker of the motion the stranger was in the room before the light revealed him. Shattuck, advancing eagerly, suddenly paused. A pang of disappointment — more, despair — quivered through his heart. He beheld a tall, slow, shambling man, clad in old brown jeans, with a broad-brimmed hat, and the heavy boots affected by the mountaineers; he had a grave, meditative face, and he fixed his eyes upon the patient on the bed with that expression of proprietorship which everywhere marks the physician. Otherwise Shattuck could not have believed his senses. "Are you—are you—" he stammered, overlooking in his agitation the slight gesture of salutation with which the stranger recognized his presence there—"are you a regular graduate of a medical college?"

The mountaineer bent a lack-lustre eye upon him. "*Which?*" he said, in amazement.

"What sort of doctor are you?" demanded Shattuck, troublous recollections of the old idea of charms and spells rising to his mind.

"I be a yerb doctor, by the grace o' God," returned the mountain practitioner. He took, without more ado, the candle from his host, and with it in one hand looked fixedly down at the white face, all streaked and stained, upon the pillow.

Shattuck, constrained by every sentiment of loyalty to his friend of which he was capable, quivering with undeserved self-reproach that he had not earlier made inquiries which might have elicited the nature of the aid to be summoned, frantic with anxiety for the result, and lest he omit some essential duty, turned hastily, and without another word went straight down the stairs. With some instinctive policy animating him, he sought out the bridegroom as most likely to be won over to his theory. This was a tall, heavily built young mountaineer, pleased with the conspicuousness of his position in proportion as his wife, a demure and staid young woman, was abashed and overcome by it. He had that universal bridal manner, intimating a persuasion that nobody else has ever been married. He received Shattuck with the kindly condescension likely to grace one who has attained so unique a distinction.

"I suppose, Mr. Pettingill," said Shattuck, craftily, "that you don't feel at home here now, as you are going away to live among the Gossams. I hear you have built a house across the creek from your father-in-law. I suppose you feel quite one with the Gossams now."

"Oh, Lord, no! that I ain't," declared the bridegroom, with the precipitate denial of one whose secret fear has been put into words, and who seeks to boldly exorcise it. "I hain't married all the fambly; one's a plenty, thanky. Ye needn't be afeared ter speak yer mind 'bout 'em ter me. I'd hev liked Malviny jes' ez well ef she hadn't been a Gossam."

The thought of the rose that by any other name would smell as sweet came incongruously into Shattuck's mind for the instant, but he rejoined hastily:

"Well, if I could get speech of any member of the Pettingill family that cares anything for the name, I would say that Mr. Pettingill has behaved very strangely—sending for an herb doctor instead of the kind of physician that Mr. Rhodes would have if he were at home."

"Lord!" exclaimed the young fellow, laying his hand on Shattuck's shoulder and looking earnestly into his eyes, as they stood on the porch beside one of the flaring windows, "Phil Craig, they say, kin all but raise the dead; he's reg'lar gifted—a plumb yerb doctor. The t'other kind—why, they *pizens* ye"— kindly didactic, **and with a rising** inflection.

"Well, people in **Colbury will** think it mighty strange that Mr. Pettingill didn't send for the kind of doctor that Mr. Rhodes would have had if he could have chosen," Shattuck retorted, with a frown. "You all vote against Rhodes, don't you?"

The countenance of the bridegroom was embarrassed and troubled. Perhaps he thought the festivities made to celebrate his happiness had been sufficiently overcast without further clouding them with political differences.

"But we-uns hain't got no gredge at Mr. Rhodes," he stipulated.

"I should be much grieved," continued Shattuck, "if Mr. Pettingill—he seems to be a worthy man— should be included in the prosecution, **or** any member of his family involved in any way; but of course Mr. Rhodes's relatives and political friends will make things hot if—if he should die here with medical attendance denied him."

"Good Lord!" the young man burst out, "*we-uns* hed nuthin' ter do with it—jes' Fee Guthrie. Do ye think they'd prosecute Fee? 'Twar jes' a fight—a sorter fight—but *we-uns*—"

"If I knew where a sure-enough doctor lives, or could find anybody that does know, I'd have him here if he had to come a hundred miles. I've asked and asked, and nobody seems to know."

"Wait a minute "—the bridegroom turned to intercept old Zack Pettingill as he came down the stairs.

Bold as Shattuck's policy had been, he quaked to witness his own suggestion of political enmity, malicious denial of medical attendance, and the possibility of prosecution, introduced as a threat into Zack Pettingill's honest and hospitable consciousness. And yet he could but laugh at the manner of it. In order to capture and speak apart to his parent, the bridegroom had drawn the old man almost behind the door. In fact, while the son stood visible, with earnest and urgent gestures and grave and deprecatory countenance, the effect of his communication upon the unseen Pettingill was only intimated by the agitation which beset the door, as the old man floundered behind it in the activities of his anger, and his contemptuous floutings of the suggested implication in crime. Now the door quivered on its hinges; now it received a blow that would have sent it flaunting wide had not the young man's hand restrained it; and finally, when it became quiet, Shattuck divined the success of his effort before the bridegroom turned away and the liberated father emerged from behind it. He was not prepared, however, for the glower of deep-seated hatred which Zack Pettingill cast upon him through the open window before he turned toward the stairs. Shattuck felt suddenly wounded; the blood mounted to his face as if he had received a blow; and if he had for the moment forgotten that in these mountains the poorest honest man holds his dignity as safe from the imputation of crime as if he were a magnate and millionaire, and resents it as dearly, what other course could he have pursued with the interests he had at stake—his own conscience and his friend's life? As he paced to and fro the short limits of the porch, there sounded almost immediately the quick thud of galloping hoofs down the rocky hill, surging through the river, becoming fainter on the opposite bank, and so dying away. In his preoccupation he attached no importance to this, as the guests were now beginning to take leave. Only when young Pettingill reappeared, a trifle breathless and with an excited eye, and the comment, "We sent fur Doctor Ganey — seventeen mile—Steve Yates rid fur him," did Shattuck connect the swift departure that he had unconsciously remarked with the success of his mission. He did not triumph in it as he had expected. His sensitiveness, with which he was well enough endowed to keep him amply supplied with unhappiness, was all astir within him; the knowledge of the wounds that he had dealt—deep, bitter, and intentional—had developed a double edge and a sharp retroaction. He doubted if in all Zack Pettingill's hard, limited, and most respectable life he had ever been brought face to face with the ignominy of such suspicions and such threats. Not that the taking of life on a grievous provocation and an implacable quarrel was held, in the mountain ethics, reprehensible; the deep turpitude lay in the suggested circumstances—a conspiracy, a political grudge, and the victim a guest. It would have been far indeed from his own roof-tree could Zack Pettingill, the very soul of hospitality, have contemplated the infamy of which Shattuck had affected to suspect him. He wondered a trifle that so ignorant, so coarse, so violent, so lawless a man should be so vulnerable in the more æsthetic sensibilities, forgetting that traits of character are as the solid wood, indigenous; and that cultivation is, after all, only surface polish and veneer, and can never give to common deal the rich heart, the weight, and the value of the walnut or the oak.

"My wife an' all her folks air a-goin' now, an' I reckon I'll hev ter hustle along an' jine 'em," drawled the bridegroom, presently. "I reckon they hev hed enough o' dancin' an' fiddlin' an' sech. Thar ain't been ez much dancin' in the cove afore I got married sence the Big Smoky war built—'thout," he qualified, meditatively, for he was a man of speculation—"'thout 'twar the Injuns. Some 'low ez Injuns war plumb gin over ter dancin' in the old times "—with the sufficient air of an ethnological authority—" war dances an' scalp dances." He smiled in slow ridicule. "Folks didn't dance none in the war ez we hed hyar-abouts—Fed and Cornfed—'thout ye call some o' them quicksteps on the back track dancin'—*they* war lively enough for ennything! But "—with the manner of resuming the subject—" they danced at the weddin' t'other night at Mr. Gossam's, an' they hev danced at the infair, an' now I hope nobody ain't goin' ter gin no mo' dances; leastwise not in complimint ter Malviny an' me. They air toler'ble tiresome ter me," he protested, with a *blasé* air. "An' I ain't s'prised none ef they air devices o' the devil ennyhow, ez ennybody mought know from the eend this one hev kem ter. Malviny ain't no dancer, an' air mighty religious, an' all this hyar fiddlin' an' glorifyin' hev been sorter terrifyin' ter her.   I ain't pious myse'f," he concluded, with an air which to Shattuck's discerning observation sufficiently identified his type as the incipient man of the world.   "I expec' ter go ter heav'n in partnership with Malviny—she's good enough fur two."

He strolled off to join a group whose departure was impeded by much hospitable insistence to remain longer, and by the presentation of bundles of the supper wrapped in paper ; for, alack! the disaster had preceded the opening of the supper-room, and its triumphs were and would ever be only a matter of conjecture.   The disappointment was stamped into the lines of Mrs. Pettingill's worn countenance.   It seemed a perversely withheld opportunity of joy in her restricted life, since it was deemed unmeet that the formal feasting should proceed while Leonard Rhodes lay up-stairs at the point of death. She could only cut great slices of cake, and press them upon her guests, with the wheezing adjuration, "Take it home, and *jedge* what luck we hed with the bakin' !"

She had been altogether despoiled of the fine show that the table in full array would have made, but the apple - brandy that had constituted Mr. Pettingill's share of the preparations, in circulation since the first arrival, had by no means been in vain.   He was disposed to offer his example as one that might with profit be adopted.   "I always b'lieved in a *handed* supper," he remarked.   "Then, ef—ef—an accident war ter happen' 'fore 'twar all over, folks wouldn't go away hongry from yer house, nohow.   But the wimmin-folks air so gin over ter pride an' fixin's that they air obleeged ter set out a *table* all tricked up an' finified off."

The violinist, however, was esteemed in some sort exempt from the rule of etiquette which necessitated the immediate dispersing of the company without the formal supper. A curious eye might have discovered him under the staircase which led to the wounded man's room. He sat with the "lap-board"—usually used in cutting out the men's clothes—across his knee, and here was ranged a liberal choice of the viands which the shed-room had contained. Most of the household dogs—there were twenty odd—were underfoot in the shed-room, presiding with a speechless frenzy of interest in the partition of the good things; but two of the younger ones sat at the fiddler's feet, and watched, with heads canted askew and the glistening eyes of admiration, the prodigies of his execution. The stiff tail of one of them—a pointer—sweeping the floor, now and again came in contact with the violin that stood on end in the corner, eliciting a discordant twanging of the strings, and a low, hollow, resonant murmur; whereupon the dog would rise with a knitted, puzzled brow and an air of irritated interruption, only to seat himself anew, and with a bland and freshened interest resume his earnest watch upon the violinist's movements. Again he would wag his tail in the joy of his heart, again strike inadvertently the strings of the instrument, and once more arise to vainly investigate the mystery of "this music in the air."

Occasionally the closed door hard by opened suddenly to disclose Mrs. Pettingill's anxious face and gray head, as she cast a searching glance to discern what havoc the fiddler had succeeded in making in the good things set before him. She added to the normal drawl of the mountaineers an individual wheeze of singular propitiations, and implying cordial and confidential relations. There may be more beautiful sounds, but none of more suave and soothing effect than that husky, "Jack, jes' try a glass o' this hyar cherry-bounce along with a bite o' pound-cake "—as she extended the " bite," which, in point of size, might have discouraged the jaws of the giant Cormoran, but never Jack Brace's. "It'll *rest* ye mightily, arter all the fiddlin' ye hev done." And again, "Jack, hev ye ever tasted my sweet-spiced peach pickles ?"

Jack had, indeed. But Jack said he never had, in order that he might renew the gustatory delights that he remembered.

Now and then less friendly eyes gazed in upon the nook. A gigantic mountaineer, slowly strolling through the half-deserted scene, came to a full halt hard by, leaned peeringly forward, took a step closer, and, with his shaggy-bearded face inclined pharisaically over the well-filled lap-board, demanded, in a tone of gruff reproof :

"What air ye a-doin' of hyar, gormandizing like ye hedn't hed nuthin' ter eat fur a week an' better, an' a man dyin' up-steers ?"

"Ye talk like I war a-nibblin' on Len Rhodes," cried Jack Brace, angered by the mere suggestion that etiquette required that he should desist. "My goin' hongry ain't a-goin' ter holp him, an' my eatin' arter fiddlin' all night ain't a-goin' ter hender. Ef he can't go ter heaven 'count o' me an' this leetle brandy peach "—as he held up the appetizing morsel both the dogs rose up on their nimble hind-legs in pathetic misapprehension of his intention, their eyes widening with dismay as he withdrew the dainty effectually from view—"why, he ain't got *enough* religion ter git thar, that's all!"

Shattuck, going up-stairs, glanced down, upon hearing the words, at the cosy nook and the fiddler, and was reminded anew of his friend's danger, his sense of achievement in carrying his point having served for a time to dull his anxiety. The room had taken on that strange, discordant, forlorn effect which is characteristic of a scene of gayety overpast, and is never compassed by mere bareness, or disarray, or disuse. There was a pervasive sense of expended forces, as if all the elation and effervescent spirit exhaling here had left a veritable vacuum. The candles on shelf and niche and table were sputtering in their sockets or burning dimly. Here and there mountaineers slouched about, awaiting their womankind, who presently flustered out of the shed-room wrapped in shawls, and with big bundles of the "supper" so unhappily transformed into a "snack." There were chairs tilted back against the walls as the spectators of the festivities had left them. A saddle or two and a trace-chain and some bits of harness were lying about the floor, where they had been temporarily disposed by the owners, engaged in "gearing up" the teams without. Now and again voices could be heard calling refractory beasts to order, but dulled by the distance, and partaking of the languor of the hour. The baby, who had danced as assiduously as the best, albeit its walking days were not yet well

ushered in, had succumbed at last, and lay, a slumbering heap of pink flesh and blue calico, upon the floor.
Its attitude demonstrated the elasticity of its youthful limbs, and its hands clutched one of the pink
feet that had done such yeoman service earlier in the
evening. An old hound, bound to the spot by the
talismanic phrase, " Guard him !"—a duty from which
only death itself could lure him—sat bolt upright by
the prostrate figure, and looked now with sleepy
eyes and cavernous yawns at the departing guests,
and now became preternaturally vigilant, and uttered
wistful wheezes of despair and envy as the hopeful
gambols of the young dogs about the munching fiddler caught his attention. The whole picture grew
dim and hazy with its flickering lights, and fluctuated
suddenly into darkness, as if it had slipped from act-
uality into a mere memory, as Shattuck went farther
up the stair and the roof-room gathered shape and
consistency before him. The window at one end
still held the glamour of the moonlight, the silver
green of the swaying foliage, the freshness and the
sparkle of the dew. He heard the pigeons cooing
drowsily. The wolf-skins swinging from the rafters
caught the gleam of the candle, and borrowed a sleek
and rich lustre. The focus of the tallow dip itself
glowed yellow in the midst of its divergent rays,
that grew dim as they stretched ever farther among
the duskily brown shadows of the place. Now and
again it was eclipsed as figures, ministering to the
wounded man, passed before it. Suddenly they
drew back. Rhodes's face, distinct upon the pillow,
caught the light full upon it. Shattuck started forward, a great throb of relief astir at his heart, and a

loud exclamation, incoherent, upon his lips. For his friend had opened his eyes, alight with his own old identity; his face, pallid, and with smears of blood faintly discernible, although much of it had been washed away, wore a languid smile. It seemed that the element of his being which was strongest in him, his sense of postulance, of candidacy before the people, was reasserted first of all his faculties.

"Did I—did I—hurt anybody?" he faltered; "I didn't mean to hurt anybody." Then, as he seemed to realize his surroundings, his memory revived.

"Where's Fee? Fee didn't get hurt, did he? Where am I?" He lifted himself upon his elbow and looked waveringly about. "Lord!" he exclaimed, impressed by the silence, "you didn't stop the dancing on *my* account, Mr. Pettingill? I've spoiled the party! Well! well! I'll never be able to look Mrs. Pettingill in the face again." And he sank back on the pillow.

The surly countenance beneath the host's grizzled shock of hair took on a milder expression. The stiff grooves and lines of the lips relaxed, and might be said to have released a smile. "We kin spare the party, Mr. Rhodes—spare it a sight easier'n we kin spare you-uns." Then, as Shattuck unwisely pressed up to the side of the bed, the old man's eyes suddenly assumed a hard glitter of triumph with the hot anger that made him breathe quickly and stertorously, and curved the lines of his stiff old mouth.

"Thar be *some*," he remarked, "ez will 'low I be jes' glad ter git shet o' bein' prosecuted. *Me* prosecuted, 'kase ye an' Fee tuk ter tusslin' in the middle o' the dancin', an' Fee war the bes' man. *Prose-*

cuted!" He snorted out the word with a repulsion that made the very tone odious.

Rhodes, visibly agitated, pulled himself into a sitting posture. "Who — who — said that — such a thing?" Still dazed and confused though he was, his eyes, sweeping the by-standers, rested with the certainty of reproach upon Shattuck. There was a momentary silence. "Understand one thing, Mr. Pettingill," he said at length, with a quick flush upon his pale face that had seemed to grow lean in the last hour—"understand this: alive or dead, no man speaks for me."

He sank back once more upon his pillow, which the herb doctor had readjusted with a hand that was as soft and listless as any fine lady's; he lifted the injured man's head into another position.

"It air mo' level," he observed, learnedly. "This slit in his head air a-goin' ter cure up right off," he continued, looking with mild blue eyes at Shattuck, who stood flushed and indignant among them all, feeling repudiated in the odd turn that affairs had taken. "'Tain't goin' ter inflame none, hevin' bled so much. He warn't shot nowhar; jes' cut on the head. His hair is singed some, whar the powder burnt it, I reckon. He mustn't git up, though, ter-day nor ter-morrow, else he'll fever."

If Shattuck, with the cowardice that is the essential sequence of a well-intentioned mistake, hoped that no more might be said by Mr. Pettingill, he understood little of the pertinacity and endurance that can animate him who presses his breast against the thorn. The host had been unspeakably afflicted by the bare suggestion of foul play. It had served as a goad when naught else might have moved him.   Even although its efficacy was nullified, he could not pass it by, but again and again in review he evoked all its capacities of poignancy.   " Ye shet up, Phil Craig," he said, his manner of rebuke palpably affected. " Ye ain't fitten ter doctor the ' quality.'   I hev hed ter send Steve Yates a-cavortin' *seventeen* mile in the midnight ter fetch a doctor ter physic Mr. Rhodes fur a leetle gash side o' the head!   May keep we-uns from bein' *prosecuted*, though ; leastwise we'll hope so."

Rhodes, appalled, could only stare with amazement at Shattuck.   How his friend could have brought himself to consider bodily health before political advantage, and yet call himself a friend, was a thing which he could not comprehend.   It was all too fresh for even the sophistical comfort of believing. that he had tried to do all for the best.   He could only look at Shattuck with eyes full of wonder and reproach, doubly effective from his reduced and prone estate ; and Shattuck, indignant and resentful, could only turn short about and walk away.   He repented that he had done aught.   And then he wondered how any man of sense could have done aught else.   His dignity was affronted by the position in which he found himself.   He despised his friend for the pusillanimous time-serving of his hearty endorsement of all that the mountaineers had done and said.   And yet he could but acknowledge that this was ample. He despised himself for his vicarious fright, his overserious treatment of the incident.   And yet, as he recalled the scene—the two struggling, swaying figures, the savage blow with the butt end of the pistol, the sudden discharge of the weapon, the heavy fall, the long insensibility—it seemed as if the issue were phenomenally fortunate, rather than such as might have been expected. Amidst all the nettling subjects of contemplation, one recurred with continually harassing suggestions—how he should meet the physician whom he had caused to be summoned in the midnight from the distance of seventeen miles, when the learning or the ignorance of the simple herb doctor had so amply sufficed for the emergency. Caused to be summoned! He thought of Steve Yates riding the horse's back sore, believing that a dying man lay in the house. As he heard Rhodes's rollicking laughter—a trifle quavering, to be sure—he quailed before the idea that there was nothing to offer the physician when he should arrive. He felt that he would have been glad of a diseased liver or an injured brain to justify his proceedings. He began in a nervous state of expectancy to pause whenever he reached the shadowy window, and to look through the silvered branches of the sycamore-tree, fearing to descry perchance a mounted figure approaching along the winding road. All vacant it was as it curved, now in the clear sheen, now lost in the black shadow, reappearing at an unexpected angle, as if in the darkness the continuity were severed, and it existed only in sinuous sections. Once adown the dewy way a youthful cavalier spurred with a maiden mounted behind him, swiftly passing out of sight, recalling to the imagination some romance of eld, when the damosel fled with her lover. An ox-cart lumbering slowly along, with its burly, nodding team, through the illumined spaces, and disappearing in intervals of obscurity, the motion of the oxen's horns somehow vaguely discerned before they emerged again from the shadow, illustrated the leisurely ideal of mountain travel.   After it had quite vanished, and even the sharp, grating creak of its unoiled running-gear had been lost in the distance, a swift canine figure, distorted by speed to a mere caricature of its species, with tail drooping, with ears laid back close to its head, darted along the serpentine curves—one of the visitors' dogs, just made aware of his master's departure, and in his haste to overtake the jogging vehicle adding farcical suggestions of comparison to its slow progress.

And then for a time Shattuck, pacing the length of the room and pausing at the window, marked neither approach nor departure.   The shadows were lengthening; the moon was low in the sky; the neighboring massive mountains were darkly and heavily empurpled against the pensively illumined horizon.   At their base the valley slept; it wot little of the opaline mists that gathered above it, and enmeshed elusive enchantments of color, which vanished before the steady gaze seeking to grade them as blue or amber or green, and to fix their status in the spectrum.   A strange pause seemed to hold the world.   Only the pines breathed faintly.   Beneath their boughs he saw suddenly Letítia Pettingill sitting on a log of the great wood-pile.   Her pale-blue homespun dress seemed white in the moonlight. She leaned back, her hands clasping her head, which rested upon the higher logs behind her, her eyes fixed contemplatively upon the slow sinking of the reddening moon.

5

Another had observed her there. It was only a moment or two before a tall figure sauntered out from the house and stood near by with a casual air, surveying not her, but the aspects of the departing night or the coming day, as retrospection or anticipation might denominate the hour. Shattuck with a frown recognized the figure; it was easily marked; its height and breadth and muscle would suffice to distinguish it, without the added testimony of the long tousled ringlets and the square, stern, martial face, overshadowed by a broad-brimmed hat. Guthrie's pistol and a knife gleamed in his leather belt. His long boots jingled with the replaced spurs, but he made no move toward departure, and his horse still stood, half in the shadow and half in the sheen, drowsing under a dogwood-tree. It was only after he had waited some time thus silent and motionless that he slowly cast his surly, long-lashed eyes toward Letitia. If she had seen him, she made no sign. Still clasping the back of her shapely head with both uplifted hands, she sat, half reclining, against the logs, and watched the moon go down. The initiative was forced upon him. There was a latent capacity for expressiveness suggested in the surprise and uncertainty and subtle disappointment depicted upon his face. He advanced slowly to the wood-pile, and sat down on one of the lower logs, his booted and spurred legs stretched out before him, one hand upon his hip, his hat thrust back, his ringleted head bare to the dew and the sheen. Still she did not move nor glance toward him. As his eyes absently traversed the space about them, he caught sight of Shattuck turning away from the roof-room window.

Whether from a full heart, or in despair that she would break the silence, or on a sudden impulse which the glimpse of the stranger roused, he spoke abruptly, reverting to the scenes of the evening.

"I reckon ye air in an' about sati'fied now with what ye hev up-ed an' done," he drawled, slowly.

She unclasped her hands that she might turn her head and look steadily at him for a moment. Her lustrous illumined blue eyes either showed their fine color in the ethereal light of the moon, or the recollection of it was substituted for the sense of it in the sudden adequateness of their expression. Her gaze relaxed, and she resumed her former attitude. The interval was so long before she spoke that the reply seemed hardly pertinent.

"Ever see *me* wear a shootin'-iron?" she demanded. Her voice was not loud, but it had a vibratory quality like that of a stringed instrument, rather than a flute-like tone.

He stared at her. "Hey?" he demanded. "What ye say?"

She did not change her posture now. "Ever see *me* pound ennybody on the head with a shootin'-iron?" she continued.

"Shucks!" he cried, slowly apprehending her meaning; "ye can't git out'n it that-a-way."

"I never war in it. When ye see somebody o' my size in a fight with one o' yer size, let *me* know it."

"'Twar *yer* fault, an' ye know that full well," he made himself plain, with an intonation of severity.

"*My* fault? *Mercy!*" she cried. "*I* wouldn't hev bruk up that dance fur a bushel o' sech ez ye an'

Rhodes!" She gave a gurgling laugh of retrospective pleasure.

A moment's silence ensued, while he pushed back his hair to look gloweringly at the half-reclining figure, which, although **not** moving, had contrived to take on an air of flouting indifference.

"Ye air a mighty small matter," he said, scathingly, "fur me an' Rhodes ter make ourselves sech fools about."

"An' sech *big* fools!" she cried, with animation. "Whenst I feel obligated ter see I'm a fool, it's sech a comfort ter know I ain't much of a fool."

He said nothing in reply, feeling too clumsy and ponderous to follow the attack with so lithe and elusive an enemy. He did not definitely realize it, but in dropping his aggressions he assumed far more potent weapons.

"O my Lord A'mighty!" he groaned, putting his head in one hand, and covering his eyes as he supported his elbow upon the log behind him; "it don't make much diff'ence whose fault 'tis. *I* hev ter suffer fur it. *I* hev ter suffer fur everything. Sufferin' air what I war born fur, I reckon. Leastwise I ain't seen nuthin' else."

Something faintly stirred the trees; it was not the wind, for it did not seem to come again or to pass further. It was as if they were awakening from some subtleties of sleep, unknown to science, that had stilled their pulses. Fragrance was in the air; the great red rose in the grass by the gate was bursting its buds. The rank weeds asserted their identity. Even the wood-pile gave evidence of walnut and hickory and the resinous pine. And still the moon, ever reddening, ever dulling, sank lower, and the stars were brightening in the darkening sky.

Once more he groaned. "I never war cut out for a fighter," he declared. "Whenst I war a leetle bit o' a boy, an' my dad married agin an' brung that everlastin' wild-cat o' a step-mam o' mine home, I war in a mighty notion o' bein' frien'ly—leetle liar—leetle cowardly fox! I knowed what war good fur me, an' whi€h side my bread war buttered on, an' she couldn't beat me hard enough ter make me hit back or sass her. I war fur givin' up an' takin' mild ez a lam' everything she hed a mind ter do ter me. But arter a while I got so ez whenst she beat my leetle brother it made me winge an' winge—she couldn't hurt sech a calloused time-server ez *me!* An' so I tuk ter hidin' him in the bresh whenst she got mad at him. An' one day whenst she fund him, an' tuk ter larrapin' him, I jes' flew at her, an' I bit her arm 'mos' through. She let Ephraim alone. She war skeered at me. I seen it. An' I tuk ter bitin' arter that like a cur-dog. My dad lemme 'lone. Vis'tors ez kem ter the house war warned off'n me. I begun ter git my growth. I hed an arm ez growed so it could lam a man like a sledge-hammer; it kep' all the boys an' everybody else off'n Ephraim, ez never war a fighter, an' let him git some growth, an hold up his head, an' try ter do like folks."

He had dropped his hand and was staring at her with surprised eyes. She was leaning forward, the golden moonlight still on her face. Her finely cut lips were smiling. She held out, with an air of gay, mysterious confidence, a tiny object between her fin-ger and thumb.

"'Hold fast what I give ye,'" she quoted, with a low, gurgling triumphant laugh.

He reached out and took from her with slow suspicion a pistol ball, turning it around, and looking at her with an air of suspended comprehension and doubt.

"I fund it hyar at the wood-pile; it never teched Rhodes. He ain't much hurt—his senses jes' knocked out'n him. They can't do nuthin' ter you-uns fur sech ez that."

"They better not try!" he cried, belligerently. Then, with the accents of scorn: "D'ye 'low ez I be a-troublin' *myse'f* 'count o' sech cattle ez Rhodes? Naw, sir! Nobody air a-goin' ter pester me! The whole mounting, an' the home folks an' all, hev got mighty perlite ter me, an' hev been fur a long time." He paused meditatively. "Yes, sir," he exclaimed; "peace hev kem ter me by the pound!" He smote his massive chest.

Then, after another silence, he sighed. "But I be troubled," he resumed, "'kase hyar one day 'bout a year ago I goes ter the church house. I always loved the Lord, fur He war persecuted, an' I knowed He felt fur me. I never war so tuk up with this worl'. I hain't hed no pleasure in it. I yearned fur a better one. An' durned ef the thin-lipped, turnip-hearted preacher didn't git up an' gin out the doctrine ef enny war ter hit ye on one cheek, ye mus' turn the tother one; fur that's religion! That ain't my policy, an' 'tain't my practice. An' I reckon I'll hev ter go ter hell jes' whenst I war a-settin' myself in the hope o' heaven."

He drooped his head upon his hand again and

groaned aloud. " I hev wondered," he resumed, his voice somewhat muffled by his attitude, " ef the cuss read that in the Good Book, or jes' made it up out'n his own head. But that sayin' hev tormented me in the midnight, an' tuk my sleep from me. I sorter feel it in me like it *mus'* be true. Religion can't be so easy ez jes' lovin' the Lord. It's this hyar hevin' ter love yer fellow-man ez makes religion so durned hard on ye."

A cloud was in the west, not continuous, but with dusky brown strata across the gilded spaces above the purple mountains ; its shadows lay on the mists below in dull streaks amidst the shining pearly tone. When the moon, so golden, so great now and glamour-ous, passed behind one of these bars of vapor, and even the sullen cloud was tenderly tinted and showed radiating verges of dull gold, one might see the be-reft world in the prosaic gray medium of the day that was to come.

Once more he looked about him and sighed. " Why," he argued, " I couldn't hev got on with all the smitin' folks wanted ter do ter me an' Ephraim, 'specially Ephraim. But then I 'low ez I hev got the mounting too much skeered ter fool with Ephraim or me nuther now, an' mebbe ef I sot out ter repent right hearty I mought make out yit. But I furgits —I furgits! I can't repent more'n a haffen hour at a time. An' hyar ter-night—jes' on account o' you-uns—I hauls off agin, an' mighty nigh kills Rhodes !"

" 'Twarn't 'count o' me," she drawled, with the musical vibration that seemed to follow each tone. She had resumed her former attitude and her air of mocking gayety. "Ye air carryin' it all wrong. 'Twarn't account o' *me* ye half killed Rhodes. 'Twar all account o' 'Tucker'!"

He caught the gleam of her laughing eyes as he sat with his elbows on his knees and glowered sidelong at her.

"I am small," she protested, in dimpling merriment. "I can't ondertake more'n my sheer. Let 'Tucker' take the blame. Ye warn't dyin' ter dance with me. Ye war dyin' *not* ter dance with yerse'f."

His face had flushed. His eyes were full of grave resentment as they met her laughing glance. "I didn't 'low ez ye war so onfeeling ez ye 'pear ter be," he said, reproachfully. "Ever sence that time at the church house whenst all were convicted of sin, or saints, 'ceptin' ye an' me settin' alongside o' one another, I hev been sorter sorry fur ye, an' 'lowed ye war sorter sorry fur me."

She only replied with a laugh, and he evidently deemed futile the bid for sympathy on the score of religious or irreligious fellowship, for he recurred to it no more.

There was a stir along the path; a great highstepping turkey gobbler was slowly coming down it, pausing now and then, and turning his wattled head askew to bring his eye to bear upon some incident of the high dewy weeds, that might promise a preliminary bit to a morning meal. The rest of his tribe, yet roosting on a bare branch of an otherwise fullleaved tree, looked big and burly against the roseate sky; each long inquisitive neck now and again stretched downward, each clutching claw ever and anon moving uncertainly along the perch with a fluctuating intention to descend, was growing momently more distinct as the gray light more and more encroached upon the moon, all obscured now by one of those cloud strata.

In this interval of eclipse Guthrie asked, suddenly, from out the dusk: "Ye know I warn't 'Tucker' by rights. Whyn't ye wanter dance with me?"

The shadow made her face uncertain. He could only see that she did not move. "Did I say I didn't want ter dance with you-uns? I don't 'pear ter remember it." Her tones, vibrant with mockery, were a trifle louder upon the air—a trifle strained; or was it that the world seemed more silent, muffled in the cloud that hid the moon?

"What's the reason ye wanted ter dance with Rhodes?" he demanded, pursuing the subject.

"Did I say I wanted ter dance with Rhodes?" She asked the counter-question with the sharp note of inquiry.

He detected its spuriousness, but her enigmatical intention embarrassed him. "Ye hed ruther dance with him than with me," he said, forlornly, losing his balance.

"Waal, it looks sorter that-a-way, now don't it?" she replied, in casual, irrelevant accents, as of an unconcerned third person.

The moon came out from under the cloud with a great flare of golden glory. Somewhere a cock's crow sounded—clear, mellow tones, delivered with the precision and aplomb of the blast of a bugle. The wind of dawn was coming over the eastern summits, and suddenly the moonlight was all superfluous above the dark, rugged western mountains, for the gray day was on the land. The little house stood distinct and forlorn, all its windows flaring to show its denuded state within ; here and there a tallow dip still sputtered. And if by moonlight and half distinguished the loom and the warping bars had looked disconsolate in their evicted estate under the trees, by daylight they wore so sorry and so consciously distraught an air that such definite expressiveness seemed oddly incongruous with their inanimate condition. All atilt and unsteady they stood on the uneven ground, and about them were many other objects of the household gear which the night had served to obscure. Pots and pans were scattered about or congregated in heaps. Chests and bedsteads, bags and bundles, quilting-frames and churns and tubs—all bore token how the behests of hospitality had stripped the house to make room for the dancing and the exigent demands of the extensive supper-tables. The dogs seemed to take much note of this unprecedented dislocation of the domestic administration, and they went about with inquisitive, exploring noses, and tails stilled and drooped in suspended judgment, amongst the various objects which they snuffingly recognized. One old fellow, the evening of his days much racked by rheumatism, seemed to discern an adequate reason in all the confusion, as he curled himself to doze on the plumpest of the feather-beds, with a large bone disposed within easy reach, to which he might refer as inclination prompted. The spinning-wheels all teetered unsteadily on the uneven chips about the wood-pile ;

now and again the wheels revolved with precipitate, erratic action as the wind stirred them. Letitia no longer looked at the moon—a mere pallid simulacrum of itself, worn thin and gauzy against the pale west; one might hardly know if it still hung there when the first red dart of the sun, yet below the horizon, was aimed at the flushing zenith. Her dress was blue again, not white; her face had something of the flush of the sky upon it, half seen though it was. She had bent forward to the little flax wheel, and had drawn out a thread, breaking and tangling it, only affecting to spin, while the whimseys of the wind turned the wheel. The light was distinct enough to show even the pistol ball in Felix Guthrie's hand as he held it up and gazed at it speculatively.

"I wisht it war in Rhodes's heart," he observed, slowly. "That's whar I wisht 'twar."

The spinning-wheel stopped suddenly; the blue eyes were bent upon him; her lips curved in laughter. "Thar ye go ter heaven!" she cried, waving her hand as if to point the way, "repentin' by the half-hour."

IV.

ALL day the slow process of the restoration of the household gods went on. For many a year thereafter all manner of losses dated from this period. "Hain't been seen nor hearn tell on sence 'fore the infair," was a formula that sufficiently accounted for any deficit in domestic accoutrement. There was no one in the Pettingill family so lost to the appreciation of hospitality and the necessity of equalling the entertainment given by the bride's relatives as to opine that the game was not worth the candle. But more than once Mrs. Pettingill, with a deep sigh, demanded, "Who would hev thunk it would hev been so much more trouble ter kerry in things agin 'n ter kerry 'em out!" She did not accurately gauge the force of enthusiastic anticipation as a motive power. Nevertheless she bore up with wonderful fortitude, considering that the triumph of the supper had been eclipsed. The inanimate members of the household were exhibiting a sort of wooden sulks as they were conveyed to their respective places—now becoming stiffly immovable, despite the straining muscles of the "men folks;" then suddenly, without the application of appreciably stronger force, bouncing forward so unexpectedly that the danger of being overrun was imminent, and cries of "Stiddy, thar! Ketch that eend! Holp up, thar!" resounded even through

Rhodes's dreams in the roof-room, as he drowsed peacefully under the narcotic influences of hop tea. The loom might have seemed to entertain a savage resentment for its supersedure, and was some two hours journeying back to its place in the shed-room, the scene alike of the blighted supper and its old industrial pursuits. After that the "men folks" took a vacation, and applied themselves with some zest to apparently incidental slumber; old Zack Pettingill nodded in his chair on the porch; the others, chiefly volunteering neighbors, fell asleep in the hay at the barn while ostensibly feeding the cattle, leaving the great skeleton of the warping bars staring its reflection in the river out of countenance as it leaned against the fence, with its skeins of carefully sized party-colored yarn the prey of two nimble kittens, who expressly climbed the gaunt frame to tangle them. Even Mrs. Pettingill, sitting on an inverted basket in the yard amongst her gear, looking a trifle forlorn, bareheaded, with her gray hair tucked in a small knot at the nape of her neck, her spectacles poised upon her nose, her hands on her knees, lost herself while gazing at her possessions in the effort to decide at which end she had best begin to rehabilitate the confusion; her eyelids presently drooped, and scant speculation looked through those spectacles. The great shady trees waved above her head. Bees robbed the clover at her feet, and flew, laden and drowsily droning, away; the light shifted on the river; the sun grew hot; the far blue mountains were like some land of dreams, so fair, so transfigured, that they hardly seemed real and akin to these rugged, craggy, darksome heights which loomed beside the little cottage. Everywhere were sleeping dogs ; now and then one roused himself to recollections of the infair and the supper, and invaded the shed-room, standing in the door and with drooping tail gazing upon the simple domestic apparition of the loom in its accustomed place, evidently having believed, in his optimistic simplicity, that the good things and the splendor and the delightful bustle of the past evening were to continue indefinitely, and infinitely disappointed to find them already abolished, the fleeting show of a single occasion.

Shattuck would hardly have acknowledged it to himself, but he certainly felt relieved of an irksome prospect by this succumbing of the Pettingills to the influence of excitement and fatigue. Conversation with his host would necessarily be somewhat hampered by the events of the preceding evening. He could not well resent the old man's indignation, and yet a hospitable forbearance and courtesy would be of even more poignant intimations. He had winced when the bridegroom had taken leave of him with a punctilious show of cordiality and a hearty handshake, as assurance that he bore no malice for those insinuations. For these reasons the guest was not sorry to note the solemn preoccupation in his host's open-mouthed countenance as he passed out from the porch to the shade of the trees, where he came presently upon Mrs. Pettingill, sitting as motionless as a monument amongst her distorted and dislocated " truck," as in her waking moments she would have phrased her belongings. He lighted his cigar as he strolled down to the river, pausing to strike the match upon the white bark of an aspen-tree. The ferns gave out a sweet woodland odor, faint and delicate, overpowered presently by the pungent fragrance of the mint as his feet crushed the thick-growing herb. The crystal river murmured as it went, and seemed to draw reflective, half-breathed sighs, as in the pauses of a story that is told. Now and again, when the banks were high on either side, the rocks duplicated the sound of the lapsing currents with a more sonorous, cavernous emphasis, as if they sought to enter into the spirit of this sentient-seeming life. The sky, looking down from its blue placidities, only here and there smote the water to azure emulations of its tint; for the shadows predominated, and the gravel gave the stream that fine brown, lucent tone, impossible to imitate, broken occasionally where some high boulder incited the impetuosity of the current to bold leaps. Then it was crested with snow-white foam, and shoaled away with glassy green waves to the same restfully tinted brown and amber swirls. The overhanging rocks were gray and splintered and full of crevices, with moss and lichen. Where they lay in great fractured masses under a giant oak, a spring gushed forth. He heard its tinkling tremor, more delicately crystalline and keyed far higher than the low continuous monotone of the river. He mechanically turned toward the sound, and saw Letitia in her light-blue dress sitting upon the gaunt gray rocks at the foot of the craggy masses, a brown gourd in her hand and an empty cedar pail at her feet. Her eyes were fixed gravely upon him, her face was fresh as the wild roses amongst the crevices of the rocks. She looked not more wilted by the excitements and heat and turmoil of the dancing at the infair than the flower blooming with the break of day. He strolled toward her, and spoke at the distance:

"You're the only member of the family awake now, I believe." He smiled, and flicked off the ash of his cigar.

The expression of her eyes changed as they still rested upon him. "Dun'no' whether I be awake or no," she observed. "I kem down hyar arter a pail o' water, an' 'pears like I can't git away agin. Disabled somehows. Asleep, mebbe, though' I moughtn't look like it."

Her uncouth garb and dialect were somehow softened by the delicacy of her proportions and the perfect profile and chiselling of her face. Her speech was hardly more grating upon him, precisian though he was, than the careless, untutored lapses of a child might have been; all the senses of comparison as readily ignored them. She looked so sprite-like as she sat in a drooping, relaxed posture by the spring in the niche of the rocks, one hand behind her head, the other holding the gourd against her blue dress; and the idea of an oread or a naiad suggested to his mind was suddenly on his lips.

Her reply instantly reminded him of her limitations and her ignorance.

"Witched an' bound ter the spot!" she exclaimed, with widening eyes and breathless tone. She lowered her voice: "Did you-uns ever *see* one?"

Her literal interpretation embarrassed and threw him off his guard.

"Never till now," he said. He was not intentionally flirting with Zack Pettingill's daughter; but elsewhere and to another of her sex the speech would have impressed him as a pretty compliment. In her quality of woman, in her possession of a heart, she was no more represented in his mind than if she had been the flower above her.

She either did not comprehend the flattery or she ignored it. Her mind seemed fixed upon the water-nymph and the oread. "Bound ter the spot!" she reiterated, with a sceptical air. "Thar's a heap o' ways o' bein' bound ter the spot. Laziness kin hinder ez totally ez a block an' chain. Mebbe they war 'flicted that-a-way, sorter like me." She stretched both arms upward in an attitude that might have been grotesque in another, but with her was a charming and childish expression of fatigue.

He sat down on the ledge of the rock, took out his watch, and looked at it. "I wish I knew whether the doctor wouldn't come or would," he said, the harassment of the earlier hours recurring to his mind. "I am sorry they ever sent for him. Doesn't he seem a long time coming?"

"Fee Guthrie axed me that question fourteen hundred an' fifty times this mornin'. I don't set my mind on doctor men whenst folks air well, only whenst ailin'. 'Pears ter me like Mr. Rhodes's main complaint air foolishness."

Shattuck flushed with a sort of loyal resentment for his friend's sake. "You think he is foolish because he wanted to dance with you?" he said, tartly.

She cast a rallying side glance down upon him. "Mr. Rhodes warn't particular 'bout dancin' with me," she protested. "I ain't in no wise a favorite 'mongst the boys. That's what makes me 'low

6

I be so smart!" She turned her head with a bird-like coquetry, more formidable for being so natural.

"Too smart for them?" he said, placated in spite of himself by her naïve arrogations.

She nodded the wise little head that she so boldly vaunted. "They all ax me, 'Hey? hey?'" — she raucously thickened her voice in drawling mimicry—"ter every word I say—every one I ever see but you-uns."

If he could compliment, she could return the courtesy. He was silent for a moment, remembering the criticisms that he had heard last night on her unexpected and contrariwise conversation. She was doubtless far too clever for her compeers and her sphere —even clever enough to know it.

"You don't think it worth while to be a favorite amongst fools. But how is poor Mr. Rhodes a fool?"

"Foolish," she corrected him, as if she made a distinction. "'Kase he wants ter git 'leeted ter office, an' he kems 'round sa-aft-sawderin' folks ez laffs, 'an laffs at him, a-hint his back. An' he dassent say his soul's his own! An' he hev ter take sass off'n everybody. He talks 'bout the *kentry*, an' ennybody kin see he don't keer nuthin' 'bout the *kentry*. I'd ruther be a wild dog down thar by the ruver-bank, an' feed off'n the bones the wolf leaves, an' be free ter hev a mind o' my own."

Shattuck seemed to revolve this caustic characterization of his friend the politician. He did not care to press her further as to her opinions. He only said, presently, once more looking at his watch, "I think it so strange that the doctor doesn't come."

"Fee Guthrie waited a cornsiderable time ter make sure ez Mr. Rhodes wouldn't die, an' 'twouldn't be desirable ter hang nobody ter-day."

Her interlocutor winced a trifle, remembering his threats last night. Her placid face, however, intimated nothing of any intention that might animate her words; it expressed only its own unique beauty.

He was charmed by it in some sort. He could see by that mentor, his watch, how long it had been that he had sat here listening alternately to the river's song and her low vibrant drawl. But he fancied that reluctance to meet the mountaineers at the house had detained him, or eagerness to descry the first approach of the superfluous physician, rather than the fascination of this rustic little creature, whose words so combined bitterness and honey. He hastened to divert her attention from the last suggestion.

"Where *is* Guthrie now, anyhow?" he said, affecting to look around as if expecting to see him somewhere at hand amongst the black vertical shadows of the noon and the still golden sunshine.

"Off in the woods somewhere, I reckon," she said; "prayin', mebbe."

"Praying?" he repeated, in astonishment.

"Lawsy-massy, yes! He's a mighty survigrous han' at prayin' an' repentin'. He repents some every day—whenst he don't furgit it."

She laughed in a languid way, once more stretching up her tired arms, the brown gourd in one of her lifted hands, and then she relapsed into silence, her eyes fixed upon the swift flow of the stream. He too was silent, gazing upon the gliding waters. Naught so unobtrusively, so sufficiently fills an in-

terval of quiet as this watching the continual movement of a current. They neither knew nor cared how
the time went by. Ceaselessly the swift swirling lines
made out to the centre of the stream, and further
down swept once more close in to the banks as the
conformation of the unseen channel directed the volume and the force. The spring gurgled; its sun-lit
branch, wherein might be seen now and again a darting
minnow, with its *svelte* shadow beneath it, flowed
timorously down to join the river till a sudden widening and a quicker motion showed that its pulses
felt the impetus of the stronger current. A kill-
deer, flying so low as to dip its wings, ever and anon
alighted on the margin, its stilt-like legs half submerged as it ran hither and thither, now and then
bending to dig in the sand with its long slender bill.
Suddenly there was a darker shadow in the water.
A young woman had abruptly emerged from the undergrowth on the opposite bank, and was crossing the
stream on the rickety little foot-bridge, consisting of
but one log, the upper side hewn; her balance was a
trifle difficult to maintain, as she carried a child in
her arms. She looked eagerly toward the two as
they sat by the spring, thus essentially differing
from "leetle Mose," who, upon perceiving them,
turned the back of his pink sun-bonnet upon them
with an air of sullen rejection, unaware how the dignity of his demonstration was impaired by the di-
minutiveness of his head-gear, and, sooth to say, of
the head within it. If he had expected to thus for-
midably crush the two spectators, he was mistaken;
but he could not observe how it affected them, for
he buried his face upon his mother's shoulder. She

seemed fatigued and travel-worn as she came near, and her face bore traces of recent weeping in the pathetic drooping lips, the heavily lidded eyes, and her pallor. She strove gallantly for a smile and to speak in a casual tone, as she said, "Howdy, Litt?" Then, although nodding to Shattuck, for introductions are not in vogue in this region, she went on, eagerly: "Did Steve kem ter the infair? He 'lowed he would." She paused, biting her lips hard to keep back the tears. Letitia looked uncertainly at Shattuck, as if expecting him to reply. The benedict, drearily superfluous to the festivities, had hardly been noticed by her as he lurked about the walls and sought what entertainment was possible to one under the social disabilities of matrimony.

"Who? Stephen Yates? Oh, yes," said Shattuck. "He talked to me a long time. You were uneasy because he didn't come home?" he asked, with facile sympathy. At the kind tones her self-control melted, and the tears began to flow afresh. "The infair broke up with a row, and Mr. Rhodes was hurt," he explained, holding out his cigar with a delicate gesture, and touching off the long ash against a verge of the rock. "Steve Yates went for the doctor on one of Mr. Pettingill's horses. It seems to me that it is time for him to be back, too," he added, his mind recurring to his own interest in the matter, and once more he looked across the river and up the section of the road which became visible for a little way along the side of a corn-field, expecting to see the dust rise beneath the hoof-beats of the messenger's horse or the doctor's buggy wheels. But all was still and silent; only the air shimmered in the heat, and from amidst the blue-green expanse of the corn he saw a mocking-bird rise in the ecstasy of its redundant song, its wing-feathers a dazzling white in the sun, and drop back quivering and still singing upon the unstable perch of a waving tassel.

Adelaide's tears continued to flow, although she sought to stanch them now and again with the curtain of her sun-bonnet, which she pressed to her eyes. She had seated herself upon one of the rocks on the opposite side of the spring, and the "leetle Moses," whom she held upon her knee, one arm passed about his sufficiently burly waist, seeing that he was not noticed, indulged his own curiosity, and from the interior of his pink sun-bonnet bent a stare of frowning severity first upon Letitia, and then transferred his callow speculation to Shattuck. Perhaps it was far less Adelaide's natural embarrassment at thus meeting in tears a stranger than her divination of the young girl's mental attitude toward her that roused her pride and the resources of her fortitude. She sought to put away the recollection, hardly less poignant than the reality, of the long sad hours of the wakeful night—spent in reviewing the quarrel, repenting her hasty words to her husband, and anon inconsistently angered anew because of the memory of his own bitter sayings— the keen expectancy of the lagging morning, and the terrible morbid fear that had grown upon her jarred and shaken nerves that he would come back no more. Far, far was all her feeling from the girl's comprehension, and she deprecated that, with that half-scoffing face, Letitia should look in upon her sorrows—disproportionate and fantastic though they might be, but none the less piercing—and seek to gauge them by the narrow measure of her own experience and her own untried, undeveloped gamut of emotions.

"I ain't a-goin' ter git married," remarked the fancy-free scoffer from her perch, "till I kin find a man ez I kin trust wunst in a while ter take keer o' hisself, a-goin' an' a-comin' from a neighbor's house. Mus' be powerful sorrowful ter set at home an' shed tears lest he mought hev stumped his toe on the road. Mighty oncommon kind o' man I want, I know, but "—with resolution—"I be a-goin' ter s'arch the mountings, far an' nigh, till I find him. I'd like ter marry a man ez could be trusted ter take keer o' hisself, an' mought even, on a pinch, take keer o' me."

Shattuck, with a smile, glanced across at the weeping wife, who laughed a trifle hysterically amidst her tears, and said:

"Oh, *don't*, Litt!" Then, regaining her composure, she once more pressed the curtain of her calico sun-bonnet to her eyes. It seemed that her dignity required some explanation. "I wouldn't hev minded it so," she said, "ef me an' Steve hedn't hed words. He wanted me ter kem with him ter the infair, but I war 'feared ter bring leetle Mose, fur he mought hev cotched the measles or the whoopin'-cough."

"He's safe now," remarked Letitia. "I be the youngest o' the fambly. I hed the measles thirteen year ago, an' I never *did* demean myself so fur ez ter hev the whoopin'-cough."

Somehow the tone of raillery, the sense of the freedom and the irresponsibility of the young girl,

roused a vague sort of protest in the other, only a
few years older, but upon whose heart were so many
clamorous demands, all the dearer for their exactions.
She felt bound to set herself right. Who had ever
a happier married life than she and Stephen, a more
contented home? And then the supreme unanimity
of their worship of the domestic god Dagon—the extraordinary "leetle Mose!"

"I 'low I wouldn't hev been sech a fool ef 'twarn't
so uncommon fur me an' Steve ter fall out," she
said, her face resuming its serene curves, her full,
luminous dark eyes fixed with a sort of recognition
on Shattuck, which his quick senses apprehended as
identification from description. "I oughtn't ter
hev set up my 'pinion 'gin his, I reckon. He war
mightily tuk up with a man—I reckon 'twar you-uns
—ez hed been a-diggin' in the Injun mounds."

Shattuck nodded in response to this unique intro-
duction.

"An'—an' "—she faltered a trifle—"ez hed a
mind ter go a-diggin' up the bones o' them Leetle
Stranger People o' ourn, ter—ter sati'fy hisse'f what
sort'n nation they used to be, an' ter git thar pearls
off'n thar necks."

There was a shocked gravity and surprise even on
Letitia's face. Adelaide had looked away toward
the road, affecting to watch for an approach, in despair of being able to fitly meet Shattuck's gaze after
saying this, which seemed to affect other people as a
commonplace matter, but to her was an accusation of
the deepest turpitude. The countenance of the infant Moses, still bent upon him with a sternly investigating stare, was the only one whose gaze had not

a covert reproach. He hardly cared to argue with their prejudice. He sought to effect a diversion—in questionable taste he might have deemed it at another time, however little taste might be considered to be concerned in his conversation with the humble mountaineers. He had often heard, and had formally accepted as worthy of credence, the popular axioms concerning the dangers of interference between man and wife. But he certainly did not anticipate the effect of his words when he said:

"I shall have to look out for you, I hear. You are such a friend to the Little People that you have loaded a rifle for me. What sort of a shot are you, now ; and how far will your rifle carry?" He cocked his cigar between his teeth, and looked at her with an air of good-natured raillery.

Her face seemed, in the shadow of her purple sunbonnet, to be slowly turning to stone, so rigid and white it was. She did not reply, but as he noted her startling change of expression he felt a sudden rush of indignation. The mountaineers, with their unconscious ignorance, their intolerance of all standpoints save those within their own limitations, their arrogations of censorship, their suspicions of occult wickedness in his motives and intentions, their overt assumption of a right to direct the public conscience, had begun to strongly anger him. His capacity for making allowances was all at once exhausted, and he found the intensity of her look strangely irksome.

" Well, what's the matter?" he asked, a trifle more roughly than he ever permitted himself to speak to a woman ; for he was a man of consciously chivalric impulses, which he had willingly permitted to agreeably tinge his manners.   He held his cigar suspended between his fingers while he waited.

"Did—did Steve tell you-uns *that* word?" she cried, in a tone like despair.

"Why, yes," he returned, promptly.

There was a moment when the vivid sunshine, the cool, dank shadows of the foliage stirring with such soft dryadic murmurs above her head, the song of the bird from the strong, rich effulgence of the corn-field, the chant of the river, even the cry of her child, were as null to her as if her every faculty had been numbed in the centuries of death that crumbled slowly the pygmy burying-ground.

"Did *he* tell that word on me?" she cried at last, her voice rising discordantly. "He hev gone—he hev gone fur good. He warned me ef I teched that rifle ter fire at them that disturbed the rest o' the Leetle People whilst waitin' fur jedgment—or said that word—that he'd turn me out'n his door. But he 'lowed 'twar the easiest way ter go hisself. An' he hev gone—gone fur good." And once more she lapsed into stony immobility.

Mr. Shattuck turned his cigar and looked down at it. It was a casual gesture, but there was a spark of irritation in his eye. He had lost all appreciation of any element of interest in her beauty, in the pictur-esque charm of the surroundings. The incongruity that he and his semi-scientific researches in his idle summer loiterings should become involved in a fool-ish quarrel between a mountaineer and his wife struck him as grotesque, and offended his every sense of the becoming. He had piqued himself somewhat upon his sensibilities, his ever-ready sympathy with

all sorts and conditions of people. He had fine abil-
ities in many æsthetic ways; he could discern the
higher values, to seek to make them his own and
assimilate them. He appreciated the correct standpoint; he felt the susceptibility to the glow of a no-
ble emotion, and he appraised its possession exactly
as he did his knowledge of the Italian language—a
fine thing *per se*, and one to grace a gentleman. His
capacity to enter into the feelings of the mountaineers, to meet them, despite the heights of his learning
and his social position, without effort and without
affectation, had extorted the admiration and emulation of his friend the politician, versed in all the
arts of currying favor. But he was not equal to this
crisis, since it bore heavily upon the fund of pride
encompassing his own personality. His consideration, his kindness, his whole attitude was to them as
themselves, not in any sort as one with himself. He
had not a word of pity for her; he did not see, with
that fine far sight which he sometimes called insight,
her long, desolate future that challenged her eye and
turned her heart cold; he had no perception of those
farthest perspectives of altruism, a share in another's
morbid terror—he so despised her folly.

And when once more she broke silence—" He hev
gone !"—" I reckon not," he said, coolly, still looking
with a smile at the end of his cigar, and presently
returning it to his lips.

The nervous strain of the moment seemed hardly
capable of extension till that most wearing and jarring sound, a fretful child's discordant wail, rose
upon the air. Perhaps her rigid arm hurt Moses;
perhaps he detected that something was going awry

with her; perhaps he merely felt too long overlooked and neglected; but the great Dagon lifted a stentorian and unwelcome cry, and paused only with an air of vengeance, as if he expected all who beheld to be properly dismayed, seized his pink sun-bonnet by the crown, and cast it from him on the ground with a great sweep of his short arm. As he gazed around, bald-headed, to note the effect, his sullen eye encountered Letitia's, who was for once in her life silenced and amazed by the turn affairs had taken. She made an effort to regain her balance.

"I ain't s'prised none ef ye want some water," she said, producing the great brown gourd, and bending down to submerge it in the depths of the cool, gurgling, crystal spring.

"Leetle Mose," emitting a piercing shriek of anger that she should take the liberty of addressing him, flung himself with averted face into his mother's arms. The tone went through Shattuck's head, so to speak; his brows knitted involuntarily with pain; he was about to rise to go in-doors, for the possible embarrassments and discomforts of conversation with old Zaek Pettingill were insignificant indeed to the hardships encountered in the society of "leetle Mose," upon whom he cast a look of aversion, forgetting that he was a specific unit of that genus, man, for whom Shattuck felt so largely.

Feminine ears seem curiously callous to that frenzied infantile shrillness. Letitia, all unaffected, brought the brimming gourd close to the shrieking Mose, who turned to find it beside him. Now the way had been long, and the sun was hot, and had burnt the great Dagon as if he had been any common person. The deep coolness of the gourd—it must have been very large to his eye—allured him. He involuntarily gave a bounce and a gurgle of delight. Few people ever saw "leetle Mose" smile, and a most beguiling demonstration it was. His elastic pink lips parted wide; his few teeth, so hardly come by, glittered; his very tongue, coyly dumb —though it was better tutored than it would admit —might be seen frisking between his gums. He waited expectantly for his mother for a moment, and as she did not move he permitted Letitia to serve him; he reached out eagerly, holding the gourd with both hands, lifting his pink feet as if he intended to stay the bottom of the vessel by those members, and after several futile, ill-directed bounces he succeeded in applying his soft lips to the verge. He stopped, sputtering, once to look up, with laughing eyes full of gladness and with a dripping chin, at Letitia, and then, as he plunged his head again to the water, they could hear him laughing and gurgling in the gourd that echoed cavernously. The specific unit became all at once more tolerable to contemplate. Shattuck, in laughing ridicule of him, glanced at Letitia. Her eyes did not meet his. She was staring intently at the section of the road visible at some little distance by the side of the corn-field. He turned to follow her gaze. He had not before noticed the thud of hoofs; the sound was upon the air now. From out the deep shadow about the spring naught was visible in the sun-flooded highway but a cloud of dust, every mote red in the dazzling radiance. The approach had been obscured by the intervening undergrowth that grew close about the river where the road came down to the bank. He could still hear the thud of hoofs. Did he fancy it, he asked himself suddenly, or was there something erratic suggested in the sound? Certainly the interval was strangely long, reckoning by the distance, while they stood and watched the close undergrowth on the opposite bank, and waited for the rider to emerge from the covert. At last, as the horse appeared, the mystery was solved. He was a bay horse, in good condition, with a long stride, and an old-fashioned Mexican saddle with a high-peaked pommel. He came down the slope and waded into the water in a slouching, undetermined way, now and then turning his head to look with wondering dissatisfaction at the heavy, swaying stirrups as his movements caused them to lunge heavily back and forth—for they were empty, and the saddle bore no rider. He paused to drink in the middle of the stream, but as Letitia ran toward him, calling "Cobe! Cobe!" he desisted, looked intelligently at her, and again at his swaying empty stirrups. He could have told much, evidently, if he had not been dumb. Then he came readily trotting through the water, which swept away from his swift strides in foamy circles, and, struggling up the bank, let her catch his bridle and stroke his head. He shook his mane and neighed with pleasure to be at home again.

Adelaide was standing, her child in her arms, gazing breathlessly at him. Letitia, still stroking the animal's head, had turned a pale face and eyes full of vague appeal upon Shattuck.

"I don't understand," he exclaimed.

"This is the horse he rode," she said.

"THE SADDLE BORE NO RIDER."

V.

The news of the horse's return with an empty saddle was received at first lightly enough by others.
The treasures of old Zack Pettingill's whiskey keg
and his wife's cherry-bounce, lavished forth on the
preceding evening, were deemed amply sufficient to
account for any eccentricities of equestrianism. But
when several days had passed without the reappear-
ance of the dismounted horseman, the slowly perco-
lating gossip touching a conjugal quarrel began to
offer another and a more exciting interpretation of
the mystery. So general was its acceptance that although a company of men organized a search and
patrolled the roads and the by-paths and the moun-
tain-sides, it was with scant hope or expectation of
any definite discovery, and inquiry of the physician
whom Yates had been despatched to summon resulted only in a verification of the popular conviction
that he had never delivered the message. Thus the
fears evoked for his safety were very promptly
merged in reprehension, and speculative gossip was
mingled in equal parts with pity for his wife.

" Who'd ever hev thunk ez Adelaide Sims, counted the prettiest gal this side o' nowhar, would hev
been deserted by her husband 'fore three years war
out?" Mrs. Pettingill said, meditatively, her pipe between her lips, as she "walked" a spinning-wheel

into the house, making it use first one and then the other of its own spindling legs to achieve progression rather than lifting it by main force. She half soliloquized and half addressed a tall, lank mountaineer who sat upon the edge of the porch, his horse grazing hard by. He had stopped on the pretext of asking for a "bite," saying that he had travelled far over the mountain, looking up some stray cattle of his, and albeit Mrs. Pettingill disapproved of his reputation, the "snack" that she could give him was one of those admirable things in itself that could not go amiss even with a sinner. He had a big-boned, powerful frame and was middle-aged; but despite that his hair was streaked with gray, and the crow's-feet about his eyes gave evidences of the lapse of time, he was the very impersonation of the spirit of "devil may care." He had a keen, hooked nose, an eye far-seeing, gray, and of a steely brilliancy, and the thin lips of his large mouth, mobility itself, curved to a vast range of expression. His manner implied an elated, ever-ready, breezy confidence; his eye now covertly measured you, then gayly overlooked you as of no manner of consequence. His reputation might, indeed, be accounted a doubtful one. He had come before the bar of justice several times: the altering of the brand on certain cattle herded upon the "Bald" had been laid at his door; the manner in which a horse had been lost, by a drover passing through the country, and found in his possession, had been called into question. On each occasion his escape had been made good by the lack of adequate evidence to convict, although little doubt existed as to his guilt. He was one of those singu-

lar instances of an undeserved popularity. Better
men, amply able to discern right from wrong, often
opined that there was no great harm in him, that in-
justice had been done him, and that much meaner
men abounded in the cove who had never been
"hauled over the coals." He had been a brave soldier, although the flavor of bushwhacking clung to
his war record. He had certain magnetic qualities,
and there were always half a dozen stout fellows at
his back—ne'er-do-weels like himself. He had been
suspected of moonshining, but this was not considered a natural sequence of his lawless habits, for
many otherwise law-abiding citizens followed this
pursuit; in defence, they would have urged, of their
natural right of possession—to make what use they
chose of their own corn and apples, as their fore-
fathers had done in the days before the whiskey tax.
Buck Cheever's suspected adherence to the popular
standpoint on this burning question might have
been considered to only lower the tone of the profession.

Mrs. Pettingill regarded him with contradictory
emotions. As a religionist, she felt that she would
prefer his room to his company; but his room was
but scant encroachment, for he only sat upon the
edge of the porch, and he by no means asserted any
equality of piety or moral standpoint; on the con-
trary, he seemed to esteem her, and, by her reflected
lustre, Mr. Pettingill, as shining lights, and vastly different from the general run of the cove. His breezy
talk was peculiarly refreshing to her in the midst of
the ordeal, still in process, of restoring the routine
of twenty years, shattered by the havoc of the infair.

7

He had a discerning palate and a crisp and flexible tongue, and she felt, with a glow of kindness, that he said as much in praise of her corn-dodgers, which formed a part of his lunch, as any one else would have said for her pound-cake.

"Mos' folks don't sense the differ in corn-meal cookin'. It takes a better cook ter make a plain, *tasty* corn-dodger, ez eats short with fried chicken, 'n a cake."

"It takes *Mis' Pettingill* ter make this kind o' one," he protested, with his mouth full. "No sech air ever cooked ennywhar else I ever see."

"I hev got some mighty nice fraish buttermilk, Buck, jes' churned," she remarked, precipitately. "I be goin' ter fetch ye a glass right off."

Old Zack Pettingill, with his shock head of thick gray hair, and his deeply grooved face, sat in his shirt sleeves in his accustomed chair on the porch, and his expression betokened a scorn of his helpmeet's susceptibility to the praises of her culinary accomplishments, and held a distinct intimation, by which Buck Cheever might have profited had he been so disposed, that he was not to be propitiated in any such wise. Little, however, Buck Cheever cared. The lady in command of the larder dwarfed her husband's importance.

"Yes, 'm," he drawled, taking up the thread of the gossip where the victualling interlude had left it; "Adelaide's been left. That's mighty bad. An' I reckon it hurts her pride too." He showed himself thus not insensible to æsthetic considerations.

"I'll be bound it do," Mrs. Pettingill agreed, as she seated herself. She cast a speculative look upon

her husband, silent and grum as if he had been thus
gruffly carved out of wood.   He had been a stum-
bling-block in many respects in his conjugal career.
He was "set" in his ways, and some of them she
felt were ways of pure spite.   She had never before
realized, however, that his continued presence was a
thing to be thankful for.   Such as he was, she had
him at hand.   Public pity, which the sensitive feel
as public contempt, had never been meted out to her
because of his desertion.   Thus, although she could
with convenience have dispensed with him, and his
loud harangues, and his overbearing ways, and his
dyspepsia—the cove said he had been fed till he
foundered — which placed an embargo on three
fourths of the dishes on which she loved to show
her skill, he was revealed to her suddenly as a boon
in that he would yet stay by her, and the phrase "a
deserted wife" had no affinity with her fully furnished estate.

"Waal, Steve always 'peared ter me a good match
whenst he war young"—she meant unmarried—
"though riprarious he war, an' sorter onstiddy an'
dancified, but I never 'lowed he'd hev done sech a
mean thing.   An' that thar baby o' theirn! well
growed, an' fat, an' white, an' strong, but, I will say,
bad ez the Lord ever makes 'em.   Waal, waal, a body
dun'no' *how* thar chil'n will turn out; them with
small famblies, or none, oughter thank the Lord—
though *that* ain't in the Bible.   'Blessed be the man
with a quibble on 'em.'   That's what the Good Book
say."

This was a new view with Mrs. Pettingill.   She
had often floutingly wished she had a "sure enough

fambly," as if her own were so many rag dolls. "Jes' *one* son," she would say; "an' him, through being in love, hed ruther eat his meals at the Gossams'— 'long o' Malviny Gossam—whar they don't know no mo' *how* ter cook a corn puddin' or a peach cobbler 'n ef they war thousand-legs; an' jes *one* darter, ez will pick a chicken bone an' call *it dinner!* an' a 'speptic husband ez hev seeh a crazy stommick that jes' ' Welsh rabbit' will disagree with him!"

What sort of chance was there here for a woman who knew what good cooking was? "Ef 'twarn't fur the visitors ez kem ter the house," she often declared, "I'd git my hand out."

"Folks raise thar chil'n wrong," said old man Pettingill in a dirge-like tone—"raise 'em for the devil's work like I raise my cattle fur the plough. Marryin' is a mighty serious business. Yes, sir!"

"A true word!" interpolated his wife, desirous of not seeming behindhand in this view of the seriousness of matrimony, in order to intimate that whatever reason he had to be solemn upon the subject, she too had cause to be sobered by it. She knitted a trifle faster, and her needles clicked resentfully.

"Yes, sir," he reiterated. "An' steddier singin' o' psalm tunes over the bride an' groom, an' a-prayin' over 'em, an' hevin' a reg'lar pray'r-meetin', repentin' o' sins an' castin' o' ashes on thar heads, we hev *dances*, an' *dancin' Tucker*, an' all manner o' eatables, an' infairs, ez ef they war a-goin' ter dance through life, when married life is mos'ly repentance."

"That it is!" exclaimed Mrs. Pettingill, forgetting her gratitude that she too had not been "left." "Repentance o' ever bein' married.   Sackcloth an' ashes is the word!"

Old Pettingill took no notice of this confirmation of the letter if not the spirit of his dogma, save by a surly baited glance, and went on: " Church members though we all war, we stood round an' watched them young folks dance ter the devil till he fairly riz up through the floor an' smit one of 'em down."

" By gosh!" exclaimed Cheever, a sudden fear and wonder upon his face; " which one war smit?"

"'Twar Len Rhodes," his host began, but Mrs. Pettingill's wheeze, persistently sibilant, dominated even his louder tone.

" Don't you-uns be 'feared, Buck.   Satan hisself didn't show up.   He struck through Fee Guthrie's arm—a mighty survigrous one.   Ye know the En'my hev got the name o' bein' toler'ble smart, an' he never made ch'ice o' a spindlin' arm."

Once more Mr. Pettingill resumed, overlooking what she had said: "An' so Mr. Shattuck hyar 'lowed the law would be down on us ef Mr. Rhodes didn't hev his own doctor-man—ez 'peared ter be the apple o' his eye!   An' bein' ez my son war the groom, an' the 'casion war the infair, I couldn't send him off, an' I jes' axed Steve Yates ter go fur the doctor, an' go he did."

" An' go war all he did," interpolated Mrs. Pettingill; " he never kem back no mo'."

" I be powerful obligated ter him ez he never tuk my bay horse-critter along; sent him home with the saddle onter him an' all.   I dun'no' but what I be s'prised.   Ef he war mean enough ter desert his wife, he air plenty mean enough ter steal a horse."

Shattuck, who was lounging with a cigar in a big arm-chair, looked frowningly at the speaker. He had felt much distress that it should have been upon his insistence that the young man was despatched upon that errand whence he had never returned. He could hardly control his anxiety and forebodings while searching parties went forth; and so earnestly he hoped that no broken and bruised body would be found along the roadside, betokening a fatal fall from the saddle, no trace of robbery or foul deed resulting in death, that when public opinion settled upon the theory of Yates's desertion of his wife he experienced a great relief, a welcome sense of irresponsibility. And yet this was so keen and vivid that he could but reproach himself anew, since he so rejoiced because of the disaster that sealed her unhappiness. His spirits had recovered somewhat their normal tone, but nevertheless he could ill endure an allusion to his share in the circumstances that precipitated the event.

"How air she a-goin' ter git along?" demanded Cheever; a sufficiently uncharacteristic question, since his was not the type of practical mind that is wont to occupy itself with domestic ways and means. "Goin' back ter her own folks?"

"She 'lows she'd ruther die. She's goin' ter stay thar in her cabin an' wait fur him," said Mrs. Pettingill. "Sorter seems *de*-stressin', I do declar'! A purty, young, good, r'ligious 'oman a-settin' herself ter spen' a empty life a-waitin' fur Steve Yates ter kem back. *He*'ll never kem. He's in Texas by now," she declared, hyperbolically; for Texas is the mountaineer's *outremer*. "Litt say she ain't never goin' ter git married," she continued, irrelevantly.

" How long d'ye reckon she'll stick ter *that?*" demanded old Pettingill, sourly, glancing up from under his grizzled eyebrows.

" Waal," his wife defended her, " she hain't never got married yit, and that's more'n *ye* kin say."

And to this taunt the unhappy Mr. Pettingill could offer no response, save an inarticulate gruffness that only betokened his ill-will and the ill grace with which he accepted defeat. The dirge-like monody to which he seemed to have attuned his spirit was but the retroactive effect of the gayety of the infair, the swinging back of the pendulum as far as it was flung forth.   More sophisticated people have encountered that melancholy reflux of pleasure, and, with the knowledge that the cure lies in " a hair of the dog that bit you," find a revival of their capacities for gayety in new scenes of mirth.   But the society of the cove had not these opportunities for extension and reduplication. There were no more infairs nor dances nor weddings.   Mr. Pettingill was constrained to recover the tone of his spirits as best he might, despite the sheer descent from the heights of the gayeties of the feast he had made to the humdrum level of his daily life, with all the zest taken out by contrast. Few people over eighteen have this experience without acquiring with it such philosophy as serves to nullify it, but it made Mr. Pettingill very sour at sixty.

" Where is Letitia?" queried Shattuck, who had missed that element which gave a different interpretation to the whole life of the house, which lent most blithesome wings to the heavy-footed hours.   He had wondered all the previous day, but until her name was mentioned he would not ask.

"Litt? She went ter stay with Adelaide," said Mrs. Pettingill, complacently knitting. "Litt air more comp'ny 'n help. I miss her powerful."

"I kin spare her easier 'n ennything round the house," observed her father, acridly.

Mrs. Pettingill burst into an unexpected laugh. Her eyes twinkled with reminiscent raillery as they were fixed upon her husband, who seemed a trifle out of countenance.

"Waal, Litt *do* make remarks," she offered in explanation.

"I have observed that," said Shattuck.

Mrs. Pettingill became all at once grave and concerned. The quality of Litt's remarks was disconcertingly satiric, and she deprecated the fact that the stranger should have acquaintance with them. Shattuck reflected her embarrassment in some sort; it suggested "remarks" upon him which he had not had the opportunity of hearing, the very recollection of which in his presence evidently confused their amiable auditor, as if the mere consciousness of them implied discourtesy.

"Naw," she went on, somewhat precipitately, addressing herself rather more directly to Cheever, "Adelaide ain't goin' home ter her folks. Steve lef' his craps all laid by, an' 'ceptin' fur cuttin' wood an' fetchin' water thar warn't much use fur him thar. I dun'no' what Adelaide wanted with Letishy; she jes' seemed ter cling ter her. I 'lowed ter Litt ez *she* warn't no comp'ny fur grief. But Litt, she 'lowed ez leetle Moses war apt ter make her sorrowful enough fur chief mourner at a fun'al 'fore he got done with her.   His temper fairly tarrified her."

Cheever suddenly seemed disposed to bring his visit to an end.   He had an inattentive look during Mrs. Pettingill's last words, an introspective pondering thoughtfulness, inconsistent with his almost suspicious and vigilant habit of countenance.   He started as if with an effort to recapture his vagrant wits, and it was a long moment of review before he understood Mrs. Pettingill's commonplace remonstrance, " What's yer hurry, Buck ?"

Mr. Pettingill, sufficiently averse, for not unnatural reasons of his own, to conversation with Shattuck alone, made haste to second her.   " Ye 'pear ter be scorchin' ter git away," he said, although under normal circumstances both would have considered Buck Cheever's society no boon.   They were aware that ordinarily he, with his ne'er-do-weel record, would have been flattered by their courtesy.   They noted, with a sort of unformulated speculation and curiosity, his indifference to it, the definite intention expressed in his face, the preoccupation with which he looked to his saddle-girth and his stirrup-irons before he mounted.   Even to their languid and half-dormant perceptions the fact was patent that he was going because he had got what he had come for.   In their simplicity they thought it was his luncheon !

Despite his lank length and slouching awkwardness afoot, he was a sufficiently imposing horseman when he swung himself into his saddle and speedily went down the winding way.   He rode with his chin high in the air, his legs stretched straight to the extreme length of the stirrup-leathers, not rising to the motion of the horse, but sitting solidly in the saddle as if he were a part of the animal, like an equestrian statue endowed with motion. A gallant horse it was, unlike the humble brutes of the mountaineers, with good blood in his throbbing veins and fire in his full eye, and a high-couraged spirit breathing in the dilatations of his thin red nostrils; he was singularly clean-limbed; his red roan coat shone like satin; he had a compact hoof, a delicate, ever-alert ear, a small bony head, and a long swinging stride as regular as machinery. If it were possible to disconcert Buck Cheever, it might be accomplished by the question how he became possessed of this fine animal —finer even than the mountain men in their limited experience were able to appreciate. He had been known to account for him as being identical with a certain lame colt, which he had bought a few years before from Squire Beamen in the valley. "I didn't gin much fur him, bein' his laig war crippled, but he cured up wonderful. An' I wouldn't sell him now. He's some lighter-complected 'n he war then, through bein' sun-burnt. That's how kem ye didn't know him fur the same. He's better-lookin' now, though I hev ter handle his nigh fore-laig keerful."

This "nigh fore-laig" was lifted and thrust forth with a vigorous, high-stepping action that would have attested much for veterinary surgery had it been a restored instead of a pristine power. Beneath it the miles of sandy road, now sunshiny, now flecked with the shadows of the wayside trees, reeled out swiftly; the landscape seemed speeding too, describing some large ellipse.

Cheever's far-seeing gray eyes rested absently on

the shifting scene as on and on he went—a certain
supercilious observation it would seem, since from
the backward pose of his head he looked out from
half-lowered eyelids. It was too familiar to him, too
stereotyped upon his senses, to produce responsive
impressions, and he was familiar with few others,
and knew no contrasts. Thus the farthest mountain's azure glowed for him in vain. The multitudinous shades of green in the rich drapings that hid the
gaunt old slope near at hand with masses and masses
of foliage—from the sombre hue of the pine and fir,
through the lightening tones of the sycamore and
sweet-gum, to the silvered verdure of the aspen-tree
swinging in the wind—might be a revelation to other
eyes of the infinite gradations, the manifold capacities, of the color. Not to his. And he was as unmindful of the purple bloom that rested upon other
ranges as they drew afar off, of the swift clear water
of the river crossing his path again and again, of the
cardinal-flower on the bank, so stately and slender,
with the broken reflection of its crimson petal glowing in a dark swift swirl below—as oblivious as they
were of him. Only he noticed the sky, the clouds,
harbingers of change, despite the azure above and
the golden illusions of sunshine in which all the world
was idealized—change, although the long, feathery,
fleecy sweeps of vapor, like the faint sketchings of
snowy wings upon the opaque blue, otherwise void,
might seem only lightest augury.

" Mares' tails," he soliloquized as he went. " Fallin'
weather."

The voice of the cataract had long been on the air,
growing louder and louder every moment—only its

summertide song, when languors bated its pulses, and daily its volume dwindled. He had heard it call aloud in the savage ecstasy of the autumn storms, when reinforced by a hundred tributaries, and bold and leaping in triumph. And he knew it, too, in winter—a solemn hush upon it, a torpor like the numb chill of death, its currents a dull, noiseless, trickling flow through a thousand glittering icy stalactites. So well he knew it that for its sake he would not have glanced toward it.

Nevertheless, he drew his horse into a walk, and gazed fixedly out of his half-closed eyes up the long gorge between the ranges, at the river, at the glassy emerald sheet of the water-fall, and at the little house hard by. Its door was closed, as if it too had been deserted ; and it seemed very small in the shadow of the great mountains, against whose darkling forests its little gray roof and its tendril of smoke were outlined ; but it was only a moment before his quick eye detected the presence of the household. Down by the water-side the three were. The great caldron betokened a wash-day ; the fruits of the industry were already bleaching and swinging in the fragrant air on the Sweet-Betty bushes. The fire smouldered almost to extinction under the caldron, which barely steamed with a dull, lazily wreathing, lace-like vapor ; the work was evidently all done. Adelaide sat upon the roots of a tree, her arms bare, her chin in her hand, her eyes, that had learned all the brackish woe of futile weeping, ponderingly fixed upon the never-ceasing, shifting fall of the water. Letitia, too, was silent as she leaned upon the paddle that was used to beat the clothes white, its end poised upon the bench.   Moses, seated in a clumped posture, with his legs doubled in a manner impossible to one of elder years and less elastic frame, now and again babbled aloud disconsolately, and ground his gums with the cruelty of rage and with great distortion of his indeterminate features.   He had so implacable an air of such crusty gravity as he sat on the fine green moss, with his obedient vassals about him, and his newly washed habiliments, ludicrously small, swinging on the perfumed branches of the undergrowth, that he might have provoked a smile from one less preoccupied than Cheever.   The keen eyes of the horseman—very watchful they were under their half-drooping lids—were fixed upon the two young women.

The horse, alternately bowing low and tossing up his head with its waving mane, moved in an easy, light walk that hardly raised a mote of dust upon the road, overgrown with the encroaching weeds, and intimating few passers.   The sound was thus muffled, and Cheever was not observed until he was close at hand.   Letitia was first to recognize him, and, as she turned toward him, her blue eyes said much, he felt, but in a language that he wot not of.   In some sort her inscrutability disconcerted him.   He was sensible of being at a loss as he reined up at the riverside.   He seemed to forget, to vaguely fumble for the motive that led him here.   The dreary indifference on Adelaide's face as she met his gaze restored in some degree his normal mental attitude.   He was conscious of a sort of vague wonder that there was no sense of humiliation, of mortified pride, in its expression.   The supreme calamity of her loss had dwarfed into nullity all the opinion of others, all the bitterness of being the theme of pitying, half-scornful gossip. The cove was nothing to her, and nothing all it could say. She was bereaved.

As to Moses, he should never feel the loss; she would be to him father and mother too. And if Moses had been unduly pampered heretofore, he bade fair now to break the record of all spoiled babies. Never a gesture was lost upon her, never a tone of his oft inharmonious voice. Now, because the horse which Cheever rode suddenly caught his attention, and his discordant remonstrance with his teeth ceased abruptly, she looked around with a wan, pleased smile curving her lips. The little biped gazed up at the great, overshadowing four-footed creature with a gasp of joy, delighting in his size and the free motion of his whisking tail. A dimple came out in Dagon's pink cheek, although a tear still glittered there. He was suddenly indifferent to his teeth, and showed them all in a gummy smile. Then, with a self-confidence in ludicrous disproportion to his inches, he pursed his lips, and giving an ineffectual imitation of a chirrup, and a flap of the paw, he sought to establish personal relations with the big animal, who took no more notice of the great Dagon than if he had been a wayside weed, but bent down his head and pawed the ground.

"The young un likes the horse," Cheever observed, leniently, conscious of sharing the "young un's" weakness in equine matters, and seizing the opportunity to so naturally open the conversation, for he was not, in a manner, received at the Yates house. "How air ye a-comin' on, Mis' Yates?" he continued, his voice seeking a cadence of sympathy.

"Toler'ble well," replied Adelaide, reticently, scarcely disposed to discuss her sorrows with this interlocutor. She turned her eyes toward the waterfall once more, and her quiet reserve would have discouraged another man from pursuing the conversation. Cheever, blunt as his sensibilities were, could have hardly failed to apprehend the intimations of her manner, so definite were they, so aided by the expression of her face ; but he had his own interest in the premises, and he was not likely to be easily rebuffed.

"I hev been mightily grieved an' consarned ter hear how Steve hev tuk an' done," he went on, his countenance readily assuming a more sympathetic cast than was normal to it, since, as they were on a lower level, his downward look seemed but a natural slant, and not the same suspicious, sneering, supercilious disparagement from under half - drooped eyelids which his usual survey betokened. "I war powerful grieved," he reiterated. "I never would hev looked fur sech conduc' from Steve."

She made no answer, but her eyes turned restlessly from one point to another ; her face was agitated. It was a critical moment. She felt as though she could scarcely forgive herself should she weep to the erratic measure of Cheever's shallow commiseration. It was an affront to her sacred grief. And she had no pretext to withdraw.

Letitia had not been addressed, but she seemed to find that fact no hinderance to assuming a share in the conversation. "Ye war grieved !" she exclaimed, with a keen, frosty note in her voice, as she swayed her weight upon the paddle, poised on the wash-bench. "I never war so *tee*-totally delighted with nuthin' in my life. Steve Yates never 'peared so extry ter me. Moses thar air fower times the man he war, an' fower times, I dun'no' but *five* times"—mathematically accurate—"better-lookin'. I never war so glad in all my life ez ter hear he hed vamosed."

A most ingenuously merry face she had, with its red lips curving, and its dimpled cheeks flushing, as she turned her clear sapphire eyes up to the rider ; but a duller man than he might have read the daring and the ridicule and the banter in their shining spheres. His look of mingled reproach and anger had, too, a scornful intimation that she had not been spoken to, as he glanced indifferently away, passing her over. This was implied also in the pause. It seemed as if he could not bring himself to make a rejoinder. It was Mrs. Yates, evidently, with whom he wished to confer. But conversation with her on this theme was apparently impracticable, and yet on this theme only would he talk. He therefore sought presently to make the best of the situation, and to avail himself of Letitia as a medium for his ideas. He reckoned for a time without his host, for he only received a superfluity of her ideas.

"Waal, sir," he exclaimed at last, in polite reproach, "I dun'no' why ye be glad he is gone. I dun'no', but 'pears ter me ye mought be more cornsiderin' o' Mis' Yates."

"Hev ye lived ez long ez ye hev in this life, an' not f'und out yit ez nobody cornsiders nobody else ?" she cried, with affected cynicism. "Waal, ye air some older 'n me," she continued, blandly smiling—conscious of his grizzled hair, he was a trifle confused by this limited way of putting the difference in years —" but I be plumb overjoyed o' Steve's caper, 'kase I git a chance ter 'company Mis' Yates. Ye know "—looking up gravely at him—" I hev hed a heap o' trouble a-fotchin' up my parents in the way they should go—*specially dad.* They air fractious yit wunst in a while. An' now ef they ain't obejient an' keerful o' pleasin' me, I jes' kin run away from home an' 'company Mis' Yates. An' ef Mis' Yates don't treat me right, an' Moses gits *too* rampagious, I kin run away ter my home folks agin, an' fetch up my parents some mo' in the way they should go—*specially dad.*"

Mrs. Yates gave a short hysterical laugh, ending in a sob. Cheever, his cheek flushing under this ridicule, looked down at the mocking little creature still leaning on the paddle as it rested upon the bench. Letitia's face had grown suddenly grave. Her blue eyes, with a strange far-seeing look in them, seemed to pierce his very soul.

"Thar's nuthin'," she said, slowly—"thar's nuthin' ter improve the health an' the sperits an' the conduc' o' yer family like runnin' away. *Tell Steve Yates that fur me !*"

He started as if he had been shot. A sharp, half-articulated oath escaped his lips. His manner betokened great anger, and his eyes burned. He could hardly control himself for a moment, and Adelaide, her pale face still more pallid with fear, trembled and sprang to her feet.

"I dun'no' what ye mean by that," he cried, in-

8

dignantly. "An' ef *ye* war a man ye shouldn't say it twicet. I ain't seen Steve Yates, an' ain't like ter see him. *I* hed nuthin' ter do with his runnin' away. Lord! Lord!" he added, bitterly, "I 'lowed some folks in the cove, specially some o' the name o' Pettingill"—he had forgotten the good corn-dodger—"hed in an' about accused me o' every-thing, but I didn't expec' Steve Yates's runnin' away, 'kase he war tired o' his wife, ter be laid at my door. Naw, Mis' Yates"—he turned toward her earnestly—"I dun'no' *nuthin'* o' the whar'bouts o' yer husband. Ef I did, I'd go arter him ef 'twar fifty mile, an' lug him home by the scruff o' his neck ter his wife an' chile."

"I b'lieve ye," said Adelaide, in a broken voice, the tears coming at last—"I b'lieve ye. Don't mind what **Litt say.** She always **talks helter-skelter.**"

Letitia stood looking from one to the other, her alert, exquisitely shaped head, with the hair smooth upon it, save where it curled over her brow and hung down from the string that gathered the ringlets togeth-er at the nape of the neck, clearly defined against the dark-green foliage of the young pines, that brought out, too, in high relief the light blue of her cotton dress. Her glance was full of gay incredulity, and she evidently found food for satiric laughter in the mental standpoint of first one and then the other. It is sel-dom that a creature of so charming an aspect is the subject of so inimical a look as that which he bent upon her. But he replied gently to Mrs. Yates:

"Don't ye pester 'bout that, Mis' Yates. Ye hev got plenty ter pester 'bout 'thout it. I jes' kem ter ax ye how ye war a-goin' ter git along 'bout craps an' cuttin' wood an' sech like. I be mighty willin' ter kem an' plough yer corn nex' week ef 'tain't laid by, an' I 'lowed I could haul ye a load o' wood wunst in a while ef ye war so minded. I 'low everybody oughter loan ye a helpin' han', now Steve is gone."

Once more her tears flowed. The generosity and kindness implied in the offer touched her heart as the deed might have done. And yet her gratitude humiliated her in some sort. She was ashamed to have the cause to be beholden to such as Buck Cheever for a kind word and a proffered service. She shook her head.

"Naw," she said, the prosaic words punctuated by her sobs; "the corn's laid by, an' the cotton an' sorghum an' terbacco." She stopped to remember that Steve Yates, constitutionally a lazy fellow, and fonder far of the woods and his gun than of the furrow and the plough, had never failed in any labor that meant comfort to the household, though he did little for profit. She recalled like a flash a thousand instances of this care for her and for Moses. Why, was not one animal of every kind—a calf, and a lamb, and a filly, and a shote—upon the place marked with little Moses's own brand? She wondered how often she had heard Steve say, as he sat meditating before the fire, "By the time he's twenty he'll hev some head o' stock o' his own, ye mark my words." And last year the cotton was soft and clean beyond all their experience, and the flax was fine, and the weaving had been successful out of the common run, and little Moses's homely clothes thus appeared to their unsophisticated eyes very delicate and beautiful, and she had been almost ashamed of Stephen's pleasure in this smart toggery—it seemed so feminine. And now he was gone! And here she, the object of this constant, honest, thrifty care of the thriftless Yates, was weeping because of a kind word, and thanking Buck Cheever for remembering that she might need to have wood hauled.

"We don't need wood," she said, "'kase Cousin Si Anderson sent his nevy, Baker Anderson—he's 'bout sixteen year old—ter haul wood an' be in the house of a night, 'count 'o robbers an' seeh, though Letishy an' me air nowise skeery."

"Naw," put in Letitia, suddenly; "an' I didn't want him round hyar, nohow. I jes' kin view how reedic'lous I'd look axin' the robber ter kem in an' help wake Baker Anderson, 'kase we-uns couldn't wake him—he bein' a hard sleeper, seeh ez Gabriel's trump wouldn't 'sturb from his slumber—so ez we could git the boy ter the p'int o' sightin' a rifle. Naw! Steve war perlite enough ter leave one o' them leetle shootin'-irons ye call pistols hyar, an' plenty o' loads fur it. It's handy fur folks o' my size. An' Moses air men folks enough 'bout the house ter suit my taste."

Cheever made no sign that he heard. His eyes still rested with their sympathetic expression—patently spurious—upon Mrs. Yates. To the hard, keen lines of his face the affected sentiment was curiously ill-adjusted. Letitia's eyes were fairly alight as she gazed at him, gauging all the tenuity of this æsthetic veneer.

"I be glad ter know ye air so well pervided fur, Mis' Yates," he said; "an' so will all yer frien's be. Ye air mighty well liked in the cove an' the mountings hyarabouts.   I dun'no' ez I ever knowed a woman ter hev mo' frien's. Ye hev got a heap o' frien's, shore."

"Lots of 'em hev been hyar jes' ter find out how she takes it," remarked the small cynic. "An' 'fore they go away they air obleeged ter see ez *I* bear up wonderful."

Letitia had dropped the paddle, and was leaning back against the silver bark of a great beech-tree. She had plucked a cluster of the half-developed nuts from the low-hanging boughs, and as she bent her head and affected to examine them she half hid and half vaunted a roguish smile.

"They hev all kem, sech acquaintances ez I hev got," said Adelaide, flustered by this attack upon the motives of the community, fearful that Cheever might repeat it, and thus eager to set herself right upon the record. "Folks hev been powerful good; everybody hev kem round-about ez knowed Steve."

"'Ceptin' Mr. Rhodes," observed Letitia. "He war toler'ble constant visitin' hyar whilst in the neighborhood ez long ez Steve Yates held forth. But ez it air agin the religion o' wimmen ter vote, an' they think it air a sin, this hyar wicked Mr. Rhodes, ez air stirrin' up all the men folks ter tempt Satan at the polls, jes' bides up thar at some folkses ez be named Pettingill, they tell me, a-nussin' of his nicked head. He knows Adelaide an' me air too righteous ter vote, so he don't kem tryin' ter git us ter vote fur him."

" Whar's Fee Guthrie?" asked Cheever, suddenly, reminded of him by the allusion to the wound he had given the candidate.

The next moment there was a sneer upon his face, for the young scoffer had changed color. It crept up from the flush in her cheeks to the roots of her hair; but she replied, with her air of mock seriousness:

"I seem ter disremember at the moment."

Adelaide was dulled by the trouble and the preoccupation that had fallen upon her. "He war hyar this mornin', an' yistiddy too," she remarked, all unconscious of any but the superficial meaning of what she said. "He 'pears ter be powerful troubled 'bout his soul."

"He seems ter 'low ez he *hev* got a soul," observed Letitia, casually. "The pride o' some folks is astonishin'."

"He 'lowed he war goin' ter the woods ter pray," said Adelaide.

"An' I tole him," said Letitia, "that the Lord mought like him better ef he went ter the field ter plough. His corn is spindlin', an' his cotton is mightily in the grass. But it takes more elbow grease ter plough corn an' scrape cotton than ter pray, so the lazy critter is prayin'."

Her complexion had recovered its normal tints, and she laughed at this fling with manifest enjoyment, although the other two failed to respond—Adelaide deprecating its tone, and Cheever preserving an elaborate manner of ignoring that she had spoken at all.

"Waal, waal, Mis' Yates, I mus' be ridin'," he said, gathering up the reins. "Good-by. Ef ye want me fur ennything jes' call on me, an' ye'll do me a pleasure. Yes, 'm."

Her recognizant response was lost in the tramp of his horse, keen to be off on the first intimation that progress was in order, and in the wail which Moses set up in logical prescience that the admirable quadruped was to be withdrawn from his enchanted gaze. He lunged forward, bending his elastic body almost double, to see the horse go, mane and tail flying, and with the sun upon his neck and his sides that had a sheen like satin. As the rider was turning at right angles to cross the rickety bridge, he looked back over his shoulder at the group. Adelaide's dark attire and the diminutive size of Moses rendered them almost indistinguishable, but the faint blue of Letitia's dress defined her figure against the sombre green of the banks as if it was drawn in lines of light. She had not changed her posture; her face was still turned toward him. He knew that she was gazing after him as the fleet hoofs of the horse with the "nigh fore-laig crippled" swiftly bore him into invisibility. He could not hear her words, but he instinctively felt that she spoke of him, and he could only vaguely guess their import. So unflattering were these divinations that he ground his teeth with rage at the thought.

"I wisht I hed never seen her," he said, as the hollow beat of the slackened hoof sounded upon the bridge. "I wisht I hedn't stopped. But *who* would hev thunk ez that darned leetle consarn would hev been so all-fired sharp ez ter guess it? I wisht I hedn't stopped at all."

An incongruous fear, surely, for a man like this; but more than once, as he rode, he looked over his shoulder with a knitted brow and a furtive eager eye.

Naught followed but the long shadows which the sinking sun had set a-stalking all adown the valley. The world was still. He heard only here and there the ecstatic burst of a mocking-bird's wonderful roulades. Then the horse, with muscles as strong as steel, distanced the sound. Once, as the woods on either side fell away, he saw the west; it glowed with purest roseate tints, deepening to a live vermilion in the spaces about the horizon whence the sun but now had blazed; the nearest mountains were darkly purple; the northern ranges wore a crystalline, amethystine splendor, with a fine green sky above them that had an opaque hardness of color, which gradually merged into amber, giving way at the zenith to azure. In the midst of all a great palpitating star glistered, so white that with these strong contrasts of the flaunting heavens one might feel, for the first time, a full discernment of the effect of white.

Another moment the deep woods had closed around, and it seemed that night had come. He presently ceased to follow the road. The jungle into which he plunged had no path, no sign of previous passing, and the earth was invisible beneath the inextricable interlacings of the undergrowth. But if the sense of man was at fault, the good horse supplied the lack with a certain unclassified faculty, and with the reins on his neck and his head alert pushed on at fair speed, stepping gingerly over the boles of fallen trees, making his way around insurmountable boulders, swimming a deep and narrow pool; and finally, in struggling up the opposite bank, he uttered a whinny of triumph and recognition that bespoke his journey's end.   The sound rang through the evening stillness of the woods with abrupt effect, repeated a thousand times by the echoes of the huge rocks that lay all adown the gorge.   The place might realize to the imagination the myths of magic castles to be summoned into symmetry out of the craggy chaos by some talismanic word.   It was easy to fancy, in the solitude and the pensive hour, castellated towers in those great rugged heights, a moat in the deep pool, even a gateway, a narrow space above which the cliffs almost met.   Buck Cheever wot of none of these things, and no fancied resemblance embellished the stolidity of his recognition of the place as "mighty handy" for his purposes.   Perhaps the horse had more imagination, for when his owner dismounted and sought to lead him through this narrow space, that seemed a broken doorway to an unroofed tunnel—so consecutive were the crags, so nearly their summits approached each other—he held back, making a long neck, hanging heavily on the bridle, and lifting each hoof reluctantly.

"D—— yer durned hide! ain't ye never goin' ter l'arn nuthin', many times ez ye hev been hyar?" cried his master.

Thus encouraged, the horse slowly followed Cheever along the narrow passway between the cliffs, that finally met in a veritable tunnel, which might have seemed an entrance into a cave, save that at its extremity Cheever emerged into a lighted space and the free out-door air, and stood facing the western skies.

Nevertheless, the ledges of the cliff extended, rooflike, far out above; its walls were on either side;

the solid rock was beneath his feet.   It was a gigantic niche in the crags, to which the subterranean passage alone gave access, one side being altogether
open, showing the tops of the trees on the low opposite bank of the river, the stream itself in the deep
gorge below, and many and many a league of cloud-
land.   This unexpected outlook, these large liberties
of airy vision, formed the salient feature of the place,
dwarfing for the first moment all other properties.
On the resplendent background of the sunset, still
richly aglow, the slouching figures of a group of half
a dozen men about a smouldering fire had an odd de-
humanized effect.   Familiar though he was with these
uncanny silhouettes, he started violently, and hesitated, as if about to turn and flee.

VI

His gesture elicited a guffaw.

"Hold on, Buck," cried one of the men, affecting to clutch him to stay his flight.

"'Stan' the storm; it won't be long,'" trolled out another, a rich stave, with the resonance of the echoing walls. "What ye feared o', Buck—the devil? He don't keer ter 'sociate none with we-uns ez long ez ye air abroad an' afoot."

"I dun'no' what ails my eyes," said Cheever, visibly disconcerted, and passing his hand across his brow, as he still stood near the entrance, the bridle in his hand, the fine head of the impatient horse at his shoulder.

"Think ye see the devil?" cried another, jeeringly.

Cheever colored, and frowned heavily. The ridicule elicited what other means might have failed to lead forth. He could not brook this merry insolence, these flouts at his momentary fright. He justified it.

"I 'lowed I seen *another man*, what ain't hyar, an' never war," he said, gruffly, looking out at them from his drooping lids, his chin high in the air. The words seemed to have subtly transferred his transient terror. It took a longer lease in the exchange.

There was a momentary silence, while they stared with sudden gravity at him. A sort of remonstrange, a struggle against credulity, was in the square face of one burly fellow, seeming less a dark, illegible simulacrum of a man than the others, since he stood at an angle where the light fell slanting upon his features.

"What man, now?" Derridge said, in a deep bass voice, and the argumentative accents of one who will tolerate in evidence only fact and right reason. His tone seemed to challenge the name of the rash being who, in corporal absence, should venture in similitude among them.

"Dad burn ye, shet up!" cried Cheever. "I couldn't see his face. He turned it away. Whenst I looked at him he turned it away."

"In the name o' Gawd!" ejaculated one of the men, in a low-toned quaver.

Another, one Bob Millroy, Cheever's mainstay and lieutenant, glanced over his shoulder. "He ain't hyar now?" he demanded, in expostulatory haste.

"Naw, naw!" exclaimed Cheever, recovering himself, the more quickly as a monition of the possible disintegration of his gang, under the pressure of this mysterious recruit to their number, flitted across his mind. "Naw; he went ez soon ez I kem. Thar, now!" he continued, more lightly; "I know how it happens." He broke into a laugh that might have seemed strained, save that the rocks made such fantastic riot in the acoustics of the place. "It's Steve Yates. I'm used ter seein' *six* men, an' whenst I count my chickens thar's *seven*. I looked ter see jes' six!" and he laughed again.

"But Steve air over yander in the shadder!" expostulated Derridge, the disciple of pure reason. "Ye couldn't hev seen him at all."

"Waal, then," sneered Cheever, "I seen double. They say thar air good men, an' ministers o' the gospel, ez kin view a few more snakes 'n air nateral ter thar vision whenst the liquor air strong; an' that thar whiskey o' old Pettingill's kin walk a mile, I reckon, ef need war."

The others had hardly recovered from the superstitious thrill induced by the explanation of the strange agitation that beset him upon his entrance. They were ill-prepared to so summarily cast the subject aside, and stood still, with preoccupied, dilated eyes, mechanically gazing at him as he turned lightly toward Yates, who rose from a saddle on which he had half reclined beside the fire. The young mountaineer's face had a tinge of pallor, despite its sunburn. His dull brown eyes were restless and anxious. He was hardly an apt scholar for scheming and dissimulation, but he sought an air of ease and satisfaction as he asked:

"Waal, did ye hear ennything o' my fambly in yer travels?"

Cheever, all himself again, clapped him on the shoulder with a heartiness that made the blow ring through the high stone vault. "I *seen* 'em, my fine young cock, I *seen* 'em. I wouldn't take no hearsay on it. I seen Mis' Yates *herself*, an' talked a haffen hour with her. An' I seen Moses."

Steve Yates made shift to glance at him once, then he turned his eyes away toward the western sky, nodding repeatedly, but silently, to the items of news with which Cheever favored him.

"Mis' Yates ain't wantin' fur nuthin', though Moses wants everything, '*ceptin*' *teeth*; like ter hev took my horse-critter away from me, willy-nilly! Mis' Yates hev got that thar ugly, leetle, frazzle-headed Pettingill vixen ter 'company her, an' Baker Anderson with his rifle bides thar o' nights. Mis' Yates war cheerful an' laffin'. 'Steve will kem back whenst he gits tired,' she say. 'He an' me had words 'fore he lef'. I'll hold out ez long ez he kin,' she say. 'I don't believe he hev done nuthin' agin the law,' she say. 'But *ef* he hev,' she say, ' he air better off away than hyar at home, 'kase lynchers air mighty lawless round these parts.' An' she say, 'I know Steve air man enough ter take keer o' hisself an' do fur the bes', an' I'm willin' ter bide by what he do.'"

Alack! that a lie can so counterfeit the truth! To this wily and specious representation Stephen Yates listened with his eyes full of tears, afraid to trust a glance upon the face of his crafty companion.

"She say," Cheever went on, " ef Steve hev done ennything agin the law, I hope he'll make hisself sca'ce.'"

The other men, now affecting to stroll about in the ample spaces of the cavernous place, busying themselves with replenishing the fire or feeding the horses, of which there were half a dozen in a shadowy nook that seemed to extend downward to further subterranean regions, all gave furtive heed to these domestic reports. Ever and again they eyed the disingenuous face of the narrator with its half-closed lids and flexible lips. Then they would look at one another, and slyly wink their recognition of his craft. One of them, standing with his hands in his pockets and with a fire-lit face above the blazing logs, after a survey of this sort, grotesquely imitated the speaker's attitude and gesture, and silently worked his jaws with abnormal activity, as if in emulation of Cheever's ready eloquence, shook his head in affected despair, and desisted amid a smothered titter from the rest.

"Moses hev got another tooth; mighty nigh ez long ez a elephint's I seen at Colbury, I told him; an' it seemed ter make him mad—leastwise madder'n he war at fust. He wouldn't take no notice o' me, 'ceptin' whenst I put my finger in his mouth ter view his teeth, an' durned ef he didn't nearly bite it off. Oh, ye needn't ter trouble, Steve; ye air all right, an' hev done the bes' ye could, cornsiderin' all."

"I reckon so! I hope so!" said Yates, with something very like a sob.

They all sat around the fire late that night, after their supper of venison broiled on the coals, and corn-bread baked in the ashes, and washed down with a plentiful allowance of innocent-looking moonshine whiskey, colorless and clear as spring water. The stars seemed very near, looking in at the wide portals of the niche; the tops of the gigantic trees swaying without were barely glimpsed above the verge. The shadows of the men lengthened over the floor, or fluctuated on the wall as the flames rose or fell. Now and again the fire-light was strong enough to show the horses at their improvised manger in those recesses where the darkness promised further chambers of the cavern. One steed lay upon the ground, the others stood, some still and drowsing, but more than once the sharp pawing of an iron-shod hoof challenged the abrupt echoes.

Outside, so sweet, so pure was the summer night; the buds of the elder-bush were riven into blooms, the mocking-bird piped for the rising moon, the katydids twanged a vibrant note, and the river sang the self-same song it had learned in the prehistoric days of the pygmies. Even so still, so calmly pensive was the time that the far-away murmur of the water-fall came to Yates's ears, or it may be to his memory only, which transmitted the fancy transmuted in sound to his sense. He lounged, half pillowed upon his saddle, in the circle about the fire, and strove to drink and laugh and talk with the rest. Many a merry jest had those walls echoed, seeming almost sentient in emulation of the boisterous joy. To-night, somehow, they had forgotten their jovial wiles. More than once the echo of laughter quavered off into strange sounds that the ear shrank to hear, and one after another of the brawny fellows looked furtively over his shoulder.

A sudden jar—only a screech-owl shrilling in a tree on the river-bank below—but one of the men was on his feet, all a-tremble, crying out, "What's that?" And this was the bold Cheever.

"Put up yer pistol, ye darned idjit!" exclaimed Derridge, the disciple of reason. "Don't ye know a squeech-owel whenst ye hear one? Ye must be plumb sodden in Pettingill whiskey."

Cheever, with a half-articulate oath, sank back upon the saddle upon which he half lay and half sat, and presently evolved an excuse for his nervousness.

He had something too in his face that implied a
doubt, a need of support, a wish for counsel.

"That gal at Yates's, I mean Litt Pettingill, sorter
purtended ez she b'lieved ez I knowed o' Steve's
wharabouts.   Now Steve's welcome to shelter with
we-uns.   But I'd hate it powerful ef jes' 'kase he fell
in with we-uns that night ez he war a-goin' fur the
doctor ter patch Len Rhodes's head, 'twar ter be the
means o' draggin' the law down on we-uns, an' gittin' it onto our trail."

"Ye mus' hev said suthin'.   *She* couldn't jes' hev
drawed the idee out'n *nuthin*'," reasoned the deep
bass voice of Derridge, who wore a severe and repre-
hensive frown.   "Ye air a smart man, Buck, an' I
ain't denyin' it none, but whenst a man talks ez much
ez you-uns he *can't* gin keerful heed ter *all* his words,
an' ye mus' hev said suthin' ez gin her a hint.   Folks
kin talk too much, specially whenst they set up ter
be *smart*."   He was a silent man himself, and was accounted slow.

Cheever sneered.   "Ye air powerful brigaty ter-
night.   I reckon I be ekal ter keepin' a secret from
enny gal folks.   Leastwise I hev knowed a power o'
secrets an' cornsider'ble gal folks.   An' they never
got tergether ez I ever hearn tell on."

This was logic, and it silenced his interlocutor.
They all sat musing for a time, while the smoke
mounted into the lofty dome of the niche, and the
fire leaped fitfully, casting its flicker on all their
faces, and the whole interior, a dull red and a dusky
brown, seemed a discordant contrast to the white,
lucent light of the unseen moon, stretching across
the shadowy landscape.   Dew there was on the trees

9

without; it scintillated now and then, and far away rose soft and noiseless mists. More than once the night sighed audibly in sheer pensiveness.

"Boys," said Bob Millroy, suddenly, "I be a believer in signs."

There was a motionless interest in every face turned toward him. A contagion of credulity was in the very word.

"Hyar we-uns hev been," he went on, "a-goin' tergether fur many a day in secret, an' sech ez our workin's air they ain't 'cordin' ter law nor the 'pinion o' the cove. An' I ain't felt 'feard nowise—though some mought say the hemp air growed an' spun, an' the rope air twisted—till this evenin', whenst Buck Cheever seen an' extry man 'mongst we-uns, ez turned away his face. Sence then the fire's cold!"

He spread out his hands toward it, shaking his head in token of the futility of its swift combustion, with its flashes and sparkle and smoke, as he chafed them together.

"Lord A'mighty, ye durned cowardly fool!" cried the leader of the party, beside himself with anxiety and many a premonition. "Didn't I tell ye agin 'twar jes' Steve, ez I never looked ter view, bein' ez he ain't reg'lar 'mongst we-uns?"

"Ye 'lowed he turned his face away," said the believer in signs.

"Waal, hev Steve got enny crick in his neck that disables him from a-turnin' of _his_ face away?" demanded Cheever.

"He war in the shadder; ye never seen Steve," said Derridge, slowly shaking his logical head.

"He turned his face away so ez ye mought not

view it," said Millroy, with a credulity that coerced responsive conviction.

Cheever was shaken. He suddenly desisted from argument. "Who air ye a-'lowin' 'twar?" he demanded from the opposite side of the fire.

The ligaments of his neck were elongated as he thrust his head forward. The fire-light showed only a glassy glitter where it struck upon the eyeballs beneath his half-closed lids. Bereft of the expression of his eyes, it was wonderful how much of suspense, of petrified expectation, of the presage of calamity, the hard lines of his face conveyed.

"'Twar him we met up with on the road that night," said Millroy, who from the affluence of his resources of conjecture could afford to dispense with mere proof and fact.

Cheever was conscious that the others were watching him with the urgent anxiety of those who have a personal interest at stake. The sense of emergency was substituted for courage.

"I wish 'twar," he said, coolly. "*He* ain't dead— a mighty pity! I'd give the bes' horse I ever see"— he nodded his head toward the gallant roan—"ef I could view *his* harnt."

There was an evident revulsion in the plastic minds of his followers. They had no sense of consistency to sustain adherence to any dogma. Millroy was in the minority when he said, still mysteriously shaking his head, "I'll bet the minit ye seen him 'mongst we-uns an' he turned his head away war the minit o' his takin' off."

"Ye air always skeered o' yer shadder, Bob," said Cheever; "an' I never knowed a feller so rich in

signs ez kem ter nuthin'. That man would be powerful welcome hyar in the sperit. I be a heap more
pestered 'kase we let him git off soul an' body tergether. I know he war shot. I dun'no' who fired
it "—he mechanically closed his right hand as upon
the handle of a pistol, his first finger extended and
crooked upon the imaginary trigger, while the observant Bob Millroy scanned with unspoken deductions the unconscious, involuntary gesture. "I never
thunk he war much hurt, though ez he went scourin' off he war bowed ter the saddle-bow, but that war
ter escape the bullets ez kem arter him. He'll live
ter lead a posse an' the sher'ff ter the spot, mos' likely; *I'm* 'feared o' that. I'd *de*light ter see his
harnt."

"Bob oughter hev a muzzle," said the reasonable
Derridge, irritably—"ter keep him from spittin' out
signs hyar, whilst we-uns oughter be cornsiderin' how
the law mought be takin' us, red-handed, with all our
plunder ter convict us "—he cast a glance at certain
saddle-bags that lay close to Cheever's side. "He jes'
sets up an' gins us a sign fur this, an' a warnin' fur
that, till we air plumb wore out with his foolishness."

"This place be safe enough, I'm a-thinkin'; no
use a-worryin' an' a-fussin'," said the unctuous voice
of Pete Beckett, always full of a hopeful content, and
like oil upon the troubled waters.

The others listened with clearing countenances,
but Cheever shook his head. "Revenuers know it;
they raided a still hyar wunst." The red fire-light
on the circle of faces showed their alarm at the recollection, the prophetic suggestion. "Old man Peake
run it."

"Ye 'low ef they war ter s'picion ennybody roundabouts, they mought s'arch hyar," said Derridge, drawing the logical conclusion.

"Edzac'ly," said Cheever, impatient of the waste of words by so patent a deduction.

"They do say," remarked Millroy, sepulchrally, "that arter Zeb Tait went deranged, he hid hyar whenst they wanted ter jail him ez a crazy."

"Too crazy ter want ter go ter jail," exclaimed Derridge, satirically.

"An'," pursued Millroy, lugubriously, "he starved hisself ter death in this place; leastwise they fund his corpse hyar, though he mought hev died from his ailment. But I dun'no' *ef* folks *do* die from jes' bein' crazy an' bereft."

"Naw, they don't," said Cheever, suddenly, "else ye'd hev been dead long ago, ez crazy a loon ez ever went a-gibberin' o' foolishness around."

Somehow his magnetic quality was at fault. The others failed to fall in with his humor. They all sat silent, staring at the red coals; the image of the distraught, solitary creature, who had in the secret stronghold of the mountains wrought out his terrible doom, was in the mind of each.

Millroy spoke rather to their thought than to the words of Cheever, when he said, "The buzzards an' the eagles flyin' an' flusterin' round the body led the sher'ff ter the spot."

The prosaic word, full of worldly omen, broke the breathless spell.

"An' the *sher'ff* knows the place, too!" cried Derridge. "Waal"—he turned his eyes, at once furious and upbraiding and full of prescient terror, upon

Cheever—"hell-fire be my portion ef I don't think ye hev tuk the mos' public place about the cove fur these hyar doin's"—he pointed at the saddle-bags. "An' a man in Colbury either dead by this time, with warrants sworn out for we-uns, or else on our track ter identify us fur the sher'ff."

"I tuk this place 'kase 'twar our reg'lar stampin'-groun'," cried Cheever, lifting his voice to defend himself against the burly, swelling tones of his accuser. "It air ez safe ez enny other. Thar ain't none o' us out o' place 'ceptin' Steve." He winked slyly at the others, for the young mountaineer lay a little in the shadow and a trifle behind him. So blunted was the conscience, the humanity in each, that the sense of possessing a scape-goat, the opportunity of profit on another's injury, had a suave and unctuous influence to heal their dissension. "*We-uns*, why, we-uns air some a-herdin' o' cattle twenty mile away on the Balds; some war in Car'liny yistiddy tradin' fur cattle"—he pointed at the mire on the boots of two of the party—"Buncombe County mud! An' *I* hev jes' got back from ridin' in open daylight about the cove, with my mouth an' eyes stretched ter hear how Yates hev disappeared. I be a-goin' home ter-morrer ter git salt fur my cattle"—he put on a waggishly virtuous air. "An' *I* war thar ter-day, ez my fambly kin testify. 'Tain't safe, though, I know, ter keep this truck hyar long"—he winked at the saddle-bags—"nor ter divide it yit."

The alert expression with which each man hearkened to the allusion of partition was eminently suggestive of the pricking-up of ears. Indeed, as they all sat indistinct in the shadow and the flicker, there was something dog-like or wolf-like in the whetted expectancy of their waiting attention.

"I laid off ter hide it hyar fur ter-night an' ter-morrer," continued Cheever, "an' whilst some gyards it, the t'others go off an' show tharsef's in place—'ceptin' Steve "—his thin, expressive lips were slightly elongated. "The news 'ain't got ter the cove yit, but time it do they will all be fur stringin' him up. *Him—knowed* ter be on that road *that* night at *that* hour, *an' 'ain't never showed up no mo'.*"

A grin of many conceits was upon his countenance, unseen by the subject of conversation, while the men in the full flare of the fire-light had some ado to suppress any facial response of relish. For in this circumstance the dullest amongst them found it easy to discern their safety. Some discussion ensued as to the best method of secreting the treasure until it should be safe to divide and use it.

"Jest ter think," remarked Cheever, with jovial hypocrisy, "o' the strange workin's o' Providence. All we-uns war arter war the man's horse—jes ter take the horse-critter an' turn the man a-foot in the road—an' stiddier that we tuk this pile o' money. It 'll buy a hundred sech horses."

Perhaps it was because of the succumbing of their fears in the drowsy influences of the hour, waxing late, perhaps because of the confidence engendered by elation and success, but a new sentiment of security, of capability, was perceptible upon the mere mention of their exploit, and several were disposed to dilate upon the future expenditure of their share rather than to devise means to properly secrete it. Here was where they seemed, strangely enough,

Yates thought, to misunderstand Cheever. He took little part in the discussion; he listened to each with a sneering negation, half masked beneath his lowered eyelids, and Yates readily divined that none probably would know the hiding-place of the plunder but himself and Millroy, his loyal henchman, and the only one of them all in whom he really reposed any confidence.

Derridge sat gazing at the embers; once he offered a characteristic observation. "I know 'twouldn't do ter keep it hyar till the s'arch be over," he said, ponderingly, accepting Cheever's suggestion, "an' 'twouldn't do fur all o' we-uns ter light out fur Texas an' sech tergether. The folks would be a-talkin' 'bout our vamosin' like Steve done, an' the sher'ff would be on our track with a requisition. An' it hev ter be hid; not in the woods, 'kase we-uns might lose the spot, or a big rain mought wash the dirt off'n it, or sech."

"I tell ye," interjected Beckett, with a swift look of inspiration. "You know old Squair Beamen's fambly buryin'-groun'. Old Mis' Beamen hev got a tombstone like a big box. Lift up the top, and put the truck in thar."

"I'd like ter put ye in thar," replied Cheever, who had stolidly eyed him during this prelection. "I wouldn't hev that truck that close ter a jestice o' the peace fur nuthin'."

"An' I hev hearn o' other truck bein' hid thar," objected Ben Tyson, indignantly. "Them men ez robbed the cross-roads store up on Scolacutta River —thar plunder war fund thar."

"Not fur a long time; 'twar powerful well hid,"

insisted Pete Beckett, as if stating an essential value. But the other two laughed, and the vexed question seemed hardly soon to be decided.

The waning moon in the skies had swung now so high that her white light lay upon the verge of the niche with a sharply drawn and jagged outline—the shadow of the roofing ledge. Momently this belt grew broader, and the glow of the coals more dully red. The two mountaineers who were deputed to watch while the others slept beguiled the tedium by a game with a greasy pack of cards, using as a table the seat of a saddle laid between them as they half reclined on the floor, and played less by the light of the fire than the clear lustre streaming in at the arched opening of the grotto. The prone figures of the others gave evidence in heavy breathing of their unconscious slumbers. All was silent without; the silver sheen made splendid the woods, although it was invested with some strange yearning melancholy, belonging only to the moon on its wane. The frogs had ceased their chanting; the katydid was dumb; the earth seemed to sigh no more; the insensate vegetation slept. Once across the white space at the verge, where fell on the floor the sharp rugged shadow of the roof, there was in the midst of the stillness a sudden movement; it came from the top of the precipice above. The two gamesters sat as if petrified, the cards in their hands, their burning eyes intent upon the shadow of the summit of the cliff. Nothing—a long moment of suspense. Nothing! And then it came again; the outline of a floating wing—a swift similitude of the night-hawk sweeping in its noiseless flight through the air to seek its unwarned prey. The two men did not so much as glance at one another as they resumed their game; of these thrilling moments, charged with suspense and danger, their lives counted many.

So still it was without that it seemed to Yates that he might lose in sleep the consciousness of those few momentous hours that had changed the whole current of his life. He went over them again and again in his scanty dreams with a verisimilitude of repetition that sufficed almost to prevent him from discerning his waking thoughts from his slumber. Now and again as he reviewed them he so realized to his imagination a different ordering of their sequence, which might have been so readily effected at the time had he but foreseen, that he experienced almost the relief of escape. Why had he not refused old Pettingill's request to ride seventeen miles for the doctor? But, indeed, had he not offered the service from the superabundance of his good-nature? "I hope the old man got his horse again, like Cheever say," he sighed; for in the interim his conscience had been loaded with every ounce that the good bay weighed. And then, again, without the fancy of what he might have done and what he wished, he would recall the circumstances as they had befallen him. Never had impressions been so burned into his consciousness as in those most significant moments of his life. He could even now recollect the glow of friendly feeling with which he said, "I don't b'lieve but what the yerb doctor kin bring Len Rhodes through; but ter pleasure Mr. Shattuck *I'll* ride fur the t'other doctor, Mr. Pettingill—*I'll* ride fur him." He could even feel again his foot in the stirrup, the quick, smooth gallop of the fresh horse beneath him. And then, the winding lengths of the sandy woodland roads, so sweet with the breath of the azaleas, all white and star-eyed in dark bosky places, so fresh with the dew, so idealized by the moon. And thinking no harm! Thinking of Adelaide, with regrets for the harsh words between them, with resolutions that they should be the last. Alack! they were likely to be the last indeed. And of Moses—proteanwise! For he could see Moses as a half-grown lad, tall and strong and straight; and then as a bearded man; sometimes as a justice of the peace; sometimes the elastic paternal ambition pre-empted for him a seat in the State Legislature; and then the image dwindled, best of all, to the small limits of the cradle where he slept, so pink and white and warm, the highest potentate in all the land! Thinking of these things Yates was as the miles sped; hearing once afar, afar, a horn wound in the stillness, and then only his horse's hoofs with the alternate beat of the gallop.

He had ridden hard, since it might be a case of life and death; but there was a bad stretch of road ahead, a long hill to climb, and the horse was blown. It was a saving of time, he thought, as he slackened the pace and went slowly, slowly up the rugged ascent. The grass was thick on the margin; he drew his horse to the side where the hoofs might fall on the smooth dank sward. He could scarcely hear his saddle creak. The animal paused at the summit to snatch a mouthful of cool wet sassafras leaves, munching with relish, despite the hinderance of the bit.

Suddenly a wild hoarse scream rang out, startling

the night; a tumult of voices sounded; a pistol shot
split the air, another; and, as he looked from the
summit of the hill down the declivity, he saw a
group of horsemen in fierce altercation in the middle of the road. Scant as the moment was, so
bright was the moon that he recognized more than
one face. And the moment was scant, for the cen-
tral figure, his whole pose vigorously resistant, fired
again, wide of the mark, the ball whizzing by the ear
of Zack Pettingill's bay horse. The animal uttered
a sharp neigh, almost articulate, wheeled abruptly,
and, heedless of either whip or spur, breaking into
an unmanageable run, fled frantically homeward.
Behind there were swifter hoofs than his. It was
hardly a moment before Cheever's splendid horse
was alongside; his burly strength re-enforced Steve
Yates's pull on the reins. Whether, in the confusion
of the moment, Cheever and his gang had mistaken
the neighing of Pettingill's horse and the sound of
his hoofs for pursuit and incontinently fled, or
whether they thus divined that they were discovered, Yates did not then definitely understand, nor
was it clearer to him afterward. Certainly they
dreaded the escape of the witness who beheld the
deed, and knew its perpetrators by face and name,
far more than that of the plundered wayfarer, who,
upon the diversion effected in his favor, made good
use of his horse's hoofs upon the road that he had
so lately travelled. Beyond a pistol ball or two, one
of which Yates thought undoubtedly took effect,
they did not offer to pursue him. They rode alongside of their protesting and unarmed captive, and
discovering shortly how efficacious was the sugges-

tion that he would doubtless be accused of the deed, since so many knew of his errand at this unusual hour and on this unfrequented road, they caused him to be pondering heavily upon the dreary possibilities of circumstantial evidence before they had gone many miles. Not that he did not offer resistance and seek flight. "What's the use o' swallerin' this bullet whether or no, Steve?" Cheever had demanded, as he presented a pistol to his captive's mouth. "I don't want ye ter eat lead, an' how would that mend the matter fur you-uns?" And when Yates sought to urge his horse into a gallop, it was but a shamble in comparison with the smooth, swift gait of the splendid animal that Cheever bestrode. He could do naught at the time, not even by screams arouse a wayside habitation, for they had soon plunged into unfrequented forests, and were far away from the haunts of men.

That they had not used him more unkindly than the interests of their own safety necessitated made no claim upon his gratitude. Perhaps, although he had not the courage to court it, he would have preferred death. He only took advantage of their leniency to stipulate that Pettingill's horse should be turned loose to return. "He mought be viewed 'mongst our'n some time. He's too close a neighbor ennyhow," said Cheever, and so he consented. Even the trivial detail of the creature's bewilderment was still in the young man's mind—how the horse persistently trotted along in the cavalcade, with his lustrous surprised eyes and his empty saddle, his erstwhile rider mounted behind one of the other men. More than once after he was driven back he reappeared from behind a sharp curve of the road, nimbly cantering and with an appealing whinny. Finally blows prevailed, and from the crest of a ridge they afterward saw him ambling erratically homeward along the white moon-lit road, now and again stopping by the wayside to crop the grass or bushes.

"Ef he keeps on that-a-way he'll git home next week," Cheever had commented.

Even now, reviewing the disaster, Yates could not say definitely what he should have done, but it seemed that some rescue would have waited upon his effort had his slow brain but devised it. More than all, above all, the sight of the saddle-bags containing a considerable sum of money taken from the stranger had a horror for him. He dwelt upon the idea that among the people of the cove he must be believed to have committed the crime, until he had a morbid sense of complicity. His mind was, as he knew, but a poor tool for scheming, but he was imperatively, urgently moved by some inward power to make an effort which might result in the restoration of the money to its proper owner. He began to feel that integrity is not a repute; it is an attribute of the mind and a spontaneous emotion of the heart. "'Tain't ter hev folks *say* ye're honest; it air ter *be* honest."

He felt himself forever blasted; he doubted if, in any event, he would ever dare to return to his home. He had known of men with far less evidence against them than these perverse lies, that masqueraded as facts in his case, strung up to a tree without judge or jury. He would do himself, his wife, his child seant favor in courting that ignoble doom. He only revolved the robbery for the sake of honesty alone, that he might devise some scheme to frustrate the highwaymen and restore the money.

Somehow, as he lay looking out at the gibbous moon, visible now, all distorted and weird in the purple sky, and no less lustrously yellow because of the sense of dawn gradually stealing upon the air, he could not disassociate Shattuck from his train of ideas despite the lack of logical connection. It was perhaps, he thought dully in recognizing the fact, because it was upon Shattuck's errand that he had gone to this dreadful fate; perhaps because the mention of a box-like tombstone had suggested to him the strange underground sarcophagi, also box-like and of stone, of the pygmy burying-ground in which Shattuck was interested. And suddenly he caught his breath and lay still, thinking, a long time.

So languid-footed was the night, but he smelt the rose in its morning blossoming! A mocking-bird sang, all faint and sweet and fresh, and dreamed again. Stars were fading; the great valley of East Tennessee was beginning to be outlined, with ridges and smaller valleys and rivers and further mountains, with a sense of space and of large symmetry that outdoes the imagination. And still the moon shone in his face.

"Buck," he said, suddenly, for all the others slept, and it was Cheever's turn to watch, "did you-uns ever hear tell o' the Leetle Stranger People?"

Cheever, smoking his pipe near at hand, as he lay on the floor, lifted himself upon one elbow. He nodded. "Many a time."

"Folks 'low they useter hev this kentry. They seem sorter small ter hev ter die."

"I dun'no' but what they do," said Cheever, impressed by the hardship of the common fate which overtook even such "leetle people." "An' folks hev fairly furgot they ever lived, too."

Yates nodded his head.

"I dun'no' ez I hev hearn the Leetle People named fur thirty year an' better. My gran'mam tole me 'bout 'em whenst I war a boy. What ailed you-uns ter git a-goin' 'bout 'em?"

"Jes' thinkin' 'bout home. Thar buryin'-groun' ain't more'n haffen mile from my house," replied Yates, casually. "Ye hev hearn tell how they coffins the dead in stone boxes, two feet undergroun', an' I reckon that fool talk 'bout Mis' Beamen's tombstone bein' like a stone box reminded me of 'em."

Cheever held his pipe in his hand. The coal had dwindled to an ash as he listened. A thought was astir in his crafty brain. Dull at scheming as Yates was, he could almost divine its processes.

"I dun'no' *when* I hev hearn the Leetle People named afore," Cheever said, meditatively.

"The old folks used ter talk 'bout 'em sometimes," rejoined Steve, apparently inadvertently, "though few knows now they ever lived, nor whar they lie. One grave air right on the south side o' that thar laurel bush—the only laurel on the slope ; I know, fur the ground sounds hollow thar ; I sounded it one day."

He cast a covert glance at Cheever. The robber's eyes, opened widely for once, were full of light as they glanced swiftly and searchingly at the sleeping men, all unconscious, about them. Then he said, in a casual tone, "I reckon thar's a heap o' lie in all that thar talk 'bout the Leetle People." And his earnest, intent, breathless face belied his words as he spoke them.

Yates sank back upon the improvised pillow of saddle and blanket, breathing quick, feeling alive once more. He had relied on Cheever's ignorance of Shattuck's intention—known, indeed, to few, and infinitely unimportant in their estimation—since the horse-thief's protective seclusion debarred him from much gossip. To this spot beneath the laurel Yates himself had directed Shattuck's attention. Now if the treasure should be concealed there, and Shattuck's enthusiasm should not fail, the discovery would be made and noised abroad, and some right at last would blossom out of all this wrong.

10

VII.

Tʜᴇ "falling weather" came hard upon its proph-
ecy. All that day the clouds mustered. Films,
lace-like and fretting the roseate heavens, thickened
as the light gradually dawned, and were dense before
the sun rose—dense, but white and semi-translucent,
and a certain focus of opaque glister, slowly mounting and mounting the sky, gave token how the great
chariot of the sun fared along the celestial highways
to the zenith. No fierce monitions in this noiseless
eclipse of the diurnal splendors of the rich summertide; the landscape lay in a lethargic shadow, and
time seemed to wait somewhere and to drowse dully,
so long the hours loitered, so little did they change;
the leaves hung still; a breathless, sultry pause bated
the pulses of the world. In the afternoon—one who
judged of time by the sun might hardly know were
it the impending cloud or the approach of night—
this long monotony of the atmosphere was broken by
a gradual darkening, and presently an almost imperceptible rain was gently falling. The air was dank,
the lungs expanded to longer and longer respirations,
and the clouds were coming down the mountain-side
—coming in fleecy ranks along the dark purple inden-
tations which marked the ravines, the vanguard with
broken flakes that suggested woolly leaders of flocks.

"Look yander at the sheep, Moses," Letitia ad-

jured the infant as he sat on the floor of the porch
—"look yander at the flocks o' the old man ez herds
the clouds on the bald o' the mounting."

Moses stared with inconceivable impressions at the
fictitious sheep, and more than once looked up with
a contemplative eye and a sensitive lip at Letitia to
hear again of the fabled herder whose flocks wore
this tenuous guise. How much he believed, how
much he understood, must ever remain a matter of
conjecture. He hearkened to all that was told to
him which trenched upon the wonderful lore of the
nursery, but maintained the while the inscrutable,
impenetrable reticence of the infant who can but
who will not talk. And now all similitude of flocks
was lost in a sudden precipitation of the cloud
masses toward the valley. Gullies, abysses, the river,
every depression seemed to exude vapors, that hung
suspended in the air, till they were met by the downward rush. All at once a louder patter was on the
little slanting roof of the porch, and upon its floor
the drops, glittering in their elastic rebound, multi-
plied till Letitia, catching Moses under the arms, bore
him within, his feet sticking straight out, conserving
his sitting posture, and placed him on the broad
hearth before the fire. And at last—whether the
night or only its dull simulacrum—darkness descended. Letitia, looking forth from the open door,
could see the pale shifting mists rather by the glow
from the hearth than by the aid of such gray and
sombre twilight as might linger without. The rain
fell invisibly in the midst of the vapors; only the
detached drops that pattered upon the edge of the
floor of the porch gave out a steely gleam as they

smartly rebounded and fell again. The room was all
the cheerier for the dull and dank aspect of the world
outside. The spinning-wheel drawn up to one corner
of the hearth promised an evening full of quiet industry and a musical whirring pleasant to hear. The
warping bars, on the opposite side of the brown wall,
were full of color, much red predominating in many
shades, for Moses had early seemed to notice the
rich, brilliant tint, and it had won his rare approval.
Indeed, so much Turkey red went into the fashioning
of his garments that the hanks of yarn and cotton designed for them and hanging from the ceiling served
to brighten the room, as if a bizarre decorative effect
had been intentionally sought. The fire blazed mer-
rily, and the light flashed back from the barrel of the
rifle that rested on its rack of deer antlers against
the chimney.

Letitia, in her faint-blue dress, moved deftly about,
giving a touch here and there to set things in their
eventide order, murmuring as she went a little song,
scarcely a tune—more like the fragmentary melodies
that the mountain brooks sing on their way to the
valley. " A cur'ous sort'n psalmin' what she makes
up out'n her own head," her mother used to say,
with that rural distrust of all out of the usual experience. An ash cake was baking under the clean silver-
gray mounds at one side of the great fire, which was
too large for comfort—for the air was not chilly, albeit both doors and windows stood open—and too hot
even for its purpose of cooking supper, for now and
again the eggs, also roasting under the ashes, gave
token by a sharp crack that one had succumbed unduly to the heat, had burst and spilled its yolk. On

each occasion Moses, sitting after his lowly habit on the floor before the fire, gave a nervous little jerk, and looked with a certain anxiety at his mother, aware that all was not well in the domestic administration. Adelaide, kneeling by the hearth, frowned almost mechanically, and forgot the mishap the next moment. Presently she looked up at the grayish blackness that filled the door and window.

"I dun'no' whether it air night or no," she said, the red live coals that she had raked out upon the hearth casting a dull reflection upon her oval face and large dark eyes. "I mought be *too* forehanded a-gittin' supper fur aught I kin tell."

"Ye'll find out whenst it air supper-time by the comin' o' Baker Anderson," remarked Letitia. "That boy air wound up ter the very minute. His folks never kin need a clock ter find out what's meal-times, nor ter look at the sun. Mus' be a great comfort ter ennybody ter hev sech a punctual stommick in the house. My mother would dote on feedin' him."

And, sure enough, presently here was Baker, a great thumping boy of sixteen, with a man's frame and a callow, square, beardless, sheepish face, as conscious of his feet as if he were a centipede, as conscious of his big hands as if he had a hundred. All the grace and the strength of his muscles deserted him at the door, where he hesitated as if he doubted how he should before all these spectators ever reach the chair by the fireside which he usually occupied. Then he made a tremulous rush, deposited himself sidelong upon it, and, looking up from under his straight eyebrows, said, with a gasp, "G'evenin', Mis' Yates."

He did not dare to address Letitia, so conscious

was he of her latent mockery, and of her knowledge
of the criticism upon the houschold which he had
made in his innocent confidences to his aunt, who
had ruthlessly repeated it to the parties in interest :
he had said that he had no objection to Mis' Yates,
but that Letitia eyed him ez ef she could sca'cely
keep from laffin' at him, an' Moses eyed him ez if he
could sca'cely keep from smackin' his jaws ; an' 'twixt
'em both he hardly knew whether he stood on his head
or his heels ; an' ef 'twarn't fur Mis' Yates, he an'
his rifle would make tharselves sca'ce at Steve Yates's
cabin.

To the manners of Moses, indeed, one far less sensitive than the guest might readily have taken exceptions.   From time to time he angrily surveyed Baker,
knitting his scanty brows, and always crooking his
fat dimpled arm above his forehead whenever he renewed his gaze ; and although this gesture is not
among the generally accepted expressions of con-
tumely, it had especial capacities to convey a flout.
Poor Baker had expected gambols with the infant to
be a means of lessening the awkwardness of his self-
consciousness, and to put him on a more easy basis
with the household.   Mrs. Yates often felt herself
obliged to apologize for the unfriendly conduct of
Moses, and even to expostulate with the great Dagon,
and beg him to mitigate his severity.   He seemed
instigated to this course in some sort by the malice
of an old dog, brindled a bluish-gray and white, who
had adopted a senile vagary that the visitor harbored
wicked intentions against the household hero, which
he evidently felt delegated to frustrate.   He always
came, upon the boy's entrance, and placed himself

between the guest and the precious "leetle Mose," who found the animal's side, cushioned with fat, a sufficiently soft and comfortable pillow, and was wont to lean upon it, resting his downy head and fine pink cheek on the dark tigerish hair of the thick neck —the formidable fangs of the brute's half-open mouth, the fiery eye and rising bristles, bearing fierce contrast to the delicate infantile curves and coloring of the child's face.   Here nightly, until Baker Anderson was led off to his slumbers in the roof-room, the dog sat immovable, now and then emitting a growl if he so much as glanced at Moses.   Mrs. Yates could only redouble her suavity to the household defender, and add some soothing dainty to the supper.   "I made this johnny-cake express fur *you-uns*, Baker," she would say.   And when he could no longer be fed, she exerted herself to entertain him in the brief interval before the young fellow, tired out with the day's ploughing or hunting, would succumb to the heat and the stillness, and nod before the fire.   Doubtless this talk was a salutary necessity for Adelaide, for the days were full of tears, and the nights of sighs and wakeful hours, and dreams of vague unhappiness and discordant, half-realized terrors.   Letitia's smiling assurance, "How ye an' Steve air a-goin' ter laff an' laff over this some o' these days!" she could not accept, although it was grateful to hear, and she would still her sobs to listen to its iteration.   But poor Baker, when awake, called for all her sympathy and countenance, thus helpless amongst his enemies, and so sorrow must needs be forgotten for a time.

They all sat thus this evening, the supper cleared away, the hearth swept, one of Moses's red stockings for winter wear growing under the needles in Adelaide's hand, the little flax spinning-wheel awhirl as Letitia drew out the long thread, the baby half drowsing on the fierce old dog's neck, the doors all aflare, when a sudden chill wind sprang up. They heard it rising far, far away—a deep, hollow murmur, all unlike the throbbing of the cataract, which was ceaseless in the darkness, beating like the heart of the night; it came stealthily down through the gap in the mountain, and the trees, hitherto silent and motionless above the little house, suddenly fell to trembling and clashed their boughs, and long-drawn sibilant sighs pervaded all their rustling foliage.

"Listen!" Letitia said, her foot pausing on the treadle, as she turned her brilliant azure eyes to the night, all black without. "Thar's the last o' the rain and the fog."

The drops were redoubled on the roof, but presently they grew fewer, discursive, and now sounded only the fitful patter of those shed by the foliage where they had lodged.

A more turbulent gust banged the batten shutters and shook the door, then went screaming, screaming through the black night, with a voice so dolorous and wild that more than once Adelaide put down her knitting, and looked up with a face pallid and agitated, as if she realized in the sound the utterance of the dreary grief that rent her heart.

"Shet the door an' bar it up, Baker," observed Letitia. "Ye air younger'n me"—with a mimicry of age—"or I'd wait on you-uns."

The boy's manner of shuffling to the door and window and securing them kindled a smile in her eyes. He could not encounter them when he was once more ensconced in the corner, so he chanced to glance at the old dog, which instantly growled, and then he was fain to stare sedulously into the fire. "I wouldn't be s'prised none ef the coals war ter hop up an' scorch me," he said bitterly to himself, for the inner man, or boy, was by no means the submissive, humble entity which the outward shy, awkward cloddishness might intimate. The gusts had sprung after him upon the door, and shook it as if a hundred beasts had lain in ambush there, baffled by his forethought.

"Oh!" cried Adelaide, all her distraught nerves a-jarring. "What do that sound like?"

"Like the wind," said Letitia, bending her smiling face to the spinning-wheel, "the wind ez air stoppin' the rain, an' the corn crap 'll be short. Don't ye see Baker thar drappin' a tear, like a good farmer, 'count o' the drought that this leetle rain don't break?"

Baker turned scarlet and shuffled his big feet and moistened his lips with his tongue, his traduced dry eyes, hot and angry, staring steadily at the fire.

"One tear, Baker, shed fur sins mought go further than that leetle tear o' yourn will go with the country's corn crap."

Letitia spoke solemnly, and looked with affected gravity at the boy, who was so lugubrious under her teasing that she could not resist, and burst into a peal of laughter. His lips mechanically distended, exhibiting two great unbroken arches of strong teeth.

"Don't, *don't* show all them teeth ter Moses, Baker," she adjured him, in pretended alarm. "Think how bent on gittin' teeth he be now, an' ef he war ter set his heart on havin' *yourn too*, how lonesome ye'd be 'thout 'em at meal-times!"

Moses, hearing his name, roused himself with an effort, looking over his shoulder frowningly, with a shrill little ill-tempered squeal, for he did not permit her to speak of him, and rarely to address him.

"Oh, oh, listen to the wind!" cried Adelaide, unheeding them all. "It sounds like the voice o' suthin' that can't rest in its grave."

"Waal," said Litt, sturdily, "I ain't 'quainted with that kind o' harnts myself, ez 'ain't got no better manners 'n ter go screechin' like the bad boys in the cove arter a day at the still—'thout the excuse o' bein' in liquor, too. We'd better make mo' stir ourselves, then we can't hear 'em. Baker, mebbe ye mought gin us a song—" she bent a beguiling smile upon him—he, who could not even talk, to be asked to sing! "I hev got a notion ez you-uns be a plumb sweet singer."

Her air of coquetry and the implied compliment were of that phase of her manners far more formidable to the callow youth than even her open ridicule. He could have sunk through the floor. He knew, however, that his blushes, his abashed and downcast eyes, were delightful to her. The indignation and resentment kindled by this reflection roused that more stalwart personality of self-respect within him, and gave him courage to mumble, a trifle surlily, that she had better sing a song herself if she hankered for singing. To this she replied, with a sudden swift transition to patently mocking glee:

"I think so myself, Baker, I *do* think so; but I didn't s'pose *ye* war so smart ez ter know it too."

And then, with the accompaniment of the musical whir of her wheel, and the sibilant fugue of the wind in the trees, and the blare of the fluctuating flames in the chimney, she began to sing in a voice low and sweet; and while she sang a strange thing happened.

As she drew the thread along, holding the end out in her hand with a graceful sweep of her arm, her blue eyes full of pensive lights, her lips parted, her tiny foot marking time on the treadle, she noted that one of the batten shutters, which had so regularly beaten in the blast against the window-frame, as the other did even now, had grown steady. All at once the fire-light leaped up with a keen glitter, and at the long narrow crevice between the shutter and the window she saw a face peering in so stealthily, a face so long and white and unrecognizable—seeming hardly human in the narrow section which the rift showed—that a sudden terror smote her heart, the words of the song rose to a scream, and, the wheel still whirling, the thread in her hand, she pointed to the window, exclaiming: "The face! the face! I'm feared o' the face!"

Adelaide had sprung wide-eyed and pale to her feet; the dog, vaguely apprehending the commotion, was fiercely growling. The clumsy boy had risen, overturning the chair with the motion, and at that instant the shutter slammed freely back and forth against the window-frame at the whim of the wayward gusts, and naught was there when the rifle was thrust to the crevice.

"Let him look down the muzzle o' that now," cried Baker Anderson, "ef he's so fond o' peekin'!"

"Don't shoot, Baker; don't shoot!" exclaimed Adelaide, her face still drawn and white. "I reckon Litt didn't see nuthin', nohow."

"My eyesight bein' sorter poorly, through agin' so much lately," the girl said, in her characteristic tone; but her own face was pallid, and as she leaned back in the chair she panted heavily.

"Don't fool me, Litt," the other adjured her, with heart-break in her voice. "War it Steve?"

"I never admired Steve," Litt gasped, "but I never thunk he war ugly enough ter be tarrified at the sight o' him."

Moses, who had turned his head upward, and looked bewildered from one to the other, now burst into a piteous wail with tears and sobs, imagining, from the excited talk, that an altercation was in progress, for, singularly enough for one of his stern and belligerent character, he deprecated a quarrel, and resented all interchange of loud words. His mother knelt by him to pat him on the back; the old dog licked his bare pink foot. Letitia still leaned back in the chair, her frightened face all at variance with her usual gay bravado.

"Who did it look like, Litt?" demanded Adelaide, not lifting her voice, and the peace-loving Moses, tolerating no quarrel that was not of his own making, turned his face, where the tears still lodged on the curves and in the dimples, to supervise the pacific answer.

"Like nuthin' I ever see afore; like nuthin' livin'," Litt barely whispered.

Adelaide's face blanched even in the red fire-light. The hand that patted Moses trembled as she knelt beside him.

Baker Anderson's blood was merely slightly stirred. The bluff courage with which he was en-dowed—no less sturdy because callow—enabled him to regard the odd incident as a welcome and ex-citing break in the monotony. He had considered his stay here with his rifle as rather the result of a senile whim on the part of his uncle than because any danger might menace the deserted Yates house-hold. He was glad to have his presence and that of his weapon justified by some simulacrum of fear and trouble. Litt fancied that she detected in his man-ner a relish of her terrors. At all events, he evident-ly suddenly thought well enough of himself to vent-ure an observation.

"Ye needn't be 'sturbed none, Mis' Yates. 'Twarn't nobody, mebbe. Ef ye'd like fur me, I'd take my rifle an' sorter tramp round the yard a leetle an' look out."

"No, no; bide whar ye air," cried Mrs. Yates. "Litt say," she faltered, "it moughtn't—be—alive," her voice quavered to silence.

"Oh, thar ain't nobody buried close enough round hyar ter git ter 'sturbin' we-uns, Mis' Yates," Baker reassured her with a capable swagger.

So fully had his sense of superiority been restored by the demonstration of the imperviousness of his courage that it seemed impossible that he should ever have quaked before that small bully in blue, even with her beautiful and bewildering eyes and her smiling lips and the keen whetted edge of her ridicule; he glanced hardily at her as she still leaned back in her chair, limp and prostrated by the fright, the overturned spinning-wheel at her feet. Oh, it was a great thing to be a man—or a boy who thought himself a man—even burdened with a pair of big clumsy feet, and several superfluous hands, and a tongue tied in the presence of small bright-eyed bullies in blue! He was emboldened to evolve a theory of his own concerning the conduct of ghosts, which was doubtless as worthy of respect as any such theories ever are.

"Harnts don't wander much ginerally," he said. "They hang round thar own buryin'-groun' mainly. Ye kin see 'em of a moonlight night, they say, a-settin' on thar graves, an' lookin' through the palin's o' the church-house yard—though I 'ain't viewed none, *myse'f*. An' sometimes whenst fraish-buried they walk in thar kin-folkses' house."

"Oh, Baker!" interpolated Mrs. Yates.

"But *ye* ain't got no fraish - buried kin, Mis' Yates," Baker hastened to stipulate. "Steve air alive an' hearty, else ye'd hev hearn 'bout him, bad news bein' a fast rider. An' thar ain't no graves in the neighborhood, an' so thar ain't no harnts o' course."

"He hev tuk a census o' sperits lately," cried Letitia, with a tremulous laugh.

"Thar air the Leetle People's buryin'-groun' nigh hyar," faltered Adelaide.

But Baker Anderson had never heard of the "Leetle People." He looked mystified, and a trifle startled, despite the resources of his courage; and, after she explained, he presently spoke with an insistent desire, most plainly to be observed, to exclude the Little People from the possibilities.

"Mos' likely it air jes' some lazy loon a-goin' home from the still or suthin', an' hearin' the singin', stopped to listen. Ez ter the *Leetle People*"— his voice drawled the words lingeringly, his eyes dwelt meditatingly on the fire, he was evidently falling under a morbid mysterious fascination — "I reckon ez they hev been lef' be all these years mebbe they won't git a-goin' at this late day."

The wind came and went in mighty surges; the trees groaned. Amongst it all one could hear the melancholy roar of the falls, and now and again a gust with a stealthy touch tried the door or the shutter, and went skurrying around the house with a rustle of the grass and the bushes to simulate a human flight.

"I wonder," said Letitia, suddenly—she had lifted the spinning-wheel, had placed it before her, and was bending her face above it, still white from the nervous shock, as she righted the confusion of the tangled thread — "I wonder, Adelaide, ef ye ever hearn that thar Mr. Shattuck talkin' much 'bout them Stranger People?"

"No—but I hev hearn Stephen tell 'bout'n it, an' how he wants thar pearls on thar necks an' thar leetle jugs an' dishes, ez they thunk enough of ter hev buried with 'em, 'lowin' they'd be thar at the las' day."

She paused in surprise. Letitia's pale face had turned a vivid scarlet.

"Adelaide!" she cried. "Do ye actially b'lieve that? Ye 'pear plumb bereft, an' ye talk like a fool.   He ain't wantin' thar pearls au' sech.   They 'ain't got none wuth hevin'!"

"Why don't he let 'em stay in thar peaceful graves, then, till the light shines in the east?" retorted the other, with spirit.

"I axed him 'bout'n it," Letitia went on; "he say he wants ter know ef they air small people sure enough, or whether they. air jes' common Injun chil'n; he 'lows he kin tell suthin' o' what nation they war by thar skulls an' jugs an' ornamints." She paused, her eyes bright with a sort of bewildered surprise.   How she had remembered this strange talk of his!   How she had laid it to heart!

"Mr. Shattuck told about one man," she resumed, "that seen the skeletons of some Tennessee pygmies, an' he writ in a book ez they war all grown up, but leetle, *leetle* folks, with thar teeth all separate an' sharp at the p'ints, like a dog's or a wolf's fangs."

Adelaide uttered an exclamation of horror.

"An' thar air lots o' cur'ous leavin's in Tennessee —bones o' big animals sech ez thar ain't none of now; an' old forts with trees many hundred year old growin' over 'em, an' built out'n stones; an' strange paintings on high cliffs, what some say war done by folks in a boat whenst a flood war in the lan'; an' cur'ous images an' weepons, an' cups an' jugs sech ez can't be fund nowadays nowhar. An' of all the queer things an' cur'ous tales in Tennessee, the Leetle People take the lead."

"What do he want ter know thar nation fur?" demanded Adelaide, stonily.   "They lived, and they air dead.   Let him take God's grace for the wisdom of it, an' ax no questions."

"Oh, ye think he air a common thief ez be arter the value o' thar truck, like the ignorant folks round hyar!" cried Letitia, repudiating kinship and the community in the pride of her new scientific acquisitions.

"Ye l'arnt *that* from him, too, I reckon—a-girdin' at yer own home folks!" said Adelaide, reproachfully.

Letitia's face was dyed even a deeper scarlet. "Oh, he be some smarter 'n folks in gineral," she protested, nevertheless. "An' Steve tole ye so, too, I'll be bound."

This allusion struck home.

"Waal, thar's been enough an' too much quar'lin' over him now, Litt," Adelaide said, sadly. "Don't let's ye an' me fall out 'bout'n him. Sing some mo'—yer singin' air powerful clear an' sweet—sing some mo'."

Letitia, only half appeased, shook her head. "My singin' 'pears ter raise harnts, or the devils, or suthin', ter-night. I can't sing no mo' with sech white queer faces ter peek through the window at me."

All her sparkle seemed quenched somehow; the airy wings of her wit were folded and trailing, and she was afoot, as it were, in the dust.

This perception, subtly realized, emboldened Baker Anderson to perpetrate in his turn a small jest at the expense of his late tormentor.

"Oh, ye mought ez well sing," he said, in a humorous, callow growl, and with an awkward wag of his square head. "I reckon ye never see nobody at the winder, 'ceptin' mebbe 'twar Fee Guthrie, 'shamed ter kem a-visitin' ye *every* night, so he mus' hev a look at ye whilst singin', through the
11

winder—he 'lows ye be so powerful pritty." And
he grinned broadly in the pride of this achievement.

For Felix Guthrie had repeatedly made one of
the small party, talking chiefly about his obdurate
soul, resistant to conversion, much as if it were an
obstinate mule, until a late bedtime turned his steps
from the door. But Letitia was neither discomfited nor roused by this unprecedented conversational
effort on the part of the shy Baker. She only replied, in a dull, spiritless tone, " 'Twarn't Fee."

Her eyes, their fine color still asserted in the glow
of the red embers, had in them a certain wonder, a
sentiment of pain, a touch of fear. The boy's words
had given direction to her thoughts. Felix Guthrie
would not have lingered to see her sing—he knew
but vaguely that her face charmed him. He had no
adequate sense of its beauty. She herself had learned it only in another man's eyes—so loath they were
to leave it, so fired with some subtle enthusiasm for
it. He could look at her silently for hours; but
surely, she thought, she could not have fancied in
that sinister apparition at the window any resemblance to him. And why should he linger without
and peer in at the fireside group when the door
would have opened willingly? It was not he; but
who was it? And this mystery bore her company
into the dull, dead hours. She could not sleep; her
eyes were open, and staring into the darkness long,
long after slumber had enwrapped all others of the
household. She was not restless, only wakeful, as
if she should never sleep again. She marked all the
successive changes of the night. A long time a

cricket shrilled and shrilled in some cranny of the room, and at last was weary, and so grew mute. An owl screamed once without, and was heard no more. Occasionally the dogs, who slept under the house, stirred and wheezed and changed their posture, bumping their heads against the floor as they moved, and were still again. The wind roved for a while listlessly about the garden bushes, and at last was lulled amongst them. And then ensued a hush so intense, so prolonged, that it weighed upon her senses, alert to catch and distinguish some sound that might break it. Naught. Not even the ashes crumbled in the wide chimney-place, where they covered the embers. So deep was the slumber of Adelaide beside her, of Moses in his crib, that they hardly seemed to breathe. Darkness unbroken and silence absolute. Thus might she feel, she thought, without sound or light, if perchance she should wake some time in her grave, after she had lain five centuries, say, quite dead; as the Little People might feel, stirred to some merely mechanical sensation of falling to dust, in those quaint coffins that had become a curiosity, bereft of human significance, of fraternal sanctity, so old, so queer they were. Thus they felt, no doubt, in the long pauses of the centuries while they waited for the judgment.

And with a sudden fear of a dull numbness stealing over her, she roused herself to a sitting posture, and slipped from the high piles of the thick featherbed to the floor. Her bare feet were noiseless as she crossed the room and sat down in a rockingchair. The stones of the hearth were warm yet, and pleasant to the touch. She heard the dogs stir once again, and a young horse that was at liberty without trot slowly around the cabin.

What sort of lives did those Little People lead here? she began to wonder anew. Was the grass so fine and soft and green in their day as now? Did the flowers bloom, and the sun shine, and the earth grow so fair of face in the long summer-time that the thought of death became inexpressibly repugnant, and one might wish it afar off, long, long to wait on this sweet existence? O Little People, that it should have come at last! O Little People, to lie so long and wait in gloom!

Somehow the thought of the eventless passing of centuries to them gave her a more adequate idea of the quietus of death—its insoluble change. She felt stifling. She rose to her feet, opened the batten shutter near at hand, and looked out upon the night. The moon had risen; she had hardly expected to see it there, hanging in the gorge of the mountains above the falls. Melancholy and waning it was. She had never heard that it was a dead, burnt-out world of spent fires; she thought it of this life, and she welcomed the sight. Stars were out, and the clouds all gone. The dank breath of herbage, sodden with rain, came to her; the mists were barely visible, hovering above the dark ravines. The shadows were long. She saw the horse whose hoof-beats she had heard, not drowsing, but standing beside a clump of bushes, his ears alert, his motionless head turned intently toward the mountains. The sound of the cataract was only a dull monotone, as if it slept in the dead midnight. And suddenly, as she stood there, with the moonlight on her white gown and her disordered hair and in her lustrous eyes, another sound smote her ear—the sound of a pickaxe striking suddenly upon stone. It came from the pygmy burying-ground. She heard it only once, for it came no more.

VIII.

Leonard Rhodes arose from the bed to which his wounds had consigned him when he was at last permitted to dispense with the vigilant care and alert fears of the " yerb doctor." The methods of Phil Craig's practice consisted largely in frustrating disastrous possibilities. " Ye can't git up ; ye *mought* fever," he replied to every appeal. " Ye mustn't think 'bout nuthin' ; ye *mought* fever !" And after the extreme limits which had been assigned to Rhodes's durance were reached, the doctor revoked his promises of liberation, and required of him one day more, quiet and recumbent, for full measure. Rhodes might hardly have submitted had he not been willing that the community should think his hurt more serious than it really was. He himself appreciated that the wound was as trivial as it might be. But there was something disastrous to the pretensions of a candidate in the disproportionate importance that had been attached to it—the insult, for its paltry sake, that his friend had offered to Mr. Pettingill, his host, and a man who habitually voted with the opposite faction ; and in a minor degree the slur cast upon the science of Phil Craig, who cared, however, not at all, looking upon Rhodes merely as an object of flesh and blood that might, under certain contingencies, perversely undertake to fever. Most

of all, Rhodes deprecated the tragic conclusion of the
midnight errand in his interest on which Steve Yates
had been despatched.   Although the community had
generally accepted the conclusion that Yates had
seized the opportunity for some unknown reason—a
quarrel with his wife was frequently assigned as the
cause—to flee the country, there were those who
shook their heads darkly over the mystery, with mis-
givings and grim suggestions and hopes that " the
body " would be found some day.   And from these
rumors Leonard Rhodes feared the defeat of all
his cherished schemes.   It was a personal popularity
which he sought to conserve.   Party feeling ran very
high, and in point of strength the two opposing factions were closely matched.   It was only by virtue of
his own superior quality of comradeship, his geniality, the fact that he was untried and had the fascination of novelty, and was held to possess certain
elements of character challenging admiration—being
esteemed brave, gay, full of generous high spirits
—that he had expected to overbear the balance,
swinging at an impartial poise, and tip it ever so
slightly in his favor.   How far this prospect had been
wrecked, how indissolubly his name was coupled with
ridicule or reprobation, he had hardly dared to consider as he lay at length watching the light and shadow play in the full-leaved sycamore-tree close by the
roof-room window, the flash of sunshine on the white
wings of the nesting pigeons by the chimney, the
wolf-skins swaying from the rafters, sometimes seeming, when the sun was low and the wind flickered, to
reassume the symmetries of life, and to lurk there,
with shining eyes and expectant motion, ready to

spring.   He could hear the river chant tirelessly its sweet low monody in its sylvan shadows ; he knew the hour by the voice of the herds, and felt scant need of his watch ticking under his pillow ; but most of all the flight of time was indicated by the sibilant wheeze of Mrs. Pettingill, often audibly conferring below stairs concerning the patient's dinner with the anxious, conscientious, cautious Craig, who seemed to consider all the disorders of the body to arise from the bad habit of eating to nourish it.   His professional interdiction was upon almost every dish in Mrs. Pettingill's répertoire; but his back would be hardly turned before her heavy lumbering step was on the stair, and her countenance, red from bending over the coals, would appear above the door in the floor, and she would emerge carrying in her hand her appetizing blue bowl, or one of her large willow-pattern plates that knew more antiquated delicacies than often grace much finer ware.   Corrugated consciousness of dereliction would be on her face, but a resolute determination to persevere in sinning.

"Ef Phil Craig hev got the heart ter starve ye, I *ain't*," she would wheeze.   "An' ef ye air so con-trairy-minded ez ter die o' this hyar leetle squab pie an' roastin' ears—roasted in thar husks—an' a small taste o' cheese and this transparent puddin', I'll jes' swear I *didn't* kill ye, an' ye hed *nuthin'* from my han' but *cold spring-water*."

And having thus adjusted her deceit to the possible pursuit of the laws of the land, she would administer her dainties, often descending heavily to her lair below-stairs for a fresh supply.

Thus it was that with all the hues of health, all

his usual vigor of step and manner, Rhodes appeared once more before the gaze of the constituents whom he fain would capture.

"Hello! Ye've been 'possumin', Len," was the surprised cry that greeted him wherever he came. And although he might good-naturedly parry it, and respond to praise the "yerb doctor's" skill, still the fact that he had been scarcely hurt at all went the rounds of the gossips and caused much speculation.

"'Twar a powerful onlucky hit fur Steve Yates," one of the mountaineers observed at the blacksmith's shop one day, where a group stood about the door. "Ef' twarn't fur that, he'd hev been hyar yit, I reckon."

"Why did that thar Shattuck hev ter sen' Steve a-skedaddlin' off in the midnight fur another doctor-man when Phil Craig war thar, handy ter physic Rhodes with everything ez grows? That 'pears powerful cur'ous ter me," said the blacksmith, "every time I git ter studyin' 'bout'n it."

"Mark my words," said an elderly wight, the smith's father, who spent much time gossiping in his son's shop—he had a grizzled head of hair, on which his hat was tilted backward; a clean-shaven face, full of the script of years; and a manner not less weighty and impressive because his opinions were in some sort impeded by a toothless utterance, so did the evidences of age and experience lend value to his prelections—"whenst ye find out *whar* Steve Yates went, an' *what* he went thar fur, ye'll know why Shattuck sent him. They air tergether in that business. Mark my words!"

The suspicion exploded like a bomb-shell amongst the coterie, doing great execution. It was so patent a possibility that Shattuck should have used his friend's temporary unconsciousness and his own affected solicitude as a blind to despatch Steve Yates upon some mysterious errand of their own, from which he was never intended to return, that it amazed all the cronies that so obvious an idea had never occurred to them before. Far more natural than that Shattuck should experience so preposterous a fear for so slight a hurt. "Why," said the old man, "Rhodes looks ez survigrous ez that thar oak-tree!" pointing to a kingly and stalwart specimen, full-leaved and flush of sap, in all its ample verdure, as it stood overlooking the barn-like place. Far more natural than that Shattuck should distrust the science of Philip Craig, famous as a "yerb doctor," and prefer Dr. Gancy, the man of nauseous tinctures and extracts, and pills and powders, who was reputed, moreover, to have poisoned people by his "store drugs," and was known to have set a man's leg, fractured by a fall, so that although he walked he could not run nor leap, and had had the good use of it never since—to send for him, with Phil Craig at hand!

There were busy times after this at the blacksmith's shop, although not much forging was done, so completely did the mystery absorb both the frequenters of the place and its working force. They made a thousand guesses far from the truth, none of which seemed, even to the projectors, sufficiently plausible to adopt, until one day a conjecture, with all the coercive force of probability, came to their minds upon the receipt of strange news, which seemed to account at once for Steve Yates's absence and Shattuck's motive in employing him on this wild-goose chase.

On the previous day Shattuck had been singularly ill at ease. He was not a man vigilant for cause of offence, and when his friendship and trustfulness had been enlisted he was even obtuse to any change in the moral temperature of his associates. It had affected his nerves vaguely, before the fact was even elusively present to his perceptions, that Rhodes had begun to regard him differently, and that the new estimate colored his friend's manner. As this gradually grew upon his convictions, he received it with a sense of injury. He had in naught justified it. His presence here was not of his own motion. He remembered how Rhodes had besought his companionship upon this electioneering tour; how he had painted the beauties of the country, the quaint character of its inhabitants; how he had promised the opening of a mound on his own land to feed his friend's archæological fad, and a monopoly of all the curios that should be found therein, floridly offering them as lures, protesting himself, too, as under infinite prospective obligations, and urging his own interest. "I have to have a friend along, and Lord knows I don't want any of those Colbury galoots, with one word for me and ten for themselves."

And when Shattuck had acceded, and the peculiarity of his manner had proved attractive to the mountaineers, and encomiums from the simple people followed him here and there, Rhodes had been impressed with the idea that his friend was an immense acquisition and a positive help in the canvass, in which small matters of personal popularity would have to count against party principles. Few men in this world could be more engagingly genial and affectionate than was Leonard Rhodes at this stage of his onslaught upon the predilections of Kildeer County. Shattuck, who gave as slight attention as might be to these circumstances and their influence upon his friend's manner, had only felt that his heart warmed in turn. Although vaguely aware for some time that a change had supervened, he experienced a shock when a surly preoccupation, an intentional espousing of an opposite opinion, which evidently had no root in conviction, a dull monosyllable in reply, that was hardly reply at all, acquainted him definitely with Rhodes's state of mind and his indifference to its discovery—nay, that he rather courted a quarrel.

The culmination came shortly after the midday dinner; they still sat in the dining-room and smoked their pipes over a small smouldering fire, for, despite the brilliance of a July day, the air was chilly. They had gone back from Pettingill's cabin to Rhodes's own house, some seven miles distant down the valley, and were re-established there. It had been unoccupied for many a year; the transient tenant merely rented the lands of the farm; the house and the furniture remained much as his grandfather had left them. It was a double frame house, with curiously low ceilings; and although it had been for fifty years amazingly fine for the district, it was not quite equal to Colbury ideals, and its owner often pondered upon getting rid of it when he should have a sufficient offer for its purchase. He had lately utilized it as a point of departure for his hill-country canvass of the two counties, being more convenient than periodic returns to Colbury, and he had in the kitchen a scornful colored couple—strictly townsfolk—languishing in exile, amazed at the lack of culture of the mountaineers, and by the fact that there was so large an extent of waste country in the world.

"Ef Len Rhodes hatter be made gov'nor o' the State, he ain't gwine ter do it by foolin' dis chile agin up ter dis hyar mizzable, destitute wilderness ter cook fur him, sure!" Aunt Chaney had remarked to the equally disaffected and lugubrious Uncle Isham, who had come to cut wood and feed the horses.

Rhodes made no inquiry as to how they contrived to get through the lonely time during his absences, nor was he moved by their reproachful dark faces in the interludes of his returns. They were fond of society, and ornaments of select colored circles in their normal sphere, and their imaginings had never pictured aught so bereft of interest as this uninhabited space in the " flat woods " so near to the great ranges.

The house itself touched Shattuck's predilections. To him a peony, highly colored, on a black ground, in a mahogany frame, made a picture full of quaint character. The tall four-post bedsteads, with paper canopy emblazoned with a wreath of morning-glories, which suggested matutinal and industrial ideas rather than slothful lingerings beneath their fading blooms; the three or four carpeted steps at the foot of the bed, a sort of movable stair to enable one to mount into its comforts; the long serpentine sand-bag, which lay at the door to keep out the draughts ; the stretch of mountains, blue far away, darkly bronze near at hand, that was visible from the tiny panes of every window—all combined to so suggest the past, to so disunite it from the present, that imagination needed little else to set these dim rooms astir again with former occupants, and to give him many an idle hour of pensive fantasies over his pipe.

He had glanced out of the door as he strolled about the dining-room, which opened on the porch at the side of the house; a mass of grape-vines twined over its dank and rotting roof; the heavy clusters of fruit had ripened here and there to a rich purple, with a silver bloom upon it, and again showed only translucent amber globules trenching upon a roseate hue. Amongst them all a tangle of white microphylla roses, their branches clambering high, was splendidly in blossom, and through the vista he saw the distant blue peaks of the Great Smoky Mountains, with the elusively glimmering mists upon them.

"Len," he said, suddenly, "you are a fool if you cut away that lot of grapes and roses. Let the porch rot. You can get a hundred such porches, but you won't come up with a tangle like that again in a lifetime."

Rhodes sat at ease, his chair tilted backward; his legs were extended at full length. His pipe was in his mouth, and his hat stuck on the back of his head; his richly brown hair was disordered on his forehead; his face was flushed, partly from the heat of the fire, partly from the smouldering irritation which Shattuck did not as yet divine; his nose, usually an inconspicuous feature, white and firm-fleshed, looked swollen and red, as if he had been drinking; his ungraceful posture drew his waistcoat into creases, and his old claret-colored coat, with a velvet collar, seemed high-shouldered and ungainly as he stayed his shoulder-blades against the back of the chair.

"Well, *I'll* undertake to do as *I* choose with my own," he broke forth, suddenly. "I'll put the axe to the root of the whole business if I want to."

Shattuck looked at him in amaze. "Why, of course, and welcome. What do you mean?" His tone was surprised and wounded, but pacific.

Rhodes, with a certain relief in liberating the pent-up tides of his vexation, went on with a visible increase of vehemence. "I mean that I have had about as much of your interference in my affairs as I have got a mind to put up with." He spoke between his set teeth, and with a toss of his hair, which was prone to fall upon his face.

Shattuck stood motionless, scarcely believing he had heard aright. A flush had mounted through his thin skin. He had a dismayed and hurt expression that was almost appealing. It was not that he found Rhodes's displeasure itself so overwhelming. That meant little to him. He was only aghast that Rhodes should make him feel it while a guest in the house. All the exigencies of hospitality hampered its recipient, and he hardly knew how to assert himself, how to lift his voice in defence.

"Will you tell me how I have interfered with you?" he asked, an almost imperceptible tremor in his tone. His eyes were fixed upon Rhodes, who did not meet them in turn, but kept his gaze upon the fire, still slowly smouldering.

"How? Well, I like that!" He cast his eyes up to the high mantel-piece, and laughed a little, showing his teeth—white and strong, but overcrowded and unevenly placed.

With all his odd bits of learning, Shattuck knew little of human nature. He had mastered more of the science of craniology than of those fine aerial transient guests that the skull may house—retroactive motives and full-winged schemes, and, strongest of all, that moral harlequin, coming and going, none knows whence or whither, the impulse. A mad bull is hardly in a state of mind or on a plane of culture to appreciate an accurately balanced syllogism, but Shattuck must needs offer logic to Rhodes:

"No stranger here could have influence enough with these people to interfere in your affairs. I am a stranger here. I could not interfere even if I would. How could I? Why should I?"

"That's what gets me!" cried his host, coarsely. "*Why* you should have undertaken to send seventeen miles for a doctor to physic a small scratch on the head, and *how* you could insinuate to an old man, whose guest I was—had forced myself on him, in fact, as well as you—that he might be strung up if I should die in his house for no fault of his—it all passes my comprehension."

Shattuck's flush grew deeper. His eyes, whose reproachful look the other never met, had a hot, hunted, harried look.

"I wouldn't have had it happen," cried Rhodes, clasping his hands behind his tousled head, the change in his attitude adding to the dislocation of his aspect and the precariousness of his posture, his chair still balanced on its hind-legs, his own legs still stretched out at full length—"I wouldn't have had Steve Yates sent on that lonely road at midnight on my errand, if I had known it, for a million—a *quadrillion* of dollars."

"Money seems really no object," Shattuck retorted, somewhat in his host's own vein. His eyes were alert now. The dull, hurt look had vanished. He was moved to defend himself against a reproach, unjust, indeed, but which his own troubled heart and tormented conscience and sensitive consciousness had often urged in their reasonless impunity. He was in naught to blame that any evil had befallen Yates—this he knew full well—and still he regretted, and still he reproached himself. And because of this he had become expert at his logical self-defence, and he sprang to its weapons as if for his life.

"A lonely road!" he sneered. "A late hour! As if I, a stranger in the country, did not travel it alone, and at midnight too, to escape the heat of a daytime journey, as everybody does who has occasion to come or go at this season. I took excellent care of myself upon it. I met nothing but a rabbit or two and a few stray cattle. It never occurred to me that Yates was not as safe on that road as in his own house. And I *did not* ask him to go. He volunteered. I *did* make too great a commotion over your being hurt, and I admit it. I was a fool for that; and I was mistaken—considerably—both in the nature of the wound and the man that got it. I gave myself too much solicitude altogether, far more than the subject warranted."

His eyes had succeeded in meeting Rhodes's at
12

last, but they saw little of what was before them. The candidate had lowered his arms to a normal posture; the fore-legs of his chair had dropped to the floor; he sat erect, looking intently and deprecatingly at his angry friend, so hard to rouse, so thoroughly roused at last. Rhodes was of that temperament best controlled by the exhibition of a counterpart emotion. Shattuck's anger quelled his own. He was eager to interrupt, wincing under the low-toned words, husky with passion. He was of versatile capacities; he could be a balance-weight were there no one else to keep the poise. His anger was only indulged under the license of impunity. It had evaporated as if it had never fired his blood. He received the demonstration with a palpable surprise— as though he had done naught to provoke it—when his friend, turning toward the door, said, ceremoniously:

"And now, Mr. Rhodes, if you will add to your kind hospitality, for which I am indebted, the favor of ordering my horse, I will trouble you with my 'interference' no more."

Even Shattuck felt that he had gone too far, that he had needlessly quarrelled on a small provocation, when the other called out, naturally:

"Why, Shattuck, I *am* surprised! You ought to be ashamed to get mad so easy, when you know how I'm bothered and tormented out of my life. And with so much at stake! And you won't let me growl a little bit here with you at home, when I can afford to growl nowhere else, confound it! You ought to be ashamed!"

Shattuck hesitated. He cast a worried, agitated glance out of the window into the large freedom of the sunshine and the wind and the flying shadows of the fleecy summer clouds. There came a day when he remembered the moment, when he regretted that he had not ridden off into the buoyant midst of these lightsome elements. But at the time it seemed impracticable. There was something ludicrous, even more, unbecoming a gentleman, in leaving a friend's house in a pet, with the host's reproaches sounding in his ears, to be matched only by the bitterness of the guest's sneering retorts. There was, it is true, that implacable pride within him to which forgiveness is an unimagined possibility, and every fibre of it was poignantly astir. He did not conceive it possible that he could ever overlook Rhodes's lapse into the blunt speech of angry sincerity, unjustified by whatever his host might have come to feel. But he must have the semblance of comity and courtesy. In fact, he could hardly bestride his horse and ride away from the man's door without this friendliness, spurious though it might be, in his farewell. His face gave such token of his train of thought that Rhodes, although seeing him hearken to the suggestion of amity, did not swing back to the half-veiled surliness, too often the effect of an accepted effort at reconciliation.

"Lordy mercy! I'll let the weeds grow sky-high if you want to see the place go to rack and ruin," he said, as he bent forward to scoop up a coal in his pipe after the rural fashion he affected. "I didn't think you'd treat me so mean — the only friend I've got left; a broken reed, sure!" with a glance of reproach. "You might afford to let me maunder, and blame you or anybody else, I should think, for the confounded affair. As I'm likely to lose my election by it, I might have the poor privilege of a scape-goat."

"I won't play your scape-goat, I thank you very much," said Shattuck, his eyes eager with his wish to go, still hovering about the closed door.

"So I perceive," said Rhodes, shortly. Then, with a change of tone and an appealing glance of his dark-brown eyes: "But, for God's sake, Shattuck, don't run away and leave me the minute I flounder into a lot of bothers! For the Lord's mercy, try to put up with me a little, and let me grumble once in a while, for I do swear to you this whole thing has put me nearly beside myself. You know it is a canvass of personalities, and there's no telling the use this will be to Devens and his friends. If I can't carry these mountain districts *I'm done*, for the party issues will beat me like hell in Colbury and round about."

He took out of the breast pocket of the old claret-colored coat the envelope of a letter, which was scrawled over with figures pertaining to the relative population of the mountain districts, with an approximative calculation of the votes which he and his opponent might respectively receive. The smoke from his pipe curled between the paper and his eyes, but not even its sinuous vagaries served to alter the obdurate result, nor had his disaffected anxious gaze any effect, however slight, although he scanned these estimates forty times a day.

"I wish to God I knew where that confounded fellow Yates was!" he exclaimed. "They'll all have it that he died on account of *my* selfishness, being forced into Lord knows what dangers in my service." Then, with the politician's instinct for a popular pose

—although at his own fireside, and with a man whom he did not care nor seek to deceive—he continued: "And for his sake, Shattuck, I'm more troubled than for my own. Why, I give you my word of honor, I hardly knew how to speak to his wife—I nearly said his widow—when I went to the house yesterday. And I couldn't look at that child of his. It's a calamity to them—a tremendous calamity—and I am concerned in it; and the Lord above knows I had no more to do with it than if I had been as dead as Hector!"

Shattuck had seated himself, his elbow over the back of the chair, his chin in his hand. He frowned heavily as he looked absently out of the tiny window-panes at the blue mountains, with so unseeing and troubled a gaze that Rhodes began to perceive that he had not only his own anxieties to restrain, but those of his friend as well. He sighed to assume the double load. He had a definite appreciation, however, that his position would hardly be bettered by his friend's desertion of him now, when he could not control the reasons therefor which Shattuck might give in his anger, and his opponent devise with so illimitable a license as speculation. He came to wish that he had let him go, but at that moment he exerted all his reserve force of geniality to heal the wound and frustrate his guest's departure.

"Oh, come on!" he cried out, suddenly, springing up actively, stretching both arms above his head, shaking out first one leg and then the other, that the trousers might slip down over his long boots, and seeking to rid himself of that stupor which waits on drowsing before a fire out of season—"come on! We are fairly baked before this fire. What ails that old nigger to build a big enough fire this weather to barbecue himself—and I wish he would! **I'll order** both the horses, and we will get out into the air, and get the cobwebs out of **our** brains. We'll ride up to Fee **Guthric's** on the mountain, and I'll do a little electioneering, and show **I bear** no malice to him. And you'll see if he **won't let** you go digging around on his land in the cove for your pygmies. **I declare** I haven't treated you **right, old fellow;"** he clapped his hand jocularly on his guest's shoulder **as they** stood facing each other, and his manner **of friendli-** ness was not impaired, although he did not fail **to see** that Shattuck winced almost imperceptibly **at his** touch. "You haven't got a thing **in** the world **but** that old **jug** out of my **mound"**—and he glanced with a careless eye at a strangely decorated jar on the high mantel-piece—"**and not a bone of a** pygmy yet. Maybe Aunt Chaney could fool you with a beef bone or two—ha! ha! ha!—hearing you **set** such store on bones, hey?"

His discretion and his intuition were at fault. There is naught of which the man of science, albeit the veriest amateur, is so intolerant as ignorant ridi- cule. His fleering laugh jarred Shattuck's nerves, made sensitive by the ordeal of the morning, and his utter lack of appreciation of the meaning of that bit of pottery was as pitiable as if he lacked a sense— that of sight, for instance, and jeered at the idea of light. The human significance of it; the lost history of lands and peoples and civilization, of which it was a dim, vague intimation; the flight of time that it so fully expressed; the idea of death, of oblivion, of which it was so apt an exponent! Shattuck could

not look at it without the thought of the hands that
had carried it; the lips that had touched it; the
strange, strange faces that had bent above it, reflected within its walls when full of water; the words,
spoken in an unknown, forgotten language, of ambition or love or homely household usage, to which
it had echoed—for a vibrant quality it had, porce-
lain-like. These immortal-seeming essences were all
gone; yet here was the dumb insensate bit of clay
left for him to turn in his foreign hands and ponder
over with his foreign fancies—the idea wrung every
fibre of feeling within him! And Rhodes's laugh
was the vulgarity of the vandal.

The state of vacuity that does not feel and cannot
know is made cognizable sometimes to the thinking
and the feeling soul by a dreary sense of solitude, for
which the consciousness of the finer susceptibility
does not compensate. It was not that Shattuck resented the fact that his friend's limitations precluded his sharing these enthusiasms, as that that burden
of isolation, that painful consciousness of a lack of
congeniality, that yearning for fellowship, so poignant to the gregarious human animal, came upon
him for the moment; a realization of being alone,
out of the reach of his companion, beset him, and he
found it bitter, albeit he recognized that his higher
standpoint created the inaccessibility.

Rhodes, once more in the saddle, was infinitely
conversable. He had on the face which he took
about with him on his canvass—his best expression,
gay, gentle, kind; his conversation was full of country jokes, which he delivered with a rural drawl, and
he was about as rustic a specimen as an educated

man can well personate. He never dropped the character for a moment, although he hardly cared to impress his friend with its value. Its lapses from his usual habit of speech revolted Shattuck in some sort, albeit the contorted language of the ignorant mountaineers never grated upon his somewhat nice philological prejudices. One was the voice of affectation—an aping of boorishness and rusticity and yeoman simplicity, which Shattuck called by the not inapt name of "poor-mindedness;" the other was the natural speech and manners of those deprived of opportunities of culture, and was entitled to respect as being the best they could do.

"Bless your soul, Rhodes," he said at last, with a touch of satire, "you needn't put so many negatives in a sentence with the kind object of pleasing me; I'm not a registered voter in either of your counties. And I love you so that I'd vote for you, if I could, just as willingly for three or four negatives in a single negation as for eight. Save 'em up, my dear boy. I remember the fate of the man who couldn't say 'No,' but I must say I *don't* think it impends for you at present."

"Hello! I didn't know you were such a schoolmaster. I'll have to mind my p's and q's, hey?" said Rhodes, with a good-natured intonation, although he had flushed darkly at the taunt.

So instilled into his blood was the instinct of policy, however, that he abated naught of his determination to conciliate his friend if possible beyond this merely outward truce. And now was illustrated how subservient is the science of propitiation to the object upon which it is exerted, for Leonard Rhodes

had been held to possess the subtle art to an extreme
degree, and so proficient had he become therein that
he was wont to find its unctuous exercise a pleasure.
He could but himself admire the dexterity with
which he brought the conversation to prehistoric
America, especially prehistoric Tennessee. He had
paused when they had reached one of the high
ridges about the base of the great mountains far
above, and he called to Shattuck to observe that,
looking back toward his place, they could distinctly
see the mound, and that, looking forward down the
multitudinous defiles amongst the ranges, the pygmy
burying-ground might be located by the proximity
of the cataract, a mere cascade in the distance, an
emerald gleam and a glittering, white, plume-like
waving. Thence the transition was easy to the
many antiquities found within the state. To his
surprise, Shattuck seemed incomprehensibly to hold
back and to grow reticent. Rhodes had material to
work upon far different from the simple unsuspect-
ing country folk. He had not thought that divination could so keep pace with most secret and supple
intention, and that his object was perfectly plain and
unglossed to the man whom it sought to mislead.
Shattuck was almost openly impatient of the topic
on which he was wont to love to talk, and which he
often could not be prevailed upon to relinquish. He
would not seriously discuss it now. When Rhodes
demanded of him a theory concerning the ancient
aboriginal races, based upon evidences of their advanced civilization, he replied with uncharacteristic
flippancy that he was never acquainted with any of
them, and that he could make a pretty pot of money

if he had been.   And when Rhodes, with that heavy
assuming ignorance which is so ready to trench upon
unknown, untried ground of laborious research, deem-
ing all things slight and of small difficulty that are
strange to its meagre acquisitions, attempted to argue
certain hypotheses upon which he had heard him
descant, Shattuck left the disquisition to his host,
not even affecting to set him right when Rhodes
himself could feel that he was floundering. The
candidate was wanting in any fine capacity to read
character or conduct in its more delicate script, and
Shattuck's state of mind was as undecipherable hie-
roglyphics. Thus at cross-purposes they at last
reached Guthrie's home, high up on the mountain.

IX.

The house was the usual small log cabin, so overshadowed, however, by trees, dense and dark, that not the whole structure, but only the tiny porch and door were visible up the dusky green vista. When the sun fell through the leaves it was in fleckings of abnormal lustre, so deep was the shade. Fowls pecked about in the long dank grass. From high up on the mountain-side came the clear metallic clink of a cow-bell. A spring gurgled close at hand in the yard, and a vessel, with butter or milk in it, covered with a white cloth, was visible among the gravelly banks that bounded the spring branch. An old woman, tall and stalwart, sitting upon the porch, furtively looking at the two visitors as they came through the bars and up the path, had so forbidding an aspect that Shattuck was reminded of the superstition of "an evil eye." She gave them no greeting, but listened silently as Rhodes, having pulled himself together again into his genial, rustic, canvassing identity, asked for Felix Guthrie. He broke off short.

"Now, I wonder if you ain't Mrs. Guthrie!" he exclaimed.

"Ye air a good guesser," she said, with a sneer. "Who else would I be, hyar in Fee Guthrie's house?"

She wore no cap. Her hair, luxuriant and gray,

was combed plainly down over her ears and caught in a heavy coil, that betokened its great length, at the back of her head.   Her face in contrast was sallow and parchment-like.   The features were singularly straight; her eyes were dark, her spectacles were mounted upon her head, and her expression was unsmiling.   It was hardly wonderful that Rhodes should have lost his balance, and he had a discomfited sense that Shattuck might relish the fact. Shattuck, however, was looking about with his usual keen susceptibility to the interest of new places and people.

"I mean," said Rhodes, confused, "the second Mrs. Guthrie."

"I ain't the *fust* one, now, sure," she said, her eyes fixed upon him with a sort of pertinacious attention.   "An' what's that to you?"

Rhodes made a mighty endeavor to cast off the influences that paralyzed his advances.   "You'd never guess, and so I'll tell you.   I have heard my grandfather talk about you enough—how he danced with you at a bran dance down on Tomahawk Creek.   Remember old Len Rhodes?   Young Len, he used to be; but I am young Len now, myself."

Her face changed suddenly, so unexpectedly that one might wonder that it did not creak, so stiff and immobile had the features seemed.   There was a new expression in her eye—a sort of glitter of expectancy.

"What did he say, this hyar old young Len Rhodes o' yourn?   What did he say 'bout'n me?" She had a cautious air, as if she reserved her opinions.

Rhodes had taken off his hat and was leaning against the post of the porch, although he still stood upon the ground. He burst into sudden laughter that seemed to startle the somnolent dark stillness of the shadows.

"Oh, no, Mrs. Guthrie," he cried, archly. "You don't catch me that way. You'll be saying next thing that because I'm running for the Legislature I'm going round the country trying to get votes by flattering the ladies. I don't know what the *t'other* Len Rhodes said to *you* that day at the bran dance on Tomahawk Creek years and years ago, but *this* Len Rhodes ain't a-goin' to repeat any of his second-hand compliments, not if he knows himself, and he think he do!"

A faint color was in her parchment-like cheek, a yellow gleam in her black eyes; the woman seemed to have grown suddenly young! A moment ago the idea might have been ridiculous, but now it was easy to see that she must have been beautiful—most beautiful. And she was determined to hear the words in which old Len Rhodes—in her day young Len Rhodes, the judge's son, and the richest and most notable man in all the county—had celebrated the fact. Her vanity still burned, albeit embers. How long, how long since fuel had been brought to feed this fire, that nevertheless would die only when her breath might leave her!

"Oh, ye air jes' a-funnin'! Ye can't remember nuthin' yer gran'dad tole 'bout the gals he danced with forty-five year ago. He couldn't tell 'em one from t'other hisself arter twenty year had passed. Gals is mos'ly alike," she added, with a consciousness that Rhodes had knowledge, as far as she herself was concerned, which contradicted this humble assertion. She smiled upon him. "Ye mus' git in the habit o' tellin' a heap o' lies electioneerin'. An' ye feel like ye mought ez well bamboozle one or two old wimmin ez not 'mongst the men. A few lies mo' or less won't make much diff'ence in the long count again ye at the jedgmint-day."

"I'll tell *you* something that's got the ear-marks of truth—something that Len Rhodes told *me* about *you*," declared Rhodes, apparently led on and over-persuaded into loquacity—"something that I couldn't know of myself. Ain't that fair, Shattuck? This is my friend Mr. Shattuck, Mrs. Guthrie. I carry him around to keep the girls from running off with me. The other Len Rhodes had no such trouble when you knew him. I'll be bound the main thing was to keep *him* from running off with the girls. Ha! ha! ha!"

Mrs. Guthrie bent her softened and unrecognizable face upon Shattuck, and said that he was "right welcome" and she was glad to see him. Then she turned to the candidate, with an anxiety which was almost pathetic, to hear that younger self praised in the repeated words of a man she had known forty-five years ago.

"Waal, I'll know the ear-marks of the truth whenst I hear it," she prompted his lagging resolve.

"Your name was Madeline Crayshaw," he began. He was gayly fanning himself with his hat.

"Ye could hev fund that out ennywhar," she said, expectantly.

"And your eyes were black," he went on, with an air of gallantry.

"They air yit," she interposed, flashing them at him.

"And for all your eyes were black, your hair was as yellow as gold, a yard long. Could I find that out *now* by looking at you?"

She shook her head.

"And Len Rhodes said you looked when you danced for all the world 'like a lettuce-bird a-flying.' "

"Who would hev thunk o' hearin' that old foolishness agin?" she cried, her eyes dim with pleasure. "I don't look like a lettuce-bird now; some similar ter a ole Dominicky hen, I reckon, stiddier a lettuce-bird. But that war the word on the tip o' Len Rhodes's tongue, for he never got tired o' talkin' o' yaller hair an' black eyes. I wonder the 'oman he married at las' warn't no better favored," she added, with a sudden hardening of the lines of her features. "Seeh a admirer o' beauty ez he war! But he war a admirer o' lan's an' cattle an' bank-stock ez well; an' yer granmam war mighty well off, ef she *war* little an' lean an' hed no head o' hair at all, ter speak of."

Rhodes did not change color. There may have been those in his grandmother's days ready to break a lance in support of the supremacy of her charms, but her grandson had no mind to enter such antiquated lists. He only said, with electioneering subtlety—the development of which Shattuck watched with the admiring curiosity and wonder that he might feel concerning some acrobatic feat which he should, nevertheless, never desire to imitate or emulate—"Yes, pretty girls had mighty little need of bank-stock and lands then, as now. Beauty always will be chosen.   If you had a daughter now, you might make it up to me for having given my grandad the go-by."

She looked at him with narrowing lids, wondering if he truly thought it possible that his grandfather had been her rejected suitor—a gay gallant, who had danced with all the country-side beauties, among whom he was a toast with his soft words and his flatteries sown broadcast, but who, when about to settle down, had chosen a staid, pious, educated wife, whose social status was such as to make his marriage a decided looking-up, even for him.   Leonard Rhodes's claim to rank with "the quality" was largely dependent upon her side of the house.   The assumptions of vanity, however, have an elastic limit. Mrs. Guthrie stretched it, convinced that he believed that the rich, dashing, flirting son of the judge was in the old days the disappointed swain of a simple mountain girl.   Thenceforward, when she set herself to boast of her youth, she claimed the trophy of his heart, dust and ashes long ago in the grave of the simple-minded old gentleman, who had grown sober under life's discipline before he was forty, and had forgotten his merry youth save for a casual reminiscence.

"Yes," continued Rhodes, "I ought to be coming up here to see some lettuce-bird of a girl, instead of those hulking step-sons of yours, Fee and Ephraim, to humbug 'em into voting for me. *Make* 'em vote for me, Mrs. Guthrie.   You owe me one now—you owe me one for the old time's sake."

"They needn't kem home ter me ef they don't

vote fur ye," she said, fascinated with this fictitious conquest. She bore herself more proudly for it to the day of her death, although she knew in her secret soul the falsity of what he seemed to believe. On such slight fare as this can the vanity of a woman subsist.

And when he turned casually and asked, " Where are the boys, anyhow ?" she directed him to a barley field, where they were cradling barley, and told him to come back that way with his friend, and she would have a "snack" for them. Shattuck marked, as they started, the alacrity with which she was rolling up the stocking that she had been knitting, and sticking the needles into the ball of yarn, her fine head, with its wealth of gray hair, distinct against the heavy vines that draped the porch. Their way took them around the side of the house in the deep lush grass, past the beehives all ranged by the fence, which was ascended and descended by a flight of steps, and surmounted by a small platform, and thence down through the orchard. Here the birds congregated in the thickly matted foliage. Only now and then at long intervals its dark green shadow was penetrated by the sun. The warm fragrance of the so-called June apples was on the July air; the clover bloomed underfoot, and the bees boomed; the call of the jay, the sweet pensive cooing of a dove, sounded; then all was silence, save for a mere whisper of the sibilant wind.

Rhodes took off his hat as he walked, with the air of a need to refresh himself, his richly brown hair slightly stirring in the breeze. He cast his absorbed glance at his friend.

"Ain't she tur'ble 'oman ?" he said, his electioneering ellipses sticking to his speech.

13

"Not so very 'tur'ble,' that I can see," said his friend, with unnoticed mimicry.

"Oh, Lord! yes, she is!" And Rhodes wagged his head with an unequivocal sincerity. "I know folks say she was an awful termagant with her first husband, who was a consumptive; and they *did* have a story" —he lowered his voice, and glanced cautiously around him—"that she hastened his end to be rid of the bother of nursing him. And then she married this fellow Guthrie's father. And she made a perfect jubilee up here a-beatin' the childern. I know the tales about it useter skeer me! I was a little shaver then, and I wouldn't go in the dark for fear of meeting her, though I had never seen her. At last one day Felix got his chance, and bit her arm nearly through, and ever afterward he clawed and bit and fought till she let him and Ephraim alone. Yes, my grandfather said she turned out exactly like he always knew she would."

"Why, I thought you said he was in love with her," exclaimed Shattuck, for Rhodes's representation had borne such verisimilitude as might deceive a casual on-looker as well as one eager to be convinced. Rhodes cast upon him an amazed glance.

"What!" he said, in his genuine "quality" voice, as if this had touched the climax of the improbabilities.

Shattuck marked the vibrations of pride and surprise ring out smartly.

Then Rhodes, hesitating for a moment, added, "My grandmother was a *lady*. As to beauty"—the sneer about beauty *had* evidently rankled — "why, such things as prettiness and coquetry were never thought of in connection with *her*. She was a *lady*, and when you've said *that* you've said it all. And she was such a superior woman! My grandfather outmarried himself more than any man you ever saw."

Shattuck was silent for a moment. "I thought," he remarked at length, "that it was the American eagle that fluttered most through the rhetoric of electioneering eloquence. I didn't know that the lettuce-bird had superseded the big national fowl."

"Oh," exclaimed Rhodes, who had waited on his friend's words with a knitted brow, and he drew a long breath of comprehension, "grandpa *did* use to say the prettiest girl he ever saw was this Madeline Crayshaw. He never saw her but once. It was at a bran dance on Tomahawk Creek—some sort of a political commotion, speechifying in favor of Henry Clay or some other old cock. He said her hair was the color of nothing in this world but a lettuce-bird, and she had the disposition of a panther. He said she reminded him of a wild woman—some sort of savage —and he wondered if she *could* look pleased, and if she were subject to the same sort of compliments that other girls like. So when she was glowering round at the other girls as if she could rend 'em with jealousy, he tried the lettuce-bird dodge. And, bless your soul, she was as pleased and sweet as pie."

"And has remembered it for forty-five years, poor thing!" said Shattuck.

"Ha! ha! ha! 'Poor thing!' She never made *you* learn to kick and bite and fight to keep a whole skin and a whole set of bones. Fee Guthrie don't say 'poor thing!' I won't go back to the first husband, for I hadn't the pleasure of his acquaintance, and he may have died simply because it was too much trouble to live."

"And *you* made her believe that you thought your grandfather was in love with her—had been rejected by her. You deceived her!"

"Man alive! how could I? She knew she never saw him but once in her life. And how can I make tenders of his affections at this late day? Tenders of affection are not retroactive. A man can't flirt as proxy for his dead grandfather. It was merely a little electioneering compliment."

"Oh, Rhodes, how do you manage to look yourself in the face in the mirror?" exclaimed Shattuck, with a laugh.

"I look at myself in the mirror with a good deal more pleasure than is proper, I expect," said Rhodes, smoothing his handsome and lustrous red - brown beard. He tipped his straw hat over his smiling, full-lashed dark eyes, for they were out of the shadows at last, and in the sun amongst a stretch of the barley. The wind bent it; long glintings of pale light pervaded it. The whole field was of a delicate, fluctuating green, with these fine undulations like quicksilver running over it. Sometimes the shadow of a cloud came, a thing swiftly scudding and noiseless too, and the green, hitherto held in indefinite solution, was precipitated into a pure emerald tint, for this was a later sowing than the spaces further down the slope, which had grown tawny with ripeness, and showed on the hither side the long swaths from the cradling, drying upon the ground. The cradles lay there too, and beneath the dark shadow of a great spreading buckeye-tree in a corner of the fence—the only one in the field that bore its pristine richness of foliage, for the rest, gaunt and bare, girdled long ago, towered into the air, dead, white, and unsightly—lounged the two brothers, loitering away the heated hour.

From the depths of the cove below, this field on the mountain slope was visible a long way. Shattuck remembered having observed it as a dull, light-tinted, tiny square in the midst of the dense primeval woods that encompassed it. Now he looked with interest to identify in turn the landmarks of the cove. So purple it was in the distance, save where the slopes rose on either hand, and the summits of the forest grew gradually into a bronze hue, and thence to the deep, restful green of the full summertide. Far away all the horizon was bounded by many a range and peak, painted in all the gradations of blue, from a dull, blurred tint to the finest turquoise delicacy, and rising tier upon tier, till at last the enamelled sky limited the climbing heights. Here and there in the depths below, vague lines marked where the fences ran. A tiny curl of smoke first betokened the Yates cabin; he saw the sun strike full on its shining roof. But most salient of all, the river gleamed a steely gray beneath the craggy walls of the gorge, and the cataract danced all white and green, like a jewel endowed with a flashing life. This only, in the sweet serenity and peace of the scene, seemed to move. The wind came and went, it is true, but with scant token of its presence; only now and again a suggestion of the pallid reverse side of the leaves bestreaked the mountain slopes and marked its path. A flock of sheep feeding in a brambly, rocky space were as motionless as a pastoral scene on canvas. Once a glow of an intense blood-bay color struck his keen eye, and made him aware that a horse was tethered a little way down from the house; the sun struck upon the glossy flank; then the animal slipped into the deep shadow, and was seen no more.

None of this had Rhodes observed. His eyes were fixed upon the two brothers as they lounged amongst the grass and weeds in the fence corner, culpably overgrown in the eyes of a farmer, but cool and sweet in the dense shade of the buckeye-tree, and with sundry long tangled vines of the purple and white passion-flowers, clear-eyed in the grass, and the scarlet trumpet-blossom flaring over the staked and ridered rail-fence. There could hardly be two men less alike, the difference accented since they were both bareheaded—the one with his grave, forceful features, at once sullen and sad, his long curling hair hanging on the shoulders of his blue cotton shirt; the other bullet-headed, close-cropped, with a twinkling, merry eye, a propitiatory expression, a broad face that would look young even when it should be withered and wrinkled like a shrivelled apple, and the coarse brown tufty hair should be as white as snow. The latter looked up with a ready-made, adjustable smile as Rhodes's hearty " Howdy, boys?" rang upon the perfumed air. The candidate did not wait for them to rise, but flung himself at length into the sweet grass, taking his hat off his head and leaning his shoulders against the big buckeye-tree.

"Waal, how do *you*-uns do, Mr. Rhodes?" said Ephraim, with smooth cordiality. "How be you-uns a-kemin' on these days? A month o' Sundays sence we hev seen ye."

He then looked quickly at his brother, with an anxious submission of his conduct for the fraternal approval. For Ephraim Guthrie labored heavily between the quick geniality of a mercurial temperament, a lack of confidence in his own judgment, and a childlike reliance on his brother's opinion: without its coincidence with his own he could not be at ease for a moment. He always spoke precipitately on the impulse of the first, was checked by the second, and waited with pathetic anxiety for the third. He was all things to all men, and this vacillating lack of consistency rendered his amiability of little value in the estimation of the candidate. Rhodes saw with disappointment the other brother, the valid object of conciliation, rise, after a mutter of salutation, to join Shattuck, who, with a nod to the two, had turned away, and stood, with one hand in his pocket, silently surveying the scene below him. He only lifted his eyes slightly in recognition of Guthrie's approach as the burly young mountaineer drew near him, and it was his uncommunicative host who spoke first.

"Glad ter see ye, Mr. Shattuck—glad ter see ye on the mounting."

Shattuck divined that he enjoyed unusual cordiality in being deemed by his host preferable for conversation to Rhodes. The injury which Guthrie had inflicted upon the candidate, and which he had been thought to so magnify, recurred to his mind, with the further fact that it was no accident. Guthrie evidently still cherished the motive that prompted it, and bore malice. It was intention that had led him to leave the candidate to talk to the plastic younger brother while he himself held aloof under the guise of joining the other guest. Nevertheless, his ear was keen for the conversation between the two, which the crafty Rhodes may have in part designed for him, and Shattuck was aware that it was only a divided attention with which he was favored. He responded, however, with equal courtesy.

"A fine view you have here, Mr. Guthrie—a very fine view. I don't know its equal anywhere."

Guthrie glanced quickly at him, then ran his eye over the scene, with the effect of seeing it for the first time. He knew no other aspect of the world. It had never occurred to him that the lives of many other people were not bounded by these fine and massive symmetries of mountain ranges in every tender phase of purest color; by infinite distances, challenging the capacities of farthest vision; by softest pastoral suggestions of cove and slope; by primeval wildernesses and stern and rugged solemnities of crags; by phantasmal chutes of flying mountain torrents. His sense of its beauty was blunted by the daily habit of its presence; paradoxically, it could be brought home to him only if it were swept away.

"Yes," he said, uncertainly, "an' we'd hev a good lookout fur corn ef we could hev mo' rain." And he cast a weatherwise eye angrily at the sky, where all the clouds seemed gadding abroad a-pleasuring only, and with no idea of utility as they dallied with the wind. "Not," he added, with an after-thought and a certain precipitation, as if he were afraid that the remark might be overheard, and forthwith acted upon—"not ez I want ter hev enny fallin' weather nuther till we-uns git in this hyar barley."

The differing interests of his crops evidently divided his affections, and he was in the normal condition of the farmer disappointed in either rain or shine.

They stood silent for a moment by the fence, and as Shattuck turned one of the great trumpet-flowers in his hand and looked down into its scarlet horn, then let the tendril spring back elastically into its place, Rhodes's words came to them as he wrestled with Eph Guthrie's presumable political persuasions against him. These were altogether assumed by the candidate for the purposes of argument, for which the plastic Eph furnished but a straw man, as it were, easily knocked down, requiring to be cleverly and surreptitiously picked up again by his insistent opponent, in order to plant still more well-delivered and coercive blows.

"Fee 'ain't got no grudge against me, I know," Rhodes was saying. "*I* don't bear no malice for a little tussle like that, and I *know* Fee don't."

"How ye know he don't?"

Shattuck was startled by hearing this *sotto voce* comment upon the dialogue by Fee in person close to his elbow. He turned and looked at the man, seeking to convey in the glance an intimation that he had spoken his thought aloud and that it had been overheard. Felix Guthrie evidently cared as little as might be. His eyes met Shattuck's unabashed.

"Fee ain't in no wise malicious," Eph piped up.

"I know it—I know that—no man better," Rhodes interrupted him promptly, for he knew that Eph could talk by the yard measure on the subject of his brother's perfections, so close was the fraternal bond. "I *know* Fee can't bear malice. I like Fee, and Fee likes me, and won't do a thing against me—not a thing !"

"Waal, ye better not be too sure o' that," the voice at Shattuck's elbow said, in that suppressed, significant soliloquy.

Shattuck, embarrassed by these confidences in prejudice to his friend's loudly expressed conclusions, was about to turn away, when Guthrie's hand was laid upon his arm.

"Stranger," he said, his head with his big broad hat and its clinging curls bent forward, "don't it 'pear a sorter cur'ous dispensation to you-uns that that man yander b'lieves so what he say whenst it air in my heart ter kill him—yes, sir, ter kill him !— if he war ter interfere with me ?"

"What !" said Shattuck, uneasily feigning. "Do you want to go to the Legislature too ?"

"Legislatur' be damned !" said the other, in a deep husky tone, and with a meeting of the straight heavy eyebrows above his intent eyes. "I ain't keerin' a minit's breath 'bout'n the kentry an' sech. But ef he interferes with me 'bout—'bout Letishy Pettingill, his life ain't wuth much purchase—not," he shook his head with a formidable look in his eye, "much purchase."

Shattuck was roused to a sense of danger. He had already interfered too much, and with disastrous results, in his friend's interests ; but here was a peril

"' YES, SIR, TER KILL HIM EF HE WAR TER INTERFERE WITH ME!'"

so patent, so immediate, that it was a most obvious duty to seek to diminish the menace. "You mus'n't be disposed to lay too much blame on Rhodes," he said. "She mightn't like either one of you, but somebody else."

"Who's *he?*" demanded Guthrie, breathlessly, with an evident instantaneous transference of the intention of vengeance and the pangs of anxiety to this myth.

"*I* don't know. Do you suppose she told *me?* Women don't tell these things; that's one of their little ways."

Guthrie drew a long sigh. "An' a mighty mean way too," he commented.

"And men are not often more communicative," Shattuck dexterously equalized the balance. "Mr. Rhodes hasn't talked to me on the subject, but I think I might undertake to say for him that he doesn't want to interfere with you in that quarter."

"He did the night o' the infair at Pettingill's," the slow mountaineer argued, with a swift application of logic.

"Oh, pshaw! he didn't want to 'dance Tucker,' that's all," said Shattuck, with a laugh, and once more seeking to turn away.

Guthrie's hand closed upon his arm; his eyes were on the stretch of barley, bending and swaying as the wind swept through its pliant blades, and shoaling from an argentine glister to green, and from green again to elusive silver glintings—what time the cove below was dark and purple and blurred, as a great white cloud hung, dazzling and opaque, high, high in the sky, and, as it passed, the valley grew graduually into distinctness again, with the privilege of the sunshine and the freedom of the wind, and all its landmarks asserted anew.

"Stranger," Felix said, lowering his tone, "she made ch'iee o' him stiddier me. *I* hed the right ter dance with her, an' she made ch'iee o' him."

"What of it? That happens every day; a woman prefers one man to another. 'Tisn't worth a quarrel."

"'Pears ter me it's better wuth killin' a man fur than all the other quar'ls that men die in daily."

Shattuck, looking into those vehement eyes, felt an uncomfortable chill stealing along his spinal column, hearing all the time Rhodes's hearty voice as he lay all unconscious on the grass, and held forth to the acquiescent, utterly unimportant Ephraim.

"Would that make her like you any better if she liked him?"

Guthrie's eyes turned ponderingly away to the roof gleaming in the cove that sheltered her at the moment.

Shattuck took confidence. "That isn't the way to make her like you, and that's what *you* want."

"Hain't Rhodes been thar lately?" demanded Guthrie. "I axed her, but she hev got sech a tormentin' way she wouldn't tell me."

"Only to talk to Mrs. Yates, and see if he could do anything to help her to hear from her husband. Oh, Rhodes would like Letitia a deal better if she could vote for him. He would go to see her every day *then*, you might be sure."

Guthrie cast a glance of frowning contempt over his shoulder at Rhodes; then, with a sudden change of tone, he said: "I hev been mightily troubled in my mind lately 'bout'n him. I war fitten ter hope in my heart ez he wouldn't git well, though I hev been layin' off ter repent some, fur I know *that* ain't well pleasin' ter the Sperit. I wouldn't hold Rhodes no gredge ef 'twarn't fur her. An' though she showed she hed ruther dance with him than with me, she *don't* 'pear ter like him noways special. An' sometimes I feel like I ought ter make myse'f easy."

The pitiable vacillations of a lover's hopes and fears appealed to Shattuck. The strength of the man's will, the sternness, almost savagery, of his character, added a force to all that he said, not lessened by Shattuck's knowledge of the object of his affections, or, rather, that upon that aerial and whimsical identity little knowledge was predicable. His disposition was to reassure, to soothe.

"Oh, you may indeed make yourself easy as far as Rhodes is concerned," he insisted. "Rhodes is thinking about nothing in this world but his election, and you ought to show a generous, friendly spirit, and vote for him, and let by-gones be by-gones."

"Oh, Lord! I'd jes' ez soon vote him inter a seat 'mongst the choir o' archangels ez not—though he'd look mighty comical thar, I'm a-thinkin'—ef I war sure ez he warn't gittin' ahead o' me 'bout Litt Pettingill."

He sighed deeply, and cast an absorbed, unseeing glance over the landscape. His strong brawny hand, still on Shattuck's arm, trembled slightly.

"I ain't like other men, stranger. I never loved nobody but her in all my life. Hate hev been my portion. Hard licks hev been my policy, an' the more ye air ready ter give, the less ye hev ter take. That's the way the world goes."

And Shattuck could not gainsay this dictum of the mountain philosopher, albeit the world from which he deduced this cogent truth was but the breadth of the cove.

"Ephraim I hed ter stan' up fur, bein' ez he war so all-fired helpless whenst small, but it air sorter of a habit o' takin' keer o' him an' speakin' him fair, account o' other folks treatin' him mean; I never sure enough keered fur him—though I don't want him ter hear me *say* that, nuther. I never knowed what love meant till I tuk ter dreamin' 'bout Litt all night an' studyin' 'bout her all day. An' I do swear it's in my heart ter kill enny man ez kems atwixt us."

"Well, 'tisn't Rhodes," Shattuck declared, easily. "And to that I'd be willing to take my oath."

"Ye see, stranger, I be mightily afflicted," said Fee Guthrie, and his strong voice trembled.

"You don't look like it, my friend," returned Shattuck, with a smile.

"Oh, I *am!*" cried the other, with a poignant intonation. "Even ef Rhodes warn't ahead of me, an' ef she liked me, she moughtn't be willin' ter marry me. Some wimmen wouldn't. I hev got that step-mam o' mine ter take keer of; many a gal wouldn't 'gree ter 'bide with her. An' I can't leave her!"

Shattuck, tiring but a moment ago, felt a freshening of interest. "Why," he said, "I have heard that she was unkind to you and your brother when you were children."

"Onkind! Lord! that warn't the word fur it till

I got the strength ter be more onkind ter her.   But she don't own nuthin'.   She 'ain't got nuthin' ter live on.   I promised my dad ter support her."

There was a pause.

" Stranger, folks tell a heap o' tales on her.   They 'low she killed her fust husband, an' hev 'witched folks, and casts the evil eye.   She wouldn't be safe.   Ef 'twarn't fur my dad fust, an' then fur me, she'd hev been made ter answer ter the folks in the cove fur her deeds.   But the Guthries hev the name o' shootin' mighty straight.   So she hev been lef' ter be."

There was another pause while he took off his hat and fanned himself with its broad brim.   With it still in his hand he resumed : " She 'witched my dad, I reckon, ter git him ter marry her, though folks said she war good-lookin' in them days.   An' dad ez good ez 'witched me ; it's an evil spell he flung around me, sure.   I knowed what he war goin' ter ax me on his death-bed ; I jes' knowed it in all my veins, in every drap o' blood.   The doctor said he couldn't live fur twelve hours more.   An' I got on my horse an' I rid away.   I rid fur an' I rid constant, an' when the horse couldn't git along no furder I rested under a tree.   I rid fur forty-eight hours—mind ye, the doctor said twelve—an' at last I 'lowed 'twar safe ter kem home.   I kem.   An' thar, propped up in the bed, war the skeleton o' a man with Death's hand on his throat, waitin' fur me an' fur my promise—an' Death waitin' too.   I reckon Death tuk right smart pleasure in that minit—he knowed he got us both through that promise, fur life couldn't mean nuthin' fur me arterward.   An'

somehow, though I hed fled that promise, I couldn't
holp makin' it.   How kin ye look in a dyin' man's
eyes an' deny him?   I promised I'd bide with her
an' take keer of her ez long ez she should live.   He
war dead in a minit.   He jes' waited till the words
passed my lips.   An' he looked at me.   An' then he
fell back dead."

Shattuck was silent.   Even his facile optimism
was at fault for the nonce.   And after another long-
drawn sigh Felix went on:

"'Tain't made my life easy.   I knowed that minit
I went into chains, fur a promise ter the dead ain't
like one ter the livin'.   An' though I owe her nuthin' but gredges, both fur me an' Ephraim, 'tain't in
gredges I be 'lowed ter pay the debt.   I never
knowed the weight of it, though, till I met that
thar leetle snip o' a gal.   'Pears ter me Litt ain't
like nobody that ever lived afore; the very way she
turns her head air diff'ent, an' the hair grows on it
not similar ter none.   Folks round about the mountings say she ain't good-lookin', but her face shines
ter me in the darkest night."

"She *is*—she is beautiful, and the rarest type of
beauty," cried Shattuck, warmly; "she is unique.
She would be considered most beautiful anywhere
else."

Guthrie turned upon him a face aglow with grati-
fication.   "That's what makes me like you-uns,
stranger," he said, cordially.   "Ye 'pear ter *sense*
things so.   But I war set agin ye some, at fust,
knowin' ye ter be Rhodes's friend," he added, frank-
ly.   "She likes ye too, Litt do.   The t'other night
whenst I war visitin' thar she talked ter Mis' Yates

an' me an' Baker Anderson 'bout nuthin' in this worl' but you-uns, an' how smart an' perlite ye be, an' book-l'arned, an' diff'ent from them in the cove."

Shattuck received this with a vague, indeterminate thrill, which he did not then discriminate as premonition, but which he remembered afterward.

Guthrie was beset by no suspicion. "Lord!" he exclaimed, his face fervent and flushed, " ef I could take that thar leetle gal's hand in mine ter walk through this life, I could make the journey well pleasin' ter the Lord, though I don't reckon I'd keer whether 'twar heaven or hell arterwards. 'Twould make up ter me fur all the troubles I hev hed in this life. An' they ain't a few—they ain't a few. But I be powerful hampered, powerful hampered, stranger, even ef I warn't so all-fired 'feared o' Rhodes. She never would abide ter live along o' my step-mam, an' I can't leave her. I hev swore a oath ter the dead." Then he seemed to shake off his fears. " It's done me good ter talk so free. I couldn't hev done it— ter a stranger too—'ceptin' I knowed what store Litt set by ye, an' how smart she 'lows ye air."

Once again that vague prophetic disquiet thrilled along Shattuck's nerves. Felix had put his hat again upon his head; his face was softened with a reminiscent smile, as his eyes dwelt upon the furthest blue peaks, most illusory semblances of mountains, faint sublimations of azure, refined almost to nullity, upon the horizon.

" T'other night, what time she could spare from tormentin' Baker Anderson—an' she do make *him* funny enough ter set a horse a-laffin'—she spent in tellin' them cur'ous tales ye hev set a-goin' 'bout the

14

folks ez war in this kentry 'fore the Injuns. An' Baker axed ef them Phœnicians warn't jes' the Fed'ral army. He 'peared ter think ez ye hedn't got the news o' the War yit. It liked ter hev killed Litt. She couldn't quit laflin'. But she tuck Mis' Yates up mighty short 'bout the Leetle People, an' 'lowed ye didn't want ter examinate thar graves fur gain, but fur knowledge fur the hist'ry o' the kentry."

And suddenly Shattuck's eyes were alight. He took instant advantage of this unexpected recruit to the ranks of scientific investigation. "She was exactly right, and shows her common-sense. And I wish, Fee "—he adopted a cordial familiarity of tone in his anxiety—" you would take that view yourself, and let me examine one or two of those graves."

Guthrie evidently experienced an inward struggle. He was divided between a sincere attraction which he felt toward the stranger, a wish to please, and a repugnant reluctance into which conscience — his queer, distorted, backwoods conscience — entered largely.

"I couldn't let ye tote the bones off, even ef they air prehistoric." He thought the word signified some sect different from Baptist or Methodist, and heterodox enough to forfeit the sanctity of sepulchre, since he had heard it so often urged by Shattuck, in extenuation of his wish to examine the graves. "I couldn't do that. *He* mought not like it whenst he wakes on the jedgmint-day ter find his bones in a strange place ; he mought never hev been out'n Tennessee in his life, an' not be 'quainted with nobody risin' at the same time 'round him. But ye may open one grave, an' "—he relented still further, looking into Shattuck's eyes, eagerly fixed upon him —" an' ef he hev got a jug like the one I seen, I'll let ye hev it, an'," his brows grew anxious with the devising of the expedient, " I'll *loan* him a pitcher from the house, so he'll hev one, though the Lord only knows what he wants with it, an' mebbe at the las' day he will hev forgot, an' won't know the diff'ence."

" I won't take the jug," said Shattuck, suddenly infected with the reluctance to rifle the sarcophagus, so strong amongst the mountaineers, so alien to the man of science. The forgotten relics lying there in that long rest became all at once, through Guthrie's homely speech, individualized, invested with the rights of property, the sense of a past and the certainty of a future, humanized as a man and a brother, rather than a system of bones that might, ethnologically considered, establish or disprove a theory, its manner of burial less significant of the universal doom of death and the hope of resurrection than of the civilization of the race and the fashion of the day. " I won't take the jug. I only want to see what this widespread story of prehistoric pygmy dwellers in Tennessee rests upon. That is all. I think they must be children—these Little People. I won't take the jug."

Guthrie's face cleared instantly. " Waal "—he drew a long breath—" I'm glad o' that. Fur ef they air chil'n, *he* mought set mo' store on his jug an' his beads 'n on his soul's salvation. I don't see ez it could hurt ter jes' lift up the top stone an' set it back agin. Bein' ez it's you-uns, I'll resk it ennyhows."

The opportunity of investigating this most unique myth, originating how and where no man can tell, of which so much has been so diversely written and said, caused every sentiment of the archæologist to glow within him.   In this secluded region it was hardly probable that the tread of science had ever before pressed the turf of the pygmy burying-ground. He should be able to speak from actual experience. There was no doubt concerning the spot.   And all the country-side confirmed the tradition with singular unanimity, with one voice.   Every detail was full of interest; the very method of coffining—the six slabs of stone in the shallow graves, the strange weavings and material of the shrouding rugs and mats, the ornaments, the weapons, the jugs with the sea-shells within—what rich intimations of the industrial status, the civilization of these people of the pygmy myth!   Ah, here indeed was history in its most unimpugnable form!   These tokens should balk oblivion, and truth prevail even in the grave.

X.

Shattuck turned with an excited, flushed face and his eyes triumphant. He had no intuition of Rhodes's anxious, disconcerted frame of mind, for the candidate was seized by a sudden fear that he was to have no opportunity to confer with Felix Guthrie anent the living issues of the election. His long ride had been taken with scant result, indeed, to flatter an old woman and to loll on the grass with the acquiescent younger brother, who would not hesitate to rescind the promise of support he had made if he fancied that it fell under the disapproval of Felix. Rhodes had had no idea that the colloquy would be so soon terminated. He scrambled sheepishly to his feet as the others precipitately passed, oblivious of the two under the tree.

"Hello! Hold on!" cried Rhodes. "Where are you making off to?"

Guthrie turned an absorbed face upon him, continuing what he was saying, but including him in the invitation extended to Shattuck to come to the house for refreshment for themselves and their horses before beginning the descent of the mountain.

"We hev had dinner long ago, but I know mam kin git ye up some sorter snack ter hearten ye up, an' ye kin leastwise take a drink 'long o' Eph an' me. An' I'll loan ye a pickaxe an' a spade, an' saddle my beastis, an' holp ye go an' dig."

It seemed to Rhodes unpardonable that his friend should be so forgetful of the interests of the election, for the allusion to the pickaxe and spade, coupled with his previous knowledge of Shattuck's chief absorption, was enough to acquaint him with the nature of the business in progress. The color had diffused itself over his handsome face to the roots of his brown hair, and his eyes were surprised and perturbed as he mechanically glanced about his attire, picking here and there a clinging barley straw from his garments. He contrived, on joining the others, to walk abreast with them, and thus end the burdensome dialogue with Eph, who, in no degree offended by his defection and accustomed to slight consideration, lagged cheerfully in the rear, chewing a straw with abnormal activity of jaw, his hat pushed far back from his broad, sunburned, fleshy face, his gait shambling and awkward, as if he still were in the furrow.

Rhodes, however willingly he might have balked his friend's preference in the choice of a subject of conversation, could hardly intimate with impunity that the enlightened voter, whose suffrage he coveted, held forth upon a theme which he considered trivial and to the last degree irksome. Nevertheless, as he walked along in the glare of the sun upon the forever shoaling waves of the silver-green grain, and listened to Guthrie droning forth his slowly forming purposes concerning the arrangements for the investigation of the pygmy graves, his irritation that the primary intention of his visit should be frustrated, and the interest appertaining to his candidacy ruthlessly thrust aside, so increased that he set himself to devise an expedient whereby he might safely disparage the matter in hand, and thus reassert the significance of his presence and the propriety of his prominence as guest.   He turned his head suddenly, archly lifting his eyebrows, and distending his eyes with a burlesque of amazement; then breaking into his joyous " ha! ha!" he clapped Guthrie jocosely on the shoulder.

" Lordy mercy, Fee!" he exclaimed, "you don't mean to say that Shattuck is devil-ing you about his confounded Little People!   Stave him off!   Gag him!   Shut him up somehow.   Don't listen to him, thinking he'll quit in the course of time.   For he won't!   I've tried him.   The more inches you give him the more ells he'll take."

Mr. Rhodes had a theory that culture is synonymous with mind and essentially coexistent.   That each assists the other, no one will deny; but that they are often largely independent, one of the other, is frequently demonstrated.   The man of more culture than capacity is painfully familiar to us all.   In the rural districts the reverse may sometimes be observed — a stalwart mental endowment, unaided by aught of alien training, seeming occasionally, in its highest development and in an uncouth subject, so incongruous as to strike one as almost inspirational.

It was none of these rare native intelligences, full-winged and of strong flight, that Felix Guthrie possessed; only a good plodding capacity, serviceable afoot, but of much sturdiness, and indeed of some slight acrobatic activity.   Rhodes was more taken aback than he had thought possible when his host, bending grave, disconcerting eyes upon him, said :

"It war *me* a-talkin' about the Leetle People. Yer ears didn't serve ye right, fur me an' Mr. Shattuck don't talk in no ways alike. Them Leetle People 'pear ter me ez well wuth talkin' 'bout ez some folks ez be bigger in stature but small-minded. Thar air a heap o' them leetle-big men lef' yit. So plenty 'tain't wuth while ter go diggin' 'em up ez cur'osities whenst dead."

There was no direct implication which of necessity conveyed offence, but Rhodes again flushed darkly, and his expression changed with the change of color. His regret had always that most nettling quality, self-reproach. No man can repent with the fervor of him who has the candor to blame himself. After an interval of tart internal colloquy with his inner consciousness, in which he called himself a fool, with the emphatic prefix of a certain strong old adjective, unhackneyed even by constant use, and upbraided himself that he should have supposed that Guthrie, like more simple-minded, ignorant men, would adopt his plausible words instead of the facts, he recovered in some degree his normal complexion and assurance, and responded glibly :

"Mountain air is mighty good for Shattuck if it's cured him of his crazy gabble about the Leetle People. Ha! ha! ha! Hey, Shattuck? I'll send him up here every few days, Fee, when the fit begins to come on again. You can hobble him out there in the orchard to keep him from running away. Ha! ha! ha! May get his wits back on your mountain air. For I swear to you he has said hardly a sane thing to me since he first heard there was any pygmy burying-ground round hereabouts.   Ha! ha! ha!"

Guthrie did not laugh, nor did Shattuck; but Ephraim, trudging in the rear, strove to be polite as best he knew how, and added a guffaw to the forced laugh of the visitor, with whom no one else would consent to be merry.

Rhodes accorded no overt attention to their silence; but his eyes, the iris of each somehow like a darkly ripe cherry in a certain red lustre, albeit merely escaping blackness, like a cherry too in its definite pronounced effect of roundness, were restless and unnoticing, and as Shattuck caught their gleam they looked angry and hot.

Shattuck was one of those people who accept the Biblical injunction touching the forgiveness of injuries, but in a purely human way.   He would not revenge himself, for this was not becoming in one acquainted in some sort with Christianity, nor did it comport with the dignity of a gentleman.   But he could not forget.   He resented Rhodes's apparently causeless anger toward him now, and it recalled the disagreements of the morning, which still galled him. The stay that he had made here, pleasant enough he had once deemed it, grew irksome in the recollection, in the light of these new relations with his host. He was saying to himself that it was time he was off; he was tired of it all, and Rhodes was insufferable.   He had no mind to bear the brunt of all the mishaps and irritation of electioneering, and this was indeed a lucky ride, since on the eve of departure it gave him the opportunity of examining the sarcophagi of the so-called pygmies at once and with the permission and aid of the man who owned the land. He had not realized how definitely he had given up this hope until the expectation was before him again in so immediate a guise. It would have been an incalculable loss to have relinquished the chance, and quitted the region no wiser than he came. His step was light, his face was sharp and eager; he looked anxiously toward the west as they neared the house, to gain some intimation through the trees how the sun fared down the great glistening concave of the western sky. The hour mattered less to him than the duration of the light.

He was hardly less impatient of interruption than Rhodes had become, and, widely at variance though the subjects were that respectively absorbed them, they both saw with unanimity of sentiment that Mrs. Guthrie, standing in the doorway, had a knitted angry brow, and a mien which betokened that they were far enough from her contemplation, and that topics of an engrossing character were in her mind and framing themselves into speech. The pervasive green tint, which seemed a trait of the very atmosphere in this dankly shady spot, rendered her white hair even whiter, her gray gown, her blue checked apron, on which she mechanically wiped her spectacles, more distinct. Her face was deeply furrowed with its frown, and there was something about her heavy jaw, her half-parted thin lips, her pertinacious eye, that gave testimony to establish the terrible stories that were told about her.

"Fee," she said, in a strained harsh voice, as soon as they were well within ear-shot, not waiting for a nearer approach, "I hev got bad news fur ye."

"I mought hev knowed it," her step-son responded, promptly. He looked at her with a reluctant face, as if by postponing to give audience to the new disaster he nullified it. He evidently held the fear of an unknown calamity as less than its realization. There was manifested none of the usual impulse to fling one's self upon the point of the sword held out. He knew too much already of that sharp edge of trouble. His many words, his dallying with the imminent discovery, bore an odd contrast to her silence, her intent ready gaze, her expectant waiting attitude. "I never knowed ye ter hev enny other sorter news. Bad news follers me. Ef I war ter go ter the eends o' the yearth—plumb ter Texas—I'd meet a man thar with, 'Fee, I hev got bad news fur ye.' Bad news begun fur me the day I war born. A body mought hev said: 'Fee, hyar ye air! I hev got bad news fur ye! Seeh a life ez ye hev got ter live; seeh a death ter die!' An' whenst I git ter hell, the devil will be thar with, 'Fee, I hev got bad news fur ye; seeh an eternity o' mis'ry ez even you-uns, with all yer speriunce o' dolefulness, hain't hed no notion of!' An' the funny part of it," he cried, with a sudden change of tone, taking off his hat and shaking his long ringleted hair backward, "none of 'em can't tell me no news. I *expect* it—'tain't news! I expec' everything bad! Torment an' trouble can't be news ter Fee Guthrie!"

His step-mother made no rejoinder, although words evidently trembled upon her lips, and all the impetus of disclosure was in her eager eye; the effort by which she constrained herself to mute waiting upon his will was intimated in every line of her hard set face. There was even drawn upon it an expression of spurious sympathy, a pretence of affectionate deprecation, infinitely sycophantic and painful to see in a woman of her age and with her white hair. She was kind enough now, doubtless, to her step-son, when all her interests hung upon his clemency. The humble Ephraim was hardly able to emulate her subservience to his brother's procrastination of the evil moment, and more than once broke out with an exclamation compounded of impatience and displeasure: " Dell lawsy mercy !" " Did ennybody ever ?" His face was red and eager, and in its round, expectant, pouting look it was positively of a porcine expression. Even the preoccupied and uninterested Rhodes was moved to a wish to elicit the intelligence.

" I hope it's nothing very serious, Mrs. Guthrie," he said, anticipating developments in reply.

But she still stood silent, looking intently with her bright, fierce eyes at Felix, who broke out instead :

" Oh, I'll be bound it's serious ! I don't look like a feller ez hev many jokes ter fill up my days. Leastwise, they ain't jokes ter me. I reckon, though, mebbe I be a joke myself—ter the devil. I'll bet all I hev got ez he fairly holds his sides whenst laffin' at me, a-goin' on like I do a-tryin' ter repent o' my sins, while all the ' bad news,' ez mam names it, in the kentry is on the hue and cry arter me all the time. I ain't got no stiddy chance ter repent." He had reached the porch at last, and leaned against one of the vine-grown posts, his hat in his hand, his frowning brow uncovered. The others stood about in expectant attitudes, the lout Ephraim the very picture of painful, agitated suspense, his mouth open, his eyes fixed on the stern, eager face of his step-mother, his hat on the back of his head.

Felix glanced up presently, and with a changed, steady voice said, "Talk on, mam."

All her forced composure gave way suddenly. She seemed metamorphosed into a fury in the very instant. "Felix, Felix," she cried, between her set teeth, "yer cattle! Somebody be arter yer cattle. Peter Brydon rid by hyar jes' now, an' tole me ez one o' yer young steers war lyin' dead yander by Injun Bluffs. An' up on the mounting that fine red cow Beauty Bess air dead, too, an' half tore up." Her teeth were grinding, one jaw upon the other; there was foam upon her lips.

"Wolves!" he said, quietly, looking up at her, a certain surprise on his face. "No use takin' on 'bout that. Hev ter lose some cattle by wolves every year. I ain't so close-fisted ez ter mind losin' a few cattle wunst in a while by accident." He cast a deprecatory glance at Shattuck, the first token of self-consciousness, of anxious regard for the opinion of others, which the young townsman had ever remarked in him. He evidently was touched by a sense of shame; he could not endure to be held susceptible of distress for a small loss of worldy goods. There was a distinct intimation of reproach in his voice as he added, "Waal, mam, I never knowed you-uns ter git inter sech a takin', an' 'low it would lay me so low, jes' kase thar be a few head o' cattle los' by wolves out'n my herd."

"*Wolves! wolves! wolves!*" She huskily jerked out the words. "Ever hear o' wolves cuttin' a beastis's throat with a knife? *Wolves!* Ever hear o' wolves cuttin' out the tenderline, an' leavin' the rest o' the meat ter spile, or ter the buzzards, till they want another feed? Then they make ch'ice o' another fat brute, an' get jes' the best cuts o' meat, an' leave the rest ter waste. *Wolves!*—two-legged *wolves!* An' they ain't much *afeard* o' you-uns, Fee Guthrie, them wolves ain't."

She had an accurate knowledge of his springs of action. He hardly cared for the loss, but as her detail progressed, the wantonness of the waste, the possible motive of spite, called a flush into his cheek and a spark into his eye. The moment the last words passed her lips, and the fact was made patent to his mind that his name was not a terror to protect his property, his whole consciousness was resolved into fire.

He stood for one instant motionless, a terrible oath upon his lips. Then he sprang off like an unleashed hound, with her exultant laugh harshly ringing through the dusky shades behind him.

"I knowed it. Fee 'll lay 'em low enough!" she cried, with the satisfaction of a Bellona, as she towered above them all, her stern, lined, dark old face so repellently triumphant that both her visitors felt a sense of recoil. "Felix will tame 'em—he'll tame them wolves. He air okal ter it." She nodded her head, with a look promissory of horrors, and then fell to rubbing her left arm, which had been partially paralyzed of late years.

Rhodes gazed wistfully into the dense umbrageous tangle whence his host had disappeared. "Now I don't think it's sensible to send Fee off that way. He might get hurt," he said.

"He ain't one o' that kind," replied the old woman, with a fierce pride in the spirit that had tamed even hers. "The Guthries—ye hev hearn them called 'the fightin' Guthries'—air a survigrous tribe. An' my step-son Felix air knowed ter be the bravest o' all the 'fightin' Guthries.' Whenst ye see him a-crawlin' out'n the leetle eend o' the horn, ye let me know."

A quick thud of hoofs, the deep-mouthed, joyous baying of a fierce hound that galloped after the horseman, gave notice to the party, whose vision was all cut off by the heavy woods, of the departure of the master of the house. Mrs. Guthrie looked at the two visitors with a smile as she listened, then fell again to softly rubbing her arm.

Rhodes and Shattuck, although from diverse points of view, could hardly have been more disconcerted than by the turn affairs had taken. The candidate was without recourse. He had allowed the golden opportunity of electioneering with Felix to evade him while he lounged under the tree in the barley field with the unimportant younger brother. He conceived a repugnant hatred of this unconscious factor in his discomfiture as he glanced at Ephraim, who stood gazing dully and blankly in the direction whence the sound of the hoofs had come, now faint in the distance. With his elastic faculty for regret, Rhodes was upbraiding himself anew, taking account of the wasted day, the long ride, and the fact that electioneering in this quarter was estopped, since the visit could not be decorously repeated; presently he was seized by forebodings that the waste of time was not at an end, for Shattuck's project was not so easily concluded. As the candidate's attention returned to the matters more immediately in hand, he became aware that his friend was declining to take luncheon with Mrs. Guthrie, on the score that he should hardly have time to get to the foot of the mountain and accomplish before sundown an errand upon which Felix had promised to accompany him.

"Ephraim, however, will do as well," he said, genially, turning to the younger brother, who instantly signified his acquiescence, and made off with alacrity for the pickaxe and spade. "But as I'll leave you Mr. Rhodes, I am sure I shall not be missed," Shattuck saw fit to add to his own excuses.

"No," Rhodes said, somewhat curtly; "if you go, I shall go too. I don't want my visitors"—he added, recovering his smile in a meagre degree, and bending it upon Mrs. Guthrie's forbidding countenance as she looked from one to the other—"to go about the mountains breaking their necks, and then putting the blame on me for not being along to advise and point out the way."

"Jes' ez yer please," she retorted, tartly, still looking from one to the other. "We ain't never considered our Ephraim plumb smart like Felix. But I never did expec' ter hear ez he warn't even fit fur a guide-post. But jes' ez ye two gentlemen feel disposed." And she reseated herself in her chair upon the porch, and resumed her knitting.

"Oh, you stay, Rhodes," Shattuck insisted, aghast at interfering so radically with Mrs. Guthrie's lunch as to remove both guests from the feast. "You can stay."

If Rhodes had been entirely at liberty, it is doubtful whether he would have remained. There was something so menacing in the old woman's eye, so coercively albeit vaguely frightful to the imagination, that the idea of spending a few hours alone with her, to eat at her board and sit by her fireside and listen to her talk, with that thin friendly veneer scarcely concealing the harsh vindictiveness of her nature, was not to be contemplated with equanimity. Whether he would have feared poison, or the stealthy stroke of a knife, or some other manifestation of a cruel insanity, although mental aberration had never been associated with her deeds, Rhodes would hardly have ventured upon the ordeal of a solitary meal served by her. Nevertheless, he noted with a pang of anger and alarm that she did not second Shattuck's insistence, and that the invitation was no longer open to him. If she heard his adieux, somewhat constrained and uncharacteristic, if she saw his outstretched hand, she made no sign except by a short nod, which he might either interpret as response, or as merely the emphasis of concluding a long row of counted stitches upon her knitting-needles.

She laid them down presently to hearken to the faint baying of Guthrie's hound on the far slope of the mountain, the echo striking back the sound, augmented like the voice of a pack in full cry, and thus, with uplifted eyes and intent, listening attitude, she was left in the deep green shadow growing duskier.

"Now see what you've done!" cried Rhodes, angrily, and all oblivious of the presence of Ephraim, as they walked away to their horses hitched to the fence. "It does seem to me you might forbear insulting my friends."

Ephraim looked with quick anxiety from one to
15

the other. On his ready impulse he spoke, forestalling Shattuck's reply. "Oh, ye can't holp makin' mam mad; she gits mad 'kase other folks breathe the breath o' life. The only way ter suit her is ter die, an' gin her the Great Smoky Mountings fur elbow-room. Nuthin' less."

"I had no idea that you would come too," protested Shattuck. "I thought that if one of us stayed, the courtesies would be amply observed; and so they would."

"You had no right to think," said Rhodes, putting his foot into the stirrup, his face scarlet under his dark straw hat. "You continually jeopardize my interests by taking the initiative in my affairs. We had accepted her invitation, and you had no right to withdraw, as I couldn't stay without you."

"Laws-a-massy, boys! don't git ter quar'lin'," Ephraim eagerly and familiarly adjured them, as he mounted an old sorrel mare, who was attended by a frisking long-legged colt. "Ye don't expec' mam ter vote fur ye noways ennyhow, Mr. Rhodes. It don't make no diff'unce. Me an' Fee ain't goin' ter hold no gredge agin ye; ye needn't mind."

The unvarnished promise, and the evident comprehension of his intentions and mission, however grating to Rhodes's more delicate sensibilities and pride, were nevertheless salutary. Once more the ground of offence was proved untenable, and he saw that a simulation of reconciliation was in order. Although he chafed under the continual constraints with which Shattuck had unintentionally burdened him, he felt that it was not yet time to boldly throw them off. Thus he adjusted himself anew to their weight.

XI.

HE was not sorry that further conversation was precluded by the necessity of riding in single file, for the road, rocky and narrow, hardly more than a bridle-path, indeed, was beset by precipices, now on one side, now on the other, and again sheer down on both, their way lying along the crest of a high comb-like ridge, above abysses veiled by the heavy growth of pines, the plumy tops waving far below. Rhodes and Shattuck found it needful to give careful heed to their steps, for their horses, bred in the "flat woods," trod this narrow ridge with a gingerly gait as if the ground were hot, with pricked-up ears, and with now and again a convulsive snort of surprise and disparagement. But the sure-footed mountain mare, well inured to the craggy heights, went deftly and carelessly along at a sharp trot, occasionally snatching a casual mouthful from the bushes that precariously clung to the wayside, while the colt, with the nimblest disregard of lurking dangers, cara-coled and curveted, now in advance and now behind the party, showing its flying, unshod heels in almost impossible attitudes against the sky, inconsistent with the laws of gravity and of standing upon the earth at all. Here could be seen the great contours of the range, invisible from the cove, or but dim-ly suggested by variant shades. The massive slopes rose on every hand ; from deep intervenient ravines came now and then silver gleams of mountain torrents among the crags and the pines. Often and often the tremors and tinklings of hidden streams struck clearly on the ear, mingled with the sigh of the rustling foliage, and their breath gave to the fragrant air freshness. A great peak near at hand loomed up high against the sky ; as the horsemen made a sudden turn the massive shoulder of the mountain intervened and the dome disappeared. The cove seemed nearer and nearer whenever a glimpse of it was vouchsafed from amidst the dark green forest that presently towered about them, for the road now ran through the woods upon a broad slope, with ever and anon a cliff beetling over their way. The dense foliage of the laurel jungles was bronzed by the sunlight, growing ever more tawny as the afternoon waned. Purple shadows were lurking in the midst of the valley. Farthest mountains, blue once, were violet now and faintly flushed. And when at last the horsemen emerged from the densities of the woods into the clifty gorge, and rode still in single file upon the swaying, hollow-sounding bridge, they found a deep red cloud reflected in the river, and all the harbingers of twilight abroad in the cove. The smoke from the Yates cabin, seeming nearer than the fact might warrant, since the undulations of the land, which plodding feet must measure, were not a part of the line of sight, curled up with a brisk convolution and a volume that heralded the evening meal. All adown the lane the cows were coming home, and the mellow clanking of their bells accented the quietude. Some night-blooming flower was awake in the woods with a sweet, wild, indefinite odor. Here and there on the purple slope, reputed to be the pygmy burying-ground, a fire-fly flickered, swift, elusive, evanescent. And on a great blooming laurel-bush the mocking-bird sang, heedless of the darkness to come, heedless of the day gone by, possessed by its fervor of music that made gloom light and all life a joyance, like some enthusiast soul in the ecstasy of a gift, unmindful of the world and of all the paltry outward aspects.

"This hyar big laurel bush air a good landmark," Ephraim said, turning in his saddle, his hand on his mare's back, that he might better reverse his posture as he spoke to the two men that followed. "About the only one thar be, too. We had better begin thar, I reckon. Fur ef ye find nuthin,' ye'd know whar ye started ef ever ye kem ter dig ag'in. The t'other trees air all too much alike." And he turned his face again toward the mare's head, and surveyed anew the space before him.

Singularly clear it was and free from underbrush; the steepness of the slope and the great draught of the gorge made it a fair field for the fierce autumn fires that annually swept over it. Only the gigantic oak and poplar and chestnut trees were spared, standing full-leaved and in a heavy phalanx upon the declivity. Beneath their boughs mystery lurked unsolved. A sentiment of awe, of doubt, of reluctance took possession even of Rhodes's prosaic mind as he reined up in the deep shadow. He drew out his watch, albeit he had resolved that he would not remonstrate.

"Will you have time, Shattuck?" he said. "Hadn't you better wait until to-morrow?"

"I war a-thinkin' ez much myself," said Ephraim, turning a hopeful face toward Shattuck, who had drawn rein, and sat motionless upon his horse, looking about him with a quick dilated eye, as if he hardly heard.

The strange place ! The thronging shadows ! How many times had they mustered here ! With what pathetic sense was the silence replete ! What tears had been shed for those who lay here hushed, and themselves would weep no more, as once they had wept in that universal heritage of sorrow ! What hearts had bled that these hearts, dust now, should cease to beat ! Time—there is no time, when man through all the vain centuries can feel so close to man, can think his thoughts and measure the throb in pulses long ago stilled. Ah ! the confusion of tongues wrought no divergence here ! The conclusiveness of the grave, however named ; the yearning sense of loss ; the insistent expectation, nay, the imperative demand of the soul that this terrible pause, this nullity, should not be the final period of that fair promise called life—all hung about the forgotten pygmy burying-ground with infinite mystery, with unassuaged pathos. Only science, of all the developments of the human mind, might fitly take account of the mere functional disabilities which it represented—might speculate and exert its fine rational inferential imagination, and construct a status from assumed facts, and promulgate dicta so founded, to be received and accepted for a time, and then demolished by a still more fine-spun theory in what is called the march of progress. These forces were astir in Shattuck as he flung himself from the saddle.

His brow was slightly corrugated, his eyes were
alight, his pulses beat at fever-heat ; not that he entertained so far-fetched a theory as that these poor mor-
tal relics were aught but the infant remains of the
American Indian, or, perhaps, of earlier aboriginal
people, but the talk of strange myths, and that inex-
plicable Tennessee tradition of pygmy dwellers, colored even his mind, which he sedulously sought to
hold blank for the correct impression, and made his
hand tremble as he laid hold of the pickaxe, extended
down to him by Ephraim Guthrie, as if he were indeed on the verge of some superlatively strange discovery discounting all human experience, and befit-
ting the realm of a fairy tale.

" Hyar they air, pick an' spade, ef ye be a-goin'
ter dig yerse'f," remarked Ephraim. He did not
realize any difference in social status that might have
relegated the manual labor to him, nor even the fact
that it was better suited to his massive and burly
frame. He had intended to perform it, in his character of host, to shield his guest from the discomfort
of the slight exertion. He relinquished the imple-
ments with reluctance, remembering this resolution ;
but superstition, now that he was upon the spot,
prevailed, and overbore even the instinct of hospitality native in the mountaineer's heart. The two im-
plements clashed together, the sound loud and metallic in the stillness; he looked a little wistfully after
his guest as Shattuck bore them away out into the
more open spot where the laurel bush grew almost to
the proportions of a tree, unimpeded by others of its
kindred. He had no wish, this simple Ephraim, to
peer in at the strange sepulchre—the six-slab stone

coffin he had often heard of in the terrible fireside stories; he cared naught for curiously woven shrouds, and feathered mantles, and carcanets of pearl beads, and jars of quaint pottery; nor for questions of race and time and civilization these may betoken and solve. Rhodes still sat in the saddle, as motionless as an equestrian statue, sharply outlined against the crimson sky, and beneath an oak bough as dark, as heavy, and as massive as if it were wrought of bronze. The light was clearer in the open space where the branches could not fling their gloom, and as Shattuck ran swiftly down through the long grass he could still see a flower here and there smile up at him—the tawny red of the jewel-weed, and the close-tufted ball of the "mountain snow." The range loomed far above. A star was on its crest, faintly scintillating. The door and window of the Yates cabin, farther down the cove, were illumined from the fire-lit hearth, a dimly fluctuating radiance, sidereal too in the midst of the gathering shadows. The falls still showed their gleaming green and white, and the mists, exhaled from the depressions between the purple slopes, wore a gentle dove-like gray. A tender hour of reveries, and blurring tints, and restful recollections of the day done, but still far from the morrow. The two men under the tree did not speak; the horses did not stir; only the vague rustling of the saddle betokened the regular rise and fall of respiration; even the frisky colt stood motionless, and gazed at the flashing river with a full and meditative eye. Shattuck had paused before the laurel on the side toward the water; neither of the other men, albeit country-bred, might have noticed that here the grass and weeds were a trifle bent—under the recent rain, perchance; a trifle withered—by the sun, it might have been. Nor did he; he chose the spot, remembering Yates's words that here the ground sounded hollow.

But no man who had ever wielded a pickaxe could have failed to discern, as he lifted it high, and the sharp point sank into the ground, that it was merely a replaced turf that yielded so readily to the blow—replaced with its mat of roots severed—and not the tough earth bound by a thousand veinous fibres to the full-pulsed herbage. He was unaccustomed to the earth save geologically or geographically considered, and to herbage except in its botanical aspects. He only lifted the pickaxe high above his head once more, and once more the point struck down into the loosened mould—struck down with a sharp metallic clangor, as of steel upon stone. It rang far through the quiet cove. A low, hollow, vibratory, vault-like resonance followed—mute, indeed, to all ears save his own, but what significance that murmur held for him! He lifted his head to look at the two men who had turned toward him upon the sudden smiting of the rock, and were gazing at him. The next moment—a moment confused forever after in his recollection—something invisible passed him in the air, singing shrilly, a high-keyed tone; a sharp report, and all the echoes of mountain and crag were clamoring. He hardly realized its meaning. He turned dully in the direction whence the sound seemed to come, and so trivial a thing as the movement saved his life. Close by his head again a rifle-ball whizzed; it kept the line unswervingly, entered the skull of the staring, amazed colt upon the slope, pierced his brain, and the creature dropped dead without a struggle on the long grass. The sight served to convince the stupefied, reluctant faculties of Shattuck that some enemy in the dusk was firing at him. He could not, in the bewilderment of the moment, distinguish the words that Rhodes shouted to him. It was rather in obedience to his gesture, as he rode a little way out from the gloom, leading by the bridle his friend's plunging and frightened horse, that Shattuck dropped pickaxe and spade, and ran toward him across the dusky, tangled grasses. He caught the reins as they were flung to him; but it was no easy matter to mount the rearing and snorting animal. The other two men were fairly in retreat before Shattuck, running by the horse's side, and hanging with all his weight upon the bridle, contrived to get his foot into the stirrup. Rhodes, riding down the smooth slopes of the pygmy burying-ground, across unnumbered graves, the heavy shadow of the forest trees shielding the party, and making further attack futile, heard at last the hoof-beats of his friend's horse at a regular gallop pressing hard behind him, and turned to see Shattuck once more safe in the saddle. He put spurs to his own steed without more ado. The dank evening air fanned his face; he could hear its silken rustle as it was stirred into seeming activity by his own quick rush through it. This vague simulation of a sound, the horses' muffled hoof-beats barely distinguishable in the thick grass, the drowsy chant of the cicada, the dull monotone of the river—all hardly impinged upon the sense of primordial stillness that pervaded the eventide; it might have seemed that

that keen, menacing note of the rifle, the sharp shibboleth of doom, was but some jarring incongruity of a morbid fancy.

The trees began to give way; the more open, level spaces of the cove were at hand; the darkness gradually diminished. Rhodes again clapped spurs to his horse, since here they were to leave the protecting shade. Foremost of the three, he was already in the lane when he became aware that he was not followed; his companions had fallen away. His first impulse, as he glanced over his shoulder into the vacant gloom, was to pursue his own way, and make good his escape. Then he reined up so suddenly that the horse, still trembling and wild and frightened, fell back upon his haunches. Rhodes sat motionless for a moment, gazing over his shoulder.

Night possessed the pygmy burying-ground, and the great phalanx of oak and chestnut-trees was lost in an indistinguishable gloom; but, here, where no shadow hindered, he could see the contours of the wide landscape, from which color had faded, and, above its dusky, blurring expanse, the dark sky embossed with a myriad of stars. The fences on either hand of the grass-grown way were dimly visible to his alert senses. Along their parallel lines naught was to be seen, save once a flash betokening the striking of a spark betwixt flint and iron; and in that moment he thought he heard the thud of hoofs. He ground a curse between his teeth as he wheeled his horse. Shattuck, it seemed, had seen fit not to follow his host's lead, and doubtless the dull Ephraim was not yet aware, as he cantered along in the rear, that Rhodes did not still guide the little party. The candidate was a brave man, and in any sufficient quarrel could have stood his ground with equanimity. To be the target, however, for a mysterious enmity that lurked in ambush and in the nightfall promised heavy draughts upon the resources of his courage. The prosaic and utilitarian phase of his mind took account of his candidacy in this connection. No man is so heavily handicapped in a race as he who bears the imputation of unpopularity. The public expectation of success is as a loadstone to the event. He sustained a positive loss in the mere fact that he or his friend had been fired upon. And whither was Shattuck bound now, and what to do? With a determination to hold him in check and to thwart his purpose, Rhodes galloped in the direction whence the faint hoof-beats sounded, albeit the darkness held unknown terrors, the thought of which shook his nerves, and although silence as profound as this had but now been rent by that tense report of the rifle. It was only for a few moments that the successive cross-stakes of the zigzag rail-fences, seeming disconnected from the rest, and high as the horse's head, flew by him on either side in relief against the lighter tones of the fields they enclosed. The river suddenly shows between its banks, gleaming darkly with the night sky, all the splendors of the stars shattered in the ripples, and is gone as he dashes on. He hears the booming of the cataract; and from the pygmy burying-ground, where late the mocking-bird sang, the sudden ill-omened shrilling of an owl. He sees above the western mountains a dull red after-glow of the sunset, and below its darkling pine-grown slopes the little Yates cabin, its windows shining squares of yellow light. The radiance issued forth so far as to reveal Shattuck alighting from his horse at the bars, and the clumsier figure of Ephraim Guthrie still mounted, and looking over his shoulder, as he perceived for the first time that Rhodes was not in the lead.

An aptitude in emergency is a natural trait, not cultivated, and Rhodes possessed it to a useful degree. He flung himself from his horse, and followed on his friend's heels with such despatch that albeit he did not hear the words with which Shattuck greeted the party within, he was on the threshold before a rejoinder was elicited. No friendly greeting had it been, to judge from the dismayed, deprecatory faces grouped about the fire. Adelaide had risen with a slow look of doubt, a sort of stunned surprise. Letitia, who had been out milking the cows, stood in the back doorway, the brimming piggin on her head, one hand lifted to stay it, the wind rustling the straight skirt of her dress, the twilight and the fire-light mingled on her face. Her blue eyes were alight with a sort of wonder, that held nevertheless an intimation of comprehension, which was at variance with the stolid amazement in Baker Anderson's countenance, as, just arrived and still breathless, he sat squarely in his chair, one hand on either knee, his jaw fallen, gaping thunder-struck at the intruder. The centre of the family group, Moses, was seated upon the floor in the fire-light, and turned himself dexterously about to survey over his small shoulder the new-comers ; he was silent in seeming recognition of the fact that their gaze overlooked him, and had no reference to his existence ; his soft face only expressed a sort of infantile apprehensiveness and suspension of opinion. A tallow dip sputtered on the high mantel-piece; there was pine amongst the fuel, and the resin flared white in the flames. Very distinct the scene was, although, as the lights fluctuated, the fire flickered in the breeze, which swayed it like a canvas: the brown walls; the purplish black squares where the night looked in through the windows, with here a feathery bough, and here a star, and here the dim contours of a dark summit against the sky; the red-bedecked warping bars; the table not yet set forth with the supper crockery, save only a great brown pitcher and a yellow bowl; the sheen of tin-ware on a shelf; even Shattuck's shadow, as sarcasti-cally nonchalant as the substance which it mimicked, as it waved its hand in mockery of courtesy, while he reiterated his bitterly merry congratulations. The white light showed the very flare of fury in his eyes that oddly dallied with the smile on his face.

"You are a courageous rifleman, Mrs. Yates," he was saying, glancing up at the rifle on the wall, glit-tering upon the rack of deer antlers. "You have set three men off at full run this evening. Few ladies could say as much, I am sure. If you would only mend your aim a little!"

With a blunt accusation she could doubtless have coped; but she could only stare at him in silent amaze-ment as he made these elusive feints. The other two men, lumbering and massive shadows in the back-ground, stared too in surprise at him, and silently waited developments.

He had his hat in his hand as he leaned on the tall back of a chair, and he looked steadily at her with

an air of graceful and good-natured raillery, all at variance with the fire in his eyes.

"Mend your aim, only a trifle, Mrs. Yates, and
next time perhaps your target won't be so unman-
nerly as to run off from so accomplished a marks-
man," and once more he laughed with a genial inflection, then caught his breath with a sort of gasp as
his face grew scarlet.

Rhodes laid a hand upon his shoulder. " Why,
Shattuck," he exclaimed, with a resonant amazement
that made the roof of the little cabin ring like a
sounding-board, " what are you thinking of ?   Mrs.
Yates to fire a rifle at us ?"

" At me, if you please !" cried Shattuck.   Then
addressing Adelaide : " Didn't you say you would—
or perhaps my treacherous memory misleads me—in
case I ventured to open the pygmy graves?   Your
husband told me this."

" Yes ; but I never—" she faltered ; then she
paused.

Letitia had placed the piggin on the shelf, and
crossed the room with a quick, light, definite step.
The clumsy rifle was off the rack and in her slight,
incongruous grasp in another moment.   She held it
up before the men ; there was the powder stain of a
recent discharge about its lock.   And then her eyes,
like blue flames, burned upon the shrinking, over-
whelmed mistress of the house, thus seemingly convicted on her own hearth-stone.

Adelaide never knew how she found the breath to
gasp forth the words ; the instinct of self-defence
alone framed them.   " I fired the rifle off at a hawk
ez war arter the chickens, early, early this arternoon

whilst ye war away," she replied to the woman who had said nothing, instead of to the man who had spoken so plainly.

Rhodes's eye was suddenly steady. His face had grown graver, indeed, but it had cleared. It wore a look now adjusted to inspection, and thoroughly in character—the pallid hue, the relaxing ligaments, and flabby flesh it showed only a moment ago were all resolved into the firm, controlled countenance of a man who has his nerves, his fears, his prospects, well in hand.

"Mrs. Yates," he said, with sober circumspection, "this is a very serious matter, to threaten to shoot Mr. Shattuck. I hope your husband told you so."

Poor Adelaide ! With that sense of responsibility for woe which is in some sort assuaged by a completeness of confession, she broke out, with all the abasement of self-blame: "Oh, he did ! he did ! That's why we quar'led ; that's why he lef' me. I know 'twar wrong, now. I reckon I never meant it then. But I wanted the Leetle People lef' be in thar graves, like they hev always been."

Rhodes's comprehension was at best but ill adapted to the reception of any subtle meanings. To his mind those words expressed a recantation of her former denial. His face hardened, but at the same time there was a look of genuine relief upon it, which Shattuck—still leaning upon the back of the chair, and airily flirting his hat in his hand as he glanced from one to the other—could not altogether interpret.

"It was indeed very wrong," Rhodes said, severely. "And might have been far worse. If your aim had been better, you might have killed Mr. Shattuck instead of Guthrie's colt."

She turned her eyes, full of a sort of confused terror, and her pallid face toward Ephraim, who stood near the doorway, a massive, stolid presentation of the rustic. He met her look with a glance of deep reproach.

"Fee hev been in mighty hard luck ter-day," he remarked. "Somebody hev been a-shootin' of his cattle—the leetle red steer, an' that thar small crumply cow named Beauty Bess." His tone was as if he recalled acquaintances to Mrs. Yates's mind, and had something of an elegiac cadence. "An' now hyar's that leetle colt ez he sot sech store by—spry leetle critter, with a powerful springy gait. Fee looked ter him ter show speed one o' these days."

Her wild eyes dilated. "Why, Eph," she cried, in a convincing, coercive voice, "I—I never shot the pore leetle critter!"

"He warn't *pore!* He war fat, fur true," asseverated Ephraim, with a farmer's pride in the state of his stock.

Rhodes burst into a sudden rollicking laugh, and Shattuck wondered at the evident change in his moral atmosphere. The candidate had found the explanation of his friend's unpopularity far more easily to be endured than the idea that he himself sustained a secret enmity. The circumstance of the rifle-shot would be felicitously accounted for by this woman's threats against Shattuck's projected investigation, her husband's quarrel with her for this reason and his subsequent desertion of her. The political status of the canvass might remain intact,

16

suffering naught from her inimical feeling against Shattuck, who had made her husband his partisan.

"But I wouldn't shoot a colt. I wouldn't be so mean," she declared, her eyes full of tears.

"You had rather shoot merely a man," Shattuck suggested, lightly.

"We ought to have you bound over to keep the peace, Mrs. Yates." Rhodes resumed his note of severity.

"For I have the permission of the owner of the land to open the graves and to search for curiosities and relics, and I shall do so, relying on the protection of the law," Shattuck added.

"You'd better do like ye done the t'other night," Letitia put in, unexpectedly; "kem whenst all be asleep."

Shattuck turned a look of questioning amazement upon her.

"Oh, I hearn ye !" she said, impatient of the denial in his face—"I hearn yer pickaxe a-striking inter the ground agin the rock coffins o' the Leetle People."

Once more Rhodes looked ill at ease. A strange ghoulish guest this seemed even to his standpoint of superior education — to haunt the vicinage of those pygmy graves in the light of the midnight moon.

But Shattuck's face had a distinct touch of anxiety upon it. "Why, who could that have been?" he exclaimed, with so genuine a note of surprise that Rhodes's suspicion was disarmed.

"Never mind, never mind," he said, with his coarse jocularity; "there'll be a few pygmies left for you, I'll be bound!   Come along, we must be getting home."

Shattuck shook off the hand which his friend placed upon his shoulder; but Rhodes turned with unimpaired cheerfulness to the others.

" Now look-a-here, Mrs. Yates, this must stop, short off, right *here*.   I'd like to think I'd leave as good a friend behind me as the pygmies have in you ; but you can't befriend with impunity people who have been dead so long that they are too funny to keep their coffins to themselves.   You look out! You don't want an action for assault with intent to kill brought against you, I reckon.   I think I may promise that Mr. Shattuck will do nothing about this offence — if it is not repeated.   At least, I would go that far myself," he concluded, with an air of prompting his friend's generosity.

But Shattuck said nothing.   His whole interest in the present moment had given way to that suggestion of a strange sound in the midnight and what it might signify.   He still hung on the back of the chair, his hat in his listless hands, but his face was turned toward the purplish black square of the window, and his meditative eyes dwelt upon the inscrutable darkness that encompassed the pygmy burying-ground.

Adelaide had seen, in a sort of numb despair, her denial of the deed swallowed up in her admission of the threat.   In her confused sense of the fact, and her loss of courage before the inexorability of the conviction, as it were, out of her own mouth, she could only reiterate : "I didn't do it!   I didn't do it !" And her stunned immobility of aspect seemed sullen, and her tone was interpreted as dogged.

"Oh, well, all right," said Rhodes, lightly. He could be casual enough now, since it could be made plain to all the country-side that it was no affair of his, but a quarrel between Shattuck and the fugitive Yates and the deserted wife. "Come, come, Shattuck," again clapping his heavy hand on his friend's shoulder, "we must be a-jogging."

Ephraim, too, had the voice of accusation in his farewell. "I ain't s'prised none," he said, looking over his shoulder, with a lowering melancholy gleam in his eyes under the broad brim of his hat, as he turned toward the door—"I ain't s'prised none cf Fee makes ye pay fur that thar leetle colt, an' takes it 'fore the court." He paused upon the threshold after a heavy lumbering step or two. "I reckon he won't make ye pay *much*, though; an' Fee ain't one nohow ter set store on courts," he added, relenting.

She stood there, arraigned on her own hearth-stone, silent, pale, her face seeming as rigid as if it were some changeless symmetry of marble, in the interval while they mounted their horses and rode way. The sound of the hoofs came, then ceased as a marshy dip intervened, and rose on the air once more from the farther side, and dulled in the distance to silence. The throbbing of the cataract asserted itself anew. From every weed growing rank about the fence corners, from amongst the vines over the porch, vibrated the voice of the myriad nocturnal insects, chiming and chiming interminably. Only the irresponsive darkness without met her eye as she still mechanically gazed through the doorway where the visitors had disappeared.

Letitia had sunk down in the great spacious high-

backed chair on which Shattuck had leaned.   It was
a half-reclining posture, to whose languors her slen-
derness and drooping grace lent a sort of individuality, and she looked like a child half recumbent in
the corner, both hands clasping one of its arms.   Her
curling hair, a tress or two falling on her forehead,
the rest drawn back and tied at the nape of the neck,
whence the ends all escaped, seemed longer as her
head drooped.   Her eyes for the moment were upon
the fire.   When she suddenly lifted them, they shone
like sapphires, with crystalline splendor, and Adelaide, in amazement, saw that they were full of tears
—saw them thus that night for the first and last time
in all her life.

"How could ye have done it?" she exclaimed.
"Ye wicked heart!   Ye cruel, evil soul!"

"Litt," cried Adelaide, aghast, "ye ain't believin'
what them men said ter me?   Ye 'ain't turned agin
me too?"

She looked down piteously at the girl; then as she
stooped to lift the baby, her hands trembled, and she
fumbled so that Moses made some shift to raise his
own indolent bulk and snuggle into her arms.

"*B'lieve them men?*" echoed Letitia, her eyes ablaze.
"I'd b'lieve *his* word agin the Bible.   I ain't keerin' 'bout t'others."   She seemed, with a toss of her
head, as if she annihilated them.

Adelaide could not account for her own words
afterward.   It was so strange a transition from her
own absorbing, tumultuous, insistent troubles to intrude into the subtle, incipient, unrealized thoughts
and feelings of another.

"Litt," she said, as calmly as if nothing of moment had happened—she had seated herself, with the child's face close to her cheek—"ye oughtn't ter talk that-a-way. That man don't keer nuthin' 'bout you-uns."

Letitia slowly turned her face. There was in its expression many a phase of bitter introspection, wonder underlying them all, and a sort of helpless despair as a finality, dumb and infinitely pathetic. Somehow, ignorant as the other was, little as she could have described or differentiated it, she became sharply aware of the wound she had dealt, the poignant rankling of the heart that received it. She sought, in a panic of regret and self-reproach, to nullify it.

"Ye don't keer, though," she clumsily tried to laugh it off. "Ye be always a-tellin' ez how ye be no favorite 'mongst the men folks, an' 'pear ter think it's a sorter feather in yer cap ter be too ch'ice an' smart fur the gineral run."

To her surprise, the girl showed no resentment. It seemed that that calamitous possibility had dwarfed every other consideration.

"I ain't keerin' fur sech ez them," she said, slowly, with a tremor in her low voice, as if she made the distinction clear to her own mind.

The sudden, heavy footfalls of Baker Anderson sounded upon the puncheons. He had repaired to the wood-pile for pine knots, and he seemed, in heaping them upon the fire, to seek to make amends for a dereliction of duty, plain to his own sense if not to others.

"I didn't know what in thunder I oughter hev said or done, Mis' Yates," he remarked, as he knelt on one knee on the hearth, his square, boyish face showing its grave sympathy as the white light streamed up the chimney. "I didn't know but what whilst them men war a-sassin' round so 'twould be the right way ter pertect the fambly ter take down my rifle ter 'em."

Letitia's face was aflame. "Thar's been too much o' takin' down rifles a'ready. Leave that ter Adelaide."

Baker, still in his humble posture, turned his eyes toward her, a clumsy sneer upon his blunt features. "Ef ye 'low Mis' Yates done sech ez that, I wonder ye air willin' ter bide with her. Whyn't ye go home ?"

Once more her eyes, with their jewelled effect, so crystalline a blue they were, shone upon him, fiery and fierce. "I'll bide with that thar rifle. I'll watch it by day, an' I'll guard it by night. 'Twon't send a ball agin soon ter scorch his head. I saw his hair all whar 'twar singed. An'"—she turned suddenly upon Adelaide, who was quaking beneath the storm her ill-considered words had raised—"ef ye tell me he don't think nuthin' of me, I tell you-uns I could think o' him a thousand years without a ' thanky.'"

She sat erect in her chair, flushed and defiant. She suddenly drooped back into her former, half-recumbent posture, and again burst into tears.

Adelaide, her nerves all strained and jarring, feeling at fault to have elicited this outburst in the presence of Baker Anderson, who was something of a gossip, and with the false accusations and reproaches, the danger and the trouble of her own position still pressing heavily on her, could but fall a-weeping too,

"I 'ain't got but one friend in the worl'," she said, clasping her child.   "An' hyar he is."

"Yes, an' he'll be yer frien' ez long ez he needs ye, an' no longer," said the tactless Baker, who had no talent for woe, and who hardly entered into the emotions of either woman, except to grasp the division of their friendship.

He thought them dreary company that evening, and that they were much given to silent tears, which were troublesome, cowardly things for which Baker Anderson had never found any use.

XII.

Felix Guthrie rode far and fast that afternoon. The pillage of his herds fired his blood, and his anger lent motive power to his sloth. Many a mile his search led him through the tangled mountain woods, and in devious ways along the craggy ledges, the sun sinking low in the sky, the reeking horse flecked with foam, before the slaughtered beef was at last found, far astray—according to the old herder's report. Long before he reached the spot the circling flight of the strong-winged mountain vultures, high in the air, served to verify the story. Others rose gibbering from their quarry as his panting horse galloped up the slope. He paused to assure himself how plain his brand was marked upon the creature's hide. It had been killed, then, in defiance of the name of Felix Guthrie, and the idea brought the hot blood into his cheek. Killed for spite or for a purpose? And what purpose? The choicest cuts only were taken, and the great carcass left to waste and for the buzzards. He pondered vaguely as he once more put his foot into the stirrup.

"Somebody ez likes ter feed on beef," he muttered his conclusion. "They 'lowed I'd never find it out till the cattle war rounded up in the fall; then think a wolf cotch 'em so fur from home." Sud-

denly the conviction smote him that the larder which
the beef had served could hardly be distant. "They
wouldn't want ter lug the meat fur," he said. He
flung himself into the saddle, riding slowly through
the pathless forest, guided only by the sun in the
sky, the shadows on the ground. He seemed as
native to these deep seclusions as if he had been
bred a savage thing in their midst. And yet he had
never before traversed their intricacies. His adap-
tation to the conditions of these unknown fastnesses
was like a worldling's facile mastery of the ways of
a strange city. He looked about him with the speculative interest of a new-comer. Once, when the
woods gave way upon the crest of a precipice, he rose
in his stirrups to gaze over the jungle of the laurel
and upon the great mountain panorama stretching to
the horizon. Here were landmarks that he recognized, and again features of the landscape all strange
to his experience.

"I never knowed ez folks lived hyarabouts," he
observed, in surprise. "Ef I ain't powerful out'n
my reckoning, Crazy Zebedee's cell mus' be somewhar nigh."

He sighed deeply for the thought as he slowly
took his way once more into the dense dark-green
leafage of the woods; the very sky was shut out, and
the ethereal blue and purple tints of the great mountain masses, that seemed to express the idea of light
almost as definitely as the luminous heavens, were
withdrawn, leaving a sense of loss and monotony,
like the vanishing mirage of a desert. And in the
more heavy glooms of the shadows he sighed again
as if they weighed upon him.

"Zeb hed ruther hev hed this than the jail in town," he muttered, "an' **so he runned away, an'** hid hyarabouts. I dun'no' ef he war **so durned** crazy; the trees air mighty green, an' it air sorter peaceful out'n the sight an' the sound o' folks."

He had a melancholy affinity with sorrow—from so long ago had its fellowship with him dated. He realized, with almost the strength of divination, the sentiments of the fate that the distraught creature had wrought out here. He gazed with a sort of vicarious recognition at the shadows, at the grewsome crags, **at the deep, dark waters of a** pool, where some riving of the **rocks suffered them to** gather lake-like. He wondered, with a morbid alertness **of** fancy, how did the forest look to the hot and fevered brain?—what strange distortions **of** fact metamorphosed these simple and majestic dendritic forms, and the crags, and the waters? It was a severe tension of the sympathetic power of reduplicating anoth**er's** sentiment. He hardly knew what hideous phan**tasy** of speculation had crept into his mind. So far it had swung from its wonted poise that when a sudden, faint, blood-curdling shriek of foolish laughter rang through the utter silence, he did not for an instant credit its reality. He only drew up his horse with a hasty convulsive clutch **upon** the rein, a cold tremor stealing over him, and sat motionless, a terrible superstition quickening his breath and dilating his eye.

Naught stirred. The gloomy primeval magnificence of the forest seemed tenantless. Adown **none** of those green ferny aisles, where the light trembled to intrude, could a willing fancy discern even a flitting dryadic shape, so native to these haunts. A fairy ring was on the grass beneath a tulip-tree. But who did see the dance? Not even the wind might come and go, for the woods would be lonely and were all a-brooding. Far, far less possible than any was the wild, dishevelled, haggard apparition that Felix Guthrie strained his eyes, yet feared, to see. And when the laugh rose again, faint, faint from the depths of the earth, ending in a wild derisive cackle, he became all at once impressed with its genuineness, and the idea of "Crazy Zeb's cell" flashed into his mind again, coupled with the recollection of his injury and the object of his search.

"The very place! Hevin' a reg'lar barbecue off'n my beef, the lazy, shif'less half-livers," he exclaimed, angrily, forgetting his terrors, although his face had not regained its wonted hue.

He was all alert now, erect in the saddle, the reins drawn closely in his hand, keenly peering to the right, and again to the left, as if he had some definite goal in mind. For alien though he was to the place, he had heard it frequently described in those horror-loving tales of the winter-night firesides.

"A gate"—he repeated the oft-spoken words—"a gate of rocks that looks like it mought open on hell; a gate, an' a windin' way walled in, an' a big hollow in the solid cliff ez would be a cave 'ceptin' it air open on one side, high, high above the ruver."

And then the pulsing of the current of a stream made its impression upon his senses. He had not heard it before, so essentially sylvan a sound it was, its monotony so germane to the silence. It was near at hand, this river; and here was the deep pool wherein its hurrying tributary was lulled, and dallied quiescent by the way. He lifted his eyes to two great neighboring crags, each beetling toward the other, the first of a tunnel-like series. A gateway? Could even fancy have wrought these simple forms into the semblance of a portal?—he marvelled with that incredulity which possesses the mind when looking for the first time upon some reputed similitude in nature to an artificial object. Nevertheless, he slowly dismounted, intently gazing all the while, and as he gazed the resemblance grew upon him. So definitely had the idea tutored his fancy that he had not a doubt when he hitched his horse in the dense covert of the laurel, and took his way across the narrowest portion of the stream by means of scrambling cat-like along a pendulous branch of an overhanging tree, and springing lightly from its elastic extremity near to the opposite bank. He waded out, his long boots full of water—a small matter to a hardy woodsman, save that he could hear the splash which thereafter accompanied each step, as his feet were lifted in the roomy integuments, thus preventing a noiseless approach. When he was at last beneath the great jagged gray rocks, with their niches filled here with moss, and again flaunting a tangled vine, he paused and looked up, a smile of iconoclastic ridicule upon his face. So this was what was thought to resemble a gate by the few who knew the place. And then he was minded to imagine how like an infinitely magnified portal it was —so gaunt, so vast, so grim and grewsome, leading down to the dark unknown! "Like the gates o' hell fur true," he muttered, plunging into the gloomy, tunnel-like way.

For one moment after the darkness had enveloped him he fancied he heard a step behind him—a shambling, stumbling step—and the snuffling snort of a frightened horse. He paused in the narrow corridor, and looked back, but the tortuous turnings of the passage obscured the entrance, and the light that it admitted was feeble and far behind. He heard his own breath in a quickly drawn *susurrus;* it echoed sibilantly. He might have counted the throbs of his heart. It was a chilly place, but the surge of excitement warmed his blood, and with another turn he had burst forth from the narrow passage.

For all his expectancy, his preparation for the emergency, he was dazed for a moment as he stood in the open space facing the great western sky. The breadth of this impression left scant room for detail—a charring fire, where only an ember glowed; a recumbent, somnolent figure wrapped in a blanket beside it; two men playing cards on a saddle; a horse's head looking out from a shadowy niche; and a cry of rage as a man who was grooming the creature turned, with the curry-comb in his hand. The sound was like a bugle call to rouse the others. It rang through Guthrie's senses with a menacing clamor. Here was matter far more significant than cattle-stealing; he had tracked home some terrible deed, he knew by the unguarded anger of the startled tones. His logic, such as he had, made itself felt in deeds. Long before the slow processes of his brain had consciously evolved the idea of danger, he had drawn his pistols, and stood, his back against the wall, a weapon in either hand.

It was an attitude that commended a temporizing policy and invited parley. Taken off their guard, the party made an ineffectual effort to secure their arms. The man beside the horse had indeed grasped a rifle that leaned against the wall, but it was an old-fashioned weapon, whose single discharge would exhaust its offensive and defensive capacities, leaving him at a pitiable disadvantage against the six-shooters which the intruder held, and therefore he forbore even to sight it. One of the card-players had struggled up on his knee, his hand behind him grasping his revolver in his pistol pocket. In view of the bead drawn upon him, he did not dare to pull it; he moved not a muscle. The other held nothing more deadly than a "bobtailed flush," which a moment ago he had regarded as the extremest spite of fate. There was something ludicrous in his petrified attitude, as he sat mechanically holding his cards before him, his mind apparently indissolubly associated with the game, his eyes fixed upon Guthrie as if he had been some amazing combination—a "show of hands" altogether uncalled for and beyond all limits of expectation. To none of them was the moment charged with such signal force as to Steve Yates, rising from his affected slumber, for it was only by feigning thus among his merry comrades that he could be alone with his own thoughts. He turned his face, full of astonished anxiety, upon Guthrie, and then he turned it away, suffused with shame, anticipating accusation. It came upon the instant.

"Hyar ye air, Steve Yates! This is whar ye hev disappeared to, hey? I'd do yer wife an' Mose a favior ef I war ter fill up yer carcass with lead. An' ef I hed it ter spare, I'd do it."

Guthrie looked about, expectant of the signs of some illegal occupation—not moonshining, for his judgment and conscience could approve of this defiance of the law, as well as his heart bear it sympathy, but something that outraged the popular sense of right. There was naught, unless those fine-limbed shadowy equine figures might suggest it.

" Hoss-thievin', hey? An' hed ter steal my cattle ter feed ye on beef whilst hid out?"

" Say, now, Fee, war *that* yer cow?" cried Beckett, the man under the insufficient protection of the " bobtailed flush." Perhaps the fact of being a helpless object of pity to his opponents both at cards and at arms quickened his sense of expedients, and lubricated his clumsy tongue. " We-uns didn't know it. Durned ef we don't pay ye fur it," with an air of unctuous sympathy.

" Naw, ye won't," retorted Guthrie—" ye won't, now. I won't tech yer lyin', thievin', black-hearted money !"

A sudden anxiety crossed the face of Derridge, who still stood by the horse's side. " It's jes' ez well ye don't want our money, *fur we ain't got none,*" he said, flashing a significant glance at the card-player, who was still mechanically holding his cards well together, although his opponent's hand lay scattered on the saddle that served as board. " Pete means we'd gin ye a beastis fur the one we tuk. But ef ye don't want her, go lackin'." He sarcastically waved his hand, and the gesture in a measure shielded the other hand as he slyly cocked the rifle. " Steve

Yates hev got inter a sorter difficult with the law, an' axed we-uns ter take him in," continued Derridge, recovering his reasoning faculties from the chaos of his fear and surprise, and adding to them the protean influences of imagination. " We-uns stop by hyar at Crazy Zeb's cell whenst ridin' arter cattle, ter swop lies, an' take a leetle drink, an' play kyerds; leastwise the t'others, not me. Them boys air gettin' ter be tur'ble gamesters, a-bettin' thar money an' gear an' sech, an' wunst in a while hevin' a reg'lar knock-down an' drag-out fight. I ain't s'prised none ef the church folks in the cove hears o' thar goin's on an' turns 'em out; they bein' members in good standing, too; an' I wouldn't blame pa'son an' the deacons an' sech. Naw, sir, I wouldn't."

" Me nuther," said Guthrie, his vigilance relaxed, his credulity coerced. All at once the gathering of the coterie in this sequestered place, that had been so mysterious a moment ago, seemed readily explicable. Jollity, companionship, card-playing, sloth—all combined to attract the mountain loafers, expert to fend off work with any odd dallying with time. He felt the pistol in each hand a cumbrous superfluity. He did not realize why he had drawn them, why he had so quickly assumed the aggressive. He wondered that, interrupted thus in their pacific absorptions, they did not reproach him. It was no longer in suspicion, but with a sort of attempt to justify his precipitancy, that he demanded, " What hev Steve Yates been a-doin' of ter run him off from home an' be searched fur ez dead?"

He had unconsciously moved several paces from the wall; the weapons in his hands were lowered and hung listlessly; the fire-light slanted athwart the place; the monstrous elongated shadows of the men extended across the floor and up the side of the niche; a bee went booming by; the river sang; and the entrance behind him was so noiseless that these trivial sounds he heard, and not Cheever's step.

The leader of the gang wore an excited face as he suddenly came in. It turned pale in the moment. He threw his arm across his eyes with a wild, hoarse cry, while the others stared in amazement, until Bob Millroy, also entering, his superstition always on the alert, was reminded of that strange intruder here revealed once before to Cheever, then visible to none else.

"Thar, now! the extry man!" he cried out, hardly less discomposed.

Guthrie, a trifle shaken by the uncomprehended commotion, reverted to the instinct of self-defence. He perceived, with a flutter of fear and a pang of self-reproach, that his remitted watchfulness had permitted him to be surrounded. They had all drawn their pistols in the interval. He spoke upon his impulse. "Lemme git out'n this!" he growled, half articulately, advancing upon Cheever, intending to push by to the only exit. Cheever, restored by the sight of the revolvers and the sudden recognition of the young mountaineer's face, laid a hand upon Guthrie's shoulder, grinding his teeth, and with a concentrated fury in his eyes.

"So ye hev fund out whar we-uns war, ye peckin', pryin' sneak; *she* tole ye ez Steve war along o' we-uns —the leetle Pettingill she-devil, that frazzle-headed vixen of a Letishy!"

Her name stunned Guthrie in some sort; he stood wide-eyed, quiescent, in amazed dismay, hearing naught of the babel of remonstrance from the others: "Hesh! hesh! he dun'no' nuthin'. **Don't tell him nuthin'!** Let him be—let him be!"

Guthrie realized the situation only when Cheever, whose grip prevented the use of the pistols, cried suddenly, "Take that!" and he heard his flesh tear under the knife, and felt a pain like the pangs of dissolution, as his warm blood gushed forth—"an' that! an' *that!*"

The next moment all the thunders of heaven seemed loosed in the cavern. How he wrenched himself away he could never say. He only knew that he was firing alternately the pistols in both hands, retreating backward through the dark tunnel. He flung himself upon the horse that stood saddled and bridled cropping the grass without, and he was miles away before he realized that the hot pursuit, which he had heard at first in full hue and cry after him, must of necessity be futile, since it was Cheever's incomparable steed that in his haste he bestrode, and not his own.

He felt a certain glow of achievement, a fervor of pride in his prowess; no slight thing it was to have escaped with his life from that desperate gang of outlaws. With a kind of valiant boastfulness he made light of his wounds as his step-mother dressed them, herself the impersonation of a panther whose young is wounded, snarling and fierce and tender. She had a sort of reverential admiration of his courage, his ferocity, that her own savagery had fostered. It was said in the cove that her semblance of kindness and affection for him was the natural outgrowth of her respect for anybody that was a "better man" than she—a pluckier fighter. She, too, would admit no efficacy in aught that Cheever could do.

"I'll be bound them pistol balls o' yourn worked many a button-hole whar thar warn't no buttons in the gyarmints ter match!" she cried, bitterly joying in the possible execution of the shots.

But Ephraim surveyed the yawning slashes with a groan, and went with averted eyes hastily out of the door, and an old house-dog stood beside Felix, and wheezed pitifully and licked his hand with an un-recked-of sympathy.

Felix was out next day, but with that singular parchment-like pallor that ensues on a great loss of blood. Mrs. Guthrie had remonstrated against all exertion, then openly applauded his decision.

"Ef 'twar you-uns, Eph," she said, looking after Felix as he rode Cheever's horse down the winding mountain way, " I mought look for'ard ter three solid weeks a-nussin' ye; ye would be tucked up in bed. But twenty yoke o' oxen couldn't hold Fee Guthrie down; he couldn't even die handy, like other folks. He hev got the very sperit o' livin' in him. Ye mark my words, he ain't a-goin' ter die handy."

And in truth it was a very spirited and gallant fig-ure that the fine, clean-limbed roan carried down into the cove. Guthrie's curling hair flaunted back from his broad shoulders; his wide-brimmed hat was cocked to one side; his spurs jingled on the heels of his great boots. And he sat in the saddle proudly erect, in defiance of the sore-rankling wounds—the knife had not had the mercy to be sharp, and in lieu of clean cuts had **torn** and jagged the flesh.   There was one wound sharper than all, that no **blade had dealt,** that was so keen, so deep, so insidious that it made a coward of him, and set astir a **chill in his blood and** a quiver in his **heart.**

It was one word—Letitia—from lips **that he had never** thought to hear it.   Letitia!   So she knew of Steve Yates's crime; **and more than once he wondered** what it might be, pausing to **look absently** down with unseeing eyes, as his stirrup-irons, sweeping through the blooming **weeds that** bordered the bridle-path, sent the **petals flying.**   Was she a party, too, to the deception the wife maintained, to her pretended **desertion,** her **affected ignorance** of Yates's whereabouts?   " Letishy **oughtn't ter be mixed up in** seeh," Guthrie **said to** himself.   " *She* **oughtn't ter** be abidin' along o' **Mis' Yates,** whose **husband air hid** out with a gang o' evil-doers, purtendin' **ter be dead** an' disappeared.   **Litt** oughtn't **ter** know **about thar** thieveries an' dens.   It can't tech *her*—thar ill-got **gains—but** she oughtn't ter **know** secrets agin the **law."**

He remembered, **with a throb between** anger and pain, the evenings that he had spent at the Yates cabin, the air of desolate sorrow that the deserted wife maintained, **even when she seemed to seek to cast it** off, and to respond **to neighborly kindness.   A flush** mounted to his pallid **cheek, he so resented** a deceit sought to be practised **upon him.   And** how ready a gull he must have seemed, he **thought, with a** sneer at the memory **of** his cumbrous phrases **of** hope and consolation, **at** which Letitia had not scrupled to laugh.   " *She* warn't **puttin' on no** lackadaisical pretence," he thought, with a glowing eye. "She hev got the truth in her too deep. She jes' busied herse'f a-spinnin' ez gay ez a bird, an' tole them queer tales ez Mr. Shattuck hev gin out, 'bout cave-dwellers long time ago, an' sun-worshippers, an' a kentry sunk in the sea, named Atlantis or sech outlandish word; tole 'em over agin nearly every evenin'. An' I could listen through eternity! She hev got sech smartness an' mem'ry. I dun'no' how she *do* make out ter remember sech a lot o' stuff. An' Mis' Yates—a deceitful sinner that woman air!—a-bustin' out cryin' agin, fust thing ye know. Litt oughtn't ter 'sociate with sech ez knows secrets agin the law."

XIII.

With all this in his mind, **the little house, coming** in sight below the massive dark-green slope of **the** great mountain, seemed to Guthrie **to hold peculiar** significance. With a poignant sentiment **which he** might not analyze, he watched it grow from a mere speck **into its** normal proportions. The sun flashed from **its** roof, still **wet with the dew, but the shadows** were sombrely green in **the yard.** Such **freshness** the great oaks breathed, such **fragrance the pines!** Adown the lane the cows **loitered, going forth to ¯** their pastures. He saw a **mist,** dully white, **move in** slow convolutions along a distant purple slope, pause **for** a glistening moment, **then** vanish into thin **air.** Away up the gorge **all** diurnal fancies trooped into the wide liberties of **endless luminous vistas of azure** sunlit mountains beneath **the shining azure heavens,** the ranges and valleys changing **with every mood of** the atmosphere, **with** the harlequinade **of the clouds** and the wind. **The river,** with **all the graces of re-** flection, presented **a kaleidoscopic comminglement of** color—it showed **the grim gray rocks, the blue sky,** the glow of the **rose-red** azalea, the many gradations of tint in the overhanging foliage and in the umber and **ochre** of the soil of the steep banks. The ponderous cataract fell ceaselessly with its keen, swift, green rush above and its maddening white swirl

below. On the bank the pygmy burying-ground
seemed by contrast the fullest expression of quiet,
with its deep shadows and its restful sheen, and naught
to come and go but a booming bee or a bird upspringing from the long grass.

All was imprinted upon his consciousness with a
distinctness which he had never before known, which
he did not seek to interrogate now. It seemed to
partake of the significance of a crisis in his life, and
every trifle asserted itself and laid hold upon him.

Letitia was sitting upon the porch in a low rocking-
chair. He recognized her from far away; but when
he had hitched the horse at the gate and came walking slowly up the path, and she lifted her eyes to
meet his grave, fixed look, there was something in
them that he thought he had never before seen—infinitely beautiful, indescribable ; a mere matter of expression, perhaps, for the luminous quality and the
fine color of the deep-blue iris were as familiar even
to his dreams as to his waking sense. It seemed a
something added ; it served, in some sort, to embel-
lish the very curve of her cheek, the curl of her delicate lip, the waving of her hair where it was gathered
out of the way at the nape of her white neck.

He had known that her beauty was generally held
in scant esteem, and he had vaguely wondered to
find himself in contradictory conviction to the popular sentiment. He had welcomed Shattuck's protes-
tation of its charm as a trophy of its high deserts.
He remembered this now. "Shattuck 'lowed she
war plumb beautiful, an' hed a rare face ; an' she
hev ! she hev ! Thar's nobody looks like her."

More than the usual interval of survey warranted

by the etiquette of salutation passed as he stood by the step of the porch, and gazed at her with absorbed, questioning eyes.   Her light, caustic laughter roused him.

" What ails ye ter kem hyar with the manners o' a harnt, Fee Guthrie ; not speakin' till ye air spoke ter ; stare-gazin' "—she opened her eyes wide with the exaggeration of mimicry—" ez ef me an' Moses war some unaccountable animals ez ye hed kem ter trap ?"

Then, with a smile that seemed to have all the freshness of the matutinal hour in it, she bent again to her work of hackling flax.   No arduous job was she making of it.   The hackle was placed upon the low shelf-like balustrade close by, and as the swaying of the rocking-chair brought her forward she would sweep the mass of flax in her hands across its sharp wires, drawing all the fibres through as she swung back again.   She had hardly more industrial an aspect than a thrush poised on a blooming honey-suckle vine that ran over the porch, idly rocking in the wind, with not even a trill in his throat to attest his vocation as musician.   A bundle of the flax lay in a chair at her side, and another in her lap ; and as she swayed back and forth some of the fine, silvery white stuff slipped down over her light blue dress and on the floor in the reach of Moses.   He was beginning to appreciate the value of occupation, and could not all day quiescently resign himself to the passive development of teeth.   He had attained the age when the imitative faculties assert themselves.   He had furnished himself with a wisp of flax from the floor, and now and again bent his fat body forward, swaying the wisp to and fro in his hand, after the manner in which Letitia passed the flax over the hackle, then sought to stuff it into his mouth—with him a test of all manner of values. Somehow the meeting of his callow, unmeaning, casual glance, for he was very busy and ignored the new-comer, disconcerted Guthrie. So forlorn was he, and little!— his future was an unwritten page, and what bitter history might it not contain! And those who were nearest to him were framing the words and fashioning the periods. But it was to be his to read! A heavy intimation of its collocations was given by the recollection of his father yesterday in the horse-thief's gang—and Stephen Yates once had an honest name, and came of honest stock! Then Guthrie thought of the deceitful mother, and he sat down on the step with a sigh.

"Mought ez well! mought ez well!" he said, lugubriously, unconsciously speaking aloud, as Letitia adjured Moses not to swallow the flax and choke himself.

"He *hedn't* 'mought ez well,'" she retorted, tartly. Then, for the infant's benefit, "I reckon, though, I could get hold o' the eend of it in his throat, but Mose would feel mighty bad when I h'isted him up on my spinnin'-wheel an' tuck ter spinnin' him all up!"

The great Dagon, not altogether comprehending this threat, listened with an attentive bald head upturned, a damp and open mouth, his two bare feet stretched out motionless, one above the other, and his *décolleté* red calico dress quite off one stalwart shoulder. But with a gurgle and a bounce he let it pass, with only his usual sharp-tempered squeal of rebuke, and then placidly addressed himself anew to discover what gustatory qualities lurked in the unpromising, unsucculent wisp of flax.

"Mose an' me air keepin' house," observed Letitia. "Mis' Yates air a-dryin' apples down yander by the spring."

Guthrie's glance discovered the mottled calico dress and purple sun-bonnet of Adelaide at some distance down the slope, as she spread the fruit upon a series of planks laid in the sun.

"It air jes' ez well," he said, gloomily. "I dun'no' ez I keer ter see her ter-day."

Letitia, as she swayed forward and flung the flax across the wires, cast a surprised glance upon him. "Ye air toler'ble perlite fur so soon in the mornin'— I notice ginerally ez perliteness grows on ye ez the day goes on—cornsiderin' ye air a-settin' on *her* door-step, an' this air *her* house."

"I want ter see jes' you-uns," he indirectly defended himself. He took off his hat, the wind tossing his curling hair as he leaned backward against the post of the porch; he started to speak again, then hesitated uncertainly.

If she noticed that he had lost his wonted slow composure, the discovery did not affect her. She still swung back and forth in her rocking-chair, as nonchalantly as the thrush swayed on the vibrating bough.

"Letishy," he said at last, "I wisht ye wouldn't 'bide hyar."

Her eyes widened. "Perliteness *do* grow on ye," she exclaimed. "Whar air ye 'lowin' I hed better 'bide?"

The opportunity was not propitious. Nevertheless he seized it. "I wish ye'd marry me an' 'bide up on the mounting at my house," he said, breathlessly.

The color flared in her face, but she still rocked to and fro, and with her casual indolent gesture hackled the flax. "Mus' be so pleasant 'long o' Mis' Guthrie," she said.

She had adopted as response the first suggestion that came, only to escape from the confusion that beset her; but as a painful flush dyed his face, she rocked a trifle less buoyantly back and forth, and looked keenly though covertly at him, when he rejoined, quietly:

"I be powerful mistaken in you-uns ef ye would gredge a shelter ter a 'oman ez be old, an' frien'less, an' pore, an' not kind, an' hev earned nuthin' but hate in a long life—ye, young, an' pritty, an' good, an' respected by all!"

She paused in her rocking. She looked steadily, motionlessly at him. "Would ye turn her out ef I did?" she asked, in a tone of stipulation.

He hesitated; then, "Naw, by God, I *wouldn't!*" he declared.

There was a momentary silence. A smile crept to the delicate curves of her lips and vivified with its light the sapphire of her eyes. "Fee Guthrie," she exclaimed, "I never looked ter have cause ter think so well o' ye!"

He gazed at her a trifle bewildered. "An' ye will marry me? Litt, ye know how much I think o' ye; 'pears like I can't tell how much I love ye."

She had thrown herself into her former nonchalant attitude, and was swaying back and forth in the rocking-chair, and gayly hackling the flax. She shook her head, smiling at him.

In his heartache, the pang of disappointment, the demolition of all his cherished hopes—and how strong they had been, albeit he had accounted them slight, had named them despair! with what throes they died! —he felt as some drowning wretch that sees a swift, unheeding bark sail past his agony.

" Account of her?" he gasped.

Once more she smilingly shook her head.

" Some other man?" his face had grown sterner ; its hard lines were reasserted.

The telltale color flared in her cheeks; he saw again, rising with the thought of that " other man," the look in her eyes which made them trebly beautiful. It was in vain that she shook her head, and carelessly flaunted the flax as she swayed back and forth.

His eyes were full of fire; his breath was quick; the fever of angry hate was in his pulses. "'Twon't be the *fust* time ye hev throwed me over fur Rhodes," he said between his teeth, the instinct to identify his rival strong within him.

She laughed aloud with such ready scorn that credulity failed him.

" Then *who kin* it be?" he demanded, expectantly.

She paused once more, gravity on her face, the shining fibrous flax motionless in her hand. " I'll tell ye—I'll tell ye, ef ye promise never ter tell."

He was dumfounded for an instant. Surely a lover never received a confidence like this!

" I dun'no' ez I want ter know till I be obligated ter find out," he said, gruffly.

" What did ye ax fur, then?" she retorted.

In his state of feeling he had scant regard for logic. It was only for the space of a moment that he sat silent, then asked, " Who, then, Litt—*who* is the man ?"

She looked down upon him with a sort of solemnity that induced a forlornly eager, palpitating expectancy, as he looked up wincing and waiting to hear.

" *Baker Anderson !*" She pronounced the words soberly. Then, with a peal of laughter, she flung herself back in the rocking-chair, swinging backward with a precipitancy that startled the idle thrush, still preening his morning wing on the honeysuckle vine, and sent him flashing through the sunshine like a silver arrow to the woods.

Guthrie stared stolidly at her for a time, hardly knowing his mind between anger and surprise. Then his stern features gradually relaxed. There was something in her merry subterfuge that savored of coquetry. The terrible vitality of his starveling hope roused itself upon the intimation. His long sigh was a breath of relief. Perhaps he should not have expected a direct response in his favor. " Wimmin 'pear ter set store on all sort'n roundabout ways ; I reckon I'll hev ter try a haffen dozen." This was his unspoken deduction. He only said, cumbrously seeking to adopt her lightsome vein, "I be powerful 'flicted ter hear it be Baker ez air the favored ch'ice. I dun'no' how I'll ever make out ter stan' up agin Baker."

And he slowly laughed again. He could hardly have expressed how much the incongruity of the idea comforted him. He was looking about with the relief that ensues upon a grave and poignant crisis happily overpast. He saw, with a sort of indiscriminating satisfaction, the dew so coolly glittering on the long grass ; in the deep green shadow of the trees the white elder blossoms gleamed. The wind came straight from the mountains, so full of strength and freshness and perfume, it seemed like the very breath of life. So often a wing cleft the blue sky, and all the nestlings were abroad ! He noted a dozen yards down a dank path a stubby, ruffled scion of a mocking-bird, standing in infantine disaffection to the prospect of locomotion, and watching with unambitious eyes the graceful example of the paternal flight, as the parent aeronaut darted across short distances from honeysuckle to glowing cabbage-rose, and called forth encouragement in clearest clarion tones, and sought to stimulate emulation—fated, like some disappointed worldly fathers, to hear only a whining vibrant declination of the mere attempt at progression from the sulky brat in the path. Guthrie, his mind once more receptive to details, observed for the first time that the little party on the porch had been joined by the old dog, who so valued the society of Moses, and who sat beside him as the infant capably went through all the motions of hackling flax ; the canine friend followed with alert turns of the head and puzzled knitted brow the wavings of the short fat arm, and kept time the while with an approving wagging tail.

"Thinks mo' of him now than Steve do," Guthrie reflected, for the very sight of Moses's bald head was pathetic in his eyes. Then his mind reverted to his own anxiety because of Letitia. "Litt," he said, and there was a sort of peremptory proprietary vibration in the tone, "I don't want ye ter 'bide hyar no longer. I want ye ter go home."

She paused, the flax motionless in her hand. A resolute light was in her eyes. She gave a decisive nod. "Mis' Yates ain't a-goin' ter shoot off that rifle at nobody agin," she said, unexpectedly. "*I* be goin' ter company that rifle closer'n a brother."

For a moment Guthrie was a trifle bewildered—the story of the mysterious shots fired at the party in the pygmy burial-ground, the slain colt, Mrs. Yates's futile denials, all detailed by Ephraim, had been superseded in interest by his own adventures and the theories that he had deduced from them. "Waal," he said at last—formally taking her standpoint into account—"that ain't nuthin' ter you-uns; ye can't guide Mis' Yates's actions. It jes' shows another reason why ye oughter be at home. Mis' Yates s'prises me; she ain't the 'oman I took her fur; but ef she kills Mr. Shattuck fur her foolish notions 'bout opening the graves o' the Leetle People, *she'll* hev ter answer ter the law. 'Tain't nuthin' ter *you-uns.*"

He was not looking at her; he had plucked a blade of the sweet-flag that grew by the step, casually tearing its delicate stripes of white and green, all unnoting that her face had turned a pallid, grayish hue; that she sat as still as if petrified, her eyes dilated, and fixed with a sort of fascinated terror upon some frightful mental picture.

"Mis' Yates s'prises me," Guthrie resumed. "Eph says she 'lows ez her husband lef' her 'kase she swore she would fire that very rifle at Shattuck ef he opened a 'pygmy' grave, ez he calls it. I'll be bound, though, Steve didn't leave fur sech ez that.   I ain't got nuthin' agin the Leetle People," he stipulated, with a quick after-thought.   "I know no harm of 'em, an' I respec' 'em, though dead an' leetle.   I wouldn't 'low nobody ter kerry thar bones off'n my lan,' not even Mr. Shattuck, though I'd do mo' fur *him* 'n ennybody else—he hev got sech a takin' way with him!   I tole him he mought hev one o' thar pitchers ez air buried with 'em, an' I'd gin the leetle pusson one o' my pitchers out'n the house.   I reckon 'twould be ez good ez his'n."   He paused, meditating on the ethics of this exchange.   "But I war glad when Shattuck 'lowed he hankered fur no pitcher, but jes' wanted ter take a look at thar jugs an' ornamints an' sech, fur the knowledge o' the *hist'ry o' the kentry.*"   He repeated these last words with a sort of solid insistent emphasis, as charged with impressiveness and importance, for the whole enterprise was repugnant to him, and he sought to justify it to himself by urging its utility, a magnified idea of which he had gleaned from Shattuck's talk.   He had torn the blade of sweet-flag into shreds, and now he cast the fragments from him.   "But it jes' shows ez Mis' Yates ain't a fit 'oman fur ye ter be with, firin' rifles an' sech, an' knowin' the hiding-place o' evildoers, purtendin' all the time ter be so desolated an' deserted.   Litt, air it jes' lately ye knowed whar Steve war, or did ye know it 'fore ye kem hyar ter keep her comp'ny?"   Then, as she sat stonily gazing at him, he added, "Did ye know it them evenin's ez I kem a-visitin' down hyar?"

She spoke slowly, with a measureless wonderment on her face.   "Air ye bereft, Felix Guthrie? I
  18

dun'no' whar Steve Yates air, an' Adelaide don't nuther."

It was hard to shake his confidence in her. Perhaps no words might have served—least of all any that Cheever could speak—save those accompanied by the savage, deep strokes of a bowie-knife aiming for his heart. The frank sincerities of the steel were coercive ; it had been thus that her name had been cut into his very flesh, a slash for each syllable. They all ached in unison with the recollection.

"Ye air foolin' me," he said, reproachfully. But even then he sought to adduce a worthy motive. "Ye air doin' it fur the sake o' yer frien's, Litt. But ye can't mend thar mean, preverted natur'. Ye oughter go home ; home is the place fur gals."

To an overbearing man, unfurnished with the authority of kindred, and restrained by even primitive etiquette from aught more coercive than advice, there was something painfully baffling in the headstrong impunity with which she cried, gayly, as she set her chair to rocking once more, " The angel Gabriel with his trumpet mought wake the dead an' 'tice 'em from the grave, but he couldn't say nuthin' ez would summons me from this spot."

So small, so feminine, and yet so easily and amply victorious !—it was hardly in his imperative nature to submit gracefully to so inconsiderable an adversary. "An' thar's daddy Pettingill," he cried, angrily, "a-quar'lin' 'kase his craps hev got too much rain, or too leetle, an' stare-gazin' the clouds, so sulky an' impident, I wonder the lightnin' don't strike him fur his sass. An' thar's mammy Pettingill makin' quince preserves, an' callin' all the created worl' ter see how cl'ar they be.   An' thar's that fool, Josh Pettingill, mus' take this junetry ter marry Malviny Gossam, an' go off ter live, an' leave *nobody* ter take keer of his own *sister.*   An' ye air lef' hyar ter 'company a 'oman ez fires off rifles at peaceful passers, an' ter know the secrets o' whar Steve Yates an' Buck Cheever be hid out.   Ef ye war *my* darter "—severely paternal—" I would put ye right now up on that horse ahint o' me, an' ride off *home* with ye; an' *darned* ef I hain't got a good mind ter tote ye back ter them absent-minded Pettingills ennyhow!"

There was no absolute intention in his words, but he had risen as he spoke, and she cowered a little; there was something in his proportions that constrained respect, and her spirit of defiance was abated somewhat.

" Fee," she said, seeking to effect a diversion, " what makes ye 'low ez Adelaide an' me know whar Steve Yates be hid out ?"

" 'Kase yestiddy whenst I run agin a gang o' fellers, hid out—I reckon they air arter some mischief —an' Steve war 'mongst 'em, Buck Cheever 'lowed ez 'twar you-uns ez told me.   They air workin' agin the law, I *know.*"

She did not at once remember the hasty chance shot—the keen divination—in the mock message she had sent to Steve Yates by Cheever; but the expression on the horse-thief's face came back to her presently, as if it had been held indissolubly in her mind for future recall.   Evidently Cheever had believed that in some incomprehensible way she had possessed herself of the knowledge, and spoke from its fulness.

She sat still, absently gazing at the flax.   "An' ye 'lowed I knowed sech ez that, an' be in league with folks ez work agin the law—thievin' or sech—an' yit ye kem down hyar an' ax me ter marry ye ?"

" 'Kase I be dead sure, Litt, ez ye wouldn't do no harm *knowin'* *it*," he replied, precipitately.   " I wish I hed faith in Heaven like I hev in you-uns.   I war jes' feared Mis' Yates an' them war foolin' ye 'bout'n it, an' hed tangled ye up in suthin' ez ye didn't onderstand the rights of."   He looked down eagerly at her, but her face was inscrutable.

" I ain't so easily fooled," she observed, succinctly.

He glanced about him, evidently on the eve of reluctant departure, but still lingering.   The infantile mocking-bird at intervals piped his strident vibrant "C-a-a-ant ! c-a-a-ant ! c-a-a-ant !"   The parent bird's keen, clear call rang out, so full of meaning that it seemed strange that it should be inarticulate, and ever and anon his white wing feathers, as he whirled in the air, shone dazzlingly in the sunshine.   Moses continued to experiment with the possibilities of flax for food, sometimes constrained to sputter by his misdirected ardor.   Guthrie would fain prolong the pleasant peaceful time.

" I mus' be a-joggin'," he said, however.   " I feel powerful foolish ridin' another man's horse.   An' I be a-goin' ter turn him over ter the constable o' the deestric', an' tell how I got him by accident, so flustered by the fight."

For the first time she recognized Cheever's horse at the gate.

" War thar a fight ?" she said.

He nodded.

"*Ye* didn't take a hand in it? Waal, I be s'prised
—*ye*, ez hev sot out ter be a saint o' the Lord!"

"That don't make no diff'unce," he said, hastily
defending his piety. "The reason thar ain't no mo'
fightin' 'mongst the saints an' disciples the Bible tells
about air 'kase thar warn't no fire-arms in them days;
I hev hearn pa'son say thar warn't none. An' that's
why peace war so preached up then, fur mighty few
men like ter kem ter close quarters with a knife."

His own wounds ached anew with the suggestion,
but with a savage pride in his prowess he said naught
of them; he would not have admitted their existence
to the man who had dealt them; Cheever might take
only what testimony he could from the blood on his
knife.

She was looking at him with that admiration, so
essentially feminine, of his valor, his ready hand, his
fierce spirit. "So ye j'ined in?" she said, smiling.

"Ef firin' a dozen pistol-shots be j'inin' in," he
replied, his eye alight at the recollection.

She changed color. "War ennybody hurt?" she
quavered.

"Listen at the female 'oman!" he exclaimed, in
exasperation, because of the contradictions of sentiment she presented. "Fairly dotes on the idee o'
other folks a-fightin',' an' yit can't abide the notion
o' nobody gittin' hurt! The Guthries hev the name
o' shootin' straight, Litt Pettingill, an' I'd be powerful 'shamed ef in twelve shots I done no damage.
'Tain't been my policy nor my practice ter waste lead
an' powder."

He stood leaning against the post, vainly specu-
lating concerning the probable execution of his re-

volvers when he had escaped, firing them with both hands. It was for a moment with absent, unseeing eyes that he mechanically regarded her, but the image that had so great a fascination for him presently broke through the absorptions of his retrospect, and asserted itself anew—so dainty, so blithe, so bird-like, so lightly swaying as she sat in the rocking-chair.

Her association with these incongruous elements of suspected fraud, and ill-favored deeds, and unfitting companions seemed a profanity, and his eager wish to have her removed far from them, shielded, inaccessible, was renewed.

"Mr. Shattuck hain't got no need o' you-uns, Litt, ter pertect him," he urged, suddenly. "He'd laff at the idee, ef he warn't ashamed of it; ennybody o' yer size an' sex a-settin' out ter pertect a able-bodied man from rifle-balls."

He looked down at her with a laugh of ridicule and a sneering eye, calculated to put out of countenance her valorous intention.

She said nothing; but determination, immobility, could hardly have had more adequate expression than in her face, her soft and delicate lips closed fast, her eyes bright and fearless.

"But shucks!"—he sought to make light of it— "Shattuck ain't a-goin' ter kem agin ter the Leetle People's buryin'-groun'—leastwise not when Mis' Yates be out an' stirrin'." A dim prospect of organizing a nocturnal expedition for Shattuck's assistance was shaping itself in his mind. "She can't be on watch night and day."

Letitia looked up, her interest in all that interested

Shattuck shining in her eyes. "That's the very word what *I* told him," she said. "He'd better kem an' dig at night, whenst the moon shines, like he done afore."

A sudden angry pain thrilled through Guthrie. It was only yesterday that Shattuck had received his permission to make these investigations upon his land; had sought it with deepening deference and solicitude, as if it were essential. And when at last it had been granted, it was in disregard of previous refusals, in despite of his repugnance, and his primitive sense of sacrilege. Thus he had been overborne by the facile influence of this suave stranger, with his ready smile and his pleasant eyes, and his frank off-hand speech. It must have been that to work freely and openly in broad daylight had become a necessary condition of Shattuck's success, for evidently he had been here before—when the moon shone!

Whether it were because of some inward monition, which by an unconscious process served Guthrie's interest, or some latent, undeveloped suspicion astir in his mind, he gave no intimation of his thought; he held himself plastic to the discovery which he felt imminent in the air. He could not, however, meet her eyes; as he sought an alternative, perhaps it was as happy an idea as any that could have come at a more propitious and reflective moment to draw out one of the pistols that he wore in his belt and turn it in his hand; he had an incidental preoccupied air as he glanced successively into the empty chambers.

"Did he find ennything *then*, d'ye know, Litt?"

"I dun'no'. I ain't seen him sence till las' night," she replied, unsuspiciously.

He had snapped the barrel in place and silently sighted the pistol at a flying bird, as if he had in view some experiment of marksmanship. Moses had ceased his femininely domestic labors, with the wisp of flax hanging motionless in his limp hand. Here was matter more to his mind, attesting his inherent masculine taste; he winked very hard at every sharp clash of the steel, but bent forward with wide up-lifted eyes, a tremulous, absorbed, open mouth, and watched the big man's attitude as he held up the weapon to a line with his eye, his whole massive fig-ure, from the great slouch hat to his jingling spurs, clearly imposed upon the fair morning sky.

A pointer, who had been asleep under the house, had rushed out upon recognizing the click of the cocking of a weapon, and stood in tremulous, wheez-ing agitation, now scanning the prospect for the threatened game and eagerly snuffling the air, now glancing up, surprised at the abnormal inactivity of this presentment of the genus sportsman.

"What makes ye 'low 'twar Shattuck, Litt?" Guthrie observed in the tone of a casual gossip.

There was a touch of rose in her cheek. "Waal, I warn't sartain a-fust. I 'lowed it *couldn't* be. Till toler'ble late, arter the moon hed riz, I hearn a pick-axe strikin' on rock up in the pygmy buryin'-ground" (he noticed that she had discarded the colloquial "Leetle People" for Shattuck's more scientific term), "an' then I knowed it couldn't be nobody but him. I didn't say nothin' 'bout'n it afore, 'kase I didn't know till las' night ez he hed got yer say-so ez he

"HE HAD SNAPPED THE BARREL IN PLACE."

mought dig on yer land." She looked up with an
unsuspicious smile; then, with the glow of mirth in
her eyes, she burst suddenly into a peal of laughter.
"Baker Anderson would hev it ez 'twar *you-uns* ez
'peared suddint at the winder whilst I war a-singin'
a song.   I wisht ye could hev seen Baker offerin' ter
take down his rifle an' go arter ye fur hevin' gin me
an' Mis' Yates sech a skeer.   Ye could run Baker
with yer ramrod !   Baker 'lows yit ez 'twar you-uns.
We-uns couldn't make out the man's face clear ; jes'
seen it fur a minit ez he looked through the winder.
But ez soon ez I hearn that pick strike on the rock,
I guessed mighty easy who hed been hangin' roun'
the porch listenin' ter the singin', waitin' fur the
moon ter rise."

A miracle could not have more stringently coerced
his credulity ; and, in truth, the circumstances wore
all the sleek probability of fact.   No man familiar-
ized by song and story since the Middle Ages with
the idea of the cavalier lingering without the castle
walls to hear a lady's lute could have more definitely
grasped its significance than did this primitive lover.
It lent a strong coherence to every word that Shattuck had uttered ; the praises of her beauty, to which
he had hearkened with such simple joy ; of her mind,
of her unique grace, so at variance with the uncouth
conditions of her life.   And what new light was
thrown upon her strangely retentive memory hoard-
ing Shattuck's words ; her eager determined vigilance
in his behalf, from which the trump that might summon the dead from their graves would be futile to
lure her ; that radiant freshened beauty in her sapphire eyes !   " Religion itself couldn't make her look

more like an angel in the eyes!" Guthrie had said to himself, with a lover's alert and receptive recognition of an embellished loveliness. And Shattuck had come, in good sooth, to listen and linger without to hear her sing while he waited for the moon to rise.

He remembered, with an angry quickening of his pulse, his own simple-minded confidences to Shattuck yesterday in the barley fields. What! in his unsuspicious folly he had even told the man how she talked of him, how she treasured his words, how she valued his great learning, for thus she was minded to regard those acquisitions which the more staid and experienced people of the country-side esteemed crack-brained fantasies. And somehow this reflection operated as a check upon the bounding fury that possessed him; it held an element of self-reproach. He had unwittingly revealed to this stranger the sentiment which Letitia would have guarded as a sacred secret—if, indeed, she herself were aware of it. His face was set and hard; but the strong hand trembled that held the pistol, silent and empty and harmless enough now, albeit so recently flinging out its fate-freighted balls and its wild barbaric shriek.

"She never war gin ter 'settin' caps' arter folks, like other gals; she sorter sets store on herse'f 'kase the common run o' boys didn't like her. She feels too ch'ice fur enny or'nary cuss; an' I reckon she'd be hoppin' mad—" And then he paused with the conviction that she did not esteem Shattuck an "or'nary cuss." This revelation would probably only result in facilitating an understanding between them. "Ef he ever sees her agin," he said, between his set teeth. There recurred to him suddenly his words yesterday, amongst the waving barley—that he had it in his heart to kill any man who came between him and Letitia. He had spoken them with other intentions, with the thought of Rhodes in his mind; but Shattuck was warned, already warned. And if he had spoken too freely, it was at least not equivocally. "Ef ever he sees her agin," he once more muttered.

"What air you-uns sayin'?" she demanded, suddenly, all unsuspicious of his train of thought. "Mose kin converse ez well ez that. The only trouble with Mose's talk is that grown folks air too foolish ter onderstan' it. Ain't it, Mose?"

But the child gave her no heed, still fixing his upturned gaze on the pistol in Guthrie's hand, as eager of expression as the uplifted muzzle of the dog, who writhed and wagged his tail, and wheezed about the great boots.

Guthrie looked down at Letitia, his eyes changed and strange, and little to be understood. She paused as her own encountered them, holding the wisp of flax motionless in her hand, vaguely and superficially aware that a crisis had supervened, albeit beyond her ken.

"I mus' be a-goin'," he said, absently, still looking at her, his eyes freighted with his unread thoughts.

Their dull solemnity grated upon her mood, so far afield was it from any standpoint yet revealed in his words. She resented his motionless, intent, pondering survey.

She sought to shake off the responsive gravity his mien induced. "Goin'!" she cried, her eyes growing brighter and deeper and darker as they dilated. "Waal, we'll hev ter try ter spare ye. Waal! waal!" with an affected sigh.

The familiar note of irony seemed to rouse him to more immediate intention. He thrust his pistol in his belt, and with a nod turned away down the path.

Moses, who could never be prevailed upon to greet a visitor, always took welcome heed of departure. To his mind the dearest behest of hospitality was speeding the parting guest. Without prompting, he sent a jubilant cry of "Bye! bye!" after Guthrie's retreating form, and beamed upon him with a damp and gummy sputtering smile, graced by all his glittering teeth.

Letitia, too, gazed after the guest, whose manner had suddenly presented an enigma. "Looked all of a suddint ez ef he hed fund suthin' he didn't want, like a rattlesnake; or hed furgot suthin' he couldn't do without, like his breakfast, or a thimble, or his brains."

He went slowly and thoughtfully along the dank path, over which the heavy long-tasselled grasses leaned. Pinks bordered it here, and anon the jimson weed; again it was enlivened by the glow of a great red rose, with the essence of summer in its fresh breath, as it swayed on a long, full-leaved, thorny wand. This clutched at his coat, and as he paused to disengage the cloth, he looked back at the house —the mountain looming behind it, with a horizontal band of mist athwart the slope; the little roof still dank and shining with dew; the tiny porch all wreathed with vines that stretched a surplusage of their blooming lengths across to the window; the little glassless square where the batten shutter swung. Here it was, he thought, that Shattuck had stood, knee-deep in the lush thick grass, when the shutter was closed, and colors were null, and the black night gloomed, and she sang within while he waited, and the moon rose all too soon ! He turned and looked at the gorge, as if he expected to see there the pearly disk amidst the dark obscurements of the night-shadowed mountains. It was instead a vista of many gleaming lights : the sunshine on the river, and the differing lustre of the water in the shadow ; the fine crystalline green of the cataract, and the dazzling white of the foam and the spray ; the luminous azure of the far-away peaks, and the enamelled glister of the blue sky—all showing between the gloomy, sombre ranges close at hand. And while he still looked, he mounted the horse at the gate and rode away.

XIV.

It was a fine sensation for the group of gossips
that always seemed an essential appurtenance to the
blacksmith shop at the cross-roads when, this bright
morning, the sheriff of the county, an infrequent and
unfamiliar apparition, rode up to the open doors, and
drew rein under the branches of the overhanging oak-
tree. So broadly spreading were these branches that
not even the diminishing shadow, ever waning as the
day waxed on to noon, had bereft the space beneath
of its gray-green gloom and its sense of dew. A
wagon, one wheel lying tire-less on the ground, and
a stout stave lashed crutch-like in its place, stood
near by in the full yellow glare, with a reduced car-
toon of itself, sadly out of drawing, on the sand beneath it, supplemented by a caricature of two men
who sat upon its pole. The interior of the shop
looked dark and cool, and the blacksmith's father,
bareheaded and in his shirt-sleeves in a rickety chair
by the door, caught the softening effect of its twilight in his aged and minutely wrinkled face. Two
or three dim figures were indistinct within ; upon a
bench outside a couple of loafers smoked, while still
another utilized as a seat the roots of the tree. The
shadow of its foliage played on the clapboards of the
roof, long ago broken here and there, and still un-
mended, for the rain and the snow were welcome to

wreak their worst, drizzling through upon the republican simplicity of the "dirt floor" within.   Hardly
a curl of smoke ascended from the chimney, and as
the officer cast his eye along the two red clay winding roads, both of a most irresponsible and vagrant-
like aspect, as if they had no goal in expectation,
there was no other sign of habitation in sight; the
woods closed in, limiting the prospect; here and
there mountains rose, seeming, as always, nearer
than reality warrants; and it was a most sequestered,
slumberous spot to which the sheriff had betaken his
brisk individuality and the energetic potentiality of
his official presence.

So welcome a break in the monotony had not occurred for many a day.   A sentiment of gratitude
merely for his company pervaded the by-standers.
They looked for no developments more striking than
the detail of the ordinary news from the town, some
good-natured raillery back and forth, and the intimation of his errand, which perchance might touch
the summoning of jurors or witnesses in some of
the more remote districts of his bailiwick; and each
idler was devoutly glad that the allurements of
plough and harrow and hoe had not availed to keep
him at work and at home on this momentous occasion, which might not be duplicated for months.
But when the officer's hard face and unsmiling eyes
betokened the more serious import of his visit, there
ran through the assembly a keen thrill of curiosity
and expectancy.

The sheriff, not perhaps all indifferent to the
flutter his advent roused, flung the reins over his
horse's head and dismounted.

"News?" He echoed the question that had been coupled with the salutation, and glanced loweringly about. "News enough. *Murder!*"

He spoke the word with a melodramatic unction, dropping his voice. He was a tall, well-built man, of a large frame, implying bone and muscle rather than fat, and promising most stalwart possibilities; and if the somewhat imposing strut, which was his favorite method of locomotion, savored of pride, it also invited attention to the many reasons which had justified him in indulging that sentiment. He turned with the blacksmith to the eager examination of the hoof of his horse which had cast a shoe, and was going a trifle lame. As the smith, this colloquy over, set about repairing the disaster, the officer, taking off his hat, lent himself with an air of consideration to heed the clamorous inquiries.

"It's a tough job, an' I ain't s'prised if I have you all on a posse 'fore night." He shook his head with serious intimations as he seated himself on an empty inverted barrel just outside the door. "Ye, Phineas!" he broke off, admonishing the smith, who had paused in paring the horse's hoof, which he held between his knees upon his leather apron, his stooping posture unchanged, his bushy eyebrows lifted as he looked up from under them in expectant curiosity at the officer. "*Ye* jes' *perceed* with yer rat-killin'. I'm in a hurry ter git away from hyar! An' I'm a-goin' ter ketch them buzzardy rascals, ef I hev ter go ter Texas." He nodded with the word as if he expressed the limits of the known globe.

"I'll be bound ye do, sher'ff!" cried the blacksmith's father, with an eagerness to bring himself to the great man's notice and impress his own importance—a characteristic of local magnates other than rural. He had seized upon the first opportunity, and thus the matter of his speech was less cogent than he would fain have had it. "Ye needn't be borryin' trouble thinkin' they air hid well. Town-folks git out'n thar depth mighty quick whenst they take ter the mountings. I be a old man now, turned sixty, an' I hev knowed a power o' sher'ffs, through not many bein' re-'lected, an' they don't hev no trouble ketchin' town malefactors ez takes ter the woods."

The sheriff bent his eyes upon the toe of his big spurred boot as his long leg swung it before him. A sarcastic smile curved his shaven lips. It seemed for a moment as if he would not speak. Then, with that respect for the old so habitually shown among the mountaineers, he said, "These are mounting folks—mounting folks, Mr. Bakewell."

The smith dropped the horse's hoof, the knife clattering upon the ground, and straightened his bent back. "In the name o' goodness," he cried, overcome with curiosity, "*who* hev been kilt?"

The sheriff, albeit his enjoyment of the frenzied interest of which he was the centre showed in every line of his gloomy, important face, was dominated by his official conscience. He pointed to the implement on the ground.

"Pick up that thar contraption an' *go to work*," he said, sternly. "Gimme a horse ter ride on, or the law will take arter *you*, with a sharp stick, too."

The smith bent down to his work once more, his eyes fixed, nevertheless, on the officer's face instead of the hoof between his knees; the horse turned

19

slowly his head, and looked back with evident surprise at these dallying and unprecedented proceedings.

The sheriff resumed: " Mounting men, 'eordin' ter
the *ante*-mortem statement."

" Air—air he *dead ?*" said one of the men on the
wagon pole, leaning suddenly forward.

" Persumed ter be, hevin' been buried," replied
the officer, his sarcastic mien unchecked now by the
mandates of decorum.

" Mighty fool ter run agin the mounting folks,
hey ?" said the old man, reflectively rubbing his
pointed chin, and with the air of tempering his regrets, as if he thought that, with this foolhardy temerity, the blood of the unknown was presumably
upon his own head.

" He war a-travellin' peaceable along the road,"
said the sheriff, suddenly entering upon the pleasure
of narrative ; "bound fur the Spondulix Silver Mine,
on the t'other side o' Big Injun Mounting.   An' the
weather bein' so durned hot, an' the moon nigh the
full, he rid at night, like mos' folks do, ye know, the
road bein' no lonesomer sca'cely 'n by day, an' he
hed fire-arms.   And he hed suthin' else ; he hed
'bout fifteen hundred dollars ter kerry, ez nobody but
the head men o' the mine an' him knowed 'bout.
Thar's the riddle of it !"   He paused, the lids drooping meditatively over his thoughtful eyes as if he
sought to pierce the mystery.

" Fifteen hundred dollars !" exclaimed the old
man, as if he could hardly credit the existence of so
many in company ; he had seen few of this welcome
denomination at a time.   His look, unguarded for

the moment, implied suspicion that the sheriff was drawing the long-bow.

"'Twar ter pay off the hands an' some o' the expenses o' the gear an' sich—they war behindhand some," continued the sheriff. "Thar ain't no express nor railroad nor nuthin', 'ceptin' jes' the mail-rider, an' they 'lowed 'twar safer in this man's hands, special ez they 'lowed ez nobody knowed nuthin' 'bout it, 'ceptin' him an' them. Mus' hev got out somehows, though." He lifted his eyes, scanning each of the group in turn as if to note the impression. "Fur he 'lowed he rid along feelin' ez free an' favored ez ef 'twar broad daylight, an' his horse travelled well, an' didn't feel the weather none, an' though he war a stranger ter the kentry, he never thunk o' sech a thing ez danger till he got 'bout two mile past Doctor Gancy's house; he war on the top o' a hill, a-beginnin' ter go down, an' the moon war ez bright ez day, an' him a-whistlin' of a dancin' chune, whenst he tuk up a notion ez thar war suthin' movin' down in the road on the level; sorter 'peared ter him one minit 'twar men, an' the nex' minit he 'lowed 'twar jes' the wind in a pack o' bushes— sumach an' blackberries an' such—ter one side o' the road. He halted fur a minit, an' didn't see nuthin', nor hear nuthin'; so he rid on, an' whenst he reached the levels thar started up in the midst o' the road— he 'lowed it 'peared ter him ez hell hed spewed 'em out all of a suddenty, fur he couldn't see *whar* they kem from—a gang o' 'bout half a dozen mounting fellers. He 'lowed he hed never seen 'em afore, an' they didn't know him, fur they called him 'stranger.' Every man pursented a pistol at him, an' look whar he would, 'twar down a muzzle. But they war all a-laffin' at him, an' purtendin' not ter be so fur on the cold side o' friendly ; they kep' callin' out, claimin' his horse, 'lowin' he hed stole it from them, an' tellin' him he hed ter gin it up, an' march afoot, an' grinnin', an' axin' him ef he didn't know they hung horse-thieves, an' sayin' they war a-goin' ter make him git down on his knees an' thank them fur his life; an' he war a-declarin' an' a - protestin', an' though he had drawed his pistol, he hadn't fired it. An' ez they war a-tryin' ter pull him out'n the saddle, one sly rascal cut the girth, an' an idee kem ter him ez the whole consarn lurched ; he slipped his feet out'n the stirrups, an' let saddle an' saddle-bags drap ter the ground, fur he 'lowed they meant ter kill him, sure, an' that way he got loosed fur a second, an' in that second he whirled his horse round an' galloped along the road, leadin' the gang that fired arter him at every jump. One bullet went through his lung—lef' lung I b'lieve Doctor Ganey say. I ain't sure now whether 'twar lef', or right, or middle, or what not ; leastwise Doctor Ganey pulled a tur'ble long face whenst the man had eluded the horse-thieves an' got inter his hands."

"Dun'no' which war the the fryin'-pan an' which war the fire, myself," commented old Bakewell.

"But he tole the man at fust he wouldn't die," continued the sheriff.

"But I could hev tole him he would whenst he called Doctor Ganey," chuckled the sexagenarian.

The officer looked somewhat surprised, for the "valley folks" thought a trifle better of science expressed in drugs than did the mountaineers, who presumed them to be the spontaneous production of the apothecary shop, and thus opposed to nature, expressed in herbs. He was, however, country-bred, hailing originally from one of the mountain spurs, and had been transplanted to the town only by the repeated success of his political schemes, resulting in his election to the office of sheriff on more than one occasion. The rural standpoint medically was thus perfectly comprehensible to him ; and, being in full health, entirely independent of aught that Doctor Gancy might or might not know, he himself leaned to facile disparagement.

" Folks in Colbury 'lowed Doctor Gancy ought not ter hev let him be brung ter town nex' day in the cool o' the mornin' on a spring bed an' in a spring wagon ; though he war turrible anxious ter be sure ter make a ante-mortem statement; the robbers hed got the saddle-bags an' money, ye see, an' he didn't want folks ter think 'twar him ez stole it."

There was a momentary pause, broken only by the sharp staccato sound of the hammer within the shop, beating into shape the shoe that must be fitted to the hoof ; the horse outside turned his glossy neck, holding up the unshod hind foot a trifle from the ground, and looked through the door into the dark interior of the forge, where the smith's figure was to be dimly discerned in the scanty flicker of the smouldering fire ; the animal watched the process with a definite anxiety and interest that seemed to bespeak a desire to superintend its proper performance. His resignation to human guidance evidently arose more from the constraint of circumstance than reliance on man's superior wisdom. More than once the blacksmith stopped to listen, and afterward the matters at the forge went awry; outside one could hear him muttering surly comments upon the inanimate appurtenances, especially when he dropped the hot iron once in taking it from the coals, letting it slip through the inadequate grasp of the tongs, and requested it to go to a hotter place even than the fire, and there to be infinitely and illimitably "dad-burned." All of which had as little effect as such objurgations usually do upon the insensate offender; but the ebullitions seemed to serve, like thunder, to clear the atmosphere, and to enable the smith better to resign himself to the terrible deprivation of the sheriff's talk, lost in the reverberations of his own hammer and the sibilant singing of the anvil.

Outside, the sound hardly impinged upon the privilege of conversation. The sheriff's lip was curling; he hastily shifted one leg over the other, and this posture enabled him to eye the toe of his boot, with which he seemed to have confidences in some sort, reverting to it in moments when at a loss, as if its contemplation in some incomprehensible way refreshed his memory.

"Waal, the bosses o' the consarn—shucks! mighty knowin' cusses—they *would* hev it 'twar some folks down yander neighborin' the mines. I won't say who, and I won't say what," he interpolated, with a sudden recollection of a seemly official reticence; "but ez 'twar thought the man wouldn't die, an' all war keen ter git holt o' the money agin, I hed ter go fust an' air thar s'picions, ez arter a-chasin' an' a-racin' an' keepin' secret an' mighty dark turned out nuthin' at all. Fust one man an' then t'other showed up in a different place that night. Every one! I lef' word with my dep'ty, Ben Boker, who 'twas *I* wanted looked arter, an' he tuk sick with the bilious fever the very day I lef', an' air a-bed yit ; so I hev got behindhand with this job, an' I hope the folks won't lay it up agin me."

"Waal," said the old man, leaning forward, his hard hands clasped, a smile upon his wrinkled face, a slender sunbeam sifting through the boughs of the oak-tree, touching the thick tufts of gray hair on his brow, and brightening them to a whiter lustre, "I'll be bound old man Ganey warn't behindhand with *his* job," and he lifted his heavy eyebrows and chuckled softly.

"Naw, sir," said the officer, respectfully. "The doctor's job tuk off day before yestiddy mornin' 'fore daybreak. The doctor 'lowed ef he could make sun-up he mought last through till evenin'. But he had seen his las' sunrise."

"Ez ef Dr. Ganey knowed sech," exclaimed the old man. "He 'pears ter me ez ef his foolishness grows on him. Ye'll die whenst yer time kems, an' it'll kem mighty quick ef ye hev in Ganey. An' yit," with a nodding head and narrowing eyes, "thar be them ez fairly pins thar hopes o' salvation on ter the wisdom, that air foolishness, o' that old consarn. Thar's a valley man, Shattuck, ez hev been 'bidin' fur a while with Len Rhodes in the cove, a-holpin' him 'lectioneer, an' whenst Len fell down a-dancin' —mus' hev been drunk—at the Pettingill infair, an' seemed ter bump his head a passel, an' shed some blood, nuthin' would do this Shattuck but Ganey mus' be sent fur. He threatened old man Pettingill with the gallus ef Rhodes should die."

"Old Zack Pettingill! Why, he's one of my *bes'* friends, an' a better man never lived," interrupted the officer, although he lent an attentive ear, for Rhodes was of the opposite party, and the sheriff was a candidate for re-election."

"Yes, sir"—the old man redoubled his emphasis —"though Phil Craig war in the house a-bathin' the wounds an' a-bindin' 'em up with yerbs ter take the soreness out. An' ef ye'll b'lieve me he cavorted so ez old Zack Pettingill, though an obstinate old sinner, hed ter gin up, an' put Steve Yates on his bes' horse, an' send seventeen miles fur Ganey. It all 'peared so onreasonable an' so all-fired redic'lous ez I couldn't holp but b'lieve ez this hyar Shattuck hed some yer-rand o' his own ter send Yates on, special ez Dr. Ganey never kem."

"P'litical bizness—bribery an' sech," suggested the sheriff, acrimoniously, for each man was phenom-enally eager for the success of the whole ticket. So closely were the opposing factions matched, so high ran party spirit in this section, that his own candi-dacy, albeit for a far different office, made him in some sort Rhodes's opponent.

"Mought hev been electioneerin'. I hev always 'lowed, though, whenst ye fund out whar Steve Yates be now, ye'll find out what Shattuck sent him fur, though some say Yates jes' hed a quar'l with his wife, an' hed run away from her."

The officer's color suddenly changed; it beat hot in his bronzed cheeks; it seemed even to deepen in his eyes, that were of too light a tint ordinarily. He pushed his hat back from his brow, where the beads of perspiration had started in the roots of his brown hair.

"Hain't Yates kem back yet?" he asked, breathlessly.

"Hide nor hair hev been seen o' him since that night."

"What night?" demanded the officer.

"Night o' the Pettingill infair, o' course," rejoined the old man, tartly; "an' that war the second day o' July—a Friday it war; they oughter hev got the weddin' over 'fore Friday. Them young folks can't expec' no luck."

"They can't hev none worse'n they *hev* hed, 'cordin' ter my view, a-marryin' one another. The Lord's been toler'ble hard on 'em a'ready, I'm thinkin'."

This observation came from one of the men perched on the pole of the broken wagon, reputed to be a rejected suitor of the bride, and a defeated rival of the groom. The opportunity for the ridicule of sentimental woe in which the rustic delights was too good to be lost, and under the cloak of the raillery the sheriff unobtrusively drew out a note-book and casually referred to it. The night of the second of July —a Friday night—the agent of the Spondulix Mine was waylaid by horse-thieves, lost his saddle and the treasure in his saddle-bags in the fracas, and received in his flight such wounds that he died thereof within a few weeks. The officer had closed the book and returned it to his pocket before the attention of the party had reverted to him anew.

"What sorter man air this hyar Shattuck?" he asked, casually, as he held a huge plug of tobacco between his teeth, from which they gnawed, with an admirable display of energy, a fragment for present use. "What sorter man?"

"Waal," said old Bakewell, narrowing his eyes and pursing his mouth critically, as he glanced absently down at a brilliant patch of sunshine, gilded and yellow in the midst of the dark olive-green shadow of the oak-tree, "I dun'no' what ter say 'bout'n a man ez goes roun' payin' folks ter dig in Injun mounds fur a lot o' bowls an' jars an' sech like, whenst fur the money he could buy better ones right down yander at the store."

The officer had faced about on the barrel and sat bolt-upright, a hand on either knee, his amazement looking alertly out of his light-gray eyes.

"He hev quit that, though, lately," the smith struck in, dropping the hoof to which he had tentatively applied the shoe and standing still, half supporting himself with his hand on the shoulder of the animal, who once more turned his head with a slow, deprecatory motion, and gazed back upon the displeasing and seemingly incompetent doings of this dilatory workman. "Baker Anderson—he's a half-grown boy ez hev been 'bidin' at Mis' Yates's of a night ter keer fur the house agin lawless ones an' sech—he kem hyar this mornin' ter git his plough sharpened, an' he 'lows ez this hyar Shattuck say he wants ter dig up the bones of the Leetle People, buried nigh the ruver on Fee Guthrie's lan'. An' Steve favored it; but Mis' Yates 'lowed she'd shoot him ef he tampered with the Leetle People's bones, an' Baker 'lows ez that war why Steve lef' her."

"The Leetle People!" echoed the sheriff in a dazed tone, as if he hardly believed his ears.

"Lord A'mighty, Tawmmy Carew! Hain't ye never heard 'bout a lot o' small-sized people, no big-

ger'n chil'n, ez hed this kentry 'fore the Injun kem—
'bout the time o' the flood, I reckon." Old Bakewell hardily hazarded this speculation, which had
about as much justification of probability as the conclusions of many other scientists of more pretensions. " Hev ye got yer growth ez a man, an' lived
ter be 'lected sher'ff o' the county, an' ter thrive on
the hope o' bein' 'lected agin, an' *yit* air ez green
ez a gourd?—so green ez never ter hev hearn tell o'
the Leetle Stranger People?" demanded the old man,
scornfully.

Thus adjured, the sheriff, for his credit's sake, was
fain to refresh his memory. " 'Pears like I useter
know some sech old tale ez that, but I had nigh forgot it," he said, mendaciously, the lie staring irre-
pressibly out of his widely opened, astonished eyes.
"I never 'lowed it war true."

" But it *air* true," said the smith, the shoe and
hammer hanging listlessly in one hand, while the
other, leaning heavily on the horse's back, sufficed to
transfer much of his weight to the animal. " They
air the nighest neighbors Mis' Yates hev got. An'
though Steve an' this man Shattuck agreed so mighty
well, Mis' Yates couldn't abide the idee o' diggin' up
the Leetle People's bones, an' swore she'd shoot ennybody ez tried it. An', by hokey "—with a sudden
excitement in his eyes—"she *done* it! Las' night,
Baker say, this man an' Rhodes war thar in the pig
buryin'-ground—he calls them humans ' pigs '—an'
she gin 'em two toler'ble fair shots. Shoots toler'ble
well fur a 'oman. Baker say the bullet cut through
Shattuck's hair good fashion."

" Waal, that's agin the law," said the sheriff, with

his bitter, implacable official expression; "assault with intent to kill."

"Oh, shet up, Tawmmy," the old man admonished him from the vantage-ground of his age and experience. "What else air fire-arms manufactured fur?"

Beyond this cogent reasoning "Tawmmy's" speculation could not go. Nevertheless, he was sworn to administer the law, albeit thrice proven a foolish device of fools, and his brow did not relax. It was with a dark frown, indeed, that he contemplated the mental image of Mrs. Yates, because he felt that it behooved women so to order their walk and conversation as to keep without the notice of the law, since it was infinitely unpalatable to him to enforce it where they were concerned, making him, rather than the culprit, the sufferer, and forcing him to endure many unclassified phases and extremes of mental anguish. He protested at times that they ought to be exempted from the operations of the law. "They ain't got no reason, nohow," he gallantly asseverated. "An' what sorter figure does a big man cut arrestin' a leetle bit of a 'oman? An' no jury ain't goin' ter convict 'em, ef they kin git around it, an' no jedge ain't goin' ter charge agin 'em, ef he kin holp himself. The law jes' devils the sher'ff with 'em; *he* hev got ter go through all the motions fur nuthin'. They say Jedge Kinnear air a out an' out 'oman's jedge. An' no man, even in civil cases, hev got a chance agin enny 'oman or enny minor chil'n, gals 'specially, in his court. Waal, now, *I'm* a *man's* sher'ff. An' I want the wimmin an' chil'n ter keep out'n my way, an' I'll keep out'n theirn."

Shattuck, however, and especially as connected

with Rhodes, offered a prospect more in keeping with his professions and views of his office. "What do he want ter dig up thar bones fur?" he demanded. "That air agin the law, too."

"Fur the hist'ry o' the kentry, Baker say," the smith suggested; the phrase seemed to have a sort of coherency that commended it generally.

But the sheriff shook his head. "I hev studied the hist'ry o' the kentry," he asserted, capably. "I hev 'tended school, an' the Leetle People hain't got nuthin' ter do with the hist'ry o' the kentry. I read 'bout the Injun war, an' the Revolutionary war, an' the Mexican war, an' this las' leetle war o' ourn, an' the Leetle People warn't in *none* of 'em."

He was silent for a moment, looking at the ground, his head tilted askew, a wistful expression on his face, so did the mystery baffle him.

The light taps of the hammer sounding on the air as the smith drove in the last nail were suddenly blended with the quick hoof-beats of a galloping horse, and Guthrie, mounted on Cheever's famous roan, came into view along the vista of the road, reining up under the tree as he recognized the sheriff.

It was a scene remembered for many a day, reproduced as the preamble of the fireside tale recited for years afterward by the by-standers. The sheriff, standing with his hand on the forelock of the captive charger, his head a trifle bent, listened with a languid competent smile as if he had known before all that the horseman recounted; Guthrie himself, pale from the loss of blood, his hair hanging upon his shoulders, his face, so fierce, so austere, framed

by his big black hat, his spurs jingling on his high
boots, his pistols and formidable knife in his belt,
began to take to their accustomed eyes the changed
guise which afterward attended his personality when
they told of the part he bore and of all that befell
him. The only exclamations came from the spectators, as they pressed close about the two restive
horses. They fell back amazed and impressed by
the official coolness when all was done, and the sheriff
turned calmly aside.

"Come, Guthrie," he only said, "you may ride
with me to-day."

And with this he put his foot in the stirrup.

"'COME, GUTHRIE,' HE ONLY SAID."

XV.

The accuracy of Felix Guthrie's oft-vaunted aim was attested by two ghastly objects that had exhaled life and found their doom in Crazy Zeb's cell. In the presence of these dumb witnesses of the struggle, lying surrounded by the charred and cold remnants of the fire, and scattered hay and corn which the vanished horses had left, and shadowed by the gloomy gray walls with their sinister resonance, the place seemed charged with the tragedies of its associations, frightful to contemplate, ill to linger about, and far removed from any possible conjunction with the idea of mirth and the festivities which a greasy, thickened pack of cards strewed about the two bodies, and a flask, broken by its fall on the rock, but still containing whiskey, might betoken. The chilly vault opened upon the serene splendors of the infinitely pellucid sunshine that glowed to mid-summer warmth. Had ever the sky worn so dense, so keen, so clear a blue? It discredited the azure of the far western mountains, and marked how the material, even attenuated by distance to the guise of the veriest vapor, fails of the true ethereal tint of the ambient spaces of the air. The birds sang from the sun-flooded trees just beneath the cliff—so limpidly sweet the tones!—and within were two men dead in their sins, in this drear place that had known woe.

Death is not easily predicable of those of a common household, and in this scantily populated region the sense of community is close. There were some involuntary exclamations from the posse upon the recognition of the malefactors, implying a sense of catastrophe and regret; especially for one of them, a young man with the down on his lips, his face and posture contorted with the agony long endured while he had lain here deserted in the darkness of the night, lighted only by the mystic moon, beside the stark figure of his comrade, who had been shot through the heart, dying in the space of a second.

"Lordy massy 'pon my soul, ef hyar ain't Benjy Swasey! What a turrible time he mus' hev hed afore he tuk off!" cried old Bakewell, his pallid face aquiver, and his voice faltering as he bent over the recumbent form.

The sight and the circumstance failed to affect the official nerve of the sheriff. "Now this is plumb satisfactory," he remarked. "I never expected ter see Buck Cheever in this fix. I 'lowed the devil takes too good care o' his own. It's mighty satisfactory. I hed planned," he added, as he looked about at the high roof and the inaccessible depths below, "that I'd blow up this place some with giant powder or sech; but I reckon I hed better let it be— it does lead the evil-doer ter sech a bad end!"

But the old man still leaned with a pitiful corrugated brow over the lifeless figure. Age had made his heart tender, and he chose to disregard the logic that spoke from the muzzles of Swasey's discharged pistols, one lying close by, and from Cheever's bloody knife still held in the stiffened clasp of the hand that had wielded it. "Fee," he said, tremulously, "ye shoot *too* straight."

And Guthrie, his hand meditatively laid on his chin, and his eyes staring absently forward as if they beheld more or less than was before them, replied, "That's a true word, I reckon."

The air freighted with tragedy, with all the ultimate anguish of life and sin and death, seemed to receive with a sort of shock the sheriff's gay rallying laughter as he clapped Guthrie's shoulder.

"Then, Fee, my fine young rooster, ef ye hedn't shot straight I'd be a-sendin' fur the coroner ter kem an' set on *you!*"

"'Pears ter me," said the blacksmith, who still had on his leather apron, having forgotten, in the excitement, to lay it aside, and gazing with dilated eyes at the blood stains on the rock floor—"'pears ter me he'd hev a mighty oneasy seat on Fee, dead or alive."

The sheriff's jaunty jubilance, in that the lawbreakers had been so smartly overtaken, attended him through the woods and down the road, as he cantered at the head of his posse, all armed and jingling with spurs — a cavalcade both imposing and awful to the few spectators which the sparsely populated country could muster, summoned out from the cabins by the sound of galloping horses and the loud-pitched talk. The elders stood and stared; tow-headed children, peeping through the lower rails of the fence, received a salutary impression, and beheld, as it were, the majesty of the law, materialized in this gallant style, riding forth to maintain its supremacy. Only the dogs were unreceptive to the

20

subtler significance of the unwonted apparition, evidently accounting it merely a gang of men, and, according to the disposition of the individual animal, either accepting the fact quietly, with affably wagging tail, or plunging into the road in frenzied excitement, and with yelps and defiant barking pursuing the party out of sight of the house, then trotting home with a triumphant mien. The tragedy that the posse had found in Crazy Zeb's cell lingered still in the minds of two or three of the horsemen, their silence and gloomy, downcast faces betokening its influence; but the others instinctively sought to cast it off, and the effort was aided by the sunshine, the quick pace, the briskening wind, and the cheery companionship of the officer. He seemed to have no receptivity for the sorrowful aspects of the event, and his spirits showed no signs of flagging until he drew rein at the door-yard of one of the escaped robbers with whose names Guthrie had furnished him.

"'Ain't he got no sort'n *men* kin-folks?" he asked, his cheery, resonant voice hardly recognizable in the querulous whine with which he now spoke. "Lord have mercy on my soul! *how* am I a-goin' ter make out a-catechisin' the man's wife an' mother 'bout'n him! *Git* off'n yer horse thar, Jim. 'Light, I tell ye, an' kem along in the house with me ter holp bolster me up."

In several of these doomed households the forlorn women, in their grief and despair, turned fierce and wielded a biting tongue; and as the hapless officer showed an infinite capacity for anxious deprecation, their guarded sarcasms waxed to a vindictive temerity. Among them he was greatly harassed, and more than once he was violently threatened. Indeed, one old crone rose tremulously up in the chimney-corner as he sat before the fire, after searching the premises, keenly questioning the younger members of the family, and with her tremulous, aged palm she smote him twice in the face. He sat quite still, although the color mounted to the roots of his hair, while her children in frantic fear besought her to desist.

"Lord knows, Mis' Derridge," he said, looking meekly at her, "I'd be willin' fur ye ter take a hickory sprout an' gin me a reg'lar whalin' ef 'twould mend the matter enny, or make yer son Josiah a diff'ent man from what he hev turned out. I reckon ye oughter hev gin *him* a tap or two more'n ye done. But ef it eases yer feelin's ter pitch inter me, jes' pitch in, an' welcome! I don't wonder at ye, nuther."

She stared at him irresolutely from out her bleared eyes, then burst into that weeping so terrible to witness in the aged, bewailing that she had ever lived to see the day, and calling futilely on Heaven to turn the time back that she might be dead ten years ago, and upbraiding the earth that so long it had grudged her a grave.

The officer found it hard after this scene to lay hold on his own bold identity again, and he had naught to say when he got on his horse and rode away. It became possible to reassert himself and his office only when he chanced upon a household where there were men and boys. There he raged around in fine style, and frowned and swore and threatened, every creature trembling before the very sound of his voice. Thus he made restitution in some sort to the terrors of the law, defrauded by his former weakness of their wonted fierce effectiveness.

The afternoon was on the wane, and no captures had been made ; the cavalcade was about turning from the door of a house—it was the last to be visited, the most distant of all—a poor place, perched high up on the rugged slope of the mountain, with a vast forest below it and on either hand, from the midst of which it looked upon a splendid affluent territory seeming infinite in extent. Peak and range, valley and river, were all in the sunset tints—purple and saffron and a suffusive blood-red flush, all softened and commingled by the haze ; and above, the rich yellow lucency of the crystalline skies. A lateral spur was in the immediate foreground, high, steep, and heavily wooded, the monotony of the deep, restful green* of its slopes broken here and there by vertical lines of gleaming white, betokening the trunks of the beech-trees amidst the dark preponderance of walnut and pine ; more than one hung, all bleached and leafless, head downward, half up-rooted, for thus the wind, past this long time, left trace of its fury. A stream—a native mountaineer, wild and free and strong—took its way down the gorge between the spur and the mountain from which it shot forth. From the door-yard might be had a view of a section of its course, the water flowing in smooth scroll-like swirls from the centre to the bank, and thence out again, the idea of a certain symmetry of the current thus suggested in linear grace—all crystal clear, now a jade-like green, and again the brownish yellow of a topaz, save where the rapids flung up a sudden commotion of white foam that seemed all alive, as if some submerged amphibian gambollings made the depths joyous. The crags stood out distinct on either hand, with here and there a flower sweetly smiling in a niche, like some unexpected tenderness in a savage heart. All was very fresh, very keenly and clearly colored; the weeds, rank and high, sent up a rich aromatic odor.

The officer, for years a farmer, and alive to all weather signs, hardly needed a second glance at the clear tint of the vigorous mould of the door-yard beneath his feet to know that it had rained here lately. "The drought in town ain't bruk yit," he said, half enviously—a mere habit, for he had now no crops to suffer from stress of weather. Here there had been copious storms, with thunder and lightning, gracious to the corn and the cotton, and not disdaining the humbler growths of the wayside, the spontaneous joyance of nature. The torrents had fallen in a decisive rhythm; the ground was beaten hard; the rails of the fence looked dark and clean; the wasp nests and the cobwebs were torn away—alack for the patient weavings!—the roof of the little cabin was still sleek and shining. As he turned on his heel he marked how the new-built hay-stacks were already weathering, all streaked with brown.

He had searched the little barn whose roof showed behind the hay-stacks, but as he glanced toward it, in the mere relapse of bucolic sentiment, he became vaguely aware of an intent watchfulness in the lantern-jawed and haggard woman of the house, who had followed him and his party to the fence, in hospitality, it might seem, or to see them safely off the place. The reflection of her look—it was but a look, and he did not realize it then ; he remembered it afterward —was in the eyes of a tallow-faced, shock-headed girl of ten.   His own eyes paused in disparagement upon her ; the hem of her cotton dress was tattered out and hung down about her bare ankles, all stained with red clay mud.   There were straws clinging to her attire, and here and there in her tousled red hair. He was no precisian, to be sure, but her unkempt aspect grated upon him ; these were truly shiftless folks, and had a full measure of his contempt, which he felt they richly merited ; and so he turned once more to the fence, facing the great yellow sky, and the purple and amber and red flushed world stretching so far below.   A little clatter at the bars where the posse prepared to mount and ride away was pronounced in the deep evening stillness ; the cry of a homeward-bound hawk drifted down as with the sunset on his swift wings he swept above the abysses of the valley ; and then the sheriff, stepping over the lower rail, the others lying on the ground, paused suddenly, his hand upon the fence, his face lifted.   A strange new sound was on the air, a raucous voice muttering incoherently—muttering a few words, then sinking to silence.

Carew looked quickly at the woman.   Her face had stiffened ; it hardly seemed alive ; it was as inanimate as a mask, some doleful caricature of humanity and sorrow, forlornly unmoving, with no trace of beauty or intelligence to hallow it ; she might seem to have no endowment in common with others of her kind, save the capacity to suffer.   The child's face reflected hers as in a mirror. The same feeble, pitiable affectation of surprise was on each when the sheriff exclaimed, suddenly, "What's that?"

The men outside of the fence paused in the instant, as if a sudden petrifaction had fallen upon the group—one was arrested in the moment of tightening a saddle-girth; another was poised midway, one foot in the stirrup, the other just lifted from the ground; two or three, already mounted, sat like equestrian statues, their figures in high-relief against the broad fields of the western sky above the mountain-tops. Once a horse bent down his head and tossed it aloft and pawed the ground; and again the silence was unbroken, till there arose anew that strangely keyed, incoherent babbling. There was an abrupt rush in the direction whence the sound came, for it was distinct this time. The forlorn woman and girl were soon distanced, as they followed upon the strides of the stalwart sheriff. He ran fast and lightly, with an agility which his wonted pompous strut hardly promised. He was at the barn door and half-way up the ladder leading into the loft before his slower comrades could cross the yard. When they reached the barn the woman was standing in the space below the loft, her face set, her eyes restless and dilated; her self-control gave way at last to a sudden trivial irritation, incongruous with the despair and grief in her fixed lineaments.

"Quit taggin' arter me!" she cried out, huskily, to the tattered little girl, who, in tears and trembling with wild fright, hung upon her skirts.

The sheriff at the head of the ladder seemed, impossibly enough, to be tearing down the wall of the

building.   He had a hatchet in one hand; he used
the handle of his pistol for a wedge, and presently
the men, peering up into the dusky shadow, understood that he was plucking down the boards of a
partition that, flimsy as it was, had seemed to them
the outer wall when they had searched the place.
Within was a space only two feet wide perhaps, but
as long as the gable end.   Upon a heap of straw lay
a man, wounded, fevered, wild with delirium.   He
had no sense of danger; he could realize no calamity
of capture; his hot, rolling, bloodshot eyes conveyed
no correlative impression to his disordered brain of
the figures he beheld before him.   He talked on, unnoting the cluster of men as they pressed about him
in the dust that rose from the riven boards, and
gazed down wide-eyed at him.   The only light came
in through the crevices of roof and wall, but these
were many.   It served amply for his recognition, if
more evidence had been needed than the fact of his
home and the careful concealment, and it showed
the attitudes of his captors as they looked around
the thrice-searched place—at the hay that they had
tossed about, the piles of corn they had rolled down,
the odds and ends of plough gear and broken household utensils in one corner that they had ransacked.
More than one commented, with a sort of extorted
admiration, upon the craft that had so nearly foiled
them.   The triumphant figure of the sheriff was the
focus of the shadowy group, easily differentiated by
his air of arrogantly pluming himself; one might
hardly have noticed the frowzy shock of hair and the
pale face of the little girl protruding through the
aperture in the floor, for she had climbed the ladder,

and with a decapitated effect gazed around from the level of the puncheons.

It was a forlorn illustration of the universal affections of our common human nature that this apparition should be potent to annul the mists of a wavering mind, and to summon right reason in delirium. The thick-tongued, inarticulate muttering ceased for a moment; a dazed smile of recognition was on the unkempt, bearded face of the wounded man.

"Bet on Maggie!" he said, quite plainly. "She kin climb like a cat. She kin drive a nail like a man! Takes a heap ter git ahead o' Maggie!"

And then his head began to loll from shoulder to shoulder, and the look of recognition was gone from his face. He was now and again lifting his hands as if in argument or entreaty, and once more muttering with a thick, inarticulate tongue.

The sheriff glanced at a twisted nail in his hand, then down at the decapitated Maggie.

"Did you holp do this hyar job?" he asked.

The child hesitated; the law seemed on her track. "I druv the top nails," she piped out at last. Then, with a whimper, "Mam couldn't climb along the beam fur head-swimmin', so I clomb the beam an druv the top nails," she concluded, with a weak, quavering whine.

He looked down with a tolerant eye at the unprepossessing countenance. "Smart gal!" he exclaimed, unexpectedly; "a mighty smart gal! An' a good one too, I'll be bound! Ye jes' run down yander ter the house, sissy, an' fix the bed fur yer dad, fur we air goin' ter fetch him down right now."

She stared at him with dumb amazement for a moment, then turning her little body about with agility, her tousled shock of hair and her pallid little face vanished from the opening in the floor.

The appearance there of an armed party of rescuers could hardly have been more unwelcome, and the sheriff breathed freely when she was at last gone.

He lifted his head presently, glancing questioningly about the darkening place, for the irregular spaces of the crevices gave now only a dim fragmentary glimmer. He turned, as if with a sudden thought, took his way down the ladder and stood in the door, slipping the pistol into his pocket, and looking out with a lowering, disaffected eye. In that short interval within the barn all the world had changed; the flaring sky had faded, and was of a dull gray tint, too pallid to furnish relief to the coming of the stars, which were only visible here and there in a vague scintillation, colorless too. The gloom of the darkling mountains oppressed the spirit, something so immeasurably mournful was in their sombre, silent, brooding immensity. The indubitable night lay on the undistinguishable valley as if the darkness rose from the earth rather than came from the sky; only about the summits the day seemed to tarry. Many a vibrant note was tuning in the woods; for the nocturnal insects, and the frogs by the water-side, and vague, sibilant, undiscriminated sounds, joined in a twanging, melancholy chorus that somehow accented the loneliness.

"Waal, night hev overtook us," the sheriff remarked to Felix Guthrie, who had joined him at the door. Then, with gathering acerbity, "'Pears like ter me ef Providence lays ez much work on a man ez

I hev got ter do, he ought ter hev daylight enough left him ter git through with it, or else hev a moon allowed him ter work by."

Guthrie said nothing, but stood solemnly watching the darkening face of the landscape.

" We air roosted up hyar fur all night, Fee," Carew continued, in a tone that was a querulous demand for sympathy. " We could sca'cely make out ter git up that thar outdacious, steep, rocky road in the day-time; ef we war ter try it in the pitch-dark with a bed-ridden prisoner, the whole posse, prisoner an 'all, would bodaciously roll over the rocks into some o' them gorges ez look ter be deep ez hell !" He paused for a moment, his light gray eyes narrowing. " I could spare the posse toler'ble well, but I could in no wise git along 'thout the prisoner." A secret twinkling that lighted his eyes seemed communicated in some sort to his lips, which twitched suddenly, as if suppressing a laugh.

Fee Guthrie's face wore no responsive gleam. He stood gruffly silent for a time, his gaze fixed uncom-prehendingly upon the sheriff. " Air thar ennything ter hender yer stayin' all night ?" he asked at last.

The officer hesitated, then moved nearer, and laid his hand confidentially upon his companion's shoulder, among the ends of his flaunting, tawny curls.

" Fee," he said, lowering his voice, and with a very definite accession of gravity and anxiety, " I hev made a mistake—a large-sized one—about the build o' that man Shattuck."

. Guthrie's immobile, unfriendly face changed sud-denly. There was a slight quiver upon it, which passed in an instant, leaving it softened and wistful and anxious. He knew naught of the officer's suspicions touching Shattuck; he only knew that this man had lingered without the window to hear Letitia sing, while he waited for the moon to rise in the great rocky gorge of the river. It seemed to Guthrie that the very suggestion of her name would have a power over him, that it would stir him if he were dead, if he shared the long death in which the Little People lay and waited for their summons to rise again. And somehow the thought of them, silent, motionless, undisturbed in their long, long abeyance, brought a qualm of remorse. "I ought not ter hev gin my cornsent ter open one of thar coffins," he reflected, his lips moving unconsciously with the unspoken words. "My head won't rest no easier in the grave fur hevin' stirred *his'n*, an' jes' fur Shattuck's cur'osity, ef the truth war knowed; 'the hist'ry o' the kentry' "—he remembered the words with a sneer—" air nowhar." "This hyar Shattuck air a mighty takin' man," he said aloud, suddenly. The sheriff cocked his head with keen attention. "Nowise good-lookin', special, but saaft-spoken. Folks like him mighty well; he pulls the wool over everybody's eyes."

He again remembered his threat for the man who should come between him and Letitia; he had unwittingly spoken it to Shattuck himself, but it was well that he was warned.

"Waal, Fee, I ain't wantin' ter arrest him too suddint—unless I hed more grounds for suspicion agin him; but this hyar thing is murder, man, *murder!* An' 'twon't do fur ennybody ez hed enny part in sech ter get away. He sent Stephen Yates on a fool pretensified yerrand the night the man war waylaid an'

kilt, an' ye seen Steve 'mongst the gang in Crazy
Zeb's cell."

"How d'ye know ez the gang hed ennything ter
do with that job? Mought hev been other folks,"
Guthrie demanded, the cause of justice urgently con-
straining him.

"Don't know it; that's jes' the reason I oughter
keep an eye, a sorter watch, on Shattuck, an' not
arrest him 'thout he war tryin' ter clear the kentry.
I oughter hev lef' a man ter look arter him."

Guthrie said nothing. He seemed to silently revolve this view.

"Would *you-uns* ondertake ter keep him under
watch till I git back ter-morrow?" Carew moved his
hand caressingly on Guthrie's shoulder amongst his
long, wind-stirred hair. "I couldn't git down the
mountain in the dark, specially lumbered up with
that man, ez 'pears ter be dyin'—ye shoot mighty
straight, Fee!—an' I 'lowed ye be 'feared o' nuthin,
an' air a mighty fine rider, an' yer horse air sure-
footed. Ye mought walk ef ye warn't willin' ter try
it mounted. Wouldn't ye obleege me, Fee?"

Guthrie's dark eyes, with their suggestions of im-
placability, were turned reflectively upon him. The
dying light did not so much as suggest their color,
but their lustre was visible in the dusk, and their expression was unannulled.

"I hain't got no nose fur game," he replied at last.
"Ye can't hunt folks down with me."

The sheriff's hand suddenly weighed heavily on
his shoulder. "What be ye a-talkin' 'bout, boy?"
he said, imperiously. "I *require* yer assistance in
the name o' the law! I war jes' a-perlitin' aroun',

and axin' like a favior, fur the name o' the thing.   I
hev got a *right* ter yer help."

"Make yer right good"—Felix Guthrie had faced
round, his indomitable eye bright and clear in the
dusk, where all else was blurred—"*ef ye kin*. Thar's
no law ever made ez kin turn *me* inter a spy ter lead
a man ter the gallus or shet a prison door on him.
Make yer right good, why don't ye?"

The strong vitality of the sheriff's self-confidence,
the belligerent faith in his own prowess—an essential concomitant of his physique and bold spirit—
tempted him sorely. The occasion was propitious,
for a collision on such a scale was a rare opportunity
to his bridled pugnacity, and with his posse at his
back the consequences of defeat were infinitely reduced. The realization that Guthrie defied his power,
even thus supported, cried aloud for due recognition,
but gentler counsels prevailed in that stormy half-
second while his broad chest heaved and his eyes
flashed. His prospects as a candidate hampered him.
Mutiny in the forces of so popular a man as he affected to be was an incongruity of insistent significance to the returns of the midsummer election.

"No, no, Fee; suit yerse'f," he said, smothering
his feelings with a very pretty show of geniality,
which, however it might fail to impose on Guthrie,
ostensibly filled the breach. "I ain't a-goin' ter make
my right good by requirin' a man ter resk his life
'mongst them slippery gorges on a night ez dark ez
the grave itself. Naw; ef ye don't want ter go, ye
don't need ter, though ye mought be some perliter-
spoken 'bout'n it. Some o' the t'others mought take
a notion ter volunteer, even though they ain't so well

used ter the mountings ez you-uns be, through livin' up on the side o' the mounting; an' that horse o' Cheever's air plumb used ter sech roads through trav- 'ellin' on 'em every day or so. But jes' ez ye choose —I ain't keerin'."

He strode forward to a group of men collected in the door-yard, and, standing with an arm about the shoulders of two of them, engaged in a low-voiced colloquy. The subject was presumably the despatch- ing of an envoy to keep Shattuck under surveillance, and, with his reasons for the keenest interest in aught that touched this stranger, Guthrie with intent eyes gazed at them. Naught could be divined from their inexpressive attitudes; their low tones baffled his hungry ears. The excitements of the day had in a measure withdrawn his mind from his own antago- nisms to Shattuck, his fear of being supplanted, his sense of injury because of the silence with which Shattuck had received his confidence, making no sign to divulge an inimical interest. Shattuck would, however, soon enough be dealt with, he reflected. And then he found, in a sort of dull surprise, that he could take no pleasure in the thought of the ca- lamities impending for his rival, because, he reasoned, they were not in direct retribution for his own wrongs.

" I'd hev liked ter hev talked ter him one more time fust," he said, mentally revolving words bitterly eloquent with anger.

Pleasure? Nay, he deprecated the coming events. " Tawm C'rew air a mighty smart man—in his own opinion," he said, still scornfully gazing at the friendly pose of the important sheriff, which had all the values of the infrequent unbending of a very great man. "He oughter know ez Shattuck never hed no hand in sech ez murder an' thievery, an'"—with a sudden after-thought—"he *would know it*, *too*, ef he hed ever seen him."

There was a sudden strange stir at his heart. He had felt it once before, when the reproachful praise of shooting too straight had first fallen upon his ear. On a rude litter four men were bearing out from the barn door and carrying across the yard the recumbent figure of Bob Millroy, looking in the drear light of the dusk like death itself, so still he lay, suggestively stark, but with a ceaseless monotonous mutter, as if he had conveyed beyond death some feeble distraught capacity of speech. The uncomprehended words had a weird effect, and the groups of men grew silent as the litter was borne past. The sheriff followed it into the house, where with his own hands he kindled a fire on the hearth, that forthwith gave light and cheer, and converted the poor place from the aspect of a hovel to that of a home; he recommended that the patient—for thus he called him, rather than the prisoner—should be fed with chicken broth, and suggested that as all the poultry had gone to roost, Maggie would find a fat young pullet an easy capture. He saw that Millroy was comfortably ensconced in bed, with his wounds newly dressed, at which process Carew presided with *ex cathedra* utterances and a dignity bespeaking the experience of a medical expert. The restless head soon ceased to roll, the thick tongue grew silent, and the prisoner sank into slumber that seemed deep and restful.

Maggie had deftly seconded the officer's efforts, and was as helpful as a woman. But the wife held back, sullen and suspicious, speaking only when she was spoken to, and moving reluctantly in obedience to a direct command. More than once she fixed a surly, mutinous gaze upon the sheriff; and when the babble of delirium was still at last, and the room seemed full of homely comfort, the fire-light flickering on wall and ceiling, she could hold her peace no longer.

" Ye air a faithful servant of the devil," she said. " Look ter him fur yer thanks—ye'll git none from me. I know ye air a-doin' all this jes' ter git Bob well enough ter jail or hang him. He's yer sheep ter lead ter slarter."

" Lawdy mighty, Mis' Millroy !" exclaimed the officer, " what air ye a-talkin' 'bout ? Ye dun'no' whether Bob hev done ennything ter be jailed or hung fur. Ef ye *do*, ye know more'n I do. All I know is that Fee Guthrie reported gittin' in a fight with a gang o' fellers, an' he shot sev'ral an' the res' run. I 'lowed I had better look 'em up an' see what sorter account they could give o' tharse'fs, ez thar hev been crimes commit in the county. Naw'm ; ye hev got ter git through with a jury, an' a pack o' lawyers, an' a deal o' palaver, 'fore I take the trouble ter make up *my* mind. Law's mighty scientific nowadays. Ye hev got ter prove a thing on a man 'fore I'll go lookin' inter the hemp market. An' Bob hain't proved nuthin' 'ceptin' that Fee Guthrie shoots straight, ez he hev hed the name o' doin' from a boy."

He looked anxiously at his interlocutor, whom he had more bestirred himself to disarm than if she could have wielded a ballot in his behalf. She gave no overt sign of being placated, but there was something in her face which reassured him, and he observed that when the child came and leaned against her knee, she did not irritably repulse her as heretofore.

"She's a good child, Maggie air," he observed, contemplating her, remembering the little creature's eager help.

The child's small friendly gray eyes were fixed intelligently upon him as he sat resting a moment on the opposite side of the hearth; the flickering firelight showed her shock of tousled red hair and threw her magnified shadow on the wall. The shutters of the low, broad window stood open to the fresh balsamic mountain air, revealing the myriads of scintillating stars in the dark moonless concave above the western ranges; the greenish-white clusters of an elder-blossom, growing close outside in a clump of weeds, looked in and nodded, as if in greeting to those within.

"An' she's a mighty smart leetle gal too," he added.

"Yes," her mother drawled, disparagingly, "but so turrible ugly. I hain't never tuk no comfort in her. But Bob, he 'lows he kin put up with her looks mighty easy."

"Waal, the bes'-lookin' gals ain't always pritty whenst little," said the sheriff, optimistically.

His plastic countenance took on a sudden absorption in graver matters, and he arose and strode to the middle of the room, stooping to glance out of the window, as if to exert some slight surveillance upon the members of his posse without.

The door-yard was all illumined. A fire of pine knots and hickory logs flared in its midst. Around it were grouped the figures of the night-bound posse, making what cheer they could for themselves. Spurred and booted and armed, they had a reminiscent suggestion for the sheriff, who had been a soldier and could look down the vistas of memory, where many a bivouac fire was still ablaze. The familiar features of the place seemed now and again to advance, then to shrink away askance amongst the shadows, as the yellow and red flames rose and fell with a genial crackling sound pleasant to hear. The rail fence showed with a parallel line of zigzag shadows; the ash-hopper, the beehives all awry, the haystack, were distinct; and the roof of the barn looked over them all, the window-shutter of the loft flaring wide, revealing the stores of hay whereon the visitors were to sleep; through the open door below their horses were visible, some stalled and at the mangers, but one or two lying on the straw. Quite outside stood another—a sleek, claybank creature—so still that, with the copperish hue and the lustre of the fire, he looked like some gigantic bronze. Around all the dark forest gloomed. Sometimes the flames were tossed so high, with a flickering radiance so bright, that the outline of a mountain would show against that dark, cloudless, starlit sky; and once were discovered mists in the valley—silent, white, secret, swift—journeying on their unimagined ways under cover of the night. The fire-lit figures sprawling about the logs wore merry, bearded faces, and jests and stories were afoot. Amongst the men were certain canine shapes, seeming to listen and to share the mirth ; a trifle ill at ease, they now and again made a sniffing circuit of the guests, wondering, doubtless, where poor Bob Millroy was, and that upon them alone should devolve the entertainment of so many strangers.

The sheriff had a keen eye ; one glance at the group and he went forward to the window, leaning his palms on the sill. The rank weeds below glowed in the fire-light; the elder-bloom breathed dew and fragrance in his face. He gave a low whistle, which a dog heard first, and turned its head, its ears cocked alertly, but nevertheless sat still, loath to leave the merry company. A second summons and one of the men sprang up, and approached the window.

"Whar's Felix Guthrie ?" demanded the officer.

The fire-light showed a surprised glance from under the brim of his interlocutor's old slouched hat. "Why, I thunk ye sent him on some yerrand. He saddled his beastis an' put out long ago fur down the mounting. An' I axed him ef he warn't afeard o' the gorges. An' he 'lowed he war 'bleeged ter go."

The officer in his turn stared. "That's all right. I didn't know whether he hed gone," he said at last, with an airy wave of the hand. He turned within, smiling. "Fee air like the man in the Bible ez say, 'I go not,' an' goes," he muttered to himself, in triumphant satisfaction.

The sheriff found it a long night. The voices gradually dwindled until only a fragmentary, low-toned colloquy could be heard beside the fire outside, so had the number of renegades to the loft of the barn increased; and when at last the drowsy converse was hushed, the impetuous flare had died away; no fluctuating glimpses of the landscape embellished the darkness; the fire had sunk to a mere mass of vermilion embers amidst the utter gloom which it did not illumine. A wind after a time arose, and hearing it astir in the valley, the sheriff, in his frequent stridings to and fro in the little cabin, bethought himself of the menace of scattered coals to the hay and straw, and now and again looked out of the window to see how the gray ash was overlapping this smouldering mass, that had spent its energies in those wild, upspringing, tumultuous flames, and had burned out to the ground. More than once he mended the fire on the hearthstone within, merely that he might have the company of the flicker on the wall; but it, too, was drowsy, and often sent up sluggish columns of smoke in lieu of blaze, and he seemed to himself the only creature alive and awake in all the spread of mountain and valley. He had contrived to keep his vigil alone. He had given a special promise that he would call the prisoner's wife at twelve o'clock to watch the latter half of the night. By no means reluctant, exhausted with the excitements of the evening superimposed upon the work and cares of the day, she and Maggie had climbed the ladder to the roof-room, and had left the officer in undisturbed possession below.

After a while he lighted a tallow dip, and surveyed the haggard face of the patient, as he still chose euphemistically to call the prisoner. The feeble glimmer illumined the room in pallid and melancholy guise, instead of with the hilarity and glow and bright good-will which the sulking fire had shown earlier in the evening. A great, distorted silhouette of his own head appeared upon the wall, leaning ogreishly over the pillow. He noted these things in the midnight. His hand on the round knob of the bedstead seemed to stealthily grasp a club. The forlorn face of the recumbent man added its significance to the shadow. A more sinister and threatening picture it was hardly possible to imagine, and after gazing at it with gruff disfavor, Carew shifted his position, and once more looked anxiously at the haggard face on the pillow. It bore certain tokens which in his ignorance he fancied were characteristic of the *facies hippocratica;* from time to time, as he lighted the candle anew, he noted them again, and his **own face** seemed to reflect them in a sort of dismay **and terror.** Once, as he struck the candle sharply downward to extinguish the flame, he apostrophized the patient out of the sudden darkness:

"**Ef ye don't** git sensible enough ter talk sorter straight afore ye take off from hyar fur good an' all, I dun'no' how in kingdom come I be a-goin' ter find out whar it war ez ye hid that plunder—ef ever ye did hide it."

He walked back to the hearth, where the gray smoke, itself barely visible, rose in a strong, steady column, now and then darting out a tiny scintillating tongue of white flame; he threw himself again into the rickety chair, his anxious eyes on the fire. A black cat, crouched upon the hearth, commented hospitably upon his proximity by a loud purring as she alternately opened and shut her witch-like yellow eyes. She recalled to his mind many a homely fire-side fable of witchcraft that held in permanent solution the terrors of his childhood which the wisdom of later years might vainly strive to precipitate and repudiate. He looked at her askance while she peacefully slept, and the wind went heavily by the window as with the tread of a thousand men. He himself was never so consciously vigilant. It seemed as if he had never slept. He could hardly realize the fatigue, the drowsiness, with which he had struggled in the earlier portion of the night. Not a stir escaped his attention from the bed where the wounded man lay, whether in the soft recuperation of slumber, or the heavy stupors that so nearly simulate death itself, his ignorance could not determine. Once, as the flame flared white from out the gray smoke, he looked to see if the hands were plucking at the coverlet, a sign familiar to him of the approaching doom. And then, as the dull, dense, unillumined column of vapor streaming up the chimney benighted the room, he heard, with his keen senses all tense, the howl of a wolf on a far-away summit.

"So durned onlucky!" a thick voice said, suddenly, as it were in his ear.

Carew gave a galvanic start that jarred his whole frame, and he had a momentary impression that he had been dreaming. As he turned his head he heard the wind surging in the infinite leafage of the vast mountain wilderness. But within all was still save the slowly ascending column of gray smoke, and all was silent—not the chirping of a cricket, not the gnawing of a mouse — till abruptly, from out the semi-obscurity of the room, the thick, unnatural voice came again, came from the pillow where the restless head was rolling once more.

The sheriff drew a long breath of relief, raucously cleared his throat, and stretched out his stalwart, booted legs comfortably upon the hearth. Then he once more turned his face toward the bed, for, whether because of the pervasive quiet or the absence of other distractions, the utterances of delirium that had hitherto seemed incoherent and mere mouthings were now comprehensible—the words, although but half formed and thickly spoken, having become articulate.

" Durned onlucky," the voice said, over and over again, with falling inflections infinitely disconsolate.

A smile was on the officer's face. In the absence of other entertainment, these queer unauthorized gyrations of the powers of speech, all astir without the concurrence of the brain, promised to relieve somewhat the tedium.

" *Onlucky!* I b'lieve ye !" he commented, with a laugh. " Onlucky fur true—fur you !"

" So durned onlucky," the weird voice rose louder.

Then it fell to silence which was so long continued that the officer relapsed into a reverie, and once more eyed the veiled fire.

" Dun'no' nuthin' 'bout them Leetle People," the voice droned.

Once more Tom Carew lifted his head with a renewed interest ; he felt as if long ago, in some previous state of existence, he had heard of those strange extinct folk ; and then he recalled their more immediate mention — for the first time that he could remember—at the blacksmith's shop to-day, and their connection with the name of Shattuck. He sat with a half-scornful, half-doubting smile upon

his face, that bespoke, nevertheless, an intent attention, and the influence of the fascination which the
supernatural exerts ; his hands were in his pockets,
his hat on the back of his head, his long legs stretched ,
out, his whole relaxed attitude implying a burly comfort.

"Buried jes' two feet deep ; shows how small they
actially war," said the thick voice, "them Stranger
People."

The face of the sheriff, revealed in one of the lash-
ing thongs of flame, had a breathless wonder upon it.
"Durned ef it don't!" he muttered, in the accents
of amazed conviction. And again he lent his ear to
the delirious exclamations as the fevered brain retraced some scene present once more to its distortions.

"Naw, Buck, naw," Millroy cried out, with sudden
vehemence. "'Twarn't me ez told. An' Steve Yates
couldn't hev gin the word ter Shattuck. Nobody
knowed but ye and me. Ye oughtn't ter hev shot
at Shattuck. It air so durned onlucky ter shoot nigh
a graveyard. Ah! ah! ah-h!" The voice rose suddenly to a hoarse scream, and he tossed uneasily
from side to side.

The sheriff sat motionless, and albeit he had assumed the functions of nurse as well as watcher,
offered no assistance or alleviation to the sufferer,
but with a puzzled face meditated for a time on this
unexpected collocation of names ; then scratched his
head with an air of final and perplexed defeat as he
listened to the groans of the wounded man gradually
dying away to silence.

He waited expectantly, but naught broke the stillness save the wind outside in the immensity of the night and the wilderness. "I wish ter God ye'd talk sense," he adjured the patient, disconsolately.

Then he fell to thoughtfully eying the fire, the simple elements of his interest in the disconnected monologue merged into anxiety and perplexity and baffled speculation. The veiled flame still tended sluggishly upward; he heard the sobbing of the sap oozing out at the ends of the logs. "This wood is mighty green," he observed, disparagingly, "an' post oak, too, I b'lieve. 'Tain't fitten ter make a fire out'n."

A vague stir was on the roof—pattering drops; slow, discontinued presently, and discursively falling again. The little cabin was on the very verge of a rain cloud. In the valley the rhythmic beat of the downfall upon the tree-tops came muffled to his ears, and he noted the intermittent sound of the wind dying away and rising fitfully and farther off. All at once his attention was deflected from the outer world.

"The Leetle People revealed the secret, Buck. Lay it at thar door," cried the weird voice of delirium.

Carew drew his sprawling members into a tense attitude, a hand on either knee, his head thrust forward, his eyes distended, staring into the gloom, his lower jaw falling.

"Thar warn't room enough fur the bones an' the jug an' the plunder too. An' that thar one o' the Leetle People's harnts hev sot out ter walk, ez sure ez ye air born—no room sca'cely bein' lef' in his grave. So durned onlucky ter meddle with the Leetle People's graves! So durned onlucky, to be sure!"

The officer sat as if turned to stone, breathless, motionless, staring fixedly into the dusky room, and seeing nothing that was before him—only the goal which he had sought—while the fevered head still rolled back and forth on the pillow, the delirious voice repeating, with every inflection of dull despair : " So durned onlucky ! So onlucky, to be sure !"

How long the sheriff sat there, unconsciously striving to realize the situation, the significance of this strange discovery, he did not know. It was with a distinct effort of the mind at last that he sought to pull himself together and turn to the consequent step. He felt as if he were dreaming even after he was on his feet, and he paused irresolutely in the middle of the floor, and looked expectantly toward the bed, where the wounded man's head still restlessly rolled as he muttered : " So durned onlucky ! So onlucky, to be sure !" But if Bob Millroy should talk all night he could add naught of importance to what the sheriff already knew. ·

" No use a-listening ter him jabber now," he said.

A sudden look of thought smote his face ; his eyes narrowed, his teeth closed firmly, as he revolved the idea in his mind, and he turned abruptly to the window. The blasts had closed the batten shutter fast, and he shook it smartly before it would open in his hand. The slow wheeling of its edges against the sky revealed a change since last he had looked out. The stars still scintillated above in the clear spaces of the zenith, but a rain-cloud hung in the south, bulging low over the ranges, its blackness differing vastly in tone from the limpid darkness where the night was clear and serene. One summit below it was distinctly defined; there it had betaken a dusky brown color, and about its lower verge a fringe of fine straight lines of rain was suggested; a moon —a belated, waning moon—was rising in the melancholy dead hour of the night, its distorted, mist-barred disk showing between the bare eastern peaks, which were all silvered and clearly outlined above the massive wooded slopes darkling below. It shone full in the officer's eyes as for a moment he steadfastly gazed upon it. Then he laid his hand upon the window-sill and lightly sprang upon the ground below. The next moment he was standing in the door of the barn, and his stentorian halloo had roused all the slumbering mountaineers amongst the hay, and hailed the echoes in many a rocky gorge far away.

XVI.

In the deep obscurity of those dark hours before
the moonrise, in the effacement of all the visible expressions of material nature, save the glitter of the
stars and the glooming of the shadows, Felix Guthrie
had been alone, as it were, with his own soul. He
had never known, native of the wilderness though he
was, so intense a sense of solitude. It was as if his
spirit had gone forth from the familiar world into
the vast voids of the uncreate. He took no heed of
the dangerous way down the steeps, but gave the
horse the rein, and trusted to the keener nocturnal
sight of the animal. His dog ran on ahead pioneer-
wise, retracing his way from time to time and gam-
bolling about his master's stirrup irons, his presence
only made known by a vague panting which Guthrie
neither heard nor heeded. Even to the voice of the
mountain torrent he was oblivious, although it seemed
louder far by night than by day, assertive, unafraid,
congener of the solitude, the darkness, and the melancholy isolations of the mountain woods. The
rhododendron blooming all unseen by the way touched
his cheek with a soft petal and a freshness of dew;
now and again a brier clutched at his sleeve; sometimes a stone rolled beneath his horse's hoofs, and
fell into the abyss at the side of the road, sonorously
echoing and echoing as it smote upon the rocky

walls of the chasm, the decisive final thud so long delayed that to judge thus of the unseen depths which lurked at either hand might have daunted him had he listened. The horse would hesitate at times, and send forth a whinnying plaint of doubt or fear when the rushing torrent crossed the way, plunging in presently, however, and, if need were, swimming gallantly, with the swimming dog in his wake.

Guthrie's thoughts made all the way heavy ; deeper than the glooms of the night they shadowed his spirit.

"Though she may sing an' he may listen, I ain't a-goin' ter spy him out fur no sher'ff ez ever rid with spurs. I ain't a-goin' ter hound him an' track him, fur I ain't no dog ; though I ain't got nuthin' agin dogs, nuther. But "—with a hardening of the face —" I'll hold him ter account ter me. I'll bring him ter jedgment. He'll 'low the law o' the lan' hev got a toler'ble feeble grip compared with the way I'll take holt o' him. He war warned. I told him ez I hed it in my heart ter kill the man ez kem atwixt Litt an' me."

When he reached the levels of the cove the springy turf served to add speed to the smooth, swinging, steady pace. He had hardly expected so soon to see before him the steep gables of the old Rhodes homestead. These were cut sharply against the sky, for the house stood in the midst of its open fields. One or two sycamore-trees swayed above its roof, and great overgrown bushes—lilac and snowball and roses —crowded the yard. A garden, overgrown too, extended down the slope at the side, and here as well were masses of shrubs blackly visible in contrast with the open spaces.

Guthrie was a stranger here. He had never before seen so great a house as the rambling old brick dwelling. When he had dismounted at the fence he was for a moment at a loss how to enter. A porch was at the front and another at the side, and while he hesitated a vague glimmer of yellow light came through the masses of the foliage that clustered about one of the windows. He opened the gate; his foot fell noiselessly upon the weed-grown path. A great white lily was waving in the gloom close by —he saw it glimmer—another, and another; and as the file stood close in the border, the heavy rich perfume seemed to make the air dense. The window glared forth suddenly—the light in every tiny pane —when he had passed a great arbor-vitæ that stood near it, trailing its branches on the ground. Within, unconscious, at ease, unprescient, a man sat by a lamp, a book in his hand, his chair tilted back, a pipe between his teeth. Save the light, vaporous curling of the smoke above his head, there was no motion. The fire dwindled in the chimney-place; the clock had stopped as if it fell a-drowsing on the midnight hour. The wind had ceased even its vague stir, and the vines that hung about the window were still. Guthrie stood for a moment as if the inertia of the scene had fallen upon him, staring at the face that he had learned to know rather in meditating upon it in its absence than in the study of its traits. It was softer than he had thought, younger; but he recognized anew, with an infinite change of sentiment, that indefinable quality of expression, to which glance, contour, pose, all contributed, which made it so likable. And if this had been patent to him, why not to others—to Letitia? **A new** standpoint had wrought a radical difference. **The** vague fascination that had once commended Shattuck kindled Guthrie's hatred now. His eyes glowed like a panther's from out of the **darkness, and** when Shattuck abruptly put up his **hand with the** quick, decisive **motion** of keen interest **and** turned **a page of** the **volume, it** broke the lethargic spell that seemed to **have** fallen upon the **mountaineer.** Guthrie moved **up suddenly close to the window, his very** touch **upon the pane.** There was an imperious look upon his face. It seemed to hail **the** unconscious reader within, who with his quick deft gesture **presently** turned another **leaf. Guthrie could see his intent** eyes, full of light, **shifting from side to side of** the page as they scanned **the lines.** He made no effort **to attract** Shattuck's attention **beyond that** long steady, glowering look, **albeit** he wondered **that** its effect should be so belated. **He** had noted often that strange mesmeric influence of the eye; **a wild beast in the woods** would **not remain** oblivious of **the presence of his natural enemy were a** human being's gaze steadily **fixed for some space upon him. Shat**tuck suddenly put **up his hand with a vaguely im**patient air of interruption, and passed **it over** his **cheek; then** he rose abruptly to his feet, crossed the **hearth** with **his** quick, sure step, and reached up **to** the high mantel-piece, dusky in **the** shadow. There was a sharp metallic **click outside** amongst the honeysuckle vines—Guthrie had cocked his pistol.

But it was no weapon **which Shattuck** had grasped from the mantel-piece. **His train of** thought was evidently still unbroken, for he came slowly back into the circumference of the light of the lamp, as it stood on the table, turning in his careful deft hands a curiously decorated jar. Then, still standing, with the other hand he whirled over the leaves of the book, and seemed to compare the jar which he held to an engraving upon the page. That serene light of a purely intellectual pleasure was upon his face, and its peculiar charm, its alertness, its mobility, its sympathetic intimations, its clear candor, its courage, had never been more individual, more marked. The man outside, with his pistol cocked in his hand, keenly alive to all impressions that mutually concerned them, sought to see him as once he had seemed. Jealousy had tampered with Guthrie's vision, and he could no longer read these patent characters; they were like a language that one has half forgotten—a vague suggestion here and there, a broken association, a dull misconception. The next moment their eyes met.

For one instant the sudden sight of that white cheek pressed close to the glass drove the blood from Shattuck's face. He stood, the jar still in his hand, his head bent down, his questioning, searching eye intent. Then, still without recognizing the features of the man outside, he placed the jar on the table, and walked slowly to the window, unarmed as he was. He laid both hands on the sash to lift it; it was thrown creakingly up, and the light fell full on the face without, its square contour, its austere, sullen expression, its long yellow ringlets, all framed by the big brim of the broad hat thrust far back.

"Is that you, Fee?" Shattuck said, in surprise. "You nearly scared me to death. Why don't you come in?"

22

His tone was untroubled and casual. It implied a conscience void of offence.

"He thinks I hain't fund him out," Guthrie commented to himself. Aloud he replied, grimly: "'Tain't wuth while ter kem in. I kin say what I hev got ter say right hyar."

Shattuck, all unnoting the pistol in his interlocutor's hand, sat down upon the window-sill, leaning almost against its muzzle. He held one of the cables of the many-stranded honeysuckle vine in his hand, by way of assisting his equilibrium, as he looked down at his guest. There was no more serious thought in his mind at the moment than the wish that he could paint, or even sketch. It seemed a pity that so massive and impressive an embodiment of the idea of manhood, of force, as that which Felix Guthrie's face and figure presented should be known only to his few and unappreciative neighbors as a "tarrifyin' critter, full o' grudges, who shot mighty straight."

Guthrie was a trifle thrown off his balance by this serene unconsciousness. He hesitated, expecting that Shattuck would ask him what had brought him hither, unaware that the etiquette in which the townsman was reared forbade him to inquire or to manifest curiosity concerning the mission of even an untimely visitor. As Guthrie said nothing, Shattuck essayed to break the pause.

"See my prehistoric jug?" he smilingly asked, pointing with the stem of his empty pipe toward the quaint jar upon the table. "I dug that out of Mr. Rhodes's mound. It's mightily like the cut of a Malay water-cooler I came across in that book on the table—surprisingly."

Before the unsuspicious suavity of his face and manner Guthrie felt a vague faltering, such as no ferocity or danger could have induced. So conscious of this was he that he sought, with a sort of indignant protest, to throw it off. He seized upon the first pretext to express his enmity, albeit his judgment failed to approve it. He felt it all inadequate to the passion which shook him, and far from what he had intended to say.

"Content yerse'f with that," he exclaimed; "fur ye shall hev nuthin' from the Leetle People. They hev tuk up thar rest on my lan', an' thar shell they sleep in peace till the last trump sounds."

The hand that trifled with the heavily twisted vine was still for a moment, and Shattuck looked down seriously into Guthrie's eyes—seriously, but without anger.

"It shall be just as you say," he replied. "I don't wonder you feel strongly about it. At first I was furious at being shot at in a way that I can't resent, by a woman "—his eyes flashed, and his lips trembled —"and I declared I would try it again. But afterward I felt we were fortunate indeed that no one was killed except the colt. It might have been your brother or Mr. Rhodes as well as myself. You see?" He turned his head toward the light. Where the hair had been clipped to the skin a red line showed that the rifle ball had grazed the flesh. "Pretty good aim in the twilight. And perhaps since there is so strong a feeling against disturbing the 'pygmies,' so called "—his second nature of scientific exactitude unconsciously qualified the phrase—" I ought to let them alone. Still, I am sorry about the little colt;

and as the disaster happened in my errand, I should like to offer some indemnity." He made a motion toward his pocket.

"I hev a mind ter take ye by the nape o' yer neck an' break it across the winder-sill!" cried Guthrie, his eyes blazing. "Ye think I keer 'bout the wuth o' the leetle critter!" He snapped his fingers scornfully in the air, holding his arm aloft with a fine free gesture. "I be sorry he is dead, 'kase he hev got no hereafter, an' he war a frisky beastis, an' loved ter live, an' we-uns will miss seein' him so gayly prancin' in the pastur'. Ye think I kem hyar ter git a leetle pay fur him?" He would not wait for Shattuck's protest that both eyes and gesture preluded. "Naw!" he thundered. "I kem hyar ter-night ter take yer life"—for the first time Shattuck marked the burnished glimmer on the barrel of the pistol that he held in his hand—"an' ter do what I hev never demeaned myself ter do afore—ter take back my promise."

"What promise?" Shattuck interjected.

"Ah, ye know! Ye know full well!" Guthrie shook his head, and in his voice was a quaver of poignant reproach. "The promise ye got by talkin' round me, 'kase ye 'lowed I war a ignorant cuss, and not able ter see through yer deceit with all yer school l'arnin'—by praisin' her looks, an' tellin' me ter keep up my courage, an' how I mought make out ter git her ter marry me, arter all. 'Twon't make no difference takin' back the promise, fur I mean ter take yer life with it. Ye surely remember the word I said ter you-uns, ez 'twar in my heart ter kill the man ez kem betwixt me an' Litt; an', by God! it is."

A sudden comprehension was dawning in Shattuck's eyes. He leaned forward, and laid his hand on Guthrie's shoulder. "Now go slow, Fee," he said, soothingly. "Who is this man? Not *I*, and this I swear!"

The imperious face, its pallor distinct in the lamplight falling upon it from within, the rest of the figure shadowy in the black darkness without, looked up at him with a scathing contempt wrought in every feature.

"An' so I swear that I'd be justified ef I war ter put a bullet through yer heart, an' let yer soul go down ter hell with that word ter damn ye ter all eternity!"

Shattuck withdrew his hand, frowning heavily. "Look here, my fine fellow, this is strong language. If I didn't believe you are under some strange mistake, I'd make you eat your words syllable by syllable. What do you mean?"

"But I don't want ter murder ye," Guthrie went on, as if Shattuck had not spoken. "I can't shoot ye down without a weepon in yer han', like Mis' Yates tried ter do, though ye richly desarve it. Git yer shootin'-iron an' come out—come out an' stan' up fur yerse'f." He waved his hand with the pistol in it toward the more open space beyond the shrubbery. "Come out, or I'll shoot ye ez ye set thar."

"Not one step will I stir until you tell me why you say that I have come between you and Letitia."

"Bekase *she* told me so."

Shattuck's unconscious reliance upon his mental supremacy, his equipment of delicate tact, his assurance of a pleasing personality, which was half his courage, began to give way. He had yet that physical self-respect which would enable him to meet his enemy without a pusillanimous shrinking, but he no longer hoped to command the adroitness to evade the event. Still he strove to be calm.

"Impossible! Now, what did she say?" he demanded, in a reasonable voice. Somehow, he had the key to Guthrie's confidence. Even now it opened to him.

"Oh!" he exclaimed, in a voice of despair, throwing up the arm that still grasped the weapon, "I knowed it ez much from what she *didn't* say ez what she *did*. I seen it in her face. I hearn it in her voice. I ain't blind! I ain't deef! An' then "—every line in his face hardened—"she tole me how ye kem an' stood outside the winder ter listen whilst she sung, an' seein' yer face suddint, lookin' in through the batten shutter, she didn't know ye a-fust—not till arterward, whenst hearin' yer pickaxe in the Leetle People's graveyard, did she know 'twar you-uns. An' ye war waitin' fur the moon ter rise. An', damn ye! what d'ye want ter hear her sing fur?"

Shattuck's face, with a startled astonishment upon it, had grown more deeply grave. Every intimation of anger had fallen from his manner. "Guthrie," he said, in a tone so coercive, so serious, that the other looked up, newly intent, "is there no way to convince you? I never heard her sing. I never was in the pygmy burying-ground but that one time with your brother. Now, think! Is there no one else who might loiter about that house; who might venture—I should never take such a liberty—to look through the crevices of a closed window?"

Perhaps it was Shattuck's influence over Guthrie; perhaps the anxiety of a lover to believe his despair unfounded, to hope against hope—at all events, his long reflective pause indicated a change of mental attitude.

"Mrs. Yates's husband," suggested Shattuck, plying his advantage; "has nothing been heard about him lately?"

"Lord, yes!" exclaimed Guthrie, his mind reverting to the sensation of the day. "I seen him myself yestiddy 'mongst a gang o' horse-thieves a-hidin' out in the woods. I hed ter run fur my life, ez they set on me, six ter one. An' the sher'ff overhauled thar den jes ter-day."

His voice faltered a trifle. He looked shamefaced and downcast. The sheriff's suspicion concerning Shattuck had recurred to him, and he could not meet the man's eyes with this thought in his mind.

"Now, don't you see, Fee," argued Shattuck, "how likely a thing it is that Steve Yates should hang around his own cabin, and peer through the window to take a look at his own wife and child, whom he probably will never see again, unless in some such way?"

Guthrie nodded, more than half convinced. Still, with his hidden consciousness of that insult to Shattuck which he carried in his recollection of the sheriff's menace, of the mission of espionage which he had refused, he could not look up.

In some subtle way he knew that when Shattuck next spoke it was not to him alone that he addressed the information, but that the fact might be made manifest.

"Now I am going to give you a reason why I do not stand between you and Letitia." At the name Guthrie lifted a listening face. "I am engaged to be married to a lady in my own city. So Letitia may sing like an oread and look like a flower, but she is nothing to me."

He said the words with a clear conscience, for if she had fixed her affection upon him—somehow the idea aroused a vague sweet thrill in that mortgaged heart of his—it had been unsought.

Guthrie, eager for his own peace of mind to believe him, drew a long sigh of relief. "I reckon I take up sech notions jes 'kase I am so all-fired jealous," he said. Then, with a half-laugh, "Litt never actially said nuthin' nohow—though she air ekal ter sayin' anything jes ter make me mo' jealous 'n I naterally be."

A mental mutiny possessed Shattuck. Was not this the conclusion that he had labored in all good faith to precipitate? Where, then, was his satisfaction in the logical result? Why should he cling in tenacious triumph to another inference, drawn from her fancy that it was he who had lingered outside her window to hear her sing? His pulses quickened with the thought that the very fallacy wore the reflected hues of her hope. There were other recollections pressing fast upon him—that she had remembered his words, had recounted his strange stories, the look in her eyes when she had caught down from the rack the rifle which she believed had endangered his life. Her dream had in some sort fulfilled itself. He had long appreciated the charm of her unique beauty, her sprite-like individuality. His feeling suddenly expanded, glowing like a bud into the rose at the first warm touch of the sun.

He looked down at Guthrie all oblivious of him, save for weariness of the importunity of his threats, his constancy of woe, his confidences. Shattuck was absorbed for the moment in his own emotion, and the world had suddenly slipped away.

Abstractions befitted the hour. One might hardly think to see it again—that sordid, dusty, daylight world, full of commerce and hard bargains, and rigorous conventions of wealth and standing, prosaic requisites of well-equipped happiness. It had rolled far away out of consciousness. Upon the low summits of the thick growths of the orchard gleamed the lustre of the dew and the yellow suffusions of the rising moon. The shadows had become dense, symmetrical, sharply outlined. The lilies, their chalices all pearl and gold, were so white and stately and tall as they stood where the moonbeams conjured them from out the darkness of the old-fashioned borders. The light drifted through the fringes of the pines, dark themselves as ever; and between their boughs, looking to the east, one could see a field of millet, glistening with all the charmed illusions of a silver lake. And how the mocking-bird loves the light! From out the midnight his jubilant song went up to meet it.

Shattuck remembered the moment, the scene, many a year afterward, the absorption that mulcted Guthrie's words of half their meaning, and more than half their weight.

"I hev got suthin' else ter say," he began, uneasily. "I dun'no' how ter tell it ter ye, nor whether

I oughter tell it at all. Ef the sher'ff hed ever seen ye he'd know he war a fool; but thar war a man robbed an' kilt on the road that night whenst Steve Yates vamosed, an' folks b'lieve he done it."

The superficial attention with which Shattuck hearkened to this deepened the next moment.

"An' ez Steve Yates hed no idee o' goin' till ye sent him, the sher'ff thinks ye might hev sent him on that yerrand."

An inarticulate exclamation of amazement, of indignation, broke from Shattuck's lips. It was not Guthrie's intention to assuage his fears, but he felt constrained to be the apologist of the suspicion.

"Ef he hed ever seen ye wunst," he observed, "he'd know better. Of course he ain't never seen ye."

"Of course not," Shattuck assented, shortly, his confidence renewed. The suspicion touching himself was not the kind of thing that a man would willingly consider, even in its most hypothetical and tenuous guise. That it should be seriously entertained was too terrifying, too odious an idea to be gratuitously harbored. To seek to throw it off was the instinct of self-respect, of self-preservation. His nerves were still sensible of the shock, but his effort was to make light of it, to treat it as the coarse pleasantry of the officer, perpetrated concerning the only stranger within the vast circuit of mountainous country. He felt no gratitude to Guthrie for his warning, as the mountaineer had expected his revelation to be construed. He looked down at him with repugnance and indignation in his eyes, and albeit Guthrie was not skilled in deciphering subtle facial indications, he understood the sentiment and deprecated it.   He did not pursue the subject further.   He cast about in his clumsy way to make amends for his offence, for thus it seemed to him now, of repeating the obnoxious suggestion.

"I be powerful sorry I kem a-devilin' ye hyar this time o' night fur nuthin'," he said.   "I reckon ye think I'm plumb gone destracted 'bout Litt," with a pathetic uplifting of his long-lashed eyes to his interlocutor, who was still sitting in the window.   "Ye see a feller like me is mighty forlorn, especially ez I oughter know ez Litt ain't one o' them ez kin be hed fur the askin'.   I reckon it 'll all come right arter a while?" wistfully interrogative.

"I reckon so," Shattuck was constrained to reply.

Guthrie was never before in so deprecatory or gentle a state of mind.   "I feel plumb outdone whenst I remember how I hev talked ter you-uns, ez be so powerful perlite an' saaft-spoken ter all, an' considerin' of feelin's"—Shattuck winced a trifle—"an' how I hev gone on 'bout takin' back promises an' sech.   Ye know I don't mean it.   Ye air welcome ter dig ennywhar ye wanter on my lan', an' I'll holp ye enny time; now, ef ye like," Guthrie protested with an effort at reparation.   "I dun'no' but what it's ez good a time ez enny.   Thar's light enough now, an' Mis' Yates mus' be off her gyard; she mus' sleep o' nights—leastwise take cat-naps."   He looked up with a propitiatory laugh on his face.   "An' I ain't 'feard o' Baker Anderson, nor Litt, nor even Moses."

Shattuck hesitated.   He had been more shaken than he would have acknowledged even to himself by the crude suggestion that his name was for a moment connected with one of the brutal and bloody mountain crimes—a mere æsthetic horror, for his mind could not compass the atrocity against probability that the suspicion should be seriously harbored by an officer of the law. He foresaw a night of sleepless irritability, revolving the idea, should he let Guthrie go, although he felt that it should fairly be considered only a fit subject of flout, of ridicule, of inextinguishable laughter. It was rather in the spirit of defending himself against his own capacities for self-torment that he readily turned toward the prospect of diverting his mind, occupying himself with alien interests.

"The spade an' the pick mus' be right thar now," Guthrie observed, by way of urgence. "Eph say he war so flustrated by Mis' Yates's shootin' that he forgot ter fetch 'em back home."

Shattuck looked out at the sober solid shadow of the old brick house, gable and chimney and porch, projected upon the thick herbage of the yard; the silver green sea of millet glimpsed between the dark branches of the pines; the winding road that led the loitering way to the mountains. "I'll get my hat," he said.

There was no light in the hall save that which the moon cast through the high window on the landing of the stairs. It seemed fibrous, skein-like, pendulous, as far as the balusters; then it fell upon the hall floor below in a distinct, motionless image of the sash and pane, all white and lustrous. By its radiance one could distinguish a hall sofa, long and hard, covered with tattered black hair-cloth; above it, hanging on the wall, the optimistic old barometer that once, perhaps, had been weatherwise, but now insisted that all signs "set fair"; the hall tree, whereon Rhodes's hat swung in its place, while its owner lay unconscious in the room above, the door of which Shattuck need pass with no solicitous tread, for, bating continuance, the pygmies themselves slept not more soundly. The door of his own room stood ajar; the moonlight and the sweet perfumes of the night came in through its open windows. It had a sort of inhabited look, full of comfortable suggestions; perhaps it was only because the fatigue of the day was beginning to hang somewhat heavily on his senses, but as he entered, he stood for a moment irresolute.

In the midst of the dusky uncertainty of sheen and shadow he was abruptly startled to see a dim figure suddenly moving at the opposite side of the room. He advanced a step, and recognized his own image in the indistinguishable mirror. It had a strange, weird effect, this half-seen simulacrum of himself, a skulking, uneasy, secret air that belied its principal, and seemed its own independent attitude, rather than reflected. It was coercive in some sort. He caught up his hat from the table, strode down the hall to Rhodes's door, and thus took those first steps destined never to be retraced. He knocked without response, then opened the door, which creaked raspingly upon its unoiled hinges, rusty with long disuse; and Guthrie, waiting at the window below, amongst the silent pensive lustres of the moon, heard the ringing round voice of Rhodes break forth in drowsy protest, incongruous, prosaic, insistently utilitarian. The interval was short before Shattuck ran down the stair, and sprang through the window, drawing the sash down behind him, and then the two set forth together.

The lilies bloomed at the gate, their chalices full of dew. The mocking-bird sang to the silent moon. Far, far away some watercourse had lifted loud a sylvan song it was not wont to sing by day.

"How still it is! Hear Wild-Duck Creek on the rocks!" Shattuck said as he buckled his saddle girth and put his foot in the stirrup. The eastern windows were all aflare with a white, opaque radiance in broadened, vitreous, distorted reduplications of the moon. The deep, elongated shadows of the house lay among the orchard boughs. He looked around at the old building when once in the saddle, to see its gables and its chimneys rise anew against the clear sky and the vague outlines of the mountains, only because it pleased him—its solid decency, even dignity, in its honest, unornamented validity, touched his receptive æsthetic sense—not because he divined that he was looking his last upon it. How finite a creature is man; how little he knows his way along these earthly paths—adown which soon or late he goes to meet his fate, never aware how near its approach—one might realize, thinking on a time like this, when these two, all unprescient, rode together to the burial-ground of the "Leetle People." The wind was in their faces—how fresh, how free! The dew glittered in the air; the moon, although yellow and waning, with a melancholy presage in her lessening splendors, made the night like some pensive, softly illuminated day of dreamtides. Their escort of mounted shadows galloped beside them; the turf stretched out into long miles behind their horses' hoofs. They met naught save a fox scudding over a stretch of sward with stealthy speed, and a bundle of feathers between his jaws. The Yates cabin, that Guthrie was first to see, a dimly glimmering gray, was as silent and still as if it housed no life within its walls—as silent and as still as that long slope, with the shadows of the great trees and the intervenient sheen of the moon all adown it, where the Little People had slept this many a day, knowing no waking.

Shattuck led the way. He had turned once more to the tall isolated laurel-bush, almost of tree-like proportions, where he had begun his labors before. He did not at once throw himself from his horse; he was taking note of a strange thing, something that he had not marked heretofore. That mass of bloom and foliage rose between the grave whose stone coffin his pickaxe had struck and any possible surveillance from the Yates cabin. A doubt for the first time stirred in his mind whether it were indeed Adelaide who had fired that murderous rifle ball. The next moment the absorptions of his intentions, his opportunity, usurped all else. He flung himself to the ground, breathless, elated, with an electrical energy in his muscles, as he seized the pickaxe on which Guthrie leaned irresolute, and struck the first blow.

The mountaineer turned his softened moonlit face upon him with a slow smile in his eyes. "I be glad ye hed the grit ter begin; I hain't." The dew had bereft his long curls of their wonted crispness; they hung in lengthened tendrils and dishevelled on his broad shoulders. He pushed his hat far back on his head. His heavy spurred boots were deeply sunken in the long grass. He slowly placed one upon the spade as he drove it down into the mould. "I can't holp bein' sorry fur the Stranger People, ez they air leetle, an' air dead, an' hev been waitin' so long in the dark fur the las' day an' thar summons ter rise."

That sharp smiting of metal upon stone jarred the moonlit quietude, and Guthrie looked up with dilated eyes, his hand quivering on the spade. "This ain't no common grave," he cried; "the ground is loose!"

He was not given to logical deductions; he did not speculate; he only stood staring with wonder; while Shattuck, all unaccustomed to the practical phenomena of digging, apprehended only cause of gratulation that the investigation was to be the less hindered. He made no reply, briskly shovelling out the earth. Presently, with a silent sign to Guthrie, he reached the topmost slab of the strange small sarcophagus. How long since it had seen the light that now fell upon the clay-incrusted stone! When it was first laid here, in what quarter was the moon? How often had it waxed and waned afterward, unmindful? The vibrations of the cataract filled the air with the full pulsings of nature's heart. The wind—wanderer!—came and went, as it did in the days of the pygmies. A flower from the laurel—a mere tissue of a bloom, so fine, so fragile of texture—was wafted down, and fell upon the slab, as transitory, as futile, as unheeded, as ye, O forgotten Little People!

Then the slab was lightly lifted, albeit with trembling hands. With averted eyes Guthrie shrank back, and, as his shadow withdrew, the moon shone straight into the tiny crypt, and Shattuck leaned forward to look. An exclamation, not of triumph, of horror, smote the air sharply.   The mountaineer, with all his pulses aquiver, looked down into his coadjutor's white, startled face.   Shattuck was kneeling beside the open grave, holding the coveted jug in his hand, full of silver currency.   The slow mountaineer, hardly mastering the idea, turned to the coffin.   If it still held bones, they lay beneath a pair of folded saddle-bags that filled the narrow space.

In the confusion that beset his senses, he did not discriminate the thunderous sound that rose upon the air: the flimsy bridge was vibrating under the reck-less gallop of a score of horsemen.   He only knew, as in a dream, that the moonlight was presently full of swift mounted shadows bearing down upon them, Shattuck still with the jar in his hand, although start-ing to his feet, and he himself leaning upon the spade.   The air reverberated with a savage cheer of triumph.   The sheriff had thrown himself to the ground, and with a smile of scornful elation held his pistol at Guthrie's head.

"Ye air no spy, air ye, Fee?" he cried out, with ringing sarcasm.   "Got a mighty good reason not ter be.   An' I reckon, my pretty Mister Town-man," turn-ing to Shattuck, "ye air no spy nuther.   But I'll gin in, Fee, I never war so fooled ez I hev been in you-uns.   I never thunk ter set a thief ter ketch a thief this-a-way."

Upon the word, Guthrie, into whose stunned con-sciousness the truth had gradually sifted, turned, with a flaring color and a fiery eye, and dealt the officer a terrible blow in the face with his whole force.   The next moment the two men, their arms interlocked, were swaying to and fro on the brink of the open

23

grave, so nearly matched in strength that it was hard to say which might have prevailed, had not a swift flash of red light sprung out in the pallid moonlight, and a sharp report rung upon the air. They fell apart, the officer staggering backward, but Guthrie sinking down upon the ground, whence he would rise no more.

A mingled clamor, terrible, full of fierce meaning, was suddenly loud upon the night. The shifting temper of the populace was never more aptly illustrated. In an instant the officer was a prisoner in the hands of his posse, and his posse was an infuriated mob. The hoarse cry, "String him up! string him up!" arose more than once. And those who spoke calmly, and with reason and argument, were equally formidable as they called upon the officer to justify his deed.

"Air this the law? No trial! no jury! Not a minute gin him to explain! Call him thief, an' shoot him down, unarmed, in cold blood!"

They pressed about him with eyes hardly less luminous than the eyes of wolves, hardly so gentle, while the officer protested first self-defence.

"With twenty men at yer back?" "An' Guthrie's pistols over yander in the holsters on his saddle?" the refutation rang out. Then, on the repetition of the terrible cry, "String him up!" the effort at exculpation shifted to a claim of the accidental discharge of the weapon. And still the fierce clamor rose anew.

Meantime Felix Guthrie lay very still in the pale moonlight, heedless of vengeance. His long hair stretched backward on the dank grass; his face, upturned to the moonbeams, was calm and untroubled; his hands were listless and limp, and one of the younger men mechanically chafed them as he now and again bent over to seek some sign of life in the fixed eyes.

Shattuck stood bewildered, looking with a sort of numb stupefaction at the prostrate figure upon the grass, and then at the agitated and furious group about the sheriff. The catastrophe, the very scene before him, he could not realize. He felt as in a horrible dream, when the consciousness of fantasy opens before the oppressed senses. More than once a touch upon his arm failed to rouse him. When he turned his head at last he saw, half hidden by the boughs of the blooming laurel, Letitia crouching tremulously in the shadow. He did not wonder how she came there now, nor note that the door of the little log cabin was open, and its inmates, roused by the tumult, were standing on the porch. He only saw her pale elfin face looking out from among the blooms as if she were native to the laurels. Her voice, though it was but a whisper, vibrated with urgency.

"Mount an' ride—*ride* for yer life!" she said; she held his horse by the bridle. "Thar'll be lynchin' 'fore day." Her tones grew steadier. "Nobody knows who, nor why."

"I'm not afraid of the law," he said, indignantly.

"This ain't law! Gin yerse'f up in town ef ye want law. But ride now—ride off in the shadder! Ride fur yer life!"

From the leafy screen she stepped forth, throwing the reins over the head of the horse, which was frightened and restive, and held the stirrup for Shattuck. The clamorous voices of those angered men rose to a hoarse scream, and the agitated tones of the officer, pleading, arguing, justifying himself, were overborne. Shattuck put his foot in the stirrup. The next moment he was in the saddle. As he looked down, he saw Letitia's face distinctly in the moonlight that trickled through a bough; something of that love of hers, which Guthrie had at once divined and denied and revealed, was expressed in it.

"Ye'll kem back again—some day—some day?" she said.

He clasped her hand as she lifted it.

"Come back? I'd come back if it were from the ends of the earth!" he protested.

A little thing to say, wrung out of the impassioned moment, when, in good sooth, there was no time to measure phrases or take heed of the cadences of the voice. It changed the world for her. He never forgot that radiant face in its sprite-like beauty amongst the moonlit flowers. If there were other eyes in the world so tender, so pathetic, so exquisite, he never saw them before or afterward. No other creature of the earth so looked like one of the air. Even as he sought his escape through the shadows, the dull sound of his horse's hoofs making scant impression in the midst of the pawing of the posse's steeds, he turned to catch through the trees a flitting glimpse of her light dress, her volant attitude, as she sped silently and secretly back to the waiting group on the porch. Then he rode away—rode for his life; as she had bidden him.

And he **had good need of speed.** How the distorted idea gained credence amongst the infuriated mountaineers **it would be** difficult to **say. It might** have been colored **by** the circumstance that **Guthrie** could logically **be presumed** to have **had no connivance** with the robbers whom he had slain, **and no knowledge** of where they had hidden their booty ; it might have been suggested by the crafty sheriff as **a** diversion of attention ; but the suspicion **presently** permeated the group that Guthrie had surprised Shattuck in the act of securing the plunder hidden in the pygmy grave. The discovery of the stranger's flight added the **semblance of** confirmation, and lent energy to the pursuit, which, leading **in diverse directions,** served to **disperse the posse, and thus annul that** formidable engine **of the law which** the strange happenings of the **night had** turned against the **sheriff,** who had himself summoned it into existence. **It was** doubtless **with** a view to his own safety **that he selected** for his share of the search **the road back to the** county town, and **with no** expectation of the result that awaited him there. The imputation of flight, and of seeking to elude the responsibility of **his act, which might** otherwise have attached to this precipitate **return,** was in a measure eliminated by the fact that the **fugitive** had **arrived** before him, and had **already surrendered to the authorities.**

It was a time to which **Shattuck** could never look back without a wincing loathing for the part he was constrained to play, although, in truth, he fared much **better than** he could have hoped. It so chanced that the justice of the peace, an old, gentle, friendly man, whom in those early morning hours he had roused, had himself the spirit of an antiquarian; his conversation was replete with the ancient and fading traditions of the Great Smoky Mountains, and he could well appreciate the strength of the archæological interest which had led Shattuck to open the pygmy grave. It seemed in the magistrate's estimation an ample justification for many risks. They were talking of these things quietly in the justice's office when the sheriff joined them. To his prosaic amaze, instead of details of the operation of the law indigenous to the office — points of examining trials and subpœnaings of witnesses, of arrest and commitment — he heard legends of the old Cherokee settlement, Chota, the "beloved town," city of refuge, where even the shedder of blood was safe from vengeance; of the mysterious Ark before which sacrifices were offered; of Hebraic words in the Indian ritual of worship; of the great chieftain Oconostota, and his wonderful visit to King George in London; of the bravery of Atta-Culla-Culla; of the Indian sibyl known as the Evening Cloud, and the strange fulfilment of her many strange prophecies.

Thus submitting his motives to no uncomprehending utilitarian arbitrament, all the rigors of the misunderstanding that Shattuck feared were averted, and he doubtless owed his admission to bail to this fortuitous circumstance. That he never came to trial he was indebted to a chance as friendly, for Millroy, before his death, so far recovered as to make a sworn statement which inculpated only Cheever and the horse-thief's gang, thus relieving Yates as well as

"EVERY DAY THAT DAWNED."

Shattuck of all suspicion of complicity in the murder and the robbery.

The mere passing remembrance that his name had ever been mentioned in connection with these crimes was like the thrust of a knife in Shattuck's heart for years thereafter, most of all as his enthusiasms abated, and the more serious interests of life were asserted, and his worldly consequence increased. Sometimes, amidst the wreaths of a post-prandial cigar, a sprite-like face, that seemed even in his unwilling and disaffected recollection supremely fair, was present to him again, and left him with a sigh half pleasure, half pain. Further than this his words were naught, and easily forgotten.

Easily forgotten! Every day that dawned to Letitia's expectant faith held an hour that would bring him. Never a sunset came that was not bright with his promise for the morrow. Down any curve in the road, as it turned, she might look to see him. For did he not say he would come?—and so surely he would! The years of watching wore out her life, but not her faith. And she died in the belief that her doom fell all too soon, and that he would come to find her gone. And she clung futilely to earth for his fancied sorrow.

Since those days the Little People's burying-ground is doubly deserted. But few pass, and they eye it askance. And by many a fireside is told the story of the heavy doom that fell on all who carried their schemes therein and sought to know its secrets. But the birds nest in its deep shades. Every year the laurel blooms anew. And Adelaide, looking with pensive eyes upon it from her home, happy once more, can still forecast the coming of that fair spring when the morning stars shall sing together in the vernal dawn of a new heaven and a new earth, and this mortality shall put on immortality.

Meantime the Little People sleep well.

THE END.

BY MARY E. WILKINS.

A New England Nun, and Other Stories. 16mo, Cloth, Ornamental, $1 25.

A Humble Romance, and Other Stories. 16mo, Cloth, Extra, $1 25.

Only an artistic hand could have written these stories, and they will make delightful reading.—*Evangelist*, N. Y.

The simplicity, purity, and quaintness of these stories set them apart in a niche of distinction where they have no rivals.—*Literary World*, Boston.

The reader who buys this book and reads it will find treble his money's worth in every one of the delightful stories.—*Chicago Journal.*

Miss Wilkins is a writer who has a gift for the rare art of creating the short story which shall be a character study and a bit of graphic picturing in one ; and all who enjoy the bright and fascinating short story will welcome this volume.—*Boston Traveller.*

The author has the unusual gift of writing a short story which is complete in itself, having a real *beginning*, a *middle*, and an *end.* The volume is an excellent one.—*Observer*, N. Y.

A gallery of striking studies in the humblest quarters of American country life. No one has dealt with this kind of life better than Miss Wilkins. Nowhere are there to be found such faithful, delicately drawn, sympathetic, tenderly humorous pictures.—*N. Y Tribune.*

The charm of Miss Wilkins's stories is in her intimate acquaintance and comprehension of humble life, and the sweet human interest she feels and makes her readers partake of, in the simple, common, homely people she draws.—*Springfield Republican.*

There is no attempt at fine writing or structural effect, but the tender treatment of the sympathies, emotions, and passions of no very extraordinary people gives to these little stories a pathos and human feeling quite their own.—*N. Y. Commercial Advertiser.*

The author has given us studies from real life which must be the result of a lifetime of patient, sympathetic observation. . . . . No one has done the same kind of work so lovingly and so well.—*Christian Register*, Boston.

By CONSTANCE F. WOOLSON.

EAST ANGELS. pp. 592. 16mo, Cloth, $1 25.

ANNE. Illustrated. pp. 540. 16mo, Cloth, $1 25.

FOR THE MAJOR. pp. 208. 16mo, Cloth, $1 00.

CASTLE NOWHERE. pp. 386. 16mo, Cloth, $1 00. (*A New Edition.*)

RODMAN THE KEEPER. Southern Sketches. pp. 340. 16mo, Cloth, $1 00. (*A New Edition.*)

There is a certain bright **cheerfulness in Miss** Woolson's writing which invests all her characters with lovable qualities.—*Jewish Advocate*, N. Y.

Miss Woolson is among our few successful writers of interesting magazine stories, and her skill and power are perceptible **in** the delineation **of her** heroines no less than in the suggestive **pictures of** local life. —*Jewish Messenger*, N. Y.

Constance **Fenimore** Woolson may easily become **the** novelist laureate.—*Boston Globe.*

Miss Woolson has **a** graceful fancy, a ready wit, a polished style, and conspicuous dramatic power ; while her skill in **the** development of a **story is** very remarkable.—*London Life.*

Miss Woolson never once follows the **beaten track of the** orthodox novelist, but strikes a new and richly **loaded** vein, which **so** far is all her own ; **and thus we** feel, on reading one of her works, a fresh sensation, and we **put down the** book with a sigh to think our pleasant task of reading it is **finished.** The author's lines must have fallen to her in **very** pleasant places ; **or** she has, perhaps, within herself the **wealth of** womanly love and tenderness she pours so freely into all **she writes.** Such books as hers do much to elevate the moral **tone of the day**—a quality sadly **wanting in novels of** the time.—*Whitehall Review*, London.

BY HOWARD PYLE.

THE WONDER CLOCK; OR, FOUR-AND-TWENTY MARVEL-LOUS TALES: BEING ONE FOR EACH HOUR OF THE DAY. Written and Illustrated by HOWARD PYLE. Embellished with Verses by KATHARINE PYLE. Large 8vo, Ornamental Half Leather, $3 00.

The illustrations fit the stories perfectly, and are as fantastic as the warmest lovers of tales of magic can desire. The artist enters so thoroughly into the spirit of the stories that his wonderful drawings have an air of reality about them. Some are grotesque, some exquisitely graceful; all are so spirited, so vigorous, so admirable in design and in the expression of the faces and figures, and so full of action, that it is hard to say which is the best.—*Boston Post.*

"The Wonder Clock" is truly a monument to the genius and industry of the author in his line of illustrated tales, and also to the enterprise of the publishers in producing choice children's books.—*Brooklyn Eagle.*

THE ROSE OF PARADISE. Being a Detailed Account of certain Adventures that happened to Captain John Mackra, in Connection with the famous Pirate, Edward England, in the Year 1720, off the Island of Juanna, in the Mozambique Channel, writ by himself, and now for the first time published. By HOWARD PYLE. Illustrated by the Author. Post 8vo, Ornamental Cloth, $1 25.

One of the most spirited and life-like stories of sea adventure that we ever remember to have read.—*N. Y. Mail and Express.*

A charming story with an Old World flavor that no one who picks it up can lay down until it is finished.—*St. Louis Republican.*

PEPPER AND SALT; OR, SEASONING FOR YOUNG FOLK. By HOWARD PYLE. Superbly illustrated by the Author. 4to, Ornamental Cloth, $2 00.

A quaint and charming book. . . . Mr. Pyle's wonderful versatility is shown in the different kinds of subjects and the various periods he treats, in every gradation of humor, mirth, and sly satire, with now and then a touch of fine sadness.—*The Critic*, N. Y.

It is beyond compare the quaintest and most entertaining book of the season. It is unique in style, and as unique in its contents, the very turning over of its leaves being enough to transport one into some unheard-of region of imagination.—*Observer*, N. Y.

PUBLISHED BY HARPER & BROTHERS, NEW YORK.

BEN-HUR: A TALE OF THE CHRIST.

By Lew. **Wallace.** New Edition from New Electrotype Plates. **pp. 560.** 16mo, Cloth, **$1** 50; Half Calf, $3 00.

Anything so startling, new, and distinctive as the leading feature **of** this romance does not often appear in works of fiction. . . . Some **of** Mr. Wallace's writing is remarkable for its pathetic eloquence. The scenes described in the New Testament are re-written with the power and skill of an accomplished **master of** style.—*N. Y. Times.*

Its real basis is a description of the life of the Jews and Romans **at** the beginning of the Christian era, **and this is** both forcible **and** brilliant. . . . We are **carried through** a surprising variety of scenes; we **witness** a sea-fight, a chariot-race, the internal economy of a Roman **galley,** domestic interiors **at** Antioch, at **Jerusalem,** and among the **tribes of the** desert; palaces, prisons, the haunts of dissipated Roman youth, the houses of **pious** families of Israel. There is plenty of **exciting** incident; **everything is** animated, vivid, **and** glowing.—*N. Y. Tribune.*

From the opening of **the** volume to the very **close the reader's interest** will be kept at the highest pitch, and **the novel will be pronounced** by **all** one of the greatest novels of the **day.—*Boston Post.***

It is full of poetic beauty, as though born of an **Eastern sage, and** there is sufficient of Oriental customs, geography, nomenclature, etc., to greatly **strengthen the** semblance.—*Boston Commonwealth.*

"Ben-Hur" **is interesting, and** its characterization **is** fine and strong. Meanwhile it evinces **careful study of the** period in which the scene is laid, and will help those **who read it with** reasonable attention **to** realize the nature and **conditions of** Hebrew life in Jerusalem and Roman **life at** Antioch **at the time** of our Saviour's advent.—*Examiner,* **N. Y.**

It **is** really Scripture history of Christ's time, clothed gracefully and delicately in the flowing and loose drapery of modern fiction. . . . Few **late** works of fiction excel it **in** genuine ability and interest.—*N. Y. Graphic.*

One of the most remarkable and delightful books. **It** is as real and warm as life itself, and as attractive as the grandest and most heroic chapters of history.—*Indianapolis Journal.*

The book is one of unquestionable power, and will be read with unwonted interest by many readers who are weary of the conventional novel and romance.—*Boston Journal.*

Published by HARPER & BROTHERS, New York.

☞ The above work sent by mail, postage prepaid, to any part of the United States or Canada, on receipt of the price.

www.ingramcontent.com/pod-product-compliance
Lightning Source LLC
Chambersburg PA
CBHW021540110726
47902CB00004B/965